The Lament of the Leprechauns

Allan C. Howarth

authorHOUSE®

AuthorHouse™ UK Ltd.
500 Avebury Boulevard
Central Milton Keynes, MK9 2BE
www.authorhouse.co.uk
Phone: 08001974150

First published by AuthorHouse 10/5/2009

ISBN: 978-1-4490-0648-8 (sc)

Printed in the United States of America
Bloomington, Indiana

This book is printed on acid-free paper.

To Tania

Without whom
None of this would have been remotely possible

Definitely not
An average
Wife and Mother

Prologue

Wayne Higginbotham would never forget his first flight; not even if he went on to live forever, which did seem very unlikely at that particular moment. Yes, that first experience of taking off, as free as a bird, into the wide blue yonder, would always remain every bit as fresh in his memory as the very moment it had happened.

Why?

Well, it hadn't exactly been the dramatically, explosive way that he had left the ground, like a powerful rocket blasting off into space, that had made it so particularly memorable.

Nor had it been the way that he had soared gracefully through the air, in a long, curving arc; a motion that could only be described as a piece of pure balletic artistry.

It hadn't even been the spectacular crash landing that had greeted him at the end. The landing that had seen him hit the ground and collapse like the front of an old banger in a head on collision, leaving him with a fractured arm, two badly bruised ribs and scars that lingered on for weeks.

No, it hadn't particularly been anything to do with any of those unforgettable things.

It hadn't even been the remarkable fact that Wayne's first flying experience had taken place in the total absence of any sort of aircraft.

What had stuck steadfastly in the forefront of Wayne's mind about that flight was that he had decided there and then, that that was it. Enough was enough!

In fact, enough was quite a lot more than enough.

From the moment that Baz's fist had hit his chin and sent an explosion of stars and sparks cascading up into his brain,

Wayne had realised that things were going to have to change. Oh yes, things were going to have to change big time.

That was the moment that Wayne Higginbotham had decided that he was going to do something about his sad, victimised, little life, his pathetically, tormented existence.

This time, Wayne Higginbotham was finally going to sort things out.

He was going to sort things out for once and for all.

This worm was for turning.

He had stood up, slowly and painfully, his left arm dangling uselessly at his side. Baz was standing in front of him, fists planted firmly on his more than ample hips, his gang of sycophants and cronies lined up behind him, laughing, giggling and mocking the bedraggled figure that Wayne now presented.

"Y'ad enough then, Dr. Spock?" Baz had sneered, gesturing for the much smaller boy to approach him.

"Come on, come an' 'ave a go then. Come an' give us yer deadly vulcan death grip, yer pointy eared, frizzy headed, little freak."

His mocking laugh had echoed in Wayne's ears, despite the horrible buzzing noise that seemed to fill his entire head.

When Baz laughed, his double chin wobbled like a huge pink blancmange. In fact saying that Baz had a double chin was probably something of an understatement; think more quadruple. Whatever, however many chins Baz had, they were all certainly wobbling a lot, as he appraised his dishevelled victim.

Wayne hated him; not disliked, not detested, but really, truly, deeply hated him.

Even so, through his sobs and tears, Wayne had still been a little bit surprised to hear his own voice say:

"I am not a Vulcan, fatso, and the "Star Trek" character, to whom you are referring, is actually called Mr. Spock and he does not have a death grip."

"Woooo" all of Baz's entourage cried, some doubling up with scornful laughter:

"What a geek!"

"Wooo, trekkie boy."

"What a Nerd."

Baz had grinned and waved his arms, encouraging his acolytes in their derision. He had then ambled up to the injured, softly weeping youngster and put his large, ugly, shaven head, right in front of his intended victim, nose to nose; eyeball to eyeball.

"D' you know what I'm gonna do now, freaky boy? What I am going to do to you for calling me fatso?"

His round face had contorted into a hideous mask, his yellowish teeth bared and his pale blue eyes narrowed to snake-like slits.

"I'm gonna rip off yer big pointy ears, like I told yer I would, yer little freak."

Wayne had looked the intimidating bully straight in the eye and had done something quite unexpected; he had smiled.

That small act of defiance had confused Baz. Doubt had suddenly crept into his eyes and his sneer had turned into bewilderment. The threatening, creased forehead had suddenly became a deep puzzled frown.

No one standing on the corner of Cavendish Street could explain what exactly happened next. It was just that one minute, Baz Thompson, a sixteen-year-old fifth former at St Swithin's Secondary Modern School, a well known local bully and self proclaimed hard-case, had been standing over a small skinny, eleven-year-old primary school kid. The very next minute, he was to be found lying on his back, staring wide eyed into space, dribbling from the corners of his mouth.

Some said that the smaller kid had swung a lucky punch with his one good arm.

Others claim that the boy had head butted the youth and that Baz had fallen over and hit his head on the ground.

There are even those who will swear to this day that they saw the boy simply raise the palm of his hand in front of the bully's face and that Baz had flown back at least eight feet, landing flat on his back, totally pole-axed.

Even Wayne himself couldn't explain it. All he remembered was a strange feeling in his head, as though all the blood in his body had suddenly surged up to a single point, just behind his eyes, literally making him "see red" and then, when he had raised his one good hand, something had just seemed to fly out of it. Something he couldn't even begin to describe. That had been it; the bully had just sort of fallen over.

Well, not fallen over exactly. He had flown a few feet through the air, just like Wayne himself had a few minutes earlier and had then landed flat on his back with a huge thump, his eyes wide open, his body twitching and shivering, as though he had just suffered a huge electric shock.

One thing was certainly for sure, Wayne Higginbotham would never forget his first flight, because his life really did begin to change that day.

Really, really, really change.

1

Wayne Higginbotham hated his name, in fact he hated just about everything about himself, which was OK, because just about everybody else seemed to hate everything about him too.

Wayne hated his thick brown curly hair, which always seemed to look a mess, even when he had spent ages brushing, or combing it.

Wayne's hair was so thick that most combs just gave in and disintegrated pathetically, on their first drag across his head. He was always finding loose brown, blue, or sometimes even embarrassingly pink, comb teeth in his hair.

To add insult to injury, Wayne's hair even took on a faint ginger hue in the sunlight.

Wayne hated his large blue/green eyes. Whenever people asked him what colour his eyes were he would say "blue." Invariably they would say "no, they look green to me." If Wayne said his eyes were green, the response was always "no they're blue."

Why couldn't he have had just one or the other?

Wayne hated his pale white skin, that seemed to turn bright red as soon as the sun popped out from behind the clouds, even for just a second and he hated the brown freckles that seemed to cover his nose and the bits under his eyes. People were always commenting on his freckles:

"Oh look at his "lickle" freckles, how cute."

This was usually followed by a pinch of his cheek, which always hurt a lot. The offenders were usually "aunts," or female friends of his mother, who would always do it on the crowded High Street in full view of everyone, while they were out shopping. Wayne would always wish that the ground would just open up and swallow him whole; it was all so embarrassing. Wayne just wanted all his freckles to join together, so that at least he could have some sort of tan.

Wayne hated his name. I mean why had his Mum and Dad called him Wayne?

What had they been thinking of?

Everyone knows that Wayne rhymes with rain, pain, brain, drain, plain, inane and insane. Even the most mediocre child poet couldn't fail to come up with anything less than a fiendishly hurtful rhyme, or spitefully accurate limerick, fed with such easy ammunition.

As for Higginbotham, Wayne thought it was probably the worst surname in the entire world. Why could he not have been born into a family of Taylors, Smiths, or Jones, anything in fact, but Higginbotham?

The "Higgin" bit wasn't too bad; in fact Higgins would have been an OK sort of name. It was the "botham" bit that caused all the problems. It was pronounced: "bottom."

Children have a naturally scatological sense of humour and any reference to a bodily function, or private part of the body, is always regarded as a source of infinite humour. So anyone with a name that could be referenced in any way to the human posterior was fair game for ridicule.

Higgybum, Higgybutt, Bumhead and much, much worse, were affronts that Wayne had got used to over the years.

Wayne hated his clothes, because his mother bought most of the things that he had to wear at jumble sales. Naturally, the clothes that people dispose of are not going to be examples of the latest fashions, so Wayne always ended up wearing the clothes and styles that had been "a la mode," about three or four years earlier.

The latest styles now involved huge flared lapels, bell bottomed trousers and wing collars and that was how everyone else turned up to school. Wayne's collars and lapels were as narrow as can be and his trousers were virtually drainpipes.

Wayne felt like a walking, talking scarecrow in his second hand clothes; all that he felt he needed was straw sticking out of his sleeves and trouser bottoms to complete the effect.

Even more embarrassing was the fact that Doris often bought his things at the school PTA jumble sale. It had frequently been the case that older kids had mocked Wayne mercilessly when they had recognised him wearing their mouldy old "cast offs." The clothes that they had discarded as being totally unfit to wear.

Wayne hated the fact that he seemed to be much cleverer than all the other kids at Gas Street Church of England Primary School. So much so, that he had been the only one from his class who had passed the "eleven plus" exam. Meaning that he would be the only one from his whole school who would be attending Wormysted's, the local Grammar School, the following September. All the other kids now delighted in calling him "smarty pants," or "clever clogs," or "swot face," or worse.

Most of all though, what Wayne really detested, what he really, really loathed, more than anything else in the whole wide world, even more than Manchester United, were his large, pointed ears; ears that stuck out from the sides of his head, virtually at right angles.

It was the ears that caused him the most problems.

It was the ears that the other kids mocked mercilessly.

"Big Ears," "Pixie lugs," "Mr. Spock" and "Dumbo" were all names he was used to being called.

Wayne had once asked his mother if he could have an operation to fix his ears. Aunty Margaret had helpfully suggested that they could be "pinned back." His Mum had said no; that it would cost money that they didn't have. Anyway what did "pinned back," mean exactly?

Wayne didn't really fancy the prospect of having drawing pins rammed into his skull.

"I mean that has got to hurt." He had said.

3

However, almost anything would have been better than the constant torment he received, because of the freakish appendages that stuck out on the sides of his head.

All in all, it had got to the stage where Wayne wouldn't venture out, unless it was to go to school, or to do a reluctant errand for his Mum.

The rest of the time, he would sit in his bedroom playing, reading, staring out of his bedroom window at the nearby grey-green northern hills, or occasionally creeping downstairs to watch one his favourite TV shows on the Higginbotham's ancient, black and white T.V.

Wayne's favourite TV show was "Star Trek." He particularly liked the resident alien character, Mr Spock. He liked Mr Spock, because he was smart and because he, like Wayne, had pointy ears.

No one laughed at Mr Spock's ears, except that grumpy old doctor and Mr Spock was a million times cleverer than him. Mr Spock was the cleverest man in the Universe.

Yes, Wayne could identify with Mr. Spock.

Wayne's dad didn't seem to have suffered the same sort of problems as Wayne. Frank Higginbotham was a very ordinary man; a very ordinary Yorkshire man. A man of few words, all of which he seemed to think about and consider intensely, before venturing to open his mouth.

Frank would ponder his response to any question, or statement, as though contemplating the very meaning of life; then slowly, he would nod and almost invariably say: "Aye."

Frank worked in a little factory in the small industrial town of Barlickwick, near the market town of Shepton, where the Higginbotham family lived. A town surrounded by the beautiful Yorkshire Dales.

Frank screwed thingummys onto widgets and then put them into boxes.

Five days a week, eight hours a day:

Thingummy, widget, box.

Thingummy, widget, box.

Thingummy, widget, box.

Wayne thought that it was little wonder that his Dad didn't say much.

There wasn't much conversational inspiration in thingummys, widgets and boxes. Amusing anecdotes about thingummys, widgets and boxes are pretty rare and Frank hadn't managed to come across a single one of them, even if they had existed, in all of his years of working at the factory.

Frank's wife had stopped asking him many years ago if he'd had a nice day, or if anything interesting had happened at work.

Although not exactly the most dynamic or witty man alive, Frank Higginbotham was kind and gentle. Wayne believed his dad was probably the nicest man in Shepton and possibly the nicest man in all of the County of Yorkshire.

Wayne's mum said Frank was so quiet, because of what had happened during the war. Frank had never been the same man, since he'd spent six years in the army, chasing some bad guy called Adolf Hitler all around North Africa and then through Europe.

Wayne didn't think that was anything to do with it. His Dad just wasn't very clever, that was all. Wayne thought that cleverness was over-rated anyway, it just meant that people had something else to pick on you for. Frank was quite lucky, not being clever.

Frank was also lucky enough to have lank, straight hair that was always perfectly groomed and laced with Brylcreem. Wayne's hair hadn't come from that side of the family.

Lucky Frank had olive skin, which tanned easily and he'd never had a single freckle in his life.

The luckiest thing of all about Frank Higginbotham was that he had quite small, neat ears that were swept back, instead of sticking out like Wayne's. There was no doubt about it. Frank's side of the family couldn't be blamed for Wayne's ears.

Wayne thought his Dad was a very lucky man, overall, despite the war and a life spent packing thingummys, widgets and boxes.

Doris Higginbotham, Wayne's mother, more than made up for his dad's quiet nature.

Doris was a firebrand. She had a temper like a hyper-active volcano and it was always advisable to run for cover, whenever it looked like an eruption was imminent, which seemed to be at least once every day.

Wayne had learned to recognise the warning signs of an eruption very early in his childhood and had become particularly adept at finding a suitable hiding place, whenever danger threatened. This allowed Doris to pour her anger out, without Wayne suffering too much damage.

Doris Higginbotham even looked a little bit like a volcano.

She was short, plump and wore long skirts, which flared out like the lower slopes of Mount Vesuvius.

Doris' head was topped by a frizzy mass of red hair, which looked, even on a good day, like an exploding scouring pad.

Wayne had long ago decided that it had been her side of the family that was responsible for the unruly mop that he was cursed with.

Inevitably, it was Doris who handled all the disciplinary issues in the Higginbotham household.

It was always Doris who handed out the "thick ears" if Wayne was considered to have been cheeky, or if he misbehaved at all.

Whereas Wayne's Dad was quiet and docile, his Mum was loud and vivacious. Doris loved to chat, loved to dance, party, drink and smoke and enjoy her life to the full.

She worked as a barmaid in the pub at the end of the terraced street where the Higgins family lived: "The Junction Inn."

Wayne had heard her say that the hours she spent working at the pub fitted in with her having to look after him, as though her having to work there was somehow his fault.

One thing about Doris Higginbotham puzzled Wayne. She might have been responsible for Wayne's hair, but she had absolutely nothing to do with his ears. Lucky old Doris, like lucky old Frank, had small ears. They stuck out a little bit, so you could see their tips through her frizzy permed hair, but they were very small and they were absolutely and definitely not pointed.

So Wayne couldn't blame her for the banes of his life.

Doris wasn't very clever either, so he couldn't blame her for that.

It was funny though, although Doris wasn't very clever, it seemed to Wayne that she was always right, she always said that she was anyway.

Yes, Doris Higginbotham might not always have been right, but Doris Higginbotham was never, ever wrong.

Wayne was the Higginbotham's only child.

The good side of this particular deal was that he got more Christmas presents than anyone else he knew at school. The bad side was that it meant that Doris had no one else to be cross with.

Wayne often wished that he had brothers and sisters, so that they could share the burden of the frequent "tellings off," but then he would look around his bedroom and realise that the Higginbotham's little house only had two bedrooms and if he did have any siblings, then they would have to share his room. Perhaps it was better to be a lonely, only child.

It seemed that Wayne had almost had a brother. Doris sometimes mentioned a baby called Trevor. Frank and Doris had had him before Wayne but he had died at a very young age. Trevor must have been a remarkable baby because Doris always seemed to mention how perfect he'd been and how, when Wayne did anything naughty, that Trevor would never have done anything like that. It sometimes seemed to Wayne that Doris had actually preferred Trevor, but maybe that was just him being a bit jealous and silly.

Wayne was never allowed to ask about Trevor. Doris just got all upset.

There was someone Wayne could almost identify with, his cousin Cedric. Cedric was also an only child, the son of Doris' younger sister, Margaret and he was a year and a half older than Wayne.

Margaret was "posher" than Doris, so Doris said, especially when she was moaning about her.

When Margaret had still been in her teens, she had married a young bank clerk who had worked hard and gone on to become an assistant bank manager, a position he had held for many years.

Uncle Stanley's respectable and steady job, which required him to wear a smart suit with a clean shirt and tie, had allowed Doris' sister to move into a house on the Beckside estate, on the edge of town, where some people even owned their own houses.

That had made Doris quite jealous.

Eventually, Uncle Stanley and Aunty Margaret had saved enough to move to the quite posh Greenfields estate, where there weren't any council houses at all.

That had made Doris even more jealous.

Recently, Uncle Stanley had been promoted to be the manager of his own branch of the Yorkshire Ridings Savings Bank.

Now Margaret Houghton-Hughes and her family lived on the Ripon Road. The Ripon Road was the really posh part of town; the part of town where the Doctors, solicitors, teachers and the big bosses lived. Uncle Stanley had even gone and bought a brand spanking new silver Ford Granada car, complete with a sunshine roof.

Now that had made Doris very, very jealous indeed.

Wayne was allowed to play with Cedric whenever the sisters got together. Although Cedric considered Wayne a bit of a pest, he was quite nice to him, nicer than the kids at school anyway. If he hadn't been nice, Aunty Margaret would have given him a thick ear. A thick normal ear, because Cedric had very small, normal ears, but then he would have, wouldn't he.

Even so, Wayne was quite prepared to accept Cedric's bossiness and constant air of superiority, because after all, it was nice to have someone to play with for a change.

The Higginbotham family visits to Auntie Margaret's huge, modern house always inevitably ended with Doris moaning all the way home.

Frank didn't have a car, so the family would walk slowly home, through the town, to the accompaniment of Doris complaining bitterly about some new item that the Houghton-Hughes' had bought and which they would never be able to afford.

She had been much worse since Uncle Stanley's recent good fortune. Doris would go on about how her little sister was:

"All fur coat and no knickers. A jumped up, double-barrelled nowt, who should remember where she came from, instead of developing such mighty airs and graces."

Wayne wondered why Doris insisted on visiting her sister if she was always going to feel so jealous and cross when she came to leave.

Wayne wondered why his Aunty didn't wear knickers when she wore her fur coat?

He had once even commented on the situation, but had received a short, sharp clip around the ear for his impudence. Doris wouldn't allow anyone else to criticise her sister.

Margaret was family, criticising her was Doris' right and her right alone.

The Higginbotham family lived right in the middle of an old Victorian terraced street, in a grey stone house, near the very centre of the town.

It was a very small house, definitely not modern, like the houses on the Beckside estate, or posh like on Greenfields and it was definitely a million miles from the mock Tudor mansions of the Ripon road; but it was sort of cosy, in a claustrophobic kind of way.

Of course, being so small, there was no room in the Higginbotham's house for unnecessary luxuries, like a bathroom, or anything like that.

The Higginbothams had eventually had one installed in the coal cellar.

Doris had insisted on it. She had had to have a bathroom installed, with a three-piece suite: lavatory, sink and bath, as soon as Margaret had moved into the house on the Beckside estate, which had a proper modern bathroom upstairs. Frank had always been quite happy with a wash down in the kitchen sink and a weekly scrub in an old tin bath, in front of the fire in the living room.

Now, Margaret had a four-piece bathroom upstairs in her house on the Ripon Road, including one of them bidet things that you could wash your feet in. The first time she had seen that huge bathroom, complete with a separate shower cubicle, Doris had taken a funny turn. She had walked all the way home in silence and had gone to bed early that night, even missing her favourite soap opera on the T.V.

The next day Wayne had been playing in the part of the coal cellar that still contained coal and had got very dirty indeed. Doris had erupted.

"Cleanliness is next to Godliness" she had screamed as she attacked her wailing son with a hard, doorstep scrubbing brush, as he stood naked in the bath. One thing no one could say about Doris Higginbotham was that she wasn't clean and house-proud and no one would be able to say it about her son either.

They might not have had much money, but she was clean and her son always would be, at least while she had anything to do with it.

Wayne Higginbotham might have hated himself, but sometimes he didn't like his mum too much either.

2

Streams of sunlight coursed through high leaded windows and glanced off rows of ancient, grey stone columns and arches. Specks of dust danced and glistened in the beams of light, like millions of tiny swirling snowflakes, occasionally settling on the grotesque face of a gargoyle, glowering down from on high.

Father James Malone gazed up at the intricately carved oak ceiling of the chamber. It was dark, being way above the streams of light, with just a few small shields, baring colourful coats of arms, to break the monotony of the age-dirty, brown wood.

The young priest fiddled with his rosary and smiled ruefully as he wondered how many men of God had looked up at that same ceiling over the centuries, waiting to be told their fate.

He considered himself lucky; some of his predecessors would have been contemplating being burned at the stake for their indiscretions.

"Good job this is the twenty-first century." He thought to himself as he heaved a heavy sigh.

Fr James Malone was twenty five years old. His hair was thick, dark and long, tumbling over his collar in a mass of curls. His sideburns almost reached down to his chin, being fashionably styled in the manner of a Victorian patriarch. His eyes were a deep, rich brown, his lashes long and girlish. He looked more like a Pop star than a priest and certainly more Mediterranean than Irish, but Irish he was and a Priest he was, although on this particular day he felt more like a naughty, little schoolboy.

The antechamber in which Father Malone stood was a part of a complex that was attached to St. Patrick's Cathedral in Dublin, one of the most important Churches in the whole of Ireland and a long way from his new Parish, in the most remote part of Western Connaught.

Father Malone shook his head ruefully:

"Why did I go and open my big mouth?" He said quietly to himself.

He shivered at the memory of his Bishop's reaction, to what had been a supposedly jocular snippet of conversation, back home in County Mayo.

That day had started pleasantly enough, with an uneventful journey to the Holy Shrine of Knock, followed by a small reception for new Parish priests at the Bishop's mansion; a nice convivial sort of "get to know you" occasion. You know the sort of thing: a small sherry, a vol au vent and a piece of quiche, sort of occasion.

All had gone well, for a while.

Many of the guests had been contemporaries of Fr Malone at the Seminary and there had been much laughter and reminiscing about old acquaintances and the exchanging of yarns, gossip and rumour.

The Bishop was a large, rotund, beady-eyed character, who seemed to have a perpetual problem with perspiration. He always seemed to be mopping his brow with a grubby grey handkerchief, even in the chill of an Irish winter. Bishop O'Leary seemed to have taken an immediate dislike to Fr Malone; a dislike, which became disturbingly apparent during what had seemed like a particularly anodyne conversation between James and one of his old friends from the Seminary.

Fr Malone had been relating his amazement at the survival of a number of traditional superstitions amongst the populace in the rural Parish that he had been assigned to. He had coloured his conversation with an anecdotal tale about a local eccentric, a farmer who lived way out in the most remote part of the mountains.

Bishop O'Leary had arrived in the middle of the narration and his round, blotchy face, already a vague shade of purple, had virtually exploded and had turned positively crimson when he had heard James' punch line:

"He said what? And what did you do? Why didn't you let me know all this immediately? Why didn't you tell Father Callaghan or Father Burke? You know what you've been told and why we must always be aware of the works of Satan, especially here in Ireland?"

The Bishop exploded, almost apoplectic with rage, over something that had seemed so insignificant to Fr Malone; something that had seemed so innocuous, that he hadn't actually even bothered to mention it to anyone else.

The creak of a nearby door opening jolted the young Priest out of his reverie.

A small, wizened man, dressed in a simple black cassock and white collar beckoned him forward into a corridor, which he proceeded to cross towards a shiny, black door.

The old man glanced at Fr Malone and quickly looked away, as though too much eye contact might spread a horribly infectious disease.

The old man's eyes flicked up and down as he examined Malone's fashionable black velvet suit, with its flared trousers. Obvious disdain oozed from the older man's every pore. He opened the creaking door and made an impatient gesture that suggested that the younger man should hurry through.

Fr Malone crossed himself and obeyed.

The room Fr Malone entered made him gasp in astonishment.

It was nominally an office, but it was the most opulent office he had ever seen in his life, a gallery would have been a more apt description.

He'd seen rooms in Palaces that were less sumptuously decorated than what was spread out before him. The artwork on the walls was probably worth more than all the money in Connaught. He certainly thought that he recognised a Titian on one wall and was that one a Rembrandt?

Where an old master did not conspicuously adorn a wall, a medieval tapestry did. Every single work of art depicted some biblical event and representations of the Madonna and Child were by far the most popular subject.

Fr Malone gawped around the room, like a penniless child standing, open mouthed, at the window of a sweet shop.

The centre of the ceiling, already imposing in its magnificent depiction of austere Biblical characters and fat pink cherubs was dominated by an enormous crystal chandelier, ablaze with the light of innumerable candles. Yet, despite the magnificent artwork, the flickering light of the chandelier and the glow cast by a couple of other candelabras, the overall aspect of the room was extremely sombre. It was full of shadows and dark corners, compared to the intense summer sunlight outside, that the priest had grown used to. Drawn, heavy purple and gold curtains obscured every window in the office. Not even the smallest chink of sunlight dared to squeeze cheekily through the hangings.

"It's a shame," thought Fr Malone; "that in a land as blighted with rain as ours, that they should be blocking out the sun with such heavy curtains."

Father Malone squinted in the darkness, a huge ornate oak desk stood against the far wall, by a curtained window. A small figure sat behind the desk, a little old man dressed in the most lavish crimson robes, with a matching crimson skull-cap perched on the top of his bald head.

The old man did not move, but watched the young priest intently, his eyes little more than dark slits, in an incredibly wrinkled face.

Malone shuddered at the old man's gaze. His narrowed eyes seemed to burn into the young Priest and seemed to glint with a light as crimson as his robes, but perhaps that was just the reflection of the chandelier, causing strange effects.

Malone coughed politely:

"Good afternoon, Your Grace." He began.

The figure behind the desk remained ominously still, like a waxwork dummy.

Malone gulped; perhaps this whole silly matter was more serious than he had thought.

He had certainly been surprised by the summons to Dublin that had followed his conversation with to Bishop O'Leary, but he had convinced himself that it was just going to be a corroboration of facts and nothing more.

After all, what had he done?

He approached the old man's desk cautiously, waiting to be greeted, or to be asked to take a seat.

"Good afternoon, Your Grace." He repeated, hopefully, as he wondered whether the old man was deaf, or not.

The old man said nothing. His hands were propping up his chin, but were clasped as if in prayer, his eyes did not move from Malone's.

Finally, after what seemed like a sizable proportion of eternity, during which he had shuffled uncomfortably on the spot and tried to nonchalantly admire some of the works of art that surrounded him, Malone broke the silence again.

"Look, Your Grace," he spurted "it would really help me, you know; if you would let me know what is going on here?"

The old man remained stubbornly impassive.

Malone gulped, again:

"I'm Father Malone, from Finaan, you know? You asked me to come."

And then before he could stop himself James drawled:

"That's Malone, James Malone."

It came out in a bad, Sean Connery sort of way, which seemed so incongruous with the setting.

Malone had to stifle a self conscious little smirk, which quickly evaporated when the old man finally did speak, in a voice that was little more than a deep croak:

"Yes,…..we've been expecting you, Father Malone."

He held out his hand and Fr Malone approached the desk, bent and kissed the ring on his finger, desperately trying not to laugh; it was probably the nerves that were making him giddy. He stood up straight again and wondered if the old man had a white cat draped across his knee and whether he should move, just in case a red button was about to be pushed to despatch him through a trapdoor into a fiery pit:

"Goodbye, Father Malone."

Suddenly, however, Malone was aware of movement behind him. He turned quickly, as a tall, sallow priest, emerged from the shadows behind him. Malone had not noticed him before, hidden as he had been, in the darkness, behind the door:

"So this is Father Malone?" Whispered the newcomer in heavily accented English.

The man looked much younger than his colleague behind the desk, yet there was something about him that appeared incongruous in a twentieth Century setting.

It was his eyes in particular, that took Malone's breath away. They were as black as coal and as cold as a winter night. They glittered unpleasantly in the candlelight; and like the old man's, there seemed to be a red glow deep down in those bottomless pits that was not attributable to any candle.

Malone could easily imagine him in one of the old masters hanging on the walls. His face was pale, long and thin, accentuated by a goatee beard and a moustache that was almost Elizabethan in style. His hair was as black as his eyes and slicked back tightly over his head, but was worn long over his ears at the sides. His lips were bloodless and thin and his

17

mouth twisted in a permanent sneer. He was wearing a simple black cassock and white collar, like the old priest who had ushered Malone into the room, but a large gold crucifix hung loosely by the rosary at his side.

The old man behind the desk reached for a piece of paper. He moved slowly, deliberately, like an ancient tortoise stretching out for a lettuce leaf. Malone thought of darting over and passing him the paper to speed things up a bit, but quickly thought the better of it.

The skin under the old man's chin rolled constantly, as if he was trying to swallow, or was chewing on invisible gum.

Malone realised that he was even older than he had originally thought.

"Yes, Father Pizarro, this is the one."

The old man croaked, his gaze never leaving Fr Malone:

"This is the one that you have come all the way from Rome to see."

If the comment was meant to impress the young Priest, it succeeded; Malone raised his eyebrows:

"Rome?" He asked incredulously, with another gulp as his mouth dried up.

"Would you like a drink, Your Grace?" The black-eyed priest asked the old man. The old man shook his head slowly.

Black eyes looked at Malone and raised a quizzical eyebrow. Malone thought it might not be wise to ask for a vodka Martini, shaken not stirred, given the present circumstances, so he murmured:

"Er, yes, a glass of water, please."

Black eyes poured a glass of water from a carafe on an elegant table by the old man's desk and handed it to Malone, before pouring a large goblet of what looked like red wine for himself. The goblet looked as if it had been forged in solid gold.

"Your Bishop wrote to me, expressing concern about your encounter with this, this er, creature, Father Malone." The ancient Bishop croaked:

"It seems that you have had congress with it on more than one occasion, but have failed to inform your superiors of the said congress."

"Creature? Congress?" Malone repeated even more incredulously.

He looked at the black eyed Priest to solicit some support, any support, but the latter quickly looked away.

The Bishop licked flecks of spittle from his lips:

"I refer to the Leprechaun, you fool."

His croak was now much more high pitched and impatient.

"With respect, Your Grace," Malone stammered: "If this is all about that conversation I was having with my old friend Charlie, that His Grace, Bishop O'Leary heard, then the world has gone mad. I was merely telling Charlie, an old mucker of mine from Maynooth, about a chat that I'd had with an old man, out in the hills. With all due respect Your Grace, it was about a perfectly innocent bit of craic I had, with a perfectly simple oul' fella, way out in the back of beyond. I don't know where all this "leprechaun" stuff has come from. It's as if the man we were talking about isn't human. We were talking about a harmless old man, an eccentric; a village idiot, a simpleton."

"With the same respect, Father Malone, young man, Bishop O' Leary seems to be thinking otherwise."

The old man retorted sharply, with an edge of venom in his voice,

"And, with respect," he mimicked the phrase sarcastically:

"He is a great deal more knowledgeable about such matters than you, young man. You will now relate the entire conversation you had with this "Charlie," and you will omit no detail, no matter how trivial it may seem to you."

Malone hung his head feeling even more like a naughty schoolboy in the headmaster's study:

"Yes, Your Grace." He answered, desperately trying to remember something that had occurred many weeks earlier:

"Well, what I told Charlie was that I was cycling over the mountain road to Westport one morning, when I bumped into a fella that I've met in the village a few times. An oul'fella called Mickey Finn. He shouted "Morning" to me. Naturally I responded with a similar greeting: 'Tis a fine day. He said. But I'd hurry if I were you, there'll be a soft rain later."

"A soft rain?"

Black eyes interrupted, but the old man held up his hand and nodded to Fr Malone, bidding him to continue.

"Well, by way of being neighbourly, I said to the old fella, it's been a few times that I'd cycled up in the mountains and I couldn't believe how remote it was, so wild and open."

"Yes, go on." The old man leaned forward expectantly.

Fr Malone continued:

"Well, I said to him: If there are still any of the little people left in Ireland at all. This was where they'd be. The oul' fella laughed at that and said that I was an eejit and did I not know that I was talking to one at that very moment?"

The old man coughed slightly and sat back in his chair, his lips twisting in a satisfied smirk.

"Condemned by his own tongue."

Black eyes licked his lips.

"Mmmm, Father Malone, do you know where you are?" The old man croaked.

"Well er, St.Patrick's Cathedral, Your Grace?" Malone replied with more than slight hint of sarcasm in his voice.

The old man's mouth moved as though he was chewing over Malone's words, but it was the younger Priest who spoke next.

"This is no place for your searing wit, Father Malone. You stand before Bishop Donleavy, the head of the "Sacred Order of Saint Gregory" in Ireland. What do you know of it?"

"Bishop Donleavy?" Malone asked, wondering what he could say about someone he had never heard of in his entire life.

"No, The Sacred Order of St. Gregory the Great," hissed the black-eyed priest, contemptuously.

"Ah" said Malone: "Now, saints were a particular speciality of mine at the Sem......"

"St Gregory the Great." Barked black eyes, as he rudely interrupted the young Priest:

"He was one of the greatest of all the early Popes. He lived around the beginning of the seventh century, when your little island was, surprisingly, one of the few beacons of Christianity in Europe. It was a time when the Lord's ministry on Earth, was threatened by pagan barbarian hordes and by stubborn adherents of the old religions. Pope Gregory set up a secret organisation within the Priesthood, within the church, to eliminate the servants and agents of Satan, an elite unit of Our Lord's army, if you like."

The bearded priest walked in front of Malone:

"I presume you have heard of such creatures as vampires, werewolves, warlocks, witches, wizards, demons, fairies, goblins and shape shifters, Father Malone? No doubt you have wasted much of your time watching the so called horror movies, at your cinema, or in Satan's very shop window; the television set? Yes, I see you are familiar with the creatures spawned by Lucifer to ensnare and destroy the Children of Our Lord. I see that you have heard of the Hell-born abominations that threaten all true believers; the creatures that live in their nightmares and haunt their souls. All those things that hark back to the pagan beliefs and practices that existed before God surrendered his only son, Jesus Christ, Our Lord, to save us."

He crossed himself, then turned and looked at the older man, who once again fixed Malone with a stare.

"For nearly fifteen hundred years, the "Sacred Order of Saint Gregory" has protected the Church and the souls of men from the teeming hordes of Lucifer on Earth. A prophecy was written, long ago that stated that it could only be such a spawn of Satan, an immortal that could stop the Second Coming of Our Lord. "

The old man croaked:

"In whatever guise these slaves of the devil wish to project themselves; and yes, such creatures as vampires and werewolves do exist, we eliminate them. We are the last line of defence, the agents of salvation."

"You mean you fight witches and so on?"

Malone suggested helpfully, although he couldn't help sounding extremely sceptical and his mind was full of images of Torquemarda and the Spanish inquisition, gleefully burning heretics.

Black eyes snorted:

"Witches have always been few and far between. We deal with real demons, real entities, real threats to the souls of men and the very real threat that they present to "Our Lord" himself. Like this creature of yours, Father Malone. Oh yes, you might think of him as a simpleton and there is indeed a small chance that he may be, but Ireland has always been the front line, in our battle against the unholy spawn of Satan. It is one of these creatures that is prophesied to sire "God's Assassin" and that must be prevented at all costs."

He crossed himself as if to protect himself from the name he had uttered.

"St. Patrick himself started the battle when he cast out all of the snakes and the scribes of the time were not just referring to reptiles, I can assure you. Our role is to continue his work and cast out all the demons that have made this dark island their home, until it is safe for Our Lord to once again, walk the earth."

Fr Malone stared at the two others in the room.

"I, I'm sure this is all meant to be metaphorical, isn't it?" He stammered:

"I mean, this fella I met, that I told the Bishop about, he really isn't really one of the little folk, he's just a sad, lonely old man, surely there's no such thing as a……."

"Silence!" The old man croaked as loudly as he could manage.

"It is possible that he is innocent, of course, but if it is likely that you have spoken to a real demon, then we must know and we must act. It is ten years since we have seen one of these creatures and nearly twenty since we got rid of the last one in Connemara. It would appear that we still have work to do. Now please sit down and tell us more of it."

"We shall judge the guilt, or innocence of this creature in due course, Father Malone." Black eyes hissed, malevolently:

"We have plenty of experience in cleansing the earth of such filth. Now pray tell us everything you know, we have plenty of time, plenty of time."

3

Thursday, the 27th of June had started off just like any other Thursday, or any other boring old school day for that matter.

Wayne's Mum had bellowed up the steep stairwell from the kitchen that it was time for him to wake up and get himself downstairs for breakfast, or he would be late for school.

Wayne had rubbed his eyes and crawled slowly, groaning and scratching out of his bed and peeked out of the curtains.

As usual, it was raining and the stone slates on the roofs of the terraced street opposite, shone wet and silvery under a heavy, grey, summer sky.

There was no sign that any thing unusual was going to happen to Wayne on that particular Thursday. No sign at all.

He had stumbled down the stairs, as he usually did and into the kitchen:

"What do you want for your breakfast then, love?" Doris had asked as she clattered around some pans. Given that the only choices of breakfast that Doris ever offered were toast and jam, or cornflakes, Wayne had yawned then grunted a preference for the latter option, prompting Doris to snap:

"You know where they are then! Come on, you're old enough and big enough now to get your own."

Wayne had sighed and climbed down from the stool that he had only just occupied. He poured a few cornflakes into his bowl and carelessly splashed some milk and a spoonful of sugar onto them and had then begun to read an article about dinosaurs on the back of the cereal packet, through tired and bleary eyes.

"Come on Wayne, hurry up!" his mother had bawled, noticing that he hadn't yet started to eat.

"You know we don't have time to mess around in the morning; Jesus, what would your grandmother have said?"

She had snatched the cornflake box away and slammed it into a cupboard with a bang. Wayne had sighed again, picked up a spoon and began to slowly munch his breakfast. He didn't know what his grandmother would have said, not a clue. Wayne hadn't known any of his Grandparents. They had all died long before he was born. He had often wondered what sort of ears his grandparents had had and whether he could blame any of them for the major curses of his life. But you could never tell what their ears had been like from the old photos he had seen, because they had either had big hats or big hair.

Doris and Frank had been quite old when he had been born. Frank had already been in his mid forties and Doris not much younger. That was probably why his grandparents were all dead. They'd got fed up of waiting for a grandchild, even him.

Doris' snatching away his cereal bowl and yelling at him to quickly clean his teeth and get himself off to school before she "clattered his ears" for being so lazy and slow had shattered Wayne's dreamy thoughts about his ancestry.

Wayne knew better than to argue with his formidable and frequently frightening mother, so he had done as he was told.

Wayne's day at Gas Street School on that particular Thursday had been remarkably unremarkable. His lessons with Mr. Braithwaite and his favourite teacher Mrs. Ball had passed without incident. He had sat next to Richard Hebden as usual. Richard was as close as Wayne had to a best friend. Richard lived on the Beckside estate, where Aunty Margaret used to live, although he wasn't posh like her. Wayne and Richard had chatted about football and TV and the things that eleven-year-old boys tend to chat and laugh about. They had played soccer in the rain soaked playground at morning break time, after lunch and then again in the afternoon. As usual Wayne had received the usual mickey taking about his ears:

"Come on lugsy, pass us the ball."

"Knock it in with your wing nuts, Higginbotham."

"If you'd have flapped those wings on the sides of yer head, you'd have reached that header, Higgybutt."

Wayne was so used to it, that he hardly even noticed.

Lunch had been totally forgettable; it always seemed to consist of lots of cabbage and potatoes prepared in a multiplicity of different ways and then a dessert consisting of some unidentifiable suet stodge, which was always smothered in thick, lumpy custard.

At quarter to four, when the school bell rang to bring the school day to an end, nothing at all had happened to suggest that anything out of the ordinary was about to take place.

Thursday, June 27th was quickly sliding into the oblivious past of Wayne's largely insignificant young life, just as every other day had, that had preceded it.

Wayne had gathered his coat and his satchel and bade his few friends and schoolmates goodbye and then had trudged out of the school gates, on to Gas Street and set off on the short walk home.

He hated the walk home these days. It was on the walk home that he occasionally bumped into his nemesis, Baz Thompson, the local bully.

Wayne passed the end of Corporation Street, as usual and then crossed on to Cavendish Street, where he lived.

It was only then that Wayne saw them: Baz Thompson and his gang, loitering in the alley, by old Alfie Lancaster's house, six doors from the safety of his own home.

Baz's Grandad was a neighbour of the Higginbotham family and Baz would often pop round to beg, borrow, or steal money from his unwitting forebear.

Usually, if Wayne was playing out in the large communal backyard, or on the front street, Baz would waste no opportunity in tormenting him. He regarded terrifying the much younger and smaller boy as good, easy entertainment. Baz had noticed a small model of the Star-ship Enterprise from the TV show "Star Trek" on Wayne's bedroom windowsill. Combining the fact that Wayne did have rather large pointy ears with his knowledge that "Star Trek" had a pointy-eared character called Spock; Baz, using every single ounce of his intellect, had wittily decided to call Wayne "Dr. Spock." He thought it incredibly amusing, as seemingly, did his friends.

Baz, or Basil as his mother knew him; had four or five friends, all a year or two younger than him, but all as equally and stunningly stupid. Stupid enough to admire Baz, because he had once been arrested for throwing bricks outside Burnley's football ground. That had made him seem extremely hard and to such morons, being hard also meant that he was very cool. Baz lapped up their admiration and the tales of his misdemeanours had gradually grown taller in his telling of them, until some of his friends were convinced that Baz Thompson was an underworld Godfather, every bit as evil as London's notorious Kray twins and equally as cool.

As soon as Baz had spotted Wayne, on that Thursday, at about ten to four, he knew he was going to have some fun. He saw the youngster stop his infantile skipping and how his face had paled as soon as he had seen Baz and his mates. He had watched the boy gulp and look around quickly, hoping that some adult might be around to save him. There had been no one.

Most of the other kids at Gas Street school lived on Beckside and so went the other way home.

Wayne was totally alone.

"Oi, Dr.Spock!" Baz had shouted:

"Come 'ere!" He glanced at his gang and grinned. Wayne walked slowly towards his tormentor who leaned down and grabbed the lapels of his jacket.

"Got any cash on yer, spaz?" Baz had leered.

"No, I'm sorry, I haven't." Wayne stammered.

"You sure?" Baz growled as his grip on Wayne's jacket tightened and he pulled him slightly off the ground, so that Wayne had had to stand on his tiptoes.

Wayne's eyes widened in fear and he shook his head nervously.

"No Baz, honest, sorry, I don't have a penny."

"Baz snorted and imitated the timid voice of his prey:

"No Baz, sorry Baz, I don't have a penny, na, na, na."

He turned to look for the approval of his acolytes who all giggled.

Baz grabbed Wayne's ear:

"Hey!" he shouted, "look at the size of the lugs he's got on him!" The gang laughed.

"They're all pointed. He looks like a lickle pixie, awwww."

More laughter.

Baz's mocking laughter turned back into a threatening grimace.

"Tell you what shrimp." Baz had sneered.

"I'm gonna do you a big favour."

Wayne gulped; he knew Baz's idea of a favour would not be a very palatable prospect.

Baz continued.

"If you go and nick a fiver from your fat, ugly mother's purse and bring it to me in the next five minutes. I'll not rip yer ears off, the next time I see you. If you don't, I will rip them both off and the favour will be that you won't look like such a spazzy little freak any more."

Baz's gang had laughed.

Wayne, his face contorted with pain as Baz twisted his ear, thought quickly about his options.

He could do as Baz asked, but then that would be theft and he would get into trouble.

Was Doris any less scary than Baz?

If Wayne did do it, Baz would only do the same thing again.

He could just say he would do it and then hide inside his house.

No, Baz wouldn't dare come and get him from his house, would he? But he would rip his ears off the next time he saw him.

No, the only thing to do was what he did.

"No, I won't." he retorted, as bravely as he could manage: "I don't care what you do, I won't steal for you."

Wayne had pulled back sharply, slipping out of Baz's grip.

Baz's gang had sniggered uncomfortably. Defiance was not supposed to be on today's programme of events.

Baz was shocked that Wayne had not simply complied with his request. No one stood up to Baz Thompson.

He was shocked that of all the people in the world who had stood up to him, it was that miserable, little, elfin geek right in front of him. A kid who wasn't even half his size and who had made a fool out of him, made him look small, in front of his tittering mates.

"Why you little........" he had snarled as he attempted to grab Wayne's jacket again, but Wayne had dodged him.

"Gerroff!" Wayne shouted as he ducked under Baz's flailing elbow. Baz spun as quickly as his bulk would allow but again Wayne avoided his grabbing hands.

Baz was apoplectic with rage. His face had gone a peculiar shade of purple as he wheeled around, trying to catch the slippery kid who had so embarrassed him.

"I'm gonna kill you!" He roared.

Finally he managed to grab the back of Wayne's collar and he pulled him back, puffing and panting. Then he re-established his grip on Wayne's lapel. Wayne wriggled desperately, but this time Baz did not let go. He swung his fist up under Wayne's chin and sent the boy flying through the air. He watched him hit the ground heavily and then relaxed and grinned as he heard the murmur of approval from his gang.

"Nice one Baz"

"Yeah that'll teach him."

"Cheeky little git!"

The bedraggled figure of Wayne climbed up slowly, obviously in great pain. Blood was pouring down his chin from his mouth.

Baz flexed his shoulders manfully and prepared to close in for the kill.

He uttered more threats and mocked the smaller boy's liking of "Star Trek," that was when Wayne had responded with his: "I am not a Vulcan, fatso" speech.

It was then that Baz had felt the first seeds of doubt taking root in his mind. He continued to play to his audience of sycophants, however, and went on threatening the smaller boy, bragging about how he was going to rip off his ears, but there was something about Wayne Higginbotham that Baz had never encountered before, something totally and utterly unexpected.

The kid hadn't seemed frightened any more.

Wayne had smiled at him.

Now Baz really was confused. His nose was inches from Wayne's. The kid should have been pleading for his life, like all Baz's victims did. But he was smiling at him.

That was when it had happened!

That was when the badly injured Wayne Higginbotham had faced down the much larger bully and had somehow knocked him out.

Knocked him out without so much as touching him, well that was what some said anyway. Wayne couldn't actually remember. The last thing he could remember was seeing Baz stretched out on the ground twitching; then he had heard someone, probably one of Baz's gang, shout:

"Quick, get his mother"

The next thing he knew, he was lying in a hospital bed.

That hadn't been the end of Wayne Higginbotham's very peculiar day, though, oh no. That had only been the start.

It got much weirder after that.

Much, much, weirder.

4

"I'm worried about young Wayne Higginbotham." Mrs. Elizabeth Ball stated, as she poured hot water from the kettle into a teapot, while staring thoughtfully out of her kitchen window.

"Mmm!"

Her husband murmured, without raising his head from behind "The Yorkshire Post."

"He's generally a happy go lucky sort of boy, but he seems to have been ever so down recently, ever since he heard that he'd passed his eleven plus." She put the lid on the teapot and turned to her husband.

"Tea dear?"

"Mmm"

"It's probably because he's going to be leaving all of his friends when he goes off to Grammar School. That can be very disturbing for a child of his age. Not that he seems to have many friends, that Hebden boy seems to be the only one he's close too. Toast?" She asked as she opened a loaf of "Tiger" bread.

"Mmm." Came the muffled response from behind the broadsheet newspaper.

"It should be the happiest time of his life. I mean he's from quite a poor family but he's very, very clever. Streets ahead of the others when he was in my class. He should be relishing the prospect of Grammar School."

"Mmm"

Mrs Ball hesitated as she poured the thick brown tea into two mugs.

"Are you listening to me?" She asked her husband, sounding somewhat exasperated.

"Mmm" came his reply as she added milk to the tea.

"I mean he could be in trouble at home, or something. You just don't know what happens once these kids walk out of that gate at quarter to four"

"Mmm"

Two slices of toast popped up in the toaster.

"Well what do you think?" She asked sharply as she slapped heaps of butter onto one of the slices of toast

"Mmmm?

A steaming mug of hot tea was banged down on the table right in front of the paper.

"John, have you been listening to a word I've said?" She barked.

"What?" John Ball asked with a touch of exasperation.

"Of course, I was listening."

"Oh yes, course you were, so what was I saying then?" Elizabeth demanded as she eased herself onto one of the chairs at the breakfast table and slammed a plate of hot buttered toast in front of her partner.

"That you're worried about this kid and er, he's usually happy."

John Ball shrugged, he thought he'd done enough to escape further discussion and his hand went back to his newspaper.

"What's his name then?" Elizabeth asked, folding her arms aggressively.

"Er, Shane Hegginton?" John suggested, with more hope than conviction.

"Wayne Higginbotham!" Elizabeth snapped and glowered at her spouse, who sighed and then slowly and reluctantly folded his newspaper.

Elizabeth Ball shook her head resignedly as she reached for the marmalade jar.

"Men!" She grumbled, cheering up as she noticed that she only needed one more cut out golly from the Marmalade jar label and she would be able to send off for an enamel golly badge. They were great little incentive prizes for the kids.

She buttered her toast and spread the marmalade on the warm butter before licking her fingers.

"I think I'll ask Mrs. Higginbotham to come into school for a chat."

"Good, right, yes, do that. Get her in and slap on the thumbscrews. Although wasn't he in your class last year?" John pondered.

"Yes, he was, what's that got to do with it?" Elizabeth asked with a puzzled frown on her face.

"Well, isn't he in old Braithwaite's class now? Surely he should be doing all the worrying."

Elizabeth gave a snort of derision:

"Braithwaite hasn't a clue what's happening anywhere in that school. He thinks he's still fighting the Second World War. They may say the battle of Waterloo was won on the playing fields of Eton, but as far as Braithwaite is concerned, El Alamein is still being fought in Gas Street's playground. I like Wayne Higginbotham. He's got a very promising future, if it's managed properly."

John Ball smiled as he looked at his wife munching her toast, her face a picture of determination as she stared at the jar of marmalade.

"That's what makes you such a good teacher." He said softly. She looked up at him:

"What?" she asked; surprised that he hadn't dived straight back into his paper as soon as the conversation had lulled.

"Because to you it's more than a job; you actually care about those kids." John gently patted her hand.

"Go and sort it out love, young Higginbotham should think himself lucky he's got a guardian angel like you looking after him. Right, now master Higginbotham's sorted, can I read my paper?" John asked, raising his eyebrows and picking up the paper again.

"By the way have you thought that he might be being bullied? Kids always pick on differences and if he's the only one going to Wormysted's, well….." He added as he disappeared back behind his paper.

That morning at Gas Street Primary school, Wayne Higginbotham was conspicuous by his absence. Wayne was never ill. Elizabeth expressed her concerns in the staff room at first break:

"Yes, not like him is it?" Mr. Braithwaite the headmaster and Wayne's class teacher stated as he absent-mindedly dropped half a Rich Tea biscuit into his cup, splashing tea all over his regimental tie.

"Punctual boy, Higginbotham, almost military in his timing. Prerogative of Kings, you know, punctuality. A much under estimated quality these days, if you ask me."

"Yes, Mr Braithwaite. Have you ever considered the possibility that Wayne might be being bullied?" Elizabeth suggested, carefully.

"No, No." Mr. Braithwaite harrumphed, shaking his head so vigorously that his thick spectacles slipped down his nose. He peered at Elizabeth from over the rims:

"I've been teaching for nearly thirty years now and I know all there is to know about bullying, I can spot it a mile off and it's not happening here, Elizabeth. I wouldn't have it. One thing I learned in the army. Bullying destroys morale, you know. You've got to stamp on it. Short, sharp, shock, what!"

Mrs. Monk who'd taught Wayne when he had been younger and Mrs McGiver, another of his old teachers raised their eyebrows conspiratorially at Elizabeth. She smiled wryly at them.

"He's certainly not been himself lately. He was always so cheerful. There was always a smile on his face."

Elizabeth looked at the other two for support, they both nodded but Mr Braithwaite stared back out of the window overlooking the playground where most of the pupils were enjoying the morning break. The screams, yells and laughter of children at play filtered through the window into the staff-room.

"No, look at 'em down there. No bullying, they've not got the time for it. Mr. Jackson keeps the boys playing football all break long. Good clean team sports. That's what they need, lots of activity, busy, busy, busy. A busy mind and a busy body have no time for mischief. It's the devil that finds work for idle hands to do. Activity, that's what stops the bullying. When I was in North Africa, I remember my C.O. saying…."

He was interrupted by the bang of the staff room door as it slammed shut.

Mrs Grimes, the school secretary, had slipped into the staff room, quickly poured herself a drink and took a spot in the centre of the staff room. She sipped from her cup of steaming hot coffee and addressing no one in particular said:

"Have you all heard?" Knowing full well, of course, that she was the only one who had heard whatever it was that she knew. Silence descended on the staff room, even Mr Braithwaite looked away from the window as his spectacles slid down his nose again.

Mrs Grimes leaned forward conspiratorially

"That Higginbotham boy's in hospital."

There was a general outbreak of shocked murmuring from the several teachers in the staff room and an audible gasp from Mrs.Ball. Mrs Grimes was obviously revelling in being the bearer of bad, albeit exciting news:

"His mother rang in about ten minutes ago. It seems….."

Her voice dropped and she leaned forward again as if whispering a secret to a confidante:

"…………it seems, he was in a fight, on the street. A veritable brawl."

Mr Braithwaite stood almost to attention, his glasses slipped down his nose again:

"Fight?" He spluttered, "Who? What? Where? When? How?"

"Last night on his way home from school, so his mother says."

Mrs Grimes pursed her lips as though there was something unbelievable about Mrs. Higginbotham's statement.

Elizabeth piped up above the general hubbub:

"Is he alright? How badly is he hurt? Do we know how long is he going to be in hospital?"

Mrs. Grimes looked offended by the barrage of questions:

"Well I don't know, do I? I'm only telling you what his mother just told me. She rang me from a pub, at this hour of the day would you believe?"

She sniffed:

"Mind you, it doesn't surprise me. You've only got to look at her."

Mrs. Higginbotham had argued with Mrs. Grimes several years earlier, over some complete triviality and had used some mild bad language, which Mrs. Grimes had neither forgotten, nor forgiven.

"Common piece of work that Higginbotham woman." She hissed maliciously.

Elizabeth Ball looked crestfallen, she had gone decidedly pale.

"Now, now, Elizabeth, no need to worry."

Mr. Braithwaite patted her shoulder.

"Young Higginbotham will be fine, I'm sure. Children are tough little devils you know. Troopers! He'll be back at school in no time."

Elizabeth grimaced:

"Bob, it's only just over three weeks until the summer holidays and after that he'll be off to Wormysted's Grammar School. We might not see him here again, and he is our star pupil this year, for goodness sake. He's the only one who's passed his eleven plus, after all. I think I'll pop along to the hospital after school and see if I can find out how he is."

"Mm, good idea Elizabeth, do a recce. A quick sortie out to see how the land lies as soon as possible. Let me know the situation so that I can strategise operations."

Bob Braithwaite straightened his back and shouted above the general hubbub in the staffroom:

"Now, Ladies and Gentlemen, about prize giving…"

Later that night Elizabeth Ball awoke with a start.

John was lying next to her, snoring like a clapped out old motorbike with the silencer removed, yet it was not that sound that had jolted her from her sleep, disturbing as it was.

Nor was she aware of having had a bad dream. She had not got to that point in a nightmare where the subconscious mind rouses you, just as disaster is about to strike. In fact she was not aware of having had any dreams at all. No, it was more just a sudden and intense uneasy feeling, a thought that had jumped into her mind and caused her to wake up for some unknown reason. Maybe, she thought, it was just a silly women's intuition, yet she was very worried about young Wayne Higginbotham; very worried indeed.

5

Wayne could hear lots of indistinct voices; some sounded strange, some sort of familiar. It was difficult to make them out because of the loud buzzing in his ears and the violent throbbing in his head.

He slowly opened his eyes.

Everything looked ever so slightly blurred.

He could tell that he wasn't at home though. It was so bright, the light was so different. He could see the vague outlines of other beds and the shapes of women in blue uniforms moving about.

Nurses, he presumed. Wayne realised that he must be in hospital.

As his vision began to clear he could see his mother, Doris, sat at the side of the bed, looking confusingly pleased, but also slightly cross.

"Waking up at last are you?" She scalded softly.

"I've been sat here over an hour. I don't know, fighting in the street. That's not how I've brought you up to behave, is it?"

Wayne opened his mouth to speak but the pain in his skull went mad, so he just shook his head gently.

"Anyway," Doris continued: "If that Baz Thompson was involved, I don't suppose it was all your fault. I've brought you some nice grapes and a bottle of Lucozade. It'll help you get back on your feet."

"Baz?" Thought Wayne and the image of the prone body of his assailant, lying on the pavement, crept slowly back into his mind.

"Ohhh" He groaned, "Baz, is he dead?"

"Dead?" Doris snapped. "Dead? No, he's not dead, but I don't think he'll bother you for a while. When his mates took him home he was grinning like an idiot and reciting Hickory Dickory Dock. He looked and sounded even more simple than usual to me. Anyway, it's you I'm worried about. You've got badly bruised ribs they say and a broken arm as well."

Doris sniffed and sighed before looking inquisitively back at her son.

"Well, are you going to tell me exactly what happened?"

Wayne groaned again and felt very, very sick. His chest hurt, his mouth hurt and his arm hurt. In fact everything hurt. He didn't want to speak and so he moaned and pretended to drift back into unconsciousness.

"Doctor!" He heard his mother screech.

"I think he's going into one of them there coma doo daas."

Wayne heard someone bustle up to his bedside and then felt that sudden horribly uncomfortable feeling as someone lifts your eyelid. He saw the Doctor standing over him. A middle aged man with a chubby, round face, bald head and circular gold rimmed spectacles, a bit like John Lennon's:

"No, Mrs. Higginbotham, don't worry. Your son is not going into one of them there coma doo daas, as you so eloquently put it."

The Doctor stated patiently, but with more than a slight hint of condescension.

"But he does need rest. I suggest you leave him with us tonight, so that we can keep an eye on him. You can pop back in the morning to see how he's doing. He's taken quite a beating you know. He is most certainly suffering from concussion as well as the severe bruising and the fracture"

From his sanctuary behind closed eyes, Wayne heard his mother reluctantly agree and surprisingly felt her plant a rare kiss on his forehead.

"See you tomorrow love." He heard her say.

Perhaps he ought to get beaten up more often.

Wayne listened to Doris' footsteps as she walked away from his bed and heard the double doors bang together as she left the ward.

He had intended to have a look around when his mother had left, but somehow the very act of closing his eyes sent him off into a deep, dark, dreamless sleep.

It was night time when he awoke. He re opened his eyes and looked around. His vision seemed much clearer now, even though it was quite dark.

He was in a small unit of four beds. He couldn't see anyone in the bed next to his, because the curtains were drawn around it.

He wondered briefly if someone had died and shuffled uncomfortably, which brought waves of pain from seemingly every part of his body.

"Ouuuuch!" He groaned quietly, before checking out the other beds.

The bed opposite contained an old, untidy looking man, who was snoring loudly. He had long, straggly grey hair, which was thinning on top and it looked like he hadn't shaved in days.

The other bed, near the huge windows, was empty and all the bedclothes were neatly folded and piled on top of the mattress.

Wayne sighed. He could see a couple of nurses and a porter by a brightly lit desk down the corridor beside his bed. He wished he'd had a bed by the window, even though the curtains were drawn and he had no idea what was on the other side.

He looked around to see if there was a telly anywhere. In a big new hospital like this they might have a new colour set like his Aunty Margaret's. He couldn't see one though, not near his bed anyway. The Higginbotham's telly was an ancient black and white thing that they'd had since England had won the World Cup nearly a decade earlier.

There was a small cupboard by his bed, which had the bottle of Lucozade his mother had brought and a glass on top. Above his pillow there was a button on the wall that had "Emergency call" written above it. There was also a switch and a set of headphones hanging off it. Wayne wondered whether he should check out what was on the radio when he noticed a peculiar sound: silence. He looked around and noticed that the old man in the opposite bed had stopped snoring. Not only had he stopped snoring, but he was sitting upright in his bed with his eyes wide open, even in the gloom they reminded Wayne of small vivid blue saucers. The old man was staring right at him, his mouth moved rapidly but no sound came out. He looked wild, quite mad in fact. Suddenly he shouted:

"Norse!"

Wayne jumped in shock and ten million nerve endings sent pain messages to his brain:

"Arrrghh" he groaned, screwing up his eyes in pain.

From somewhere opposite, the old man yelled again:

"Norse!"

Wayne heard the clatter of someone walking rapidly down the adjacent corridor and then bustling into the four bed unit. He opened his eyes a little.

"Now, now, mister Lydon. There's no need for such shouting, you'll wake other patients."

Wayne peered out of his slit like eyes. A nurse was moving the old man's pillows and trying to calm him down with soft shushing noises, but the old man continued to stare wild eyed at Wayne.

"By all the Saints!" The old man muttered and then quickly pointed at his head, then either side of his chest and down at his belly.

"Holy Mary, Mother of Jaysus. Norse, do you not see that over there?"

"What are you talking about Mister Lydon?" The nurse replied, somewhat tersely.

"In the bed, Norse, the boy in that bed."

"Yes, mister Lydon, very good, there's a boy in the bed over there. There's nothing wrong with your eyesight, is there."

Wayne realised that when the old man said "norse" he wasn't talking about the language of the Vikings, but was in fact referring to the nurse. His accent was strange and went up and down in all the wrong places. Wayne thought where he had heard that accent before and realised that it had been on the news, when stuff had been on about the troubles in Ireland. So that was it, the old man was Irish. Wayne snapped back into listening to the conversation opposite:

"Now Mister Lydon, please do calm down, there are no such things. He's just a poor young boy who has been beaten up by some thug. Please calm yourself, or I will have to get the sister."

The nurse busied herself around the old man who was still staring at Wayne. She pulled up his blankets and tried to get him to lie down.

"He's one of 'em, I'm telling you, by the blood of Our Lord, Jaysus."

The old man crossed himself again and Wayne remembered he'd seen religious people do it on the TV.

"I'm tellin' you norse, I've seen one before, long ago, and that is one, over there, as sure as Saint Patrick chased all the snakes out of Ireland. I was in Kerry, on the way home from the pub and….."

"Yes, yes, Mister Lydon, you do seem to spend a lot of time in pubs, don't you?"

The nurse continued to shush the old man whose babbling got quieter and quieter as he was gently pushed back down on to his pillows. Once the old man's mad stare had been broken, Wayne felt confident enough to re open his eyes. The nurse, eventually satisfied that the old man was asleep by the sudden outburst of a loud snore, glanced over at Wayne. She smiled:

"I'm sorry love, did he wake you?"

Wayne nodded and blushed. The nurse was very young and pretty and had such kind brown eyes.

"He's an old drunk, I'm afraid, who quite literally fell out of the pub at lunchtime yesterday and broke several ribs. I'm not sure that he's quite sobered up yet."

The nurse smiled reassuringly and tucked up Wayne's bedclothes.

"Go back to sleep, love. You'll feel much better in the morning. Don't mind him. Little people, indeed. I've never heard such nonsense."

Wayne smiled at her then closed his eyes.

What had happened to Baz?

How had he knocked him out?

It must have been the blow he had received to his head when he had landed from Baz's punch that was making him forget the details.

He could remember raising his hand and feeling a jolt, like a small electric shock and then Baz had flown backwards through the air.

Wayne opened and closed his fist; it didn't feel sore at all.

His knuckles didn't feel like they'd made contact with Baz's wobbly chins. How had he done it?

Wayne began to drift off, back into a fitful sleep.

He dreamt that Baz was busily ripping off his ears and tossing them to his cronies, but that the ears kept growing back, bigger and bigger and Baz was getting madder and madder and his gang was laughing, louder and louder. Then a mad, staring, old Irishman was standing in the school hall during assembly pointing at him and screaming:

"He's one of them. He's an alien. He's here to eat our children!"

All the kids were laughing, not at the mad old Irishman, but at Wayne, who was stood in the middle of all of his school friends, stark naked. He quickly moved his hand down so the girls couldn't see his willy, which just seemed to make everyone laugh even more.

Wayne raised his hand and suddenly, all of the kids who had been laughing were now screaming and being blown out of the school hall windows, one by one. Even Annette Welsh, who Wayne was secretly in love with, had been laughing at his private bits.

Wayne felt a tear roll down his cheek as he inadvertently blasted her over the headmaster's lectern.

Suddenly, Wayne was aware of two strange voices talking nearby, he wasn't quite sure whether he was still dreaming, or awake. He felt the warmth of a hand as it was placed softly on his forehead. A man spoke quietly in a very deep, posh voice:

"Yes, this is the Higginbotham boy. Concussion, severe bruising, fractured arm. Temperature seems normal."

Another male voice, equally proper, asked:

"So what happened to him?"

The first voice answered, sounding a little bit cross:

"Street brawl, seems like a kid can't go to school today, without some hoodlum trying to beat seven shades out of him. Mind you, it's a funny business, but by all accounts the little tyke seems to have given as good as he got."

The other voice laughed:

"Good for him! The little chap doesn't look big enough to say boo to a goose. Any history of allergies? Penicillin?"

"No, no, although the mother was unable to supply any hereditary info...."

"Really?"

The voices began to get quieter as the men moved away.

Wayne realised that the voices belonged to a couple of doctors doing the night rounds and felt a little bit mean that he hadn't opened his eyes and thanked them for looking after him.

It was then, just before the voices became totally indistinct, that a simple statement was made, that rendered everything else that had happened to him that day seem almost irrelevant. And what had happened to Wayne Higginbotham thus far, on that Thursday, the 27th of June, could hardly be judged normal.

One simple statement was made, that would stick in Wayne's mind forever. In fact, the statement didn't just stick in his mind; it pierced his very consciousness, like an arrow passing straight through his heart.

Everything that he had ever known was ripped apart and every certainty rendered totally and utterly meaningless.

It was the first whispered voice he had heard which uttered the simple line:

"Yes, the mother knows nothing about his ancestry at all, seems she adopted him as a small baby"

Then, after a brief pause the voice added:

"Did you notice the ears by the way? Never seen anything like them!"

6

Father James Malone sipped his tea from a china cup and stared out of the large sash window. Boggy green fields, dotted by grey rocks, stretched almost as far as the eye could see, all the way to the distant grey mountains, which reached up towards the blue, lightly clouded sky, like the stubby finger tips of a giant hand stretching out from the earth.

"They'll be telling me there are such things as giants next." James muttered to no one in particular. He watched a small fluffy white cloud skid across the sky as though it had somewhere important to go. One thing was for sure; it was the only thing in a hurry in this part of the world. It couldn't have been more different to Dublin. In the weeks since his return from the Irish capital and his own home town, Father Malone had found himself getting more and more restless in this, his Parish, in an area that had once been viewed as the very edge of the known world.

"What was that, Father?"

An unexpected voice behind him made him turn in surprise.

"Oh sorry, Father Dermot. I was just talking to myself." Malone mumbled with more than a little embarrassment, suddenly conscious that his colleague had entered the room while he had been lost in thought.

Fr Dermot Callaghan laughed:

"It's the first sign of madness you know."

Fr Malone's eyes widened:

"What?"

"The talking to yourself." Fr Dermot replied flatly as he picked up a copy of "The Irish Times" from a coffee table and sank down into a tatty old arm chair with a grunt of satisfaction.

Malone smiled at his older colleague and turned back to the window.

"No Dermot. The first sign of madness is surely the belief in the existence of the little people. The confirmation of madness is in then talking to one of the self proclaimed little people and then being stupid enough to go and mention it to a Bishop, who just happens to be a sort of informer to the Papal witch burning, demon hunting, vampire slaying, flying squad."

Fr Dermot Callaghan was one of the two other priests with whom Fr Malone shared a large old rectory, in the quiet village of Finaan.

The village sat on the borders of County Mayo and County Galway, in that part of the West of Ireland known as Connemara.

A wild, remote and ruggedly beautiful area, popular with tourists and artists alike, because of its dramatic mountains, coastal scenery and it's ever changing quality of light.

At that moment, Fr Malone would have given anything to swap the tranquil beauty of the landscape before him, for the hustle and bustle of a busy Dublin street.

He had been born and raised in Ireland's capital, but had been eager to leave once he had graduated from the seminary, in fact, he couldn't get away fast enough.

The young James Malone had held dreams of being sent to Africa, or South America as a missionary, somewhere exciting, where he could do something really worthwhile. Instead, he had been despatched to Finaan, a backward village at the absolute back end of nowhere.

In Dublin, at least he had felt a part of the twentieth century, instead of being lost somewhere that seemed to exist in a timeless, twilight zone.

To Fr Malone, Finaan should not have been real. It was the faux, idyllic Ireland of Hollywood movies, the Ireland that time and reality had almost forgotten.

To him, it was the Ireland that should only really have existed in the fond, folksy, idealised memories of the Diaspora. Yet here it was: A place where friendly people passed pleasantries with the passing clergy, outside their whitewashed stone, thatched cottages.

Where the village main street had more bars than shops and each building was painted a different, bright, gaudy colour.

Where there were still almost as many horse traps as there were motor cars and where sheepdogs chased both.

Where the Church was regarded as being almost as important as the pub and the priest was second only to the landlord in the village hierarchy of affection.

To Fr James Malone, Finaan was an anachronism in an age when man had already walked on the moon.

There were times, when he was out on his bike on some fuschia hedged country road, when the light was fading and the mist rolled in over the hills, that he could almost believe that he was in some lost age of myth, magic and legend. A land where standing stones stood testament to noble warrior kings, where barrows brooded in rain-soaked fields and leprechauns might just be hiding behind every rock.

That feeling was going to be even more prevalent now, in the wake of all the fuss about a simple, innocuous conversation with one of his more colourful parishioners. He was a rational and scientific man, for goodness sake, a thoroughly modern man of God.

The young James' background had been quite secular, for Ireland. Both of his parents had been teachers and although the family attended Mass most Sundays, that was about the only time religion encroached on their lives. Malone's elder brother, Dan, had gone to Trinity and become a lawyer.

Jimmy, as he had been known at home, hadn't known what to do and sort of just drifted into the Seminary, after he had finished at the local Christian Brother's School. It certainly hadn't been a vocational decision. Once there, however, he convinced himself that he had a mission, a purpose on earth and had graduated top of his class. Those days seemed as if they'd happened a hundred years ago.

Fr Malone liked heavy metal music every bit as much as he liked traditional Hymns and psalms, much to the annoyance of his two older house mates, Father Dermot Callaghan and Father William Burke.

He liked Gaelic football, rugby and soccer, especially his beloved Leeds United.

He liked dancing with girls, watching the latest movies and drinking copious amounts of Guinness.

He liked all the things that most blokes of his age liked.

How had he got himself into a situation where ancient superstitions were taking up more of his time than his pastoral duties?

He shook his head as another lonely cloud skimmed franticly across the sky outside, caught on the wings of a stiff breeze, coming straight off the Atlantic.

"When's he coming then?"

Malone was dimly aware of Fr Dermot's question coming from somewhere behind him.

"What?" He asked turning towards the older priest, who was sat somewhere behind a fog of pipe smoke, "The Irish Times" neatly folded on his knee.

"When's he coming, this famous Spanish Exorcist?" Fr Callaghan asked, with that twinkle in his eye that meant he was teasing the young priest, but instead of finding it annoying as he usually did, Malone found it oddly reassuring.

If Father Callaghan was taking the whole matter with a pinch of salt, then maybe he should too.

Fr Malone sighed heavily, turned from the window and plonked himself carelessly in another armchair that had clearly seen better days.

"Tomorrow!" He replied morosely: "He had to go back to Rome, to the Vatican City itself, would you believe? To be filing a report and discussing the matter with his superiors. I mean can you believe it?"

Father Dermot laughed:

"It's not the end of the world you know, James. I'm quite sure he'll go to see this oul' fella with you, get him to say a few Hail Mary's and then he'll be back off to Rome on the first available plane. He'll find it too cold and inhospitable in our little corner of the World to hang around too long. He'll be far too used to the good life of the fine wines and all the Vatican comforts to want to hang around. You'll see."

Father Malone nodded, but another sigh passed his lips.

Father Callaghan leaned forward and patted the younger priest's knee:

"I tell you what Father, we'll get him and Lord Burke together; the two of them'll probably be getting on like a house on fire before the week is out."

He winked and then stood, put the newspaper down and crossed over to an old sideboard upon which several liquor bottles stood.

Father Dermot Callaghan was a man in his late fifties, almost bald, but with lots of thick, fluffy white hair around his ears and across the back of his head. His bulging middle was a testament to his taste for the finer things in life and his ruddy cheeks an indicator of a boisterous good humour.

He had been the local priest for more than a quarter of a century, almost as far back as the emergency and had seen just about everything in his time. He was always willing to share his experiences with his young charge.

"Talking of fine wine, I could use some of Lord's rich bounty myself, would you be sharing a wee whiskey with me, my young and troubled friend?" He asked, glancing at Malone as he poured himself a large glass of "Paddy's."

Father Malone shook his head:

"No thank you Dermot."

He wiped his forehead with his hand and twisted his face into a look that reminded Fr Callaghan of a time when he had been severely constipated.

"What if he does more than make old Mickey say a few Hail Mary's? I tell you Dermot, there was something obsessive, almost insane about this Spaniard. Something madder even than the old Bishop whatsisname and he was about as mad as a March hare, drunk on poteen."

Fr Dermot took his pipe from his lips and savoured a large sip from the glass of whiskey. He swilled the amber liquid around his mouth contentedly a couple of times and then swallowed. He grimaced and closed his eyes tight, as though he had just swallowed a pint of sulphuric acid.

"Aaah" he sighed "pure nectar. Thank you Lord."

Then he placed his pipe back into his mouth and strolled slowly, over to the fireplace, leaving a trail of thick smoke hanging behind him, like a rusty, old branch-line steam engine.

A couple of peat briquettes burned in the grate, even in what was the middle of the Irish summer. He put the tumbler of whiskey down on the mantelpiece, took a last huge lungful of pipe smoke and then banged the pipe out on the fire grate, pouring the contents of the bowl onto the peat.

He put the pipe down on the mantelpiece next to his whiskey and slowly and methodically began to blow his nose on an old grey handkerchief.

Fr Malone sat expectantly. This was the usual pre-amble to one of Fr Callaghan's "State of the Nation" lectures.

Fr Dermot tucked the hanky into his trouser pocket, cleared his throat and began.

"The Church is like the government of a great Country, young James. It has a department for everything that can affect the life of man. This "St. Gregory" bunch, are a bit like an arm of the CIA, you know, those fellas in the black suits who supposedly appear after UFO sightings. Some poor fool sees a flying saucer and wham, there they are, as quick as a flash, saying it was a weather balloon, a surplus of whiskey, or some such nonsense. This Spanish Fella will come over, check out the old man and tell you that he's nothing but an old Irish simpleton who's been out on his own in the wilds too long and that you've been wasting everybody's time. He'll say that, even if he finds him wearing a green suit, sitting on a shamrock, playing a fiddle and singing "Patrick McGinty.""

Father Malone shook his head:

"That's what I'm hoping, but it wasn't the impression they were giving me." He said, shaking his head slowly:

"It was like being interrogated by the FBI, or the Gestapo even. These guys were serious, Dermot, deadly serious. I mean they really, really, believe in all this "little people" stuff."

Fr Dermot smiled:

"There are many more within the boundaries of our own Parish that would take such things equally seriously, young man, but I wouldn't worry if I were you. I think old Mickey Finn is a lot smarter than any of our colleagues in Rome. An awful lot smarter."

Fr Malone stood and began to pace around the room:

"I can't believe they dragged me out to Dublin and that someone is coming all the way from Rome to deal with something that is so ridiculous. I mean this is the Twentieth Century for goodness sake. Men have walked on the moon and the Roman Catholic Church is out on a Leprechaun hunt?"

He stood by the window and stared out into the void.

Fr Dermot Callaghan raised his eyebrows and took a large sip of whiskey.

53

"Yes, it's hard to believe, young fella. Hard to believe indeed." He muttered, so quietly that Fr Malone didn't hear.

Something else escaped Fr Malone's notice too. Despite his reassuring words, his humour and confident manner, Fr Callaghan was sweating, sweating profusely. He stood, refilled his whiskey glass almost to the top and took a large gulp. Had Fr Malone turned and looked at his colleague, he would have been shocked by the look on his face. Fr Dermot Callaghan looked totally and utterly terrified.

The next day Fr Malone took the old battered Morris Minor that the three priests who lived in the old rectory shared and drove to Shannon Airport, a journey of nearly two hours, given the cars maximum speed of forty miles an hour.

Fr Malone had spent every inch of the journey worrying about whether the old girl would actually get to Shannon, without collapsing into a rusty heap of tortured metal. Three times he had been convinced that he was being shot at as the old car back-fired leaving clouds of exhaust fumes in the middle of the road. So, by the time he got to Shannon airport, it was with more than a little trepidation that he greeted the black eyed priest who he now knew as Father Francisco Pizarro.

There was no warmth in the greeting that the Spaniard gave to the young Irish priest, merely a nod and a limp handshake:

"Did you have a good flight Father?" Malone asked pleasantly.

He figured that if he was going to have to spend some time with black eyes, he might as well make it as enjoyable as possible.

Pizarro scowled:

"Yes" he replied curtly as he strolled through the busy terminal towards the exit:

"You have made the necessary preparations?" Pizarro asked as they both sat down in the old Morris. Malone nodded, remembering the instructions he had been given before leaving Dublin.

"Yes. My colleague has told me the names of two local men who are experts in local folklore. I know them both, they are both God fearing men who attend Mass regularly and take the Sacrament."

"Good!"

The black-eyed priest nodded his head. He ran his hand through his greased back, black hair and put on a pair of black sunglasses. Once again Malone was reminded of a Bond villain. All Pizarro needed to do was to pull on some tight black leather gloves and he would look like the archetypal hit man.

Pizarro reached into his briefcase and took out a pair of tight, black leather gloves.

"Err, Ok, Let's go." Malone stammered, ramming the gearlever of the old car into first gear and slowly moving forward towards the car park exit. The car immediately back fired. Pizarro did not seem to notice, he didn't even flinch. Malone apologised, but Pizarro just ignored him and closed his eyes behind his dark glasses. In fact Pizarro spent almost the entire journey to Finaan with his eyes closed. Malone wasn't sure whether he was praying, asleep, meditating, or just plain ignoring him.

It was just before they got to Finaan that Pizarro finally awoke and addressed his companion, his gaze, however, seemed to remain fixed on the windscreen of the car:

"Tonight I would like to rest and make some preparations. Tomorrow, we shall visit the men that you have identified as experts on the phenomena that we are called upon to deal with. We shall begin to put an end to this evil for once and for all. As far as I am concerned, too much time has been wasted since your audience with His Grace. Such is the nature of modern Vatican bureaucracy."

Black eyes paused, took off his sunglasses, carefully folded them and then turned towards Malone:

"I should warn you Father; that I expect your total co-operation in every aspect of this matter. Your very life, indeed your eternal soul, may depend on it. However, you will stay back when I finally confront the beast. They are far more dangerous than you might think."

Fr Malone nodded.

"Oh yeah." He thought silently to himself:

"The beast? We're talking about an old man. He may have been incredibly dangerous once, about fifty years ago. In his young and vital days, the most he could possibly do now is hit you with his walking stick, or fall on top of you as he suffered a heart attack and died."

The black eyed priest studied Fr Malone carefully. It felt to Malone like he was reading his mind, as though he was able to hear the sarcastic thoughts that he was thinking.

Despite the slivers of sunlight that stole through the rolling clouds and illuminated the passing lush Irish landscape, Malone felt a cold shiver run up the entire length of his spine.

Pizarro turned back towards the windscreen. From the corner of his eye Malone was sure the Spaniard was smiling. Indeed, it was more of a grimace than a smile, with colourless thin lips, that made Malone's stomach turn a little. The first time Malone had seen anything but a sneer on his long, tanned face.

Another, deeper, colder shiver ran down his spine.

7

Wayne returned home to the Higginbotham's little terraced house on Cavendish Street after just one night in hospital, with his chest tightly strapped, his arm in a plaster cast and his mind in turmoil.

Adopted?

Him?

What did that mean?

Wayne knew what the word adopted meant, of course, but he just couldn't help being unable to relate it to himself.

Doris and Frank were his Mum and Dad.

They always had been his Mum and Dad.

Doris and Frank had been his Mum and Dad for as long as he could remember.

But that was it, though, wasn't it?

There was a time when he had been a baby and hadn't known what was going on. That was when it must have happened. But what did it all mean?

If Doris and Frank weren't his Mum and Dad, who was?

What did they look like?

Did they have funny ears and freckles?

Did they live in Shepton?

Did they have any other kids?

Wayne's mind whirled and questions just kept flooding into his consciousness, a million "what ifs."

He didn't say anything to Doris and Frank of course. If they hadn't told him that he was adopted, they must have had their reasons and it would be pointless and probably hurtful to talk about it.

Hurtful to him anyway, because Doris would probably fly off the handle and start screaming and shouting about him keeping his nose out of such matters and how none of it was any of his business.

He had once mentioned, in the most rational and unemotional terms, that he found it strange that he didn't seem to physically resemble either Doris, or Frank, in the way that Cedric seemed to be a virtual carbon copy of his father, Stanley Houghton-Hughes.

Neither Doris, nor Frank had the humungous, pointed ears.

Neither Doris, nor Frank had curly auburn hair, unless Doris had had one of her fashionable, frizzy perms at the old lady's hairdressers on Rosamund Street.

Frank had brown eyes, Doris blue-grey, so where had Wayne's blue-green eyes come from?

He had asked, very politely if there was any particular reason for his having such radically different physical features?

Wayne knew a black boy, two years above him at Gas Street Primary School, who had been adopted and had wondered, very briefly, if that could possibly be the reason behind his differing characteristics.

Doris had typically exploded on that occasion, accusing Wayne of disloyalty and of being ungrateful:

"How dare you ask such stupid questions?" She had bellowed.

"Do you not think we would have told you? We have slaved for you. We have given you the best of everything we could afford. We have worked night and day to feed you, clothe you and buy toys for you and you have the barefaced cheek to ask if you are really our son. How dare you?"

When he came to think about it, sitting in the ambulance on the way home, Doris hadn't actually, categorically, stated that he hadn't been adopted.

So Wayne smiled weakly at Doris as she attempted to make something of a fuss of him as he climbed out of the ambulance delivering him home. He gave Frank a manly: "Aye" when his father asked him if he was alright and grinned knowingly as though Frank would understand that he had now entered an exclusively male fighting club.

Doris clucked around like an old hen and ushered him up to bed to rest.

She asked what he would like for his lunch and must have been feeling sorry for him, because she even offered his favourite meal of fried egg, chips and beans, in bed.

When Frank had left for work and Doris had busied herself in the kitchen, Wayne's mind filled up again with all the questions. His brain was buzzing so much that he began to get a headache and feel sick. Even so he ate his lunch with gusto and cleared his plate in what seemed like seconds:

"Well done love." Doris beamed: "at least that bully didn't damage your appetite."

She took the tray of dirty dishes from his bed and sat down beside him:

"I'm glad you stood up to him, love." She said, smiling.

"You're your father's son alright. Frank did a bit of boxing in the army, you know."

Doris prattled on but Wayne had stopped listening during her first sentence.

"No I'm not." He thought to himself, "I'm nothing like my Dad. If that Doctor was right, he isn't even really my Dad at all."

"So will you be alright on your own for a few hours?" He heard Doris ask eventually.

"You see I've got to go to the pub to work and I'm a bit worried about leaving you on your own."

Wayne smiled and patted her arm:

"I'll be fine." He said, trying to sound as grown up as possible.

"I'll just stay here and rest. I didn't get much sleep in the hospital. There was an old Irish loony opposite me, who was either snoring, or ranting and raving all night."

Doris nodded:

"Aye, I know what it's like in those places. I didn't sleep properly for a week when I went in for my big op. Anyway I better get myself off. I'll see you later love…you know where I am if you need me."

Wayne nodded and closed his eyes. He felt her warm, soft lips as she kissed him on the cheek.

"Bye Mum" he heard himself say. Perhaps it had all been a dream. Perhaps he hadn't been adopted after all. Perhaps the Doctors had been talking about someone else and Wayne had just got hold of the wrong end of the stick.

"Yesterday was a very strange day," he thought to himself, "maybe I slept better than I thought and all the adoption stuff was just my mind playing tricks on me."

He struggled to get more comfortable, but couldn't. His ribs ached, his arm ached and his head ached.

"Adopted, adopted, adopted, adopted.

The word just kept repeating itself as though he had a record player on in his brain and the needle had stuck.

Finally, totally exasperated, he climbed out of bed as carefully as he could manage and limped through to Doris and Frank's bedroom.

His heart pounded against his chest, making his ribs ache even more.

In the corner of their bedroom, stood an old brass, fireside log box, with three sailing ships on each face and one mighty galleon on top.

Wayne gulped as he moved towards it and his breath seemed to come in short little gasps as though he had been running. He felt beads of sweat beginning to burst out on his forehead and drip down the sides of his face. The brass box was where Doris and Frank kept all their important papers.

Stuff from the bank and the building society; private stuff, he had been told more than once; stuff that wasn't anything to do with him.

Grown up stuff.

Wayne reached down and opened the lid. There was no lock. Frank and Doris were confident that having been told to stay out of the box, Wayne would do as he was told. Inside, he could see piles and piles of paper.

He reached down and picked up a few official looking forms:

"Shepton Building Society, The Yorkshire Penny Savings Bank, Dalrymple, Boggett and Close, Solicitors."

Wayne whispered the title of each letter, or form, as he leafed through them, placing them carefully in order, on the bed. After he had examined about fifteen boring pieces of paper, Wayne's broken arm, which he was using to support the lid of the box, began to ache.

"There's nothing in here." He decided, putting the papers back carefully.

He closed the box with a sigh of relief and went back to bed.

"It must have been a dream. Adopted? Me? What nonsense."

The words drifted through his mind as he closed his eyes to go to sleep.

He dreamed of laser beams blasting out of his hands, reducing Baz Thompson to a small pile of smoking ash.

"Ha!" The Wayne Higginbotham in his dream laughed: "That'll teach you to mess with Captain Yorkshire!"

Nearly three weeks passed without incident and the adoption issue began to fade in importance.

Wayne's cast and bandages were eventually removed, just in time for him to attend Gas Street School for the last day of term and the leaving celebration.

Everyone seemed delighted to see him, especially Mrs. Ball who beamed with delight when she saw him walk through the school gates and gave him a huge, enthusiastic hug, which hurt his still tender ribs:

"Oh my God, I'm so sorry" She exclaimed, as he gasped with pain:

"I totally forgot your injuries, I'm just so pleased you've come back to see us all, before you go off to that Grammar School. I was so worried about you."

She gave him another softer hug.

Wayne noticed that everyone seemed to treat him with something like respect, awe even, though he did notice kids gathering in corners, whispering and pointing:

"That's him, that's the kid that beat up that sixteen year old." He heard somebody say.

The morning passed unexceptionally. Wayne played football at break as usual, despite his sore ribs. The other boys demanded that he passed the ball, as usual; the only funny thing was that they addressed him as "Wayne" and not "Lugsy, fluff" or "Fuzz," or any other derogatory nickname.

That afternoon there was to be a special leaving assembly and prize giving ceremony in the main hall of the school, which also doubled as a gym, a canteen and an assembly room. It was the main reason Doris had made him go to school for the last day of term.

Parents had been invited to watch the prize giving and Doris had taken time off from the pub specially. It wasn't just Doris who was going to be there, though, everybody's parents were coming.

Wayne just knew that he would be called out to make the long walk to the teacher's table. As the only kid in Gas Street School who had passed his eleven plus, he was bound to get a prize and he was more than a little nervous about it.

He could imagine all the kids in the school and all the grown ups, sitting in the endless ranks of plastic chairs, staring at him, all pointing at his ears or his freckles, all whispering about him, just like in his dream.

All too soon the morning session and lunchtime passed. Prize giving was set for half past two, to give the staff and the caretaker time to clear away the dining tables and benches and set up the ranks of chairs.

At twenty past two, Mr. Braithwaite's class, including Wayne trooped into the hall to take their seats. As the eldest children in the school, they were the last to enter and Wayne noticed the parents sitting at the back, although he couldn't see Doris. He also noticed the stares of the smaller children as he passed.

As soon as the last pupil had taken his seat, Mr Braithwaite stood, pushed his spectacles up his nose and began to speak:

"Good afternoon, Ladies and Gentlemen, boys and girls and welcome to this, the last day, of what has been another successful school year at Gas Street."

Wayne's concentration lapsed as Mr. Braithwaite droned on and on. He looked around the hall with its high church like windows, its wall bars and its hanging ropes, which the children used to climb up in P.E.

The school was well over a hundred years old and looked even older, built as it was of dark Yorkshire stone, which had gone black over the years given the schools proximity to the old railway shunting yard.

Wayne had been at Gas Street since he was five years old. Six years was more than half his life and now he was leaving to go off to Grammar School, all on his own.

He looked at the head table of teachers, which was on a small stage in front of all the plastic chairs. All the teachers were sat there, in a row.

At the end of the table sat Mrs Wickens, an old lady with steely grey hair, an unsmiling face and black horn rimmed spectacles. She had taught him in his first year and had been very fierce and scary. Strange, she didn't look that scary now. Next to her sat the jolly round, ruddy featured Mrs. Monk, who had been his second teacher, she had been great fun. Next to Mrs Monk sat Mrs. Ball who looked so much younger than all the others. Mrs. Ball had been Wayne's teacher last year, the year that he had really excelled. She was very pretty with long dark hair and, as all the boys in class six seemed to have noticed, a stunning figure. She was looking round the audience and for a moment she caught Wayne's eye as he stared at her. She smiled and Wayne looked away quickly, his face flushing bright red in embarrassment.

On the other side of Mr. Braithwaite, who was now drawing an analogy between running a school and running an army platoon, sat Mr. Jackson, the sports teacher. As far as Wayne was concerned, Mr. Jackson must have been one of the Nazis that Mr. Braithwaite often referred too. He wouldn't miss his bald head, mean little piggy eyes and his constant barked commands. Although he did like the fact that Mr. Jackson rated him the best footballer in the class. Yes, old Wacko Jacko wasn't that bad he supposed.

The last two teachers on the table were Mrs. McGiver and Mrs Jones who had been Wayne's teachers in years three and four. They were both elderly and kindly spinsters who had helped Wayne enormously.

Wayne's dreaming was shattered by an outbreak of applause and by Mr. Braithwaite sitting down for a moment as he sipped a glass of water. When he stood up again, with a long list in his hand, Wayne knew that it was almost the moment he had been dreading.

Child after child, starting with the very youngest was called out to the front to receive an award for some outstanding achievement over the year. Mr Braithwaite would shake their hand and mutter:

"Jolly well done, good show" as he handed over the prize.

Then each of them had to turn and walk back, self consciously, to their seat. Some grinned inanely as they faced the audience, tightly clutching their prize, others tried to coolly ignore the smiling faces and rippling applause.

Wayne's stomach had never felt so empty, except for the thousand butterflies that were whizzing around in there.

This was worse than facing Baz.

What if no one applauded?

What if they all laughed at his hair, his ears or his freckles?

What if his trousers weren't zipped up? (He checked).

Suddenly, he was aware of a boy in his own class getting a prize for good work. He felt his mouth dry up like a creek bed in the desert, after a summer storm.

"Now a very special prize for a young man who has made everyone at Gas Street School enormously proud. A young man who has been rewarded for his humungous efforts with a place at Wormysted's Grammar School, only the second Gas Street pupil to achieve that honour in the last five years. The Prize for outstanding academic achievement goes to: Wayne Higginbotham."

Mr.Braithwaite announced as he peered over the top of his spectacles, looking for the star of the school.

There was an explosion of applause and a few cheers and whoops.

Wayne stood and marched slowly to the front of the hall, his head down.

He imagined Mr. Braithwaite wearing a Judge's wig and robes and glowering at him over the spectacles perched on the edge of nose:

"It is my sad duty, to sentence you to seven years hard labour at Wormysted's Grammar School, young man; where you will be kept in solitary confinement until the very day of your release. May God have mercy on your soul."

Eventually he reached the head table where a smiling Mr. Braithwaite shook his hand:

"Jolly well done, good show, young man. Enormously proud of you," he mumbled, as his spectacles slipped down his nose.

Wayne noticed Mrs. Ball beaming at him and managed a nervous grin back. Another tumult of applause broke out, but Wayne could hardly hear it for the nervous ringing in his ears.

Mr. Braithwaite handed him his prize; a beautiful full colour encyclopaedia. Wayne couldn't help the tear that rolled down his face as the headmaster made a short speech wishing him well at Wormysted's and he saw that Mrs. Ball's eyes had also welled up. He shook Mr. Braithwaite's hand again and whispered a tremulous:

"Thank you Sir."

Then he turned to face the audience and marched as quickly as possible with his head down to re-take his seat next to Richard Hebden, who whispered

"Are you alright?" from the corner of his mouth.

"Yes" Wayne replied unconvincingly.

"You don't want to go to that Grammar School, do you?" Richard whispered, while Mister Braithwaite was making another boring speech about the bright future of Gas Street Primary School.

Wayne thought for a moment and then shook his head slowly:

"No, not really. Not on my own."

Richard nodded and patted his arm.

"Good luck Wayne. You're not as bad as they say you are, you know."

"Thanks."

Wayne smiled, wondering what it was that they were saying about him that he hadn't heard.

At the end of the ceremony the children went to their classrooms to collect their belongings and say their "goodbyes."

Even Mr. Braithwaite had to clear his throat as he shook Wayne's hand for the last time and wished him the best of luck.

Mrs. Ball made him gasp again as she hugged him just a little too eagerly:

"Keep in touch Wayne." She choked, her eyes full of tears:

"Let us know how you get on at Wormysted's."

"I will." Wayne smiled bravely, trying not to burst into tears.

Richard Hebden grinned as they walked out of the front door for the last time, struggling with bags, rolled up artwork and paper mache models.

"You lucky devil Higginbotham. I wish Mrs Ball had hugged me like that; she's got the best bosom in Shepton. Good luck mate."

Wayne grinned back, wished Richard all the best and then started to laugh. He'd survived, no one had laughed at him.

Some of the kids were running round singing:

"No more school, no more stink, no more stinking arithmetic."

Wayne smiled:

"Not here anyway."

Doris was stood in the playground in her best two piece suit. She wiped a tear away as she took a couple of bags off him.

"Well done love, I'm very proud of you. That'll show our Margaret that it's not just her Cedric who can get to that Grammar school. That'll show her that we're every bit as good as they are."

The proud expression on her face made Wayne feel particularly pleased with himself. He had done something good for once!

It was during the second week of the interminable summer holidays that boredom and an insatiable curiosity caught up with Wayne.

He decided that he just had to have another look in that old brass box and clear up his parentage issue for once and for all. He might never know what had happened in his fight with

Baz Thompson, but he felt that he ought to finally address the issue of his parentage. The catalyst for his rekindled interest in his background had been a row with Doris over something he had said.

Well, it wasn't just what he had said; it was the way he had said it, which had caused Doris to do her erupting volcano impression.

It had all started while the Higginbothams had been watching TV and the announcer had mentioned that an Elvis film would be shown the following night.

"I don't know why they show that Elvis Priestley's films over here."

Doris had moaned:

"He won't come to England. We aren't good enough for him."

"Presley." Wayne had stated simply.

Doris had glared at him:

"What?"

"Elvis Presley, his name is Elvis Pres....ley, not Priest.. ley."

Wayne had explained with a little too much condescension for Doris' liking.

"And just who the hell do you think you are, young man? Talking to me like that, you little know it all. Just because you've passed for that there Grammar school and that Mrs. Ball thinks you're the cat's pyjamas, doesn't mean you can come showing off in here, as though nobody else knows nowt."

"Anything, actually." Wayne had muttered, which when he considered it later, had probably been more than a little unwise:

"Get yourself off to bed until you learn some respect you cheeky little so and so…" Doris had screamed as she tried to hit Wayne round the back of his head, only to miss as he ducked:

"And for your information, Mr clever clogs, I knew about Elvis Priestley long before we got you. You jumped up know it all!"

A second attempt to land a slap on Wayne had been more successful as she connected with the side of his head. Wayne had glanced at Frank, whose gaze had not left the TV screen.

"No support there then?" Wayne had thought to himself, as he gritted his teeth and steeled himself not to cry.

As he had trudged upstairs to bed, Doris' last few words had begun to take on some new significance in Wayne's train of thought. She had said: "before we got you." He wouldn't have given it so much as a second's thought before, but now what would have previously seemed a perfectly innocent and innocuous phrase took on a whole new significance:

"Before we got you."

Not "Before you were born," but: "Before we got you."

Wayne had added two and two.

The following afternoon, as soon as Doris had left for work, leaving Wayne alone in the house, he set about his task of finally finding out if he was really a Higginbotham, or not.

This time he would go straight to the bottom of the brass box. If there were papers in the box that referred to him having been adopted, then that was where they would probably be.

He lifted the lid and carefully took out a huge pile of paper, laying it on his Mum and Dad's bedroom floor. That left just a few envelopes that he hadn't examined in his last search.

He took a particularly large brown envelope out and opened it. A few black and white photos fell out; photos of a young Frank Higginbotham in a Second World War army uniform. Wayne smiled and put them back in the envelope.

The next brown envelope contained old birthday cards to Doris from her mum and granny.

"This is going nowhere." Wayne thought with a sigh.

"I don't know why I'm wasting my time."

He lifted out another envelope containing several premium bonds.

Wayne shook his head and picked up the last brown envelope at the very bottom of the box. An old, tatty looking specimen with the Higginbotham address printed on the front. Funny, it wasn't the Cavendish St. address but one in the nearby town of Barlickwick. Wayne shrugged; inside the envelope there was a brown card and a folded, official looking piece of paper. Wayne examined the card first.

It had a coat of arms at the top, the abbreviation MCW.109 and then the titles:

London County Council

Public Health Department.

Division No......

Immunisation record of Michael Sean O' Brien

Born on 24/3/1963

Address: 24 St. Joseph's Road, Hammersmith

Wayne pursed his lips, who the heck was Michael Sean O'Brien?

Whoever he was, he had the same birthday as Wayne.

Was that a coincidence?

The first entry stated:

"Immunisation against Whooping cough – Diptheria – Tetanus."

It had been ticked and initialled by a doctor, the date and time had been itemised and even the place:

The Chiswick Road Clinic, Hammersmith.

The next entry was for immunisation against Polio, it too was signed by a doctor, dated and timed. This one had taken place at the Shepton surgery, on Ilkley Road, Wayne's own surgery.

Wayne felt the hairs on the back of his neck rise up and his mouth went very dry, as a cold feeling began to grow in his belly. He opened up the folded, official looking piece of paper. It had lots of boxes on it, all outlined in red ink.

Wayne felt almost numb, his ears were buzzing, all of a sudden the feeling in the pit of his stomach that he had felt when Baz Thompson and his mates had accosted him nearly a month earlier; and when he had had to walk to the front of the entire school to pick up his prize, came back.

The feeling was not worry or even fear, it was nothing less than pure unadulterated terror.

Wayne carefully began to read the piece of paper.

8

The white washed cottage stood by the side of the road, its doors and windows brightly painted and its roof covered in thick new golden thatch. The two black robed priests walked up to the front door.

A disembodied voice came from over a tall hedge on the other side of the lane:

"I'm in the field, if it's me you'll be looking for."

Both Priests turned and looked from left to right, unable to discern the origin of the voice.

An old wizened face appeared around the corner of a tall hedge, opposite the cottage.

"Top o' the Morning to ya." The face beamed toothlessly.

An old man emerged from behind the hedge and began a sprightly climb over a five bar gate.

"Good Morning, Liam." Father James Malone smiled.

"And what can I be doing for two such fine gentlemen of the cloth, this morning?" The old man asked.

Pizarro regarded the man carefully, his black eyes travelling from the tip of his head to the soles of his well worn boots. Liam shook Fr Malone's hand:

"Hello Father, how are you keeping? Is it a cup of tea you'll be wanting? Or can I be getting you something a little bit stronger?"

"Tea would be most welcome Liam. Can I introduce Father Pizarro, all the way from Rome. Father Pizarro, this is Liam Fogerty."

Pizarro held out his hand somewhat disdainfully. The old man shook it with equal distaste.

"Rome is it now?" He said as he marched sanguinely up to his cottage, opened his front door and beckoned the Priests to enter.

"Finaan is now of interest to the Holy Father himself, is it?"

Pizarro smiled weakly:

"Every good Catholic in the world is of interest to His Holiness." The priest said, smoothly.

"A good Catholic?"

Liam laughed, closing his door behind them:

"It's many a year now, since I could be described as a good Catholic. I only attend Mass on Sundays and I've not been to confession in nearly twenty years. I've nothing to be confessing about."

He walked across his small, but nicely furnished living room and bellowed through a door into the kitchen:

"Roisin, will you be making tea? We have visitors."

A white haired old lady peered around the kitchen door.

"Oh my goodness." She declared:

"If it isn't Father Malone and a friend and me in me working clothes and all. Sit yourselves down Fathers. Liam why are you leaving the gentlemen standing in the living room like unwanted strangers?"

Liam laughed:

"Sure they're not here for you old woman, get on with the tea, will you."

The old woman gave him a withering glance, grinned nervously at the Priests and disappeared back into the kitchen.

The priests sat down together on a comfortable old sofa.

Liam, who looked to be in his early seventies, with his leathery, wrinkled face and steely grey hair, plonked himself into an armchair, took a pack of Carroll's No 1 from his pocket and offered both Priests a cigarette, both refused; Malone with a smile, Pizarro with a horrified raising of the hand.

"So, if Fr Malone told me right, I believe it's the "little people" that you'll be wanting to be discussing?" Liam asked Pizarro, shaking out a match, lighting a cigarette and puffing out a plume of smoke, a glint of mischief in his eye.

Fr Pizarro regarded the old man with a cold stare while Malone nodded eagerly.

"Yes, as I said, that would be grand, Liam. Would you be telling us all you know about all that stuff?" Malone asked.

The old man cleared his throat:

"To understand the little people is to know something of the history of Ireland."

He looked directly at Fr Pizarro again.

"Do you know much about Ireland, Father?"

Fr Pizarro shrugged:

"Maybe a little." He responded, "But I need to know much more."

Liam smiled.

"Ah, it's good to know that you think about us over there in Rome."

He then fell back into his chair and began to speak, his voice losing any semblance of age as he adopted a deep resonant tone to tell the tales that his grandfather had told him. The same tales passed down by his grandfather's grandfather:

"Long, long ago, before the Celts came to Ireland, before the Vikings, the Normans, the English and the Germans and Dutch in their tourist caravans; Ireland belonged to a race called the Fir Bolgs. Now these were small hairy people, squat and ugly in the eyes of modern men, but they made great and beautiful things. They were skilled in the working of metals and stone and in the mining of jewels. The fort of Dun Aengus on the Arran islands is one of their works, so it is said. So are the standing stones and the circles in the fields. They lived here contentedly for many years, until the "Tuatha" came. Nobody knows where they came from, some say from the "High Air," some say from the sea, but wherever it was they they came from, they came. Now, the "Tuatha de Danaan" were a fine and noble race and it is said that they were immortal, unless killed in battle. They were tall and fair and beautiful to behold. The "Tuatha" were unlike any people that have ever lived, before, or since. Their women could steal a mortal man's heart just by looking at him. They could become invisible at will and change their shape into whatever manner of man, bird, or beast took their fancy. They could fire an arrow into an eagle's eye from one mountain to the next. Their horses could run like the wind and overtake any other steed on earth. The "Tuatha" had but one weakness, they were very few in number. It is said that because they were immortal, they did not multiply like the other races. Many were killed in the battles against the Fir Bolg and their numbers declined so much that by the time the war was won, they could be counted only in scores. Legend has it that their last battle was at Moytura, over near Cong, not more than twenty miles away."

Liam's story was interrupted by his wife, Roisin bringing in tea for himself and for the clerics, tea which Fr Pizarro initially refused.

"Go on" Roisin urged the Spaniard. "Go on, have a nice cup of tea, it'll do you good."

With a sickly smile Pizarro finally accepted a cup of black tea, which Malone noticed he then pointedly failed to raise to his lips. A glass of amber liquid was also on the tray for Liam, which he despatched with one eager gulp.

Roisin bustled over to the fire and gave the smouldering peat briquettes a good poke, so that flames leapt up the grate and a blast of heat flooded into the compact, already snug room.

Liam Fogerty took a gulp of tea and then, with a deep breath resumed his history.

"Now, the Fir Bolg didn't go down without a holy hooley of a fight. Although they were mere mortals they were as tough as old boots. Lugh of the Longhand, the Prince of the "Tuatha de Danaan" was killed in the battle, which was taking four days to be won. If you go to the village of Cross you'll find the cairns where it is said that the bodies of the Fir Bolg warriors are buried."

Fr Malone had heard the stories of the Fir Bolg and the "Tuatha" before and having just read Tolkein's "The Lord of The Rings" his head was full of pictures of the Elvish "Tuatha" and Orc like Fir Bolgs running around the fields of ancient Ireland lopping each others' heads off.

He glanced at Pizarro and noted that the habitually disinterested Priest was listening to Liam's oration with rapt attention, leaning forward in his chair and taking in every word.

The heat of the room seemed to grow and the air became heavy with Liam's exhaled cigarette smoke and that from the blazing peat. Pizarro's interest was more than Malone could manage as his eyelids drooped and seemed to get heavier with every passing second.

Liam coughed which snapped Fr Malone back into consciousness as Liam then began to name "Tuatha" heroes:

"Then there was Luchtaine, who could make anything out of wood, spears that would never snap and unbreakable shields. Then there was Aillen Mac Midhna, the bard whose harp was magical and sent anyone listening straight off to sleep."

"Mmm" thought Malone."

"Aine, the Princess who started the line of the Desmond's and Cliodna who…."

Fr Malone could understand how the old bard had sent everyone to sleep. Liam seemed equally as somnambulistic even without the aid of a magical instrument. The old man reeled off name after name:

"……then there was Fionnbharr, or fair head, who took over as King by deposing Mac Moineanta and his wife Oonagh. Oonagh was the most beautiful female ever seen in this island with her long golden hair that shone like the sun and her silver raiment.....''

Malone thought of Galadriel, the Lady of Lothlorien as his eyes seemed to close for just a few seconds. They were beginning to sting in the smoke.

"....then came Aillen Mac Fionnbharr who was the King who took the Tuatha underground when the Celts came."

Fr Malone felt something wet grow in his lap and his drowsiness suddenly evaporated into acute embarrassment as he realised that he had spilled half a cup of tea quietly into his lap. He snapped awake and glanced at Pizarro who was still listening intently to Liam Fogerty and had not noticed Malone's little accident.

If he stood up, he would look like he had wet himself.

"Oh well," thought Fr Malone philosophically: "It might dry by the time Liam's finished."

Over two hours and two more cups of tea later, Liam did indeed bring his tale to an end.

"And so gentlemen, the little people as we call them, are in fact the Sidh, or the Shee, named after the hills they were hiding themselves in, after the Celts took over Erin's isle, five hundred years before the birth of Our Lord."

Fr Pizarro stroked his chin.

"Do you believe that these "Sidh" still exist, Mr Fogerty?"

Liam stared at the Spaniard:

"If you're asking me if I believe in fairies, Father, I would be all for telling you no. The Sidh are not fairies like you see in children's picture books, or like the leprechauns on the tea towels. They are not pretty little things fluttering around on butterfly wings. They are people, real people but with magical powers. They are different from us, but no less real than you and me and Father Malone."

Pizarro's mouth curled into that thin lipped smile that looked about as friendly as a cobra on a hotplate.

Pizarro stroked his beard:

"Is there any way of recognising one of these creatures if they are as skilled at shape shifting as you say?"

Liam frowned and after a few seconds, nodded:

"They say that the Tuatha de Danaan can not be changing the shape of their ears if they adopt human form. I don't know why that should be, but...."

"Do you know of any such creatures?" Pizarro demanded, rudely interrupting the old man.

Liam began to chuckle, just a little at first, and then he began to laugh. Malone joined in.

"If, Father," Liam managed to say, wiping a tear from his eye, "if I did know any such creature, what would I want to be telling yourself for? Is it the pot of gold you're after?"

Pizarro stood:

"No, Mr Fogerty, it is not, but please, if you have love for Our Lord and his blessed Mother, please respect the cloth and tell me: do you know of such a creature?"

Liam Fogerty stopped laughing and his pleasant demeanour turned into a quizzical scowl.

He glowered at Fr Malone:

"Would you be telling your foreign friend, Father, that we might all be in the Common Market now, but some things are peculiar to Ireland and the Irish. A true Irishman will be keeping the secrets of the land to himself. Some things are older than the Church of Rome, Father, and some things have more of a calling on the heart. Father Callaghan knows my thoughts on the matter. I'll be bidding you gentlemen good day."

Liam opened his front door allowing a welcome blast of fresh air to flood into the cottage. Father Malone took a deep breath as he walked over the threshold; Pizarro had been the first out and he now turned towards the cottage front door.

"Thank you Mister Fogerty." He said with that weak, insipid smile:

"May the Lord protect you."

He turned and walked away.

Fr Malone shook his head as the Spaniard disappeared around the corner:

"Thank you Liam, please don't be offended, your history lesson was marvellous."

Liam Fogerty grinned:

"He's a barrel of laughs, that one. He'd sour the milk more than any Sidh. I'm telling you, Father. He's a nasty piece of work our Spanish friend from Rome. There's something of the dark about him. I'd be watching my back if I were you."

Fr Malone shook Liam's hand and walked slowly after Fr Pizarro. Liam waited until they were well out of sight before he turned back into his cottage.

"I wasn't liking that dark fella at all." Roisin Fogerty said, as Liam scratched his head in front of the fire.

"He seemed to think himself better than us."

"Yes, yes, so he did. He did that." Liam agreed thoughtfully, then, as if he had just had a flash of inspiration, he stepped to the front door and grabbed his cap from a hook:

"I'll be at Maire Duke's, woman. I've some business to be attending to."

And with that he went out, slammed the door climbed onto his bicycle, which was stood leaning on the garden wall and sped off up the lane, his little legs pumping the pedals like pistons.

9

Fields and farms, towns and villages, woods and forests, thickets and heaths, hills and dales, rattled past the window of the express train.

A small boy sat by the train window and stared out at the ever-shifting leaden grey sky.

Wayne Higginbotham, or rather the boy who used to think of himself as Wayne Higginbotham, but now didn't know who the hell he was, agonised about the possibilities. His mind was in turmoil, thoughts barged each other aside for prominence and consideration, but each was discarded in turn as an entirely new possibility entered his head.

He had been adopted.

He had been given away.

He had been rejected.

He hadn't been wanted.

He had been wanted but someone couldn't afford to bring up a baby.

He had been wanted but a baby would have caused a scandal.

He had been wanted, but……..

He just couldn't get the subject out of his mind; adopted. He had looked the word up in the dictionary:

"To take (a person) into a relationship, especially another's child as one's own."

The only salient facts of the matter were that Frank Higginbotham wasn't his real Dad and Doris Higginbotham wasn't his real Mum.

The only people he'd known his whole, entire life.

The people he had always thought of as his Mum and Dad.

How could they have done this to him?

Why had they lied to him for all these years?

That meant that he had been born and surrendered by some other woman. Some other woman was his real mother. Why?

Why had she given him away?

Had she not loved him?

Why had he been rejected?

Was it because of his ears?

His hair?

When had he been rejected?

The folded piece of paper in the envelope had been an adoption certificate. It was dated some six months after his birth.

Had his real parents kept him until then?

Maybe his real parents had loved him and intended to raise him as normal parents raise their children, but maybe then they had been killed in some horrific accident.

Or, maybe they had been murdered.

Maybe Doris and Frank had kidnapped him and they had killed his real Mum and Dad, because they hadn't been able to have a baby of their own.

Maybe his parents had been rich and had been on holiday, driving around Yorkshire and Doris and Frank had done away with them, so that they could have the baby and his real Mum and Dad's money?

But what had they done with the money to still be so poor?

No, his Dad wouldn't have done that, not Frank; but then Frank wasn't his real Dad, was he?

Maybe his real parents already had too many children and just couldn't afford any more.

Maybe his real mother was a drug addict, or a drunk and had lost him in a drunken stupor. No, how would the person who had found him have known his name?

Maybe his real mother was an innocent young serving maid who had been duped by a wicked Squire, or an evil Lord and had been forced to give up her baby in shame. He had seen old movies about that sort of thing.

What about his real name?

It wasn't Wayne Higginbotham that was for sure. After years of hating his name, Wayne suddenly felt very uncomfortable to have lost it.

Was his real name: Michael Sean O'Brien?

Or was the name on that card just a co-incidence. It certainly seemed likely that that was his real name, especially as Michael had the same birth date as him, but how was he to know?

Somehow, it just didn't sound right.

He didn't feel like a Michael.

Wayne thought of Michael Parker at school; he had been the baddest boy in Gas Street. He just couldn't be a Michael. That would mean people would call him Mick or Mike. Well maybe that was better than being called lugsy, or fuzz.

As for Sean, or "Seen" as Wayne thought that it was pronounced, like bean or mean; well, that was just weird.

Perhaps Michael Sean wasn't his name at all.

Maybe he had just made too many assumptions.

Perhaps he had had a twin brother?

Maybe his twin had been called Michael Sean and maybe they had been separated at birth?

Maybe his brother had been adopted by someone else, or worse, had been kept by their real Mother, while only he had been rejected.

Did he have any brothers and sisters?

Did he still have a real mother and father?

Maybe they were dead, or maybe just his mother had died and maybe he looked like his mum and his father had been so heartbroken that he hadn't been able to raise him and had him adopted because of that.

Maybe it had been the other way round and he had looked like his Dad and his Mum had been too broken hearted?

There were more "maybes" in his mind than brain cells.

He'd seen something like that on the telly once.

Where was he really from?

Had he been born in London?

He had always thought that he was a proper Yorkshire man, as Yorkshire, as Yorkshire pudding, or Harry Ramsden's Fish and Chips, or Ilkley Moor bah't'at.

He had believed he was as much of a Yorkshire man as Freddy Trueman, the famous cricket player. If he was being realistic, however, it was now entirely possible that he hadn't even been born in Yorkshire. Especially if he was the Michael Sean O'Brien on that immunisation card and had once lived at that address:

24 St. Joseph's Road, Hammersmith.

Yorkshire Cricket Club wouldn't let people who hadn't been born in the County play for them, so that was his career as a cricketer up the spout then.

That was OK though because Wayne didn't really like cricket.

It did ruin his "Captain Yorkshire" fantasy.

Wayne had seen a comic book character called "Captain America" in a comic at the Doctors. "Captain America" was a masked crime fighter like Batman and he had a "stars and stripes" shield. Ever since the Baz Thompson incident, Wayne had fantasized that he might have superpowers and that he would wear a black suit and mask and bear a shield with a white Yorkshire Rose on it. So that career choice was up the spout too!

Maybe he wasn't even English.

Michael Sean O'Brien sounded sort of Irish, but no, his address had been in London and anyway, he didn't even have an Irish accent.

Maybe he was the victim of a major conspiracy.

Maybe he was being raised in secret because his Dad was a spy like James Bond and the bad guys would use the child to get at Bond, so he was being raised in secret, somewhere safe. Well, Shepton was definitely safe. Nothing ever happened in Shepton.

No, that was just plain silly.

Maybe he was the product of a doomed love affair?

Maybe he was the secret love child of someone famous?

That sort of stuff was in the Sunday Papers every week, especially that one with the naked ladies in that always made him feel a bit sweaty.

Maybe he was a Royal.

Doris had said that the Prince of Wales had big ears. No, that was even sillier.

Had his real parents been rich, or poor?

Maybe he................

The train began to slow down. Wayne suddenly became aware that instead of green fields, the landscape passing by had been solid ranks of grey houses and factories for ages. He was nearly there, nearly in the great big city of London.

Wayne had been to London once before, with his Mum and Dad, no, he had been with Doris and Frank. He found himself checking his thoughts and separating the concepts of Mum and Dad from Doris and Frank. It was just so incredibly hard to do, after all Doris and Frank had been his Mum and Dad for all of his life, well, every bit of it that he could remember.

Maybe this was all a total mistake, a misunderstanding of some sort.

Ever since he had heard the Doctors whispering and had then found that official adoption certificate and his immunisation record in that envelope, he felt like he had been waiting to wake up from some weird dream. When he had been in the hospital and he had heard the doctors talking, he really hadn't been sure at first whether he had dreamed it or not. Yet now he had seen some proper legal paperwork, it all seemed far too real to be a dream.

A platform appeared by the side of the train and people began to stand and take their coats and bags off the overhead baggage rack, some shuffled down the corridor towards the carriage doors. Wayne had clutched his duffle bag on his knee all the way from Shepton station, except of course during the change at Leeds. He had been terrified that someone might steal it, for it contained not only his most important possessions, but also the considerable sum of money that he had "borrowed" from Doris and Frank. The moment of truth was drawing near.

Wayne Higginbotham took a deep breath, then another.

Why was his mouth so dry?

Wayne hoped that the ticket collectors and guards in London were as gullible as the man in the booking office on Shepton station, or even the one on the train who had punched his ticket.

At Shepton, the clerk had peered at him suspiciously and had asked if he was travelling alone.

"Oh no, that's my mum at the other end of the platform." Wayne had blurted quickly, pointing towards a blonde woman who was fiddling with her lipstick and peering into one of those little mirror things women kept in their handbags.

"She's not feeling too well and would you believe…" He had said, leaning towards the little glass hole in the ticket office window and winking conspiratorially at the ticket office man:

"…that she forgot to get me a ticket."

The man had scowled and got up off his seat to get a better view of the woman. He turned back to Wayne, scowling suspiciously.

"I don't think……."

Wayne looked directly into the man's eyes and concentrated:

"Please, please, please." He had wished silently.

The clerk had looked slightly confused; then he had shaken his head before sitting down and laughing:

"Women eh?"

"Aye." Wayne had sighed: "Women!"

Wayne had been well into his journey when the ticket Inspector on the train had approached him.

The Inspector had smiled kindly at him:

"Travelling alone, young man?" He had asked cheerfully as he checked and punched a hole in the boy's ticket.

"Oh no," Wayne, had lied:

"My Mum's just popped to the loo. I don't think she's gone for a wee, she said she was going to powder her nose. That's what women always say though, isn't it? She'll be back in a minute or two."

The Inspector smiled wryly at the boy.

"Aye they allus say that." He agreed solemnly; then he nodded, winked conspiratorially and moved on through the coach.

Some ten minutes later Wayne heard the Inspector's voice and the click of his ticket-punching machine as he came back through the train. Wayne turned and saw him through the gap between the headrests, approaching from behind. He was only a couple of seats away.

Wayne's heartbeat had quickened and his mind whizzed through plausible scenarios and possible means of escape. To get to the toilet he would have had to pass the Inspector, now that was risking it. Maybe if he just closed his eyes tightly and pretended to be asleep the man might not notice him. He was aware of the man's approach but just kept thinking:

"I'm not here, I'm not here, I'm not here."

The Inspector chatted to the people behind Wayne. Then Wayne heard him chatting to the old man opposite. He screwed his eyes tighter and waited for the inevitable shake of the shoulder. He heard the Inspector laugh and then say something; his voice was moving into the distance. Wayne heard the click of the punch at a table further down the coach. Even so, it was several minutes before he dared to open his eyes and by then there was no sign of the Inspector at all. Wayne let out a relieved sigh and went back to watching the scenery as it whizzed past at a phenomenal rate.

Lying hadn't been the only crime that Wayne had committed that day. He had also stolen sixty pounds from the top draw in Doris and Frank's sideboard. Well, he hadn't exactly stolen it. He had left a note saying that he was treating it as an advance from his building society account and that Doris and Frank were welcome to empty the said account to make good his debt. The fact that he only had thirty-five pounds in the account seemed almost immaterial in the circumstances. He would definitely make it up to them as soon as he could.

Well, all of that was forgotten now as he climbed down off the train.

It seemed to Wayne that a thousand people must have been on that train as he was swept along the platform at King's Cross Station. There were more people than he had ever seen. Except for that one time Frank had taken him to see Manchester United play at Old Trafford when he had been about eight.

He remembered being terrified that day too, especially as he supported Leeds.

Hardly anyone noticed the one small boy in the crowd that crushed through the small gap at the end of the platform. Everyone handed their tickets over to the big, black man and rushed off into the metropolis to do whatever it was they had travelled to London to do and one small boy seemed no different.

No one approached him. No one questioned him. It was almost as though he was invisible.

Wayne had planned this trip meticulously, right down to the finest detail. Ever since he had found out that he had definitely been adopted, two weeks earlier, he had been planning to get to the address he had copied off his immunisation record: 24 St. Joseph's Road, Hammersmith.

Wayne didn't know what he'd find there, but he certainly felt that it would be a good start in finding out just who he was. He certainly had had no idea that he would be able to do it all so soon. He just hadn't been able to believe his luck, when Doris had said to him the previous week, that she would be working all day on the following Tuesday and would he be alright left on his own. She had promised to leave him a pound, so that he could get some fish and chips for lunch.

"I'll be fine Mum, don't worry. I'm nearly at that Grammar School now you know. I'm not a kid anymore." He had chided her.

So it was that on the Monday, the 12th of August, while Frank was putting thingummy's onto widgets and then into boxes at the factory and Doris was doing her couple of hours at the pub over lunchtime, he had gone to the station and picked up a timetable of trains to London.

The timetable told him that there was a train from Shepton station to London, via Leeds, every day except Sunday. It left the town at 9:30 am and got to London at 3:30pm. It could not have been more perfect. Doris was due to work from 8:30 in the morning until around 5:00pm; while Frank's shift was 8:00 am to 4:00 pm. By the time anyone realised he was missing, he would already be in Hammersmith.

He had also managed to find a London street map, complete with a map of the London underground, in one of his Dad's drawers.

The Higginbotham's had used it on their last family visit to London to see the sights, but Frank had not been able to make head nor tail of the tube map and had relied on Wayne for directions.

Wayne had been concerned about getting the money to be able to afford to make the trip. He knew that he had an account at the Shepton Building Society, but he was also aware that Doris, or Frank had to sign papers to get his money in or out. How could he do that without arousing their suspicions?

Then he had realised that he had seen Doris taking money out of the top drawer of the sideboard in the living room many times.

He checked the drawer on the Friday lunchtime, there was a hundred pounds in it. He decided that he would fund his trip from the top drawer and leave an I.O.U. He wouldn't take it all though, that would be greedy. He had a ten pound note that his Aunty Margaret had given him for his last birthday and a five pound note that Frank had given him for passing the eleven plus, hidden in his bedside table. If he borrowed just sixty pounds from Doris and Frank, that would give him a fund of seventy-five pounds, a veritable fortune and it would leave Doris and Frank forty pounds, just in case they needed it.

The fateful Tuesday had arrived at last and as he walked through King's Cross Station, Wayne, reflected that it had all gone totally to plan so far, but now he felt as nervous as he had ever felt in his life.

Was he just a tube train trip away from finding out who he really was?

Or had he wasted a considerable amount of time and money travelling all this way for nothing?

What would Doris and Frank do to him when he got home?

This time Doris would not just erupt, she'd explode, she'd go up like Krakatoa.

The explosion would probably wipe Shepton and half the Yorkshire Dales straight off the map.

The grumpy man in the ticket office on King's Cross Underground station didn't bother asking him if he was OK, whether he was travelling alone, or where his Mum and Dad were when Wayne asked for his ticket to Hammersmith. In fact, the ticket man didn't speak to him at all. He just took the proffered pound note and stuffed the ticket and change back through the hole at the bottom of his window. No smile, no thank you, nothing. His Mum and Dad obviously hadn't taught him any manners, Wayne could have told you that for nothing.

It was strange but most people in London seemed to be very grumpy, tired, or downright weird looking. Maybe it was all the shandy that made them grumpy. Frank had once said that people down south were all shandy drinking, southern poofters. Neither Frank, nor Doris, seemed to like Londoners.

"They all think they're sommat when they're nowt!" Doris would say when someone from London was on the news, talking in that funny accent that sounded Australian, or that one that sounded posh like the Queen.

Frank and Doris didn't like the Irish either, or the French, or the Italians and they hated the Japanese and the Germans, because of the war. They hated all of them almost as much as they hated the Americans, which confused Wayne because he knew the Americans had been on our side.

Weary tourists, bearing backpacks and clutching maps crowded around the tube system plans on the station walls, peering myopically at the strange, squiggly symbols.

Hippies with amazingly long hair and improbably wide flared jeans sauntered around casually. Some were wearing those coats made out of dead dogs, they were called afghans, or something.

Unbelievably beautiful girls strolled by wearing skirts so short that Wayne could almost see their knickers, others wore them so long that you couldn't even see their feet.

Busy people in business suits dashed everywhere as if they were in a race. One be-suited individual almost fell over Wayne in his haste. The businessman didn't apologise, of course, he was far too busy for that. Obviously a shandy drinker, Wayne decided. The man had just grunted, steadied the almost bowled over boy by grabbing his shoulders and had then continued on his way.

Wayne straightened his duffle bag, which was strung over his shoulder, checking as he did so that it was still intact. Doris had warned him at least two hundred times to keep his wallet in his jacket pocket and not in the back pocket of his jeans when the Higginbotham family had last visited London:

"The underground is full of pickpockets" she had said.

So Wayne glowered menacingly at everyone, no matter what age, sex, or race, just to demonstrate that if they did intend to steal his wallet, then he wasn't going to lose it without a fight. He had "taken out" Baz Thompson. Wayne Higginbotham was well hard.

His wallet was safely tucked away in his jacket pocket and his jacket safely tucked away in his duffle bag.

It was a pleasant enough summer's day, warm, albeit cloudy.

Wayne was quite surprised that he was OK just wearing a T-shirt and jeans. It was definitely warmer in London than it had been in Shepton, but, of course it had been quite early when he had set off.

As Wayne boarded the Metropolitan line train, he had to confide to himself that everything seemed incredibly intimidating without Doris and Frank.

For a moment he caught himself wishing that they were there, but then that wasn't the point of all this, was it?

Although it wasn't as busy on the tube as he had expected, it felt like everyone was staring at him:

"Thief, runaway, you'll be for it when you get home, young man."

That was OK though, because he was staring back at them thinking:

"Weirdo, pickpocket, posh pants."

One thing he did decide on the tube, after a momentary panic when he incorrectly thought he'd boarded a train going in the wrong direction, was that he would think of himself as Wayne until he definitely found out that he was called something else; Michael Seen, or whatever his real name turned out to be.

Tube station after tube station passed in a blur of darkness and sudden flashes of light.

Wayne's hands were getting clammy and the butterflies were back in his tummy, just as they had been when he had opened that brass log box in Doris and Frank's bedroom. His mouth was like a birdcage bottom, as Doris would say the morning after she had drunk one too many Babychams.

Hammersmith was getting nearer and nearer. Fear began to replace the eager anticipation and excitement that he had felt when he taken his place on the express train that morning.

"Should I turn back? It's not too late." He thought to himself. The thought of the trouble he would be in when he got home, however, persuaded him that he had to continue. After all if he gave up now, then he would never get the chance to do anything like this again. Doris would certainly see to that.

The train slowed to a stop and the red and white sign on the dirty white tiled wall outside said: "Hammersmith."

Wayne, his throat dry and his stomach churning, got off the tube and proceeded up the escalators. Once out of the station, he took out his London A-Z, looked around to get his bearings and began to walk down the busy, dirty streets towards his objective.

More than once, irritating specks of dust got in his eyes, as smoke spewing big red double-decker buses, black taxis and Lorries roared past him. He had never seen so much traffic in his life; it was crazy, so much crazier than even Bradford, or Leeds where Doris took him shopping sometimes. Just getting across the road was a nightmare.

Eventually, however, Wayne found himself outside a tall grey house on a terraced side street. He looked around; the street was so much quieter than the main roads, some kids, not much bigger than him, were playing football further down the road. Cars were parked on both sides of the street. One looked an awful lot like his Uncle Stanley's Ford Granada.

How would Aunty Margaret react to all this Wayne wondered?

It was too late now to worry about things like that.

The boy formerly known as Wayne Higginbotham, the only son of Doris and Frank Higginbotham, of 18 Cavendish Street, Shepton, took a piece of paper out of his bag, checked what he had written there, then walked slowly up three steps and knocked on a green panelled front door.

The front door of number 24, St. Joseph's Road, Hammersmith.

10

The chime made an unearthly howling sound as the westerly wind whistled through it. It was a cold, stiff breeze, straight off the Atlantic Ocean, that rushed over the green bog land, quite unseasonable for the time of the year. The chime was one of several gaudily coloured wind toys that stood, mounted on sticks, by a dry stone wall, on the side of a single track road, just before, or just after, depending which way you were going, a tiny hump backed bridge. The only other sounds, besides the weird howl of the chime, were the gentle trickle of the mountain stream that passed under the bridge and the occasional cry of a lost, solitary gull.

The road seemed to go on and on forever, across the expanse of the bleak, barren, moor-land valley, which was surrounded on all four sides by distant mountains. Not snow capped Alpine peaks, like on old peoples' jigsaw puzzles, humongous chocolate boxes, or the covers of winter holiday brochures, but mountains all the same.

One of the road side toys looked like a windmill. It whirled around in a blaze of colour, while another represented a workman manically digging a hole with a spade. Only one toy made a noise, however; a toy that represented an ancient warrior blowing a huge horn. It was an eerie noise, that some likened to the cry of a banshee; but only those who had never heard such a thing. The wind toys seemed oddly lost, standing in such a wild, desolate and lonely place, seemingly devoid of any sort of human habitation. Almost hidden, however, in a small, thickly wooded hollow on the opposite side of the road from the toys, there stood an ancient, ramshackle, old cottage.

At first sight it looked like a long abandoned ruin; the whitewashed plaster was green with mould in places and was falling off in others, exposing the bare stone walls. The door and window frames had once been painted a bright shade of red, but the paintwork had long-since peeled and now just small spots of colour remained. The only clue that someone might live in the cottage was the fact that all the windows were still intact, and the tiny wisp of smoke that curled up from the chimney, before it was swiftly whisked away across the valley on the wings of the wind.

The front door of the cottage creaked open and an old man emerged.

He blinked in the light and then sniffed the air. He looked towards the chimes, nodded and smiled:

"Thank you, old friend." He said, puffing out a large cloud of smoke, having just taken a long stemmed pipe from his mouth.

The old man looked to be about seventy with white whiskers and thick white hair, upon which a flat cap was precariously balanced. His trousers were held up with a belt of rough string, his shirt was collarless, grey and grubby, while his jacket had once been tweed, but was now so grimy as to be almost indiscernible.

"So old Liam was right when he was telling me I'd soon be getting a delegation of important visitors. I'd better be making myself scarce."

The old man muttered as he disappeared back inside the cottage.

"I wouldn't want such worthies to be seeing me in this state, especially considering how far some of them have come."

A chuckle emerged from behind the closing door.

In the far distance, an old green Morris Minor 1000 chugged slowly down the road from the high mountain pass.

"This is the most miserable, desolate place I have ever seen in my life."

Fr Francisco Pizarro almost spat as he glowered at the vista from the Morris' windows.

It was the first thing he had said since he and Fr Malone had left the house in Finaan.

"Ah, it has a charm all of its own." Malone smiled:

"You could call it unspoiled and you know it's not a bad old day. The sun is shining and although it's not exactly warm, it's pleasant enough."

Pizarro curled his lip:

"You call this pleasant; I call it beyond terrible. The sun is embarrassed to shine in such a place. It will remain unspoiled, as you call it, so long as there is one square metre of decent land left anywhere else in the world."

Fr Malone sighed:

"There used to be a lot of people here once: farms, cottages, villages. This was once a busy area, you know. Cromwell forced many Catholics off the land in the more affluent and desirable parts of Ireland, so that he could settle his English troops on the decent land.

"To Hell or Connaught." He would say to the despised native Catholics, often before despatching them to the former without even letting them make the decision themselves. So, the survivors of his persecution came and settled here and tried to eke a living out of this inhospitable land, but then of course, along came the potato famines, especially the 1840's and almost all the people left, or died. You can almost feel the sadness and melancholy in the air. A million people died and a million left Ireland forever in that famine period."

A snort from the passenger side of the car indicated Pizarro's views on the matter.

"How long until we get there?"

Fr Pizarro seemed impatient.

"Not long now," Malone answered, "in fact, do you see that clump of trees in the dip down there? That's where we're going. That's Mickey's place."

Pizarro smiled his thin lipped smile.

"Good." He hissed: "Excellent. Stop the car as soon as you can."

Fr Malone nodded and pulled over on a patch of stones by the side of the road. Pizarro took a pair of powerful binoculars out of his bag and got out of the car.

Malone climbed out of the old Morris and sat on the front wing. In the distance he could see Croagh Patrick, Ireland's Holy Mountain, from where it is said, St Patrick banished all the snakes in Ireland; beyond that lay Clew Bay and the wild Atlantic Ocean. Between the coastal mountains and the range they had just crossed, lay mile after mile of peat bog and soggy fields. Clouds raced overhead as if they were joyfully fleeing the ocean, intermittent patches of blue sky appeared and shafts of sunlight caressed the landscape.

Pizarro concentrated his binoculars on the trees in the dip. He stood for ages, just staring, until, at last, he took the instrument from his eyes. Without even looking at Malone, he said:

"It is as I thought. Let's go."

The car bumped and bounced slowly along the narrow road, until they eventually got near to the hollow. Malone parked in a gap in the wall, where an iron gate had once stood. He could wait no longer, a question had been burning in his brain since Pizarro had arrived at the airport and now seemed the opportune moment to ask it:

"Father Pizarro. Er, what do you intend to do, you know, now that we're here?"

Pizarro turned his face towards Malone and the young Irish priest once again felt those cold, black eyes dissecting him, as unemotionally as a scientist dissects a frog in a laboratory.

"I intend to find out the truth of this matter, Father Malone. If this being is indeed a Sidh, then I can begin the process of exorcism and elimination. This devil will be full of tricks and surprises, like all the others. Today, I will find out how clever he is. Do not forget that this is a war, Father Malone, a Holy War."

Malone scowled and looked down at the steering wheel:

"Exorcism and elimination, that's quite a mouthful, Father. Doesn't it sort of mean, like kill?"

The black eyes narrowed to slits.

"I would never kill one of God's creatures, Father, but I am more than happy to kill the devil's spawn, very, very happy."

He turned and pulled the lever to open the car door. The conversation was obviously over.

A strange noise filled the air as the two priests climbed out of the car. Malone smiled and nodded to Pizarro, indicating the wind toys.

The black eyed priest scowled and took a briefcase from the boot of the Morris.

"Let's get to work." He growled, setting off to walk the few yards to the cottage by the bridge.

James Malone sighed, raised his eyebrows and followed him.

The two priests walked up to the door of the old cottage.

"Mickey." Fr Malone shouted.

Pizarro spun and glowered at him.

"Silence, fool!" He barked; then he gently knocked on the door.

On the other side of the stream, which ran by the trees next to the old cottage, a donkey peered curiously over the hedge, chewing lazily on fresh hay.

There was no answer from inside the cottage.

Pizarro turned the handle.

Malone's mouth dropped open:

"What are you doing Father? You can't just go walking into some fella's house, this is private property." He gasped.

Pizarro ignored him and opened the door, peering around the edge into the cottage.

"Is anyone here?" He shouted, in his thickly accented English:

"Is there anyone home?"

He stepped fully inside the cottage.

Malone stood outside, hopping nervously from one foot to the other and looking around to see if anyone could see them breaking into somebody's home. Only the donkey was watching.

After several seconds, Malone cursed under his breath and followed the Spaniard into the cottage.

It took several moments for the young Priest's eyes to adjust to the darkness inside the building. The interior was every bit as dilapidated as the outside. Newspapers and magazines were scattered haphazardly around the bare stone floor, while the only furniture was an old tatty armchair, a table upon which stood an antiquated portable T.V. and an ancient dresser, which seemed to be leaning against the wall, or was supporting the wall, one of the two.

An ancient hearth filled an entire end wall. It contained a cast iron structure, suspending a brass kettle over a smouldering turf fire.

Pizarro knelt before the fire and prodded one of the briquettes:

"It was lit this morning." He stated flatly, before wandering through into what must have been the kitchen. It seemed to be a wooden structure loosely attached to the original stone cottage and roofed with corrugated iron. A door comprised almost one full side of the structure. Pizarro tried it, it opened, but the priest did not step through, he merely peered outside and then closed the door, turned and ran a finger along a vaguely modern sink unit, besides the T.V. it was the only concession to the late twentieth century.

Pizarro strolled around the cottage, passing through the dust filled streams of light sneaking in through the filthy windows, with a look of total disdain etched on his features:

"This one lives like a pig." He hissed.

There was a plain wooden door in the back wall that appeared to lead off into a bedroom or some other original part of the cottage. Pizarro tried the round bronze knob; the door was locked. Father Malone gasped in astonishment as the Spaniard walked over to the table and removed a small mallet and chisel from his bag.

"What the? You cannot be serious Father? This is somebody's….." Malone's outburst was stopped in mid sentence by the loud retort of the mallet as it hit the head of the chisel.

The bedroom door burst open.

Fr Pizarro stepped smartly inside, but if he had been expecting the owner of the cottage to be cowering somewhere in the room, he was sorely disappointed.

An ancient cast iron bed stood in the room, upon which some old grey sheets were untidily rolled up as though someone had left the bed exactly as he had got out of it. A table with a bowl, a jug and a hand towel of indeterminate colour stood next to the room's filthy window.

"For goodness sake Father," Malone whispered urgently, his eyes wide:

"Do you not think all the breaking and entering is uncalled for?"

Pizarro's dead black eyes burned into Malone:

"Maybe, Father Malone, you should think about which side you are on.

We deal with forces here that you do not understand. You are a rural village priest and probably always will be. I am at the right hand of our Holy Father and I have been chosen for this work. The enemies of Our Lord and the One True Church will perish and be cast into the flaming pits of hell. I am working for the greatest of causes. Please leave me to get on with that work in the best way I see fit."

His eyes widened as his voice rose into a sort of crescendo, which peaked at the end of his sentence. Malone decided there and then that his Spanish colleague was totally insane:

"Have you ever thought of debating with Ian Paisley?" Malone muttered cheekily.

Pizarro scowled:

"What?"

"Nothing Father, nothing at all!"

Malone sat down in the armchair, while Pizarro strolled back to the fireplace:

"What exactly are you looking for?" Malone asked.

Pizarro leaned into the enormous hearth again and started prodding the bricks behind the grate. Suddenly he let out a satisfied sigh:

"Aaah!"

He pushed the side of a loose brick, which swivelled freely. A small ornate wooden box was hidden in a cavity behind. Pizarro opened the box and breathed a soft satisfied sigh.

"Nothing! Father Malone. I have found what I wanted." He declared as he replaced the box behind the brick and turned from the hearth, smiling, his hands clutched tightly behind his back.

"What was that?" Malone asked. Pizarro smiled, like the cat that got the cream.

"Let us just say I have found the hiding place of the "crock of gold," my young friend. It has confirmed my suspicions."

Malone took a deep breath:

"Look Father Pizarro," he began, "I don't know what makes you so sure that this oul' fella is in league with the devil. I only mentioned to the Bishop that some oul' farmer, out in the hills, had pulled my leg by saying that he was one of the little people. All of a sudden I'm getting letters telling me to report to Dublin. You and that Bishop Donleavy interrogating me as if I had committed a cardinal sin and now I'm involved in breaking into people's homes. I mean what in the name of the Holy Mother is going on?"

Pizarro spun towards Malone, his black eyes now ablaze:

"Do not use Our Lady's name in vain." He spat:

"What is going on, had you listened in Dublin, is that we are purifying the earth; clearing the World of all the worst, foulest monsters that you can imagine. It is a good job that we exist, little village Priest. Only we know how Satan's minions work. It is also good that our sources are so reliable and that our agents know how to interpret the tittle-tattle of the minor clergy and the peasantry. These creatures are not the pretty, mischievous, little things of fairy tales. They are evil, pure unadulterated evil."

His eyes seemed to have grown, round and immense, even blacker than usual, but suddenly he stopped speaking and closed them. His face looked pained. After a short silence he started to speak again, but quietly and calmly.

"My mother died soon after I was born. It seems she haemorrhaged and because we were far away from a mid wife or doctor, she bled to death. I was raised by my elder sister and my father in the hills above Sarria, in Galicia. We were poor, but we knew no different, so we were happy.

One beautiful spring morning, when I was a small boy, my sister came home and told me that she had seen a beautiful woman, with eyes as blue as summer skies and hair as black as a ravens wings, while she was out picking flowers in the meadow above our house. She said that the woman sang like an angel and had asked her to come away with her, to a magical place full of fruit, sweet pastries and honeyed cakes. I laughed at her and said that she was mad. I knew all the local village girls and all the girls in the villages around us, not one of them could have been described as being beautiful with raven hair and blue eyes. She cried and said that she had seen what she had seen and that I was the mad one for not believing her. She asked me to go with her, to meet this fine lady. She said she would prove that she was not crazy. I refused, I was afraid, I knew even then that this woman was either a gypsy or some other stranger intent on kidnapping children and doing them harm, either that, or she was a Xanas."

Fr James Malone raised his eyebrows:

"A what?" he asked, bemused.

Fr Pizarro stroked his chin patiently, his black eyes misty, his gaze distant.

"A Xanas, it is a, how do say it? A nymph, a fairy, a sprite? That is how we call her in the North of Spain, like the Sidh that the old man described. She is always beautiful with long flowing hair and fine silken dress. She is like Basa-Andre who sits in a cave and combs her hair, waiting to snare the unsuspecting child. Either that, or this woman was an Aatxe, an evil shape-shifting demon. My people, to scare their children in their beds, often used the stories of the Xanas and the Aatxe. They used them to persuade the children not to be naughty. One thing was certain to me; this being was an evil creature and not one of God's children. My sister begged me not to tell our father, that he would think her crazy and have her taken away. I told her to stay away from the meadow, but she would not. Many times she came to me that spring and told me the same story. About how she had just been picking flowers in the morning dew, when this beautiful creature came and talked to her, laughed with her and made her feel good. I told her that she was a fool and that her imagination had got the better of her. Eventually, one morning in the early summer, we had a big fight about it. I said that she was mad and I forbade her to go to the meadow ever again. I said that I would tell our father and that he would put a stop to all this nonsense. She said I was the fool and that she was going to go away with the beautiful Lady."

There was along silence and Pizarro seemed to need to compose himself.

Fr Malone shifted uncomfortably in the chair. Then Pizarro suddenly began again:

"I went and told my father. I remember to this day how white his face went when I described the woman: "Xanas," he wailed. I had not even finished speaking when he rushed out of our house, but he was too late. My sister had already gone to the meadow and she had disappeared. She was never seen again. My father died of a broken heart soon after and I was left to be raised by the local Priest. I vowed then that I would devote my life to destroying such creatures and that is exactly what I have done."

Father Malone grimaced, for a moment he actually felt sorry for the Spanish Priest:

"I'm sorry about your sister and your mother." He said sensitively, in the way he might talk to the recently bereaved.

Pizarro glowered at him:

"I do not need your sympathy, Irishman."

Malone shrugged: "I'm not doubting what you said, but surely, I mean, come on, there isn't really such a thing as a, what did you call it? A Xanas, is there?" He suggested quietly:

"Is it not just someone who's maybe a bit simple? You know, mentally ill perhaps, who think they are, well, whatever?"

Fr Pizarro studied the Irishman intently:

"Why did you become a Priest, Father Malone?" He asked.

"Was it not to spread the word of Our Lord?"

Malone shrugged again:

"Well, yeah, of course?"

Pizarro moved closer to him:

"Do you believe in heaven and hell?"

"Well, I ...."

"What proof do you have that they exist?" Pizarro interrupted him impatiently. He prodded Malone gently, with a pointed finger. Malone moved his mouth but before he could utter a word Pizarro continued:

"None, only the faith that has been imbued in you, in your very soul, by your elders, your parents, your priests. You accept Our Lord's words without question but you are…"

He struggled for the right word:

"Sceptical, yes, sceptical. You believe in the Holy Ghost do you not? What about the rest of the supernatural phenomena that inhabit our world?"

Malone rubbed his forehead and then ran a hand through his hair:

"I suppose I hadn't thought of it like that."

Pizarro snorted contemptuously:

"Perhaps you just do not think much at all, Irishman. Left to the likes of you, the ancient prophecy would come to pass and we would all be doomed to hell on earth."

"Prophecy? What Prophecy?" James asked, suddenly confused.

Pizarro snorted:

"That is the business of the "Order" and the "Order" alone. Come, I have found all that I need to know. Let us go and……"

He was interrupted by a sudden, loud and totally unexpected knock at the door.

"Jaysus." Malone exclaimed, his face taking on a panicked expression. Pizarro, however, strode over to the door and opened it as though he were the owner of the cottage.

"Yes?" Pizarro demanded of the visitor.

Malone could see a man in early middle age stood outside. He looked as surprised to see the Spanish Priest as Malone had been to hear the knock:

"Oh, er, Good morning, Father. I was just passing and I thought I'd be looking in. You know, on ould Mickey. Is he here, is he? Has something happened to him at all?"

The weather had taken a turn for the worse, a fine drizzle of rain now poured on the man's working clothes.

"No." Pizarro stated easily: "Nothing has happened. We needed to see him; and as there is no shelter anywhere nearby, we took the liberty of inviting ourselves in. My colleague here is a friend of his. I am sure Mr Finn would not mind."

The man, Malone could see over Pizarro's shoulder looked like a farmer in early middle age, plump with a ruddy complexion and a thatch of bright red hair under a flat cap. He was dressed roughly, tweed jacket, well worn shirt and shabby trousers, but that was the usual garb of an agricultural worker in the Ireland of the early Nineteen Seventies. He nodded:

"No, yer right, he wouldn't be minding. But, be telling me now. What business would my Uncle Mickey have with two Priests like your good selves?"

Before either Malone or Pizarro could answer, he roared with laughter:

"Not planning to get married is he, the old divil?"

The farmer pushed past Pizarro and entered the cottage.

Pizarro's glowered at his back venomously.

Fr Malone laughed:

"No, no, of course not, no, not Mickey."

The visitor held out his hand:

"It's grand to be in, out of the rain. Hello there, Father Malone isn't it? I saw you at a wedding in Finaan, did I not?"

Malone, his smile fading, shook his head:

"Err sorry, but I've no recollection….."

The farmer chuckled jovially at the young Priests discomfort:

"Don't go worrying yourself at all, Father. We weren't introduced. Dan Joyce is the name. I'm a good friend of Fr. Dermot's. Me Uncle Mickey told me all about you and the little chat you had."

Dan shook Fr Malone's hand so vigorously that Malone thought he'd wrenched his shoulder.

He wasn't surprised that Dan was a good friend of Fr Dermot Callaghan. Everyone knew Fr Dermot.

Dan Joyce then turned to Pizarro and held out his hand:

"And you would be?"

Pizarro smiled a cold smile, but did not offer his hand in return.

"I am Father Francisco Pizarro. Let us just say that my colleague and I are here on Church business."

"Have we met before, at all? " Dan asked jovially:

"There's a sorta familiar look about you; although, it must have been a long time ago."

His smile faded, and he scowled as if desperately trying to remember something, but shook his head as recollection failed him. His hand dropped.

Pizarro shook his head dismissively.

"No, I think not."

Dan Joyce nodded:

"Sure, the business of the church, is it?"

His face suddenly lit up:

"No one expects the Spanish Inquisition eh?"

His laughter echoed around the cottage's interior. Malone couldn't help the smirk but Pizarro looked horrified:

"What?" He hissed, incredulously.

Dan Joyce managed to compose himself a little:

"Do you not watch that Monty Python show on the oul telly, Father? It makes me almost wet myself with the laughter, although you'll probably not be having it in the rectory at all. Now, that's an awful shame."

Pizarro looked at the farmer as though he was insane.

"As Mr Finn is not here and there is no sign of the weather improving, we may as well get on with our work." He stated flatly and turned to the still smirking Fr Malone:

"Are you ready to leave, Father?"

Malone squirmed and coughed:

"Oh yes, of course. Look Dan, would you be doing me an almighty favour?"

James Malone patted the farmer on the arm:

"Would you be telling Mickey that we were here?"

Dan nodded eagerly:

"Not a problem." He boomed: "Will the both of you be coming back at all?"

Pizarro who was already half way up the short path to the front garden gate, turned quickly:

"Oh yes, we will be back. Mr. Hoyce. We will be back, very soon."

He emphasised the word "very" as though it was a threat. His black eyes burned into Dan Joyce's ruddy face.

"Joyce." Dan laughed, "That's Joyce, you know, with a "J."

Pizarro glowered, turned and stomped off.

Fr Malone shook Dan Joyce's hand again.

"If you do see Mickey." He whispered: "Tell him to keep his head down. I think there's going to be some funny business."

Dan Joyce smiled:

"Sure I'll be seeing him, Father, but why would he be wanting to be keeping his head down? And what exactly do you mean by funny business?"

Fr Malone looked nervously at the Spaniard who was marching up the road towards the old Morris.

"Trust me." He whispered: "This really is like the Spanish Inquisition."

Dan Joyce nodded thoughtfully:

"Ah, I will be telling him, Father, I will that. You can rely on me."

Joyce grinned and squeezed Malone's shoulder affably and then watched as the two Priests, their black cassocks floating in the breeze, walked separately back along the road to the old Morris car, parked by the side of the road. He watched the Morris turn painfully in a multi point manoeuvre, before it trundled away, back along the narrow, wet road.

Neither Priest seemed to have noticed that the donkey that had been watching them with such a degree of interest had disappeared.

Nor did they notice any other car, tractor, or anything else for that matter parked nearby, from which Dan might have alighted.

Dan Joyce stood in the doorway of the cottage and watched the red tail lights of the Priest's car get smaller and smaller, until they disappeared from sight into the clouds on the mountain road that led eventually to the village of Tourmakeady.

Then he turned and walked into the ramshackle old cottage. He walked over to the fireplace, swivelled a brick and checked the box hidden behind it. He gave a small grunt of satisfaction then he gave the turf on the fire a good prod with a poker, making it glow brightly. He turned slowly and sat down with a contented sigh in the battered, old armchair took a long pipe out of his pocket and lit it methodically, soon he blew a great big ring of smoke out towards the ceiling. He began to chuckle.

"Monty Python indeed."

Dan Joyce shook his head; chuckling louder, he put the pipe down on the arm of the chair, stood, took off the tweed jacket and hung it on a peg on the back of the front door:

"Spanish inquisition." He chuckled some more.

He was still chuckling when he sat back down in the armchair, but it was an old man with a shock of wiry white hair that picked up the pipe and began to puff contentedly.

"And now for something completely different."

He laughed until the tears began to roll down his face.

11

The short, fat, ruddy faced policeman sat ponderously down in the armchair, took off his hat, straightened a few spindly strands of long hair over the largely bald top of his head and said:

"Aye, that would be gradely, Missus. Milk and two sugars, please."

Doris Higginbotham disappeared into the kitchen of the little terraced house on Cavendish Street and ·commenced making a pot of tea.

Frank Higginbotham sat uncomfortably on the long couch between the kitchen and cellar doors, puffing nervously on a cigarette. The policeman took a notebook out of his top pocket, sniffed, licked his thumb and used it to turn the pages until a clean sheet was found.

"Now then, Mr. Higginbotham," he began: "When exactly did you notice that your boy was missing?"

Frank rubbed his eyes and sighed heavily:

"It would have been about a quarter past five, when I got in from work. I was later than I expected because I'd had to pop to the shop on me way home."

The policeman's pen scribbled and squeaked as it raced rapidly across the page, leaving an almost unintelligible black squiggle:

"Five: fifteen P.M." He repeated, stabbing a heavy full stop onto the paper:

"And Mrs. Higginbotham hadn't noticed that he'd gone?"

Frank shuffled in his chair:

"She only got home, at about half past."

The policeman looked up from his notebook:

"Half-past?" he repeated, frowning incredulously.

Frank nodded:

"Half past Five" he clarified.

It was the policeman's turn to nod:

"So the boy had been left on his own then? So, exactly how long had he been left? You know it helps us to get a picture of how far he might have got?"

"Doris left him at about quarter to nine this morning."

Frank almost whispered. The policeman looked up again, his eyebrows raised:

"So he'd been on his own all day?"

Frank nodded. The policeman continued to stare at him:

"He's eleven years old, you say?"

Frank Higginbotham had never felt so embarrassed:

"He's very grown up for his age, very mature. We've left him before and he just gets on and reads or plays. He's got loads of books and toys and he had money for fish and chips and…"

"Slow down please, Mr Higginbotham, I don't do shorthand." The policeman muttered.

"So he would have been likely to pop out for fish and chips at about dinner time. What time do you call dinner time Mr Higginbotham?"

Frank heaved a sighed and shrugged:

"Twelvish, probably," He suggested.

"Twelvish probably," repeated the policeman with a slight sarcastic edge to his voice as he noted down the word.

"I suppose, if it should come to a search that gives us something to work on. And he's never done anything like this, you know, run away before?"

"No." Frank shook his head, "he's never done owt like this before."

The policeman grunted and continued to scribble notes:

"You can get a long way in over eight hours, Mr Higginbotham, a long, long way." The policeman mumbled, before looking back up at Frank:

"And he left a note, Mrs. Higginbotham tells me."

Frank looked perplexed for a moment and then a flash of realisation brightened his face:

"Oh aye."

He stood and picked up a small piece of paper from the sideboard, he handed it to the policeman.

"Dear Mum and Dad,

I'm sorry to be so naurty and such trouble. But there is something very important I must do. I will not be back for tea tonight and maybe not for bed but I will be back.

Please do not worry about me. I have borowed some money from the drawer and will pay you back or take it from my building society. I promise I am not in trouble and I am sorry to be a pest.

Love
Wayne"

Having read the note carefully, the policeman pursed his lips and then rubbed his chin. He was still rubbing his chin when Doris brought the tea through into the living room.

There you are Officer." She said as she passed him one of her best china cups and saucers.

"Oh ta, very nice." The policeman smiled, after sipping the tea and carefully placing the cup on a small round table that Doris placed by the armchair.

"May I take this?" He looked at Frank and indicated Wayne's note.

"Yes, aye, of course." Frank nodded.

"How much money did he take?" The policeman asked, frowning.

"Sixty pounds." Frank replied.

The policeman put his pen to his mouth.

"Lot of money." He stated thoughtfully:

"Why would he have taken so much money?"

Frank shook his head:

"I've no idea, not a clue."

"You don't think owt's happened to him do you?" Doris croaked, as tears filled her eyes,

"If he's been done in, I don't know what I'd do."

Frank put his arm around his wife and gave her a squeeze:

"He'll be alright, love." He whispered comfortingly.

The policeman cleared his throat:

"No, no love. Looking at this note there's something upset him and he's just gone to sort himself out, by the looks of it. Have you any idea what might have upset him? A family row, or sommat like that?

Doris glowered at the policeman:

"I hope you're not saying we don't treat him right." She blasted:

"Nothing's too good for our Wayne."

The policeman realising that maybe he had put a match to a rather short fuse held up his hand:

"No, no love, but we all have our little domestic disagreements, don't we?"

Doris sniffed loudly:

"I'll tell you what this is about. It's that Baz Thompson, that's who you should be after, the one who put our Wayne in hospital."

The policeman nodded and started writing furiously:

"Oh yes." He said nodding his head vigorously, "We know all about young master Thompson. He was the one who put your lad in t'hospital wasn't he? Oh aye, I remember, when was it that this incident that resulted in the hospitalisation of your son take place again?"

He spoke the words in a flat monotone as he wrote each one down.

"Nobbut a few weeks ago." Doris blurted:

"Just before the summer holidays. You should have seen the mess our lad was in, bruised ribs, broken arm. He needs putting away that Thompson lad."

The policeman's pen looked as if it would set his notebook on fire the speed it was moving:

"Aye, he's a right nasty piece of work, that Thompson. Sounds to me like this may be related; I mean it's very recent. It could be a matter of extortion, or sommat. Oh yes, sounds like our friend Baz might be involved alright. He's the type to demand money with menaces."

The policeman said as he firmly dotted a full stop.

"Do you know if there was owt else upsetting him?"

Doris and Frank looked at one another. Frank nodded reassuringly. Doris looked back at the policeman:

"I think he might be upset about leaving all his friends. Our Wayne's the only one from Gas Street School who's passed his eleven plus. You know, to qualify for that Grammar School. I'm not sure he wants to go. I mean the only person he knows there is his cousin Cedric and he's a year older."

The policeman continued to scribble furiously, occasionally pausing to lick his thumb and turn a page of his notebook. In his head, he had this case almost solved already; small boy, either getting bullied by a local hooligan, or worried about his next school, so he runs away. It was quite a straightforward case.

"Now, Mrs. Higginbotham, Mr. Higginbotham, can you think of anywhere where he might have run away to? You know, a grandparent? A relation? A favourite place he liked going to? Somewhere he might have felt safe."

Doris and Frank looked at one another again.

Frank shrugged, his face creased in thought:

"His grandparents are all dead and my sister in law, Margaret, would have brought him straight back home."

Frank scratched his head:

"He's always liked Blackpool, hasn't he love?" Frank muttered to Doris.

"Aye, he likes the sea." Doris agreed:

"Or there's Boston Abbey, he likes to go there and walk by the river."

"Blackpool" the policeman repeated as he scrawled it down, "or Boston Abbey, river."

"He likes to go walking up on t'moor as well." Frank added helpfully.

Doris started to weep at the mention of the word moor.

Some years earlier a number of children had been horrifically murdered about forty miles away, in a case that became known as the "Moors murders."

The policeman took another sip of tea:

"Don't worry Mrs. Higginbotham. I'll lay a pound to a penny that he's just gone off a wandering, to get his head straight about all this Grammar school stuff and Baz Thompson business. What time is it now? Half past ten. I wouldn't be surprised if he's not back before midnight, with his tail between his legs, shivering and terrified of the dark."

The policeman nodded his head towards the Higginbotham's front window:

"Look it's nearly pitch black now. You just watch. He'll be back."

He put the cup and saucer back down on the chair, stood and brushed down his uniform.

"If he's not back, first thing in the morning though, do let us know and we'll start looking in the places you've mentioned. One thing that I think you can be sure of. He won't be walking the streets all night. He doesn't sound the type, not at his age. In the meantime I'll make a few enquiries about young master Thompson, just in case. I'm sure him taking the money is a bit of a possibility."

As he was about to leave, the policeman turned to Doris:

"Just one thing love, when he does turn up. You know I wouldn't leave an eleven year old alone all day, even if they do seem mature. You never know what mischief they can get up to. I'm Police Constable Hartley by the way; P.C.107, ask for me, or my number, if he doesn't turn up and you do have to come by the station tomorrow, could you bring a recent photograph?"

When the policeman had left, Frank slumped in the armchair and stared mindlessly at another Constable, the cheap print of the Hay Wain that was mounted on the wall above the Higginbotham's mantelpiece.

He had not felt so worried since he had been pinned down behind a crumbling wall by the guns of a marauding German Tiger Tank, during the Second World War.

No, this was worse, much worse. He had been terrified on that occasion, but also strangely exhilarated. He had been young, a warrior, battle had been exciting, as well as horrific; his life had been in his own hands. All he had had to do then; was get across the street, to gain shelter behind some ruined houses, where the rest of his company were dug in. The huge Nazi war machine had rumbled ominously closer, its metal tracks clanking and squeaking, its engine growling and roaring.

Frank couldn't remember why he had decided to risk throwing a grenade at the seemingly impregnable machine. All he could remember was pulling the pin, calmly counting to three, and then sprinting out from behind the wall and hurling the pineapple like grenade at the tank.

He could still remember the whistling sound of bullets whizzing just past his ear and pinging into the ground, as he had run for all he was worth.

He could clearly remember the feeling of adrenaline pumping through his body, making his heart sound as if it was pounding in his brain.

He could remember watching the grenade bounce, seemingly harmlessly, off the tank's armour, before fortunately spinning up and dropping past a shocked looking officer, right into the open hatch.

Although he could only have glanced at the tank as he ran, everything had seemed to happen in slow motion. He could remember diving through a ruined doorway and his shock as he had felt the building shake as the tank had exploded. He could certainly remember the sheer ecstasy of relief as he had realised that he was still alive and unhurt.

He remembered the cheering and the slaps on his back as his mates had laughed at how lucky he had been and how he had cheated death.

Fear and excitement had seemed to go together, when he was young.

Now he was so much older, feeble and middle aged; a man who lived only to put thingummys onto widgets and then put them into boxes.

He was not a proud young soldier any more, he was a packing machine, an assembly line tool and he was totally powerless to do anything to help his son. Now there was no excitement; just fear. Gut wrenching, mind numbing, bowel twisting fear. He was suddenly aware that Doris was weeping. He turned and saw her leaning on the sideboard, the top drawer open:

"You don't think he's a wrong'un do you Frank?" She wailed.

"I mean he's taken sixty quid. That's two weeks wages. You don't think he's going to turn out a thief do you? I mean you never know what they're going to be like. Not when they're not your own."

Frank tenderly put his arms round her:

"No, he's not a wrong'un." He whispered softly. "I just don't know what's going on inside his head though."

Doris pushed him away slightly:

"That bloody copper was useless. I mean they're not going to do owt until tomorrow. He could be dead by then. Him and his bloody red herrings."

Frank smiled:

"Wayne will be fine," He said: "and the policeman did say he was going to check up on Thompson tonight."

"It'll be too bloody late." Doris moaned:

"I'll tell you sommat. If our Wayne does come back alright and doesn't bring back every single penny of that bloody money, I'll bloody kill him myself. Our Trevor would never have done owt like this."

Frank nodded. Vesuvius was erupting again and for once he actually felt sorry for her.

12

The boy who had once been Wayne Higginbotham, but now wasn't at all sure who he was, stepped back after his firm knock on the bright, green door of number 24, St Joseph's Road, Hammersmith and waited and waited.

Nothing happened.

Wayne heaved a heavy disconsolate sigh.

Had he travelled hundreds of miles for nothing?

Had he risked his life, his future happiness and the threat of the wrath of Doris Higginbotham on nothing?

He waited a little while, then he knocked again, a little more firmly this time.

Nothing!

Nobody came to the door; there was no noise inside; no response, nothing at all.

Of course, he knew that this had always been a possibility.

Wayne's nervousness began to turn into a sort of wretched hopelessness.

He had come all this way, spent a lot of the money that he had, in effect, stolen and got absolutely nothing in return. Doris would definitely kill him when he got home. He could almost hear her bellowing:

"Our Trevor wouldn't have done owt like this."

He knocked one more time and then retreated to sit on the small wall in front of the house. He was very close to tears, but big boys don't cry, so he sucked his teeth and tried to be good Yorkshire kid with a stiff upper lip.

But he wasn't a Yorkshire kid, was he? That was why he was here.

What the hell was he going to do now?

He wasn't quite sure how long he had been sat there, his heart sinking so low that he was convinced that it was going to fall out of his bottom, when he heard the voice of an angel:

"Hello, you look upset. Can I help you?"

It was a soft, gentle, girlish voice.

Wayne looked up, squinting in the late afternoon sunlight and saw a vision. An incredibly beautiful girl with long, straight, shiny golden hair was staring at him curiously:

"Er, no. well I, er, maybe." He stammered, as his mouth suddenly got even drier.

The girl smiled, a beaming, toothpaste commercial-like smile that sent his heart soaring from the pit of his gut to somewhere high up in his throat. Perfect, pearly white teeth, luscious red lips that curled upwards at the edges and big blue eyes that danced and sang.

"Well?" She asked, breaking into a soft laugh: "Can I help you or not?"

"Please be my mum, please be my mum." Wayne thought to himself as he heard himself say:

"I'm looking for a Miss, or maybe a Mrs. O'Brien. I think she lives here, or at least, I think she used to."

The girl smiled again and Wayne forgot all about Doris and punishments and wasted trips. In fact he felt all sort of sweaty and embarrassed like he had when he had peeked at the rude pictures of the nudey ladies in the "News of the World."

"I live in the top flat here," the girl said, waving a key to indicate one of the upstairs windows:

"And I'm sorry, but I don't know a Miss, or even a Mrs O'Brien. There's just me up there and some bloke that lives in the flat downstairs, but he's hardly ever there."

The girl spoke sympathetically, but her words knocked Wayne's reverie off kilter, like someone aggressively knocking the needle off a record.

"Oh" Wayne gasped; his disappointment almost palpable.

The girl frowned at him:

"What's your name?" She asked, "Are you lost?"

"No, me, no!" Wayne blurted nervously.

"I know exactly where I am. It's just that, I'm just, just looking for my mum. My name is Way, no it isn't, it's Michael, Michael O'Brien, Michael Sean O'Brien"

He thought he might as well try the name out, it sounded strange to him.

The girl looked concerned:

"Are you sure? You don't seem very certain young man. What a very strange boy you are. What was it that made you think your Mum would be here?"

She asked, kneeling down, so that she could look straight into the boy's blue-green eyes.

"I found this address on my old immunisation record." Wayne replied dully, pulling a piece of school writing paper from his bag, as he looked disconsolately down at the pavement.

The girl took the piece of paper from him and examined the address Wayne had copied out in his best handwriting:

"24, St Joseph's Road, Hammersmith. That's here alright."

She crouched down again.

"Look it's none of my business, but did you say you found this address on your immunisation record?"

Wayne nodded.

Mandy sucked her gorgeous teeth:

"It's just that you get the immunisation record when you're a tiny baby. I know I shouldn't ask, but have you not seen your mum since you were a baby?" The girl asked softly.

Wayne gulped and shook his head:

"No, I just live with my Dad and he won't tell me anything about her." Wayne replied, thinking quickly.

"That's why I came here. This is where she used to live. I thought she might still be here, but I suppose eleven years is a long time, isn't it?"

The girl stood and smiled reassuringly:

"That's awful, and your Dad won't tell you about her? God, men! Come with me." She said, taking Wayne firmly by the hand:

"I know someone who might be able to help."

The girl marched confidently up the steps of the neighbouring house and rang the doorbell, dragging Wayne behind her. After a few moments, a white haired old lady opened the door, which was fastened on a safety chain, and peered out myopically:

"Oooh it's you. Hello Mandy." The old lady called cheerfully and smiled at the girl. She lifted the chain off its catch and opened the door fully.

"Come in, dear." The woman said as she beckoned Mandy into her home.

The girl smiled back:

"Hi Agnes, I wonder if you could help this young man. He seems to have lost his mum?"

The old lady looked down at Wayne and pursed her lips:

"Ooo er, that's a bit careless sonny. You should look after your mum, you know, come on in."

The girl, Mandy, smiled down at Wayne and ushered him inside:

"Agnes has lived here forever, well, fifty years, or something."

Mandy whispered

"She would have known your mum, if it was only eleven years since she lived next door."

The house smelled of cats, not totally unpleasant, but not particularly nice. Framed photos stood on every available surface and Wayne's eyes widened at the eclectic taste of the old lady: Chintz lace covers on green flowery armchairs, red patterned carpets, pink fluffy edged rugs and a large, brown, three seat leather sofa.

The old lady motioned for Wayne and Mandy to sit down on the sofa:

"Would you like some tea dear?" She asked Mandy:

"Yes please, black no sugar." The stunning girl replied pleasantly.

"Got to look after my weight." She laughed.

Wayne couldn't imagine anyone with a more perfect figure than Mandy.

Agnes peered at the boy:

"And what about you, young man? Some orange juice?"

"Yes please." Wayne nodded eagerly, as he realised that he hadn't eaten, or drunk anything since he had made toast for breakfast that morning, at home in Shepton.

The old lady bustled off into the kitchen and Mandy gave Wayne a reassuring smile, which wrinkled the top of her nose and made her look even more beautiful. Wayne decided there and then that he was in love.

Most of Agnes' photographs were of a man in uniform and a couple of straight-laced boys at various stages of growing up. They all seemed to be black and white and some were quite faded.

A skinny tabby cat brushed itself against Wayne's jeans, but fled when he tried to reach down and stroke it

After a couple of minutes, Agnes bustled back in from the kitchen with a couple of cups of tea, a glass of orange and a plate of biscuits. She handed a cup of tea to Mandy and the glass of orange to Wayne and then sat down with a sigh:

"I think my bones are getting old." She groaned, albeit light heartedly.

Mandy laughed easily and Wayne thought that he should too.

"Help yourselves to a biscuit. Now, what's all this about you losing your mother, young man?" Agnes asked Wayne, as she picked a pair of spectacles off a table by her chair. Before Wayne could say anything but "er," Mandy interrupted:

"I found him sitting outside, on the wall when I came home from work. It seems his mum used to live at number 24, when he was a baby. She was called O'Byrne or something?"

She looked quizzically at Wayne:

"O'Brien." Wayne corrected her.

Mandy continued:

"Anyway Agnes, it seems his Mum and Dad are divorced and can you believe it? His Dad won't tell him anything about her."

She looked at "Michael":

"Isn't that right?"

Wayne nodded enthusiastically; his mouth was too full of biscuit to speak, although he felt a knot of guilt in his stomach at lying to such a beautiful girl when she was trying to help him.

"Anyway" Mandy continued "you've seen everything and everybody who's lived next door, since God's dog was a pup, so I wondered if you could help him? He looks so lost, poor little thing."

She turned and smiled sympathetically at Wayne.

Every time Mandy smiled at him, Wayne could feel the butterflies doing somersaults in his stomach.

Agnes sipped her tea and frowned thoughtfully:

"O'Brien, O'Brien." She repeated, shaking her head.

"I don't remember anybody called O'Brien. How long ago was it you said she lived here?"

Wayne blew out a deep sigh and frowned:

"I don't know really. I'm eleven, so I suppose it must have been about eleven years ago."

Agnes frowned even harder, making her forehead look like a neat pile of carefully folded skin sheets.

"I don't know; it's a funny old world nowadays, where a man can take a boy from his mother and keep him from her."

She shook her head:

"I don't know what things are coming too. O'Brien, O'Brien, there was an O'Grady once, but no that was just after the war. Nice man he was, always very dapper, in a smart trilby and a nice de-mob suit. I did think he might have been a spiv, but he was always ever so polite. Yes, nice man. Eleven years ago. Why, that would have been when Molly and that husband of hers, now what was his name? Oh yes, John, that was it, Molly and John, they lived in the top flat. They were there for five years at least and they've been gone six or seven years now. O'Brien, that's Irish isn't it? They were Irish, but they weren't O'Brien. No, definitely not O'Brien."

She frowned, deep in thought, straining every sinew in an effort to remember. A sudden flash of realisation hit her so hard that she jumped forward in her seat, spilling tea into her saucer:

"O'Malley, yes that's what they were: O'Malley."

She chortled delightedly:

"That's it! I remember now, Molly and John O'Malley. Nice couple they were. Now I come to think about it, Molly's sister came and stayed with them for a while. Now if I remember correctly, she was pregnant, but..."

Agnes almost seemed to have forgotten that she had visitors as she racked her memory for any possible links with an O'Brien. Her musings had almost become whispers. Wayne and Mandy were both leaning forward eager to catch every word that Agnes had to say:

"One day, she, the sister that is, pretty little thing, just disappeared. Molly and John wouldn't talk about it. Well, well, well. Now, what was she called?"

Wayne sat open mouthed. Could that was his mother she was talking about? The woman who had carried him in her body as a baby?

The woman who had given birth to him?

Agnes shook her head:

"Do you know, I think it's my age, I find it difficult to remember anything these days. I'm sure her name was Tanya, Tamsin, Theresa or something like that. Yes pretty thing she was, a bit like you Mandy, with reddish, blonde hair and the most stunning huge blue-green eyes. Irish you see."

Again a sudden realisation hit her:

"Oh my goodness, if that was her, then that baby she was carrying could have been you, young man."

Her mouth had dropped open and she was looking at Wayne as if he was a ghost.

"That baby could have been you." She repeated, before shaking her head and continuing:

"But you said that your mum and dad were divorced, so that must rule her out."

Wayne couldn't contain himself:

"Please miss, do you know what happened to her? Do you know where I could find her?"

He demanded, excitedly.

Agnes sighed heavily and shook her head:

"No dear, I'm so sorry. When she disappeared, Molly wouldn't say what had happened to her." She cast a conspiratorial glance at Mandy:

"I think there was a bit of shame, embarrassment, you know, them being Catholic and all, about the baby being born out of wedlock. That's why I don't think it's relevant to this young man. I did once hear Molly say something about having a younger sister in America, or somewhere and that was long after this girl had left. I'm sorry."

She was staring at him in the way that people stare at accident victims.

Wayne's heart sank like a stone again. America!

That was the other end of the earth. He would never find her if she'd gone off to America. He had got so near, he had possibly found out what was possibly her sister's name, his own Aunt. Now, however, it sounded like he had hit a brick wall, a large brick wall called America.

He hardly heard Mandy asking if she had heard correctly that Molly had definitely been the Tanya, or was it Theresa's sister.

"Oh yes" Agnes replied, finally turning her gaze from him.

"Do you know she still sends me a Christmas card every year, lovely woman Molly O'Malley."

Mandy smiled patiently:

"Do you send her a card Agnes?" She asked.

Agnes' eyes lit up:

"Oooooh yes, of course, silly me. I must still have her address somewhere, you know. Just wait a minute, I'll go and find it."

The old lady slowly levered herself out of her chair and tottered off over to a large bureau in the corner of her living room. She took a book out of a drawer and started to methodically leaf through the pages.

Wayne and Mandy both jumped when, above the only sound in the room, the ticking of an enormous Grandfather Clock, Agnes gave a triumphant cry:

"Ha! There it is: Molly and John O'Malley, The Old Barn, Quay Road, Oughterard, County Galway."

Wayne's mouth dropped open.

County Galway? That was in Ireland.

Ireland was abroad.

Once again a cold nauseous feeling began to creep into his stomach.

"Would you mind writing it down for me?" He asked politely, while his hopes began to wither and die all around him for the second time in ten minutes.

Mandy smiled again.

"Thanks Agnes. You're a dear. Well, Michael, I hope that's the lead you need. Although it doesn't quite match the story you told me about your parents having been together here."

She gave him an admonishing grin, which just made Wayne love her all the more.

Wayne smiled guiltily:

"I didn't mean to mislead you, Mandy." He stuttered just after they walked out of Agnes' front door, having thanked the old lady profusely for her help.

"Dad wouldn't tell me any of the details of him and mum, so I didn't know whether they were married or not."

Mandy shrugged:

"I don't suppose it matters. It sounds like this girl with the name beginning with T could well be your mum. I mean Agnes is the expert on the street and the timing sounds about right. You'll have to write to the lady in Ireland. She just may have all the answers. Now, we better get you off home. I think someone is going to be very worried about you."

13

The atmosphere in the Old Rectory in Finaan was not exactly great at the best of times.

Fr Malone's colleagues: Fr Dermot Callaghan and Fr William Burke were not exactly what could be called good friends and although both tended to be somewhat paternalistic to Fr Malone, it manifested itself in very different ways.

Fr Dermot was the classic caricature of an Irish Priest in his mid-fifties. He could have had a walk on part in a 1950's Hollywood movie about the old country and he would have been totally typecast, fond as he was of a few pints of Guinness, a glass of good Irish whiskey and the craic.

Fr Dermot's most defining characteristic was his unerring and mischievous good humour. He was loved by everyone in the village and the surrounding countryside. He seemed to know everyone and everyone knew him. Of course, the Bishop would have preferred it if the extremely popular Fr Dermot could have been a little bit less fond of the drink, but at least his habit was relatively harmless. He would often be found by Mrs. Dolan, the housekeeper, when she came in to work in the morning, still asleep in his armchair, fully dressed, a glass in his hand, snoring contentedly; with a beatific smile on his face, even in slumber.

It was well known in South Mayo that any wake in Fr Dermot's presence was one of the best parties in town.

Father William Burke was as piously pompous as Father Callaghan was amiably jovial. Tall and thin, with an aristocratic, long face, hooked nose and a perpetual look of imperious superiority, Father Burke was respected rather than revered. He had a patrician air about him that suggested that he had been meant for better things, the highest offices in the Catholic Church.

Perhaps he might have made the highest office, had some misdemeanour not put paid to his career as a Monsignor. Indeed, it had only been the swift intervention of the Archbishop, a few well-chosen words in the ears of a local politician and a Gard officer in Limerick that had prevented Monsignor Burke from being involved in a major national scandal.

That had been many years ago, however, and plain old Father Burke had long since lost any element of the humility that he had nurtured in the aftermath of his fall from grace.

Fr Burke looked after a church in a village near Finaan. He was not a popular priest, but seemed strangely satisfied by his flock's distaste for him, it matched his own aversion to them as no more than a bunch of irritating peasants.

Despite his irritating demeanour, Fr Burke seemed fond of Fr Malone, in a Fatherly sort of way and often tried to advise him on the best course of action whenever Fr Malone raised a problem that he had encountered.

Usually, of course, the advice was the exact opposite of whatever Fr Callaghan had recommended, but Fr Malone had got used to that and often found that a line taken somewhere between the two conflicting opinions, was as close to right as possible.

With Fr Pizarro staying as a guest in the house, the atmosphere became absolutely poisonous.

Fr Burke seemed to find in Pizarro, a long lost soul-mate. The fact that Pizarro had influence in Rome was nothing to do with his sycophantic courting of the Spaniard, of course. The fact that Pizarro seemed to despise the local populace every bit as much as Fr Burke, was also a source of unanimity between the two.

Fr Dermot seemed to dislike Pizarro far more than Fr Malone had imagined. His usual exuberance seemed to disappear almost as soon as Pizarro arrived. He began to appear grouchy and grumpy, even snapping at Mrs Dolan and Fr Malone, which he had never done before.

Fr Malone had noticed the impact of Pizarro's arrival at dinner on the third evening of Pizarro's stay. On the evening of his arrival, Fr Pizarro had gone straight to his room and had not even appeared for breakfast the next morning, materialising in the middle of the kitchen mid-morning, just in time for his trip to see Liam Fogarty. That evening he had again shut himself in his room with a selection of books on local folklore that Fr. Malone had had instructions to collect for him. On the third evening, however, after the trip that Fr Pizarro and Fr Malone had made over the mountains, to the little cottage in the hollow, Fr Pizarro joined the other three Priests for dinner.

Fr Burke had asked Pizarro if the journey had been fruitful. Pizarro had smiled that thin smile of his and his eyes had glittered as he had stared at Fr Malone:

"Ah yes, Father Burke. Our trip was most worthwhile, was it not Father Malone?"

Fr Malone screwed up his face:

"I'm not so sure at all. I mean we didn't even see Mickey, so I don't really know what we achieved."

Fr Dermot did not raise his head from his soup.

Pizarro turned to Fr Burke:

"The young are so innocent in the real ways of the world, Father. Would you not agree?"

Fr Burke smiled, a little uncomfortably:

"Oh yes, the young are sometimes too innocent for their own good."

He coughed and cleared his throat. Pizarro warmed to his theme:

"Take today, for example. We visited a little peasant shack high in the mountains. A little cottage lost in a wooded hollow with some eccentric wind toys outside. It was strange, the occupant of the cottage was nowhere to be seen, but a visitor arrived while we were there, in this most remote of places. He too was looking for this Mickey Finn person. Is that not so Father Malone?"

Fr Malone nodded. He hadn't heard anything yet that had made the days events seem at all unusual let alone supernatural. Fr Dermot continued to sip his soup with his head down.

Pizarro broke a piece of bread:

"Men of our, experience, Father Burke......"

"William, call me William."

Fr Burke interrupted, unaware of the brief flash of annoyance that passed the Spaniard's eyes:

"Yesss, William," he hissed:

"Priests of our experience are able to recognise the Devil's work in what might seem the most incongruous of situations."

Fr Burke agreed, nodding his head furiously:

"Indeed, Francisco, indeed."

Pizarro's lips curled in a poor imitation of a smile and he continued:

"We know when the servants of Satan are trying to, how do you say it? Ah yes: pull the wool over our heads."

"Eyes" Fr Malone suggested quietly.

Pizarro flashed him a malevolent glance:

"Pull the wool over our eyes." The Spaniard repeated, a sarcastic edge to his voice."

"Tell me Father Malone." He fixed the young Priest with a stare as he sipped a spoonful of soup.

"What did you think of Mr. Hoyce"

Fr Malone shrugged his shoulders:

"Dan Joyce?" He put special emphasis on the "J"

"Seemed a nice enough fella. Genuine sort."

He shrugged and twisted his mouth as if to say that's all I have to say on the subject.

Pizarro's black eyes burned into his own:

132

"You did not notice anything, peculiar, about this Dan Hoyce?"

Fr Malone shook his head and turned to Fr Callaghan:

"No. You'll be knowing Dan Joyce, Dermot?"

Fr Callaghan raised his head from his soup and took a deep breath:

"I think so. The name rings a bell." He mumbled quietly.

Pizarro stirred his soup around with his spoon:

"I think I can assure you, Father Malone, Father Callaghan, that Dan Hoyce does not exist." He stated confidently.

Fr Callaghan raised his eyebrows and put his head back down over his soup, which he began to slurp noisily.

Fr Malone took it as a gesture of annoyance at the madness of Pizarro's statement:

"So who was that we met this afternoon at Mickey's cottage?"

Fr Malone asked Pizarro, folding his arms defensively across his chest.

Fr Pizarro smiled patronisingly:

"That, my young friend, was the creature known as Mickey Finn."

Fr Malone splattered soup over his bowl:

"What? How can you say that? You haven't even met Mickey. He's ancient. He's a white haired old man."

He turned to Fr Dermot Callaghan for support, but Fr Callaghan appeared to have gone bright red as his face seemed to get nearer to his bowl of soup.

Fr Burke's face bore an expression that looked as though he had just smelt, or stepped in something extremely unpleasant.

Pizarro nodded, smirking:

"Your "nice enough" fellow, Mr. Hoyce, is a shape-shifter, Father Malone. A Sidh, an aatxe, he and this Mickey Finn are one and the same person. Did you not notice the one thing he can not change accurately, his large, pointed ears?"

Fr Malone slumped back in his chair, his face a mask of disbelief.

"The whole world is going mad." He said, shaking his head:

"I think I've heard absolutely everything now."

Pizarro snorted:

"Oh I do not think so, young man. I am sure Father Callaghan can tell you an awful lot more about our Mr Finn. Oh yes, by the way Father, Bishop Donleavy sends his regards."

He glared at the older Priest who wiped the corners of his mouth with his napkin and stood abruptly, making his chair scratch noisily on the wooden floor:

"The Bishop knows what he can do with his regards. I'll have no part in your witch hunts Pizarro" He said quietly, but firmly; then he turned to James:

"And I would suggest James that you also distance yourself from all of this. I am sorry; I thought the Church was above all this sort of thing nowadays. I really thought that your visit was going to be a cosmetic exercise Father Pizarro. I see now that I was wrong. The church has learned nothing in the last twenty years. Indeed if it is still using such people as you, it has learnt nothing in fifteen hundred years. If you will please excuse me, I will bid you good night."

And with that Fr Dermot Callaghan stormed out of the dining room.

Mrs Dolan had just entered with two entrees:

"And what is the matter with our Father Dermot? Such a show is most unlike him." She asked of no one in particular, before turning and leaving the room.

Fr Pizarro took a sip of wine and then dabbed his lips with his napkin:

"Sometimes Satan's servants appear when least expected."

Fr Malone stood so quickly that his chair almost fell over:

"Father Callaghan is the finest Priest I have ever met, Father Pizarro. I will not hear a bad word spoken against him."

He also stormed out of the dining room.

Father Burke took a sip of wine:

"He is young and naïve, as I told His Grace, the Bishop. Callaghan, however, has consorted with this Finn for many years." He whispered, breaking off when Mrs Dolan bustled back in from the kitchen:

"Well I never. Down to just the two of you now, is it?" She exclaimed: "And a fine welcome this is for Father Pizarro, for the life of me, I don't know what's got into those two."

Pizarro nodded and proffered his weak smile:

"Thank you, Mrs. Dolan. The soup was very good, compared to most of the food I have tasted in this country. Would you be offended if I asked that Father Burke and I be allowed to talk privately now?"

"No, no of course not. You can do what you want." Mrs Dolan sniffed, obviously offended having provided most of the food that Pizarro had eaten since he had arrived in Ireland. She picked up the soup bowls and disappeared into the kitchen without looking back.

Pizarro filled his glass and that of Fr Burke:

"I find it very sad, very sad indeed, that the role that the "Sacred Order of St. Gregory" has played in protecting mankind over the past centuries has not been more acclaimed and eulogised by our mother church. I do not seek glory, Father, but if it was not for the thin red line of noble volunteers, which the Order pits against the enemy, then civilisation would have fallen long ago and the Second Coming would never take place. Here we stand on the very edge of our ultimate victory, yet we are still ignored and taken for granted."

He waved a dismissive hand in the direction of the door through which Fathers Callaghan and Malone had exited the room.

"We cannot even rely on our own peers and supposed comrades within the Holy Church of Rome."

He clicked his tongue, then sighed sadly and shook his head.

"Now, Father Burke, about that ancient prophecy and the possibility that this, creature Finn, is the one that it refers to.

14

The boy who had been Wayne Higginbotham was now pretty much convinced that he was, in fact, really someone else. Someone called Michael Sean O'Brien.

Agnes had said that the girl who had stayed at 24, St. Joseph's Road, Hammersmith, eleven years ago had been pregnant.

Wayne was now almost beginning to hope that he had been adopted; the embarrassment of being wrong would have just been too much to bear. Thoughts cascaded through his mind as he and Mandy walked the short distance back to her front door, not all of them were about his adopted status.

Wayne had not been able to stop himself staring at Mandy while they had been sat in Agnes' living room. Her long legs that seemed to go on forever and her almost indecently short skirt, her beautiful long shining golden hair, her cherry red lips, the white brilliance of her smile, but most of all those incredible blue eyes: Eyes that seemed to let you see right into her soul, kind and gentle, yet funny and mischievous at the same time, eyes that shone with sheer vivacity. Oh how Wayne would have loved to have been a Prince on a magnificent white charger that came to some evil Lord's tower, to rescue this vision of loveliness.

Oh how he would have loved to ride away with her, basking in the glow of her eternal gratitude.

"Well, Michael, as I said you better get yourself home, before it gets too late. Your Dad'll be wondering where you are."

He heard Mandy say as she stopped outside number 24. Wayne gulped:

"Oh yes, I suppose so." He mumbled.

Mandy smiled, the top of her nose crinkled again and Wayne's heart melted a little bit more.

"Come on, I better walk you home. Do you live nearby?"

Wayne's mouth dropped open:

"No, er, it's OK, er I'll take the bus, er no the tube." He gabbled.

Mandy frowned:

"Where do you live, Michael?"

Wayne looked horrified:

"Er, not far away, I'll be OK, really. I'd better go. You're right, my Dad'll be worried. Very worried."

He edged away from the girl who now definitely looked somewhat suspicious.

He looked at his watch:

"Gosh, yes, is that the time? Er, thank you very much for your help. Mandy. You've been beautiful, I mean brilliant, sorry."

His edging away had almost turned into a trot. Mandy folded her arms, scowled and twisted her beautiful mouth suspiciously:

"Michael, you haven't run away from somewhere, have you?"

Wayne shrugged and gave a half hearted laugh:

"Who me? Run away? No of course not. Look, thanks, you've been really brilliant. Taraah."

He waved, turned from her and with a deep breath started to walk quickly away. The last thing he needed now was to be hauled off to a police station and returned to Shepton, in disgrace, with nothing more to show for his adventure than a name and address, scrawled on a piece of paper.

After about ten paces, he turned to wave again. Mandy had not moved and was watching him, a concerned frown etched on her beautiful features. His confident wave seemed to break the spell, however. She smiled, shook her head and waved back, the frown disappeared and once again Wayne's heart did a double somersault and a back flip. Then she turned and walked towards her door.

Wayne turned too and walked briskly down St Joseph's Road.

When he reached the junction of the Chiswick Road he looked back, Mandy had gone. Wayne bit his lip and his acrobatic heart flopped down into his belly.

"I will probably never see her again as long as I live." He thought mournfully.

"The most beautiful girl I have ever seen in my life and the kindest and the nicest and now she's gone forever."

Wayne suddenly felt very, very lonely and an awful long way from home. The Chiswick Road was extremely busy and noisy as the evening rush hour was at its peak. The smell of diesel filled his nostrils and specks of dust assaulted his eyes. Buses and taxis, cars and lorries, beeped their horns and crawled slowly along the road. People bustled past him, all rushing to get home in time for tea and TV. In Shepton people would say "hello" to each other all the time as they passed in the street. Here, everyone seemed anxious to avoid everyone else's gaze. No one seemed to notice the boy, wandering alone down the street.

Wayne looked at his watch; it was nearly half past six.

Wayne was now faced with the prospect of the long journey home, he grimaced, then turned and saw a small boy in a shop window looking at him, his own reflection in the plate glass window, one small boy in a crowd of what seemed like millions.

One small boy, who wasn't even sure what his name was anymore, who didn't know what he was going to do next, or where he was going to go.

One small boy, with horrid huge pointy ears, thick brown curly hair and freckles.

Nothing had changed really had it?

Wayne had bought a return ticket from Shepton and the temptation to try and avoid going home was enormous, but what was his alternative. Sleeping rough on a park bench?

What would be better, staying in London or going back?

Back to what?

The inevitable humiliation and severe punishment?

The endless lecturing and permanent mistrust?

Back to: "Our Trevor would never have done owt like this to us."

Wayne stifled a rapidly rising sob as he realised for the first time that he had probably been adopted as a replacement for Doris and Frank's first baby, Trevor. He was no more than a mere substitute for the Higginbotham's own perfect baby that had died. The life he was leading had really belonged to someone else. Shepton wasn't his real home, this was. The hustle and bustle, the smoke, grit and grime of old London town.

London was where he had been born, it was his real home.

He had been tricked into believing that he was some kid called Wayne Higginbotham, when they had known that he wasn't really that person.

Wayne felt angry as well as disappointed and more than a little sad.

The tears were welling in his eyes, but the boy had learned something in Yorkshire. He had learned how to be resolute and stubbornly stoic in the face of adversity.

He had gained something out of his trip too, a name and address in Ireland; the name and address of someone who was possibly really related to him. It sounded far-fetched, but it was possible. This Molly O'Malley woman might know who his real mum was. She might even be his Auntie or something and she probably knew who his dad had been too. Maybe she knew who he really was, as well.

Yes, it was a disappointment that he hadn't found his real mum still living at 24 St. Joseph's Road. That she had not answered the door and pulled him into her arms and welcomed him home after all those years. That had never really been a possibility, had it?

24 St. Joseph's Road wasn't his home. Nor had it ever been, really. It had just been somewhere his Mum had once stayed, temporarily.

Maybe it would be better just to go home and face the music. To continue the pretence that he was Frank and Doris' only son.

Pretty soon the evening shadows would descend and the last train north would leave and he would be stuck in London overnight, with nowhere to stay.

In his wildest dreams the night had not presented any problems. He had packed his toothbrush and Pyjamas into his duffle bag and had sort of expected to stay at 24 St Joseph's Road, tucked into a nice warm bed by his overjoyed long lost mother. Now here he was, staring at himself in a shop window, lonely, angry, sad, lost and very, very confused.

A solitary raindrop hit his head:

"Great, that's all I need." Wayne muttered as he turned from the shop window. He sniffed back a rising sob and walked resignedly back towards the tube station.

The call of his supposed home was getting louder with every footstep. The thought of sleeping rough in London did not appeal to him at all and getting mugged and murdered was definitely worse than getting a sound beating from Doris and being "in the doghouse" for the foreseeable future.

It would even be something of a relief to hear the name of Trevor invoked again. At least he was used to it, although he had never realised its significance before.

Before long, Wayne found himself crushed like a tinned sardine on a much busier tube train than he had experienced earlier and then, as if in a dream he found himself back in King's Cross Station.

"Excuse me." He asked a passing guard: "Could you tell me what time the next train to Leeds leaves?"

The guard glowered at him:

"Bit young to be travelling on your own aren't you son?" The guard growled.

"Oh, I'm not alone my Mum's just buying us a sandwich in the buffet." Wayne lied glibly. He was getting quite good at lying, too good.

The guard looked at his watch:

"Seven thirty-five, platform three."

Wayne thanked him and looked at his own Timex watch.

"Twenty past seven" he noted.

Now that he had mentioned sandwiches, he remembered that he was ravenously hungry. The only thing that had passed his lips since breakfast had been Agnes' orange juice and biscuits. At that moment Wayne could have even devoured one of Doris' favourite dishes:

Tripe and onions cooked in milk and soaked in vinegar, broiled pigs' trotters, cow tongue, or even her infamous potted meat sandwiches, laced with butter half an inch thick.

Then again, when he did come to think about it, hunger did have its benefits. He marched purposefully towards the station buffet, his stomach rumbling, but he found it closed:

"Bum!" he said out loud, much to the shock of a passing, bowler-hatted commuter.

As Wayne despondently turned from the boarded up buffet, he noticed a poster on the station wall:

"GETAWAY TO IRELAND" it proclaimed, in big bold letters over a picture of a lush, green, coastal landscape. Wayne meandered slowly towards the poster as if transfixed:

"Take a break in Ireland's peaceful, unspoilt countryside.

Visit the vibrant cities of Dublin, Cork, or Galway, or lose
yourself on the most beautiful coastline in Europe.
Travel by rail from London Paddington, or Euston, to
Rosslare, or Dun Laoighere via Fishguard, or Holyhead."

Wayne's breath came in short sharp bursts and his heart was pounding in his chest again. Now he knew what he had to do:

"In for a penny, in for a pound." He thought, as he raced straight out of Kings Cross Station on to the Marylebone Road. He knew that Euston Station wasn't far away, because he had walked past it with Doris and Frank the last time they had been in London.

Wayne bit his lip as he walked along the Marylebone Road. He was not going to be anybody's substitute. He was going to find his real mum and take back his own destiny. He was not a replacement Trevor Higginbotham. He was Michael Sean O'Brien. His entered the much more modern façade of Euston station with his teeth clenched and his face set. Yet as soon as he saw the enormous station concourse, his courage and determination began to fail him again. How would he be able to get away with travelling to Ireland alone? He didn't even have a passport.

"Never mind" He said to himself: "I'll cross that bridge when I get to it."

He steeled himself and marched determinedly up to the huge ticket office and took his place in a short queue. Soon it was his turn to approach one of the kiosks:

"Hello." Wayne said brightly. "I'd like a half ticket to Ireland please."

He smiled at the man in the ticket office. The man looked at him blankly:

"What?" The man grunted.

"A half ticket to Ireland please." Wayne repeated, still smiling.

The ticket office man stared at him, incredulously:

"What, you want half a ticket? One that takes you half way there? Or a half fare? Single or return? And where exactly in Ireland is it you want to go, sonny? It's a big place you know."

The ticket office man raised his eyebrows and looked at Wayne as if to say:

"Please don't waste my time sonny, go and play your pranks somewhere else."

The man looked directly over Wayne's head as if to ask the next customer what he wanted.

Wayne's stomach seemed even emptier and the smile fell from his face.

He was now too cross to be intimidated, however. Who was this toad who was trying to stop him from finding his real Mum and Dad?

Wayne felt anger bubbling up inside and he was aware that he was glaring at the man behind the counter. A red mist seemed to descend in front of Wayne's eyes:

"That would be a half fare to Dublin, one way, Mr smarty pants." He stated, very slowly and very clearly.

Then "Please!" Wayne hissed sarcastically as he remembered his manners.

It was a bit weird because the voice hadn't sounded a bit like his, it had seemed far too deep and sonorous; it wasn't even the sort of thing he'd say anyway. Wayne was quite impressed, however, especially when it seemed to do the trick.

The man looked down at Wayne, his eyes glazed over and his mouth dropped open. He nodded, turned, punched some buttons and asked for an enormous amount of money in a weird way, sort of like a robot in a sci-fi movie. Wayne, blanched, pulled his wallet from his duffel bag and paid the man. All of a sudden, seventy five pounds didn't seem such a fortune any more.

The man wordlessly gave Wayne his ticket and his change, which the boy grabbed and stuffed back into his wallet. He turned to get away before the ticket man changed his mind but a sudden thought had crossed his mind:

"What time is the next Holyhead train?" He asked politely.

The ticket vendor stared straight ahead:

"The next Irish boat train leaves platform four, at eight thirty-seven." He recited, in a perfect monotone.

"Thanks." Said Wayne, with an expression on his face that said:

"What a weirdo."

As Wayne walked away, the ticket vendor shook his head and wiped his eyes. The next customer was already stood at the kiosk waiting to buy his ticket. The vendor stood up off his stool and, wiping his brow, said:

"I'm sorry, this kiosk has just closed. I think I'm having a funny turn."

He then proceeded to faint.

"Just my bloomin' luck." Moaned the disgruntled traveller:

"Typical bloody British Rail!"

Wayne took his seat on the boat train and tried to ignore his rumbling stomach, the aches in his recently broken arm and his sore ribs, his sore feet and the headache that was gathering like a storm in his brain. He also tried to ignore the stares of his fellow passengers who seemed concerned that he was travelling alone. As the train rattled through the evening twilight, a woman who had been sitting opposite him, asked:

"Excuse me love, are you travelling on your own?"

Wayne knew that he couldn't get away with the "my mum's in the loo" routine again, so he smiled, as best as he could through his mist of pain and said:

"Yes, my Mum is meeting me in Holyhead. My dad put me on the train, they've just got divorced."

The woman looked mortified:

"Oh, I am sorry, love. That must be awful for you?"

Wayne shrugged:

"Well, you get used to it, you know." He sighed.

The woman made a sympathetic understanding face and then asked:

"Would you like a biscuit?"

Almost every day, since he could first remember, Doris had warned Wayne not to take sweets, or anything else for that matter, from strangers, but Wayne was so sick with hunger that he felt he had no choice.

"Thanks" he said taking the proffered item.

The rattling, rocking, dee diddly dum, dee diddly dum, motion of the train soon sent Wayne off into a deep, deep sleep. He dreamed that Mandy was his mum and that Doris was trying to kill her. Then he dreamed that Mandy wasn't his mum and that she wanted to kiss him. Now that was the best dream. He dreamed of the old man in the hospital, screaming about "little people." He was vaguely aware of the train stopping occasionally and the noise of guards shouting, doors slamming and the murmur of conversations and muted laughter. Then he dreamed of being in bed at home in Shepton.

It came as quite a surprise to him when he was shaken gently awake, in what seemed like the middle of the night:

"Wake up love." a woman's voice said "We're in Holyhead."

Wayne half opened his eyes:

"Yes mum." He drawled, sleepily closing his eyes again.

"Your mum will be waiting for you," he heard the voice say.

"Mmmm." He replied, before snapping suddenly awake with a jolt.

The voice belonged to the woman opposite, not his Mum and when he looked at his watch it was the middle of the night, in fact it was early morning. He turned and looked out of the train window into a darkness broken by a few scattered lights:

"Holyhead" the sign on the platform proclaimed.

15

Doris and Frank Higginbotham, along with Doris' sister Margaret, sat forlornly in the foyer of Shepton's small police station.

A sergeant scribbled silently on a pad behind the counter, as policemen and women buzzed around noisily somewhere in the background. An occasional roar of laughter could be heard through an open door behind the sergeant.

Doris, her eyes red and swollen, sniffed:

"I don't know what they're laughing at back there. They should be out looking for our Wayne, instead of fooling around and behaving like big kids." Margaret agreed and whispered back:

"Most of 'em are kids themselves; they hardly look old enough to be out of school."

At the sight of the sergeant glancing her way, she looked quickly at the notice board with its "wanted" and "missing" posters.

"Why do these places make you feel like a criminal, when you haven't done anything?" She whispered to Doris, her stomach churning, partly through guilt at having been heard criticising the police by the desk sergeant and partly out of worry over her missing nephew.

Margaret had been there on the day that Doris and Frank had collected Wayne from the Catholic adoption agency in London. Stanley had only been a clerk in the bank at that time, but had owned a shiny new Ford Anglia and it had been the Houghton-Hughes that had driven Frank and Doris down to London to pick up their new baby.

Margaret genuinely loved Wayne, even though he wasn't really a blood relation. She felt sorry for him in some ways.

She had really felt sorry for him on that day; the day that they'd collected him. Doris had cried all the way home because she thought he was ugly:

"Just look at those ears." She had wailed. "They're awful. He's a freak, like Dumbo or something. People will laugh at him. He's not like our Trevor. Trevor was such a lovely baby."

Eventually Margaret had berated her big sister:

"Don't be ridiculous Doris. Dumbo had big ears; his ears aren't that big they're, well, just a bit misshapen that's all....a bit stuck out and pointy."

Trevor had been Doris and Frank's first attempt at adoption. The adoption had failed after a six month trial period when he had contracted meningitis and in a fit of sympathy, the baby's birth mother, supported by her own mother, had had a change of heart and had decided to keep her baby and nurse him through the disease. The Higginbotham's had been distraught when Trevor, as they had named him, had been collected by the agency to be returned to his mother. Trevor had been so beautiful, according to Doris. Wayne was definitely inferior in the looks department.

Doris inability to have children was probably all her own fault anyway, well, so rumour had it. Doris had been unable to have a baby of her own because of something that had happened during the war. Something about an American, an unwanted baby and an operation that had gone wrong. That was what some said in the village of Carelton, outside Shepton, where the girls had been raised. Margaret had been too young to understand any of it at the time, she just remembered Doris going away for a little while.

Poor Wayne, Doris had always been hard on him. Now it looked like she'd pushed him too hard and he'd done a runner.

"What are they doing?" Doris asked Frank in a low voice, but loud enough for the desk sergeant to hear:

"Are we going to have to sit here all day?"

"Constable Hartley knows you are here and will be with you shortly, Mrs. Higginbotham." The desk sergeant announced somewhat testily and with the slightest hint of a glower at the three inhabitants of the wooden bench opposite his counter.

"He said that when we came in ten minutes ago." Doris whispered to Frank from the corner of her mouth, before sniffing loudly and wiping her eyes with a tissue that she had found, only by digging noisily to the bottom of her handbag. She blew her nose loudly and crossed her legs for the hundredth time.

Frank sighed and nodded. He looked at the barred window by the police stations front door. The sound of the occasional car or lorry passing on the main road outside could just be heard over the occasional song of a bird in the trees opposite. Light shifted annoyingly as clouds passed over the sun. It was annoying, because life was going on as normal for most people; it was just another summer's day, as would the next day be and the day after that.

Frank, however, was beginning to think that no day would ever be the same again. All of Frank Higginbotham's tomorrows were doomed to be spent in mourning, in passing thoughts of "what ifs" and "if onlys."

Frank Higginbotham knew his adopted son; knew that he was as steady and well balanced as himself, even if he didn't have Frank's blood running in his veins. Wayne would not have run away, or done anything that stupid without the sort of provocation that Frank couldn't even begin to imagine. Therefore, Frank's only reasonable conclusion was that Wayne had been abducted and probably murdered by now. He hadn't said anything to Doris though. It was best that she still had hope, just in case he did turn out to be wrong.

Poor Doris, she had spent the night sitting on the settee in the living room waiting; waiting for a knock on the door that never came. He put his arm around her shoulder and she leaned her head on his.

"I do hope he's alright." Doris wailed as her chest heaved and she began to weep.

The sergeant looked up, took a deep breath and did his best to ignore the blubbering on the other side of his counter.

"The last thing we need now is a murder or kidnapping." The desk sergeant thought to himself;

"Loads of press wallahs arriving, asking endless questions and the C.I.D. sticking their noses in everywhere. Life would be turned upside down for weeks and as for social life, well that would be ruined. The overtime would come in handy though."

He wiped the smile off his face as quickly as it had spread and glanced up, guiltily at the trio on the bench; phew, they hadn't noticed.

Suddenly a short, rotund constable and a tall policewoman emerged from the doorway behind the desk sergeant. A grim looking Constable Hartley nodded at Frank and Doris as he opened the counter:

"No sign then?" He asked as he held out his hand.

Frank and Doris both shook their heads at the same time as each took his hand:

"This is me sister, Margaret."

Doris introduced her younger sibling with a nod.

Constable Hartley nodded in turn at Margaret and shook her hand:

"Pleased to meet you." he said quietly:

"This is WPC Harrison" he nodded in the direction of the taller policewoman.

"She's dealt with this sort of thing before."

The policewoman smiled encouragingly and nodded a greeting, as she shook all three proffered hands.

Constable Hartley beckoned the small party through the gap in the counter that he had created by lifting a section of the surface and opening a small gate.

"Please tell us if you've heard anything?" Doris pleaded, as the two officers ushered the distraught Higginbothams and Margaret Houghton-Hughes into an interview room.

"Would you get us some tea love?" Constable Hartley asked WPC Harrison. She glared at him momentarily, as if to say: "Why don't you get it?" before taking milk and sugar instructions from the three gaunt looking people, who were dragging plastic chairs noisily out from under the table.

Frank looked around the room. He'd seen rooms like this on the telly; a room where the cops would play good cop, bad cop, until the villain was convinced that he could confide in the good cop and confess his crime. A single light bulb hung, un-shaded, from the ceiling just like in the introduction to the TV show "Callan."

Constable Hartley pulled a chair out and swivelled it, so that he could sit and lean his elbows on the chair back. He grimaced and addressed Doris directly:

"No sorry, love. Absolutely nowt, I'm afraid. But I do have to tell you that our friend Thompson isn't involved."

Frank raised his eyebrows and tilted his head back sceptically:

"Aye, our Thommo is currently undergoing assessment in the Menston Psychiatric Hospital, you know, the loony bin on the way to Leeds. It seems that since the little fracas with your lad, he's done nowt but sit in a corner, reciting nursery rhymes and picking his nose."

Doris started to wail again:

"Now, now, Mrs. Higginbotham" Constable Hartley said softly:

"He can't have gone far. Have you got that photograph?"

Doris fumbled in her handbag and brought out a grainy black and white photograph of a small boy, grimly holding on to a reluctant looking monkey.

"It were taken on the prom in Blackpool, last year when we were on us holidays." She explained.

"It's the most recent one we've got. He loved Blackpool, our Wayne."

WPC Harrison re-emerged with a tray full of mugs of hot steaming tea, which she passed around while trying to remember who had asked for what.

"I was just saying" Constable Hartley informed her, after taking a swig of tea:

"I don't think he'll have gone far."

WPC Harrison sighed and sat down. She took a notebook from her pocket and then looked at the Higginbothams:

"I think Constable Hartley here, is right. I don't think Wayne will have gone far. He doesn't seem the runaway type. We have a list of his favourite places and that is where we will look first. The first thing I have to say though, is don't worry. We will do absolutely everything we can to make sure that Wayne is brought home safe and sound. Every officer on duty at this station has been given a description of Wayne and will bring him home, if they see him."

Constable Hartley coughed and stared at his mug of tea.

"Now why didn't I say that?" He thought.

WPC Harrison continued:

"Now, my colleague took some details last night, but as Wayne hasn't come home of his own volition, I'm afraid we're going to have to step things up a bit and go into a lot more detail. Have you got a recent photo of Wayne, Mrs. Higginbotham?"

Constable Hartley cleared his throat and pulled the black and white photograph out from under his notebook, he pushed it over to WPC Harrison, who let out a small gasp:

"My, he does have distinctive ears doesn't he? Well unusual features are quite a boon in a case like this. It gives people more of a chance to recognise him."

It was over two hours later when the Higginbothams finally emerged from the police station. They looked totally shattered.

Doris' red and swollen eyes were even more red and swollen than they been that morning. Even Frank was dabbing his eyes with a handkerchief. Margaret smiled reassuringly:

"They're going to do everything they can, Doris love. They'll find him, he'll be alright, you'll see." She looked at Frank; the look in her eyes belied the confidence of her words.

Back in the interview room, WPC Harrison looked hard at Constable Hartley:

"Why didn't you tell me that he was adopted?" She demanded, running a hand through her short dark hair. Hartley half smiled, a sickly smile that hinted at his embarrassment:

"They didn't tell me." He said with a shrug.

"That's the sort of thing you're supposed to damn well find out." WPC Harrison scalded her colleague:

"I'll bet you a pound to a penny that this is to do with the adoption."

Hartley shook his head:

"No" he blustered:

"No way! The Higginbothams categorically stated that the boy has absolutely no idea that he's adopted and all the information about the adoption is secreted away, under lock and key, somewhere safe in their room. No, Lesley, this is about bullying and the fact that he doesn't want to go to that Grammar school. I know, I can tell. I can feel it in me water."

WPC Harrison stood, put her pad in her pocket and pursed her lips:

"We've got half a day to see if your waterworks are right. If he's not back by dark we're going to have to get C.I.D. involved. Let's go and have a chat with his headmaster.

Constable Hartley nodded his agreement:

"Aye I suppose so."

Frank Higginbotham lifted the lid of the old brass log box in his and Doris' bedroom. He could hear Doris wailing in the living room below and the soothing voice of Margaret attempting to comfort her. It was strange how Doris had seemed to veer between anger and sorrow over the last twelve hours or so. One minute she had been describing how she would "tan Wayne's hide" when he came home and beat him so hard that he'd never steal anything again. The next minute she would be sobbing about her poor lost little boy and how she would kill anyone who had forced him into running away. That was women for you, always changing their minds.

Frank lifted the first few bits of paper out of the box: Mortgage details, bank and building society information; all just as he remembered leaving them. Below them came a pile of old Christmas and birthday cards, a few photos and newspaper cuttings.

Frank reached down and lifted out a large brown envelope, full of photos of him in the army. He smiled at the sight of the gawky young man in khaki. This was not the time for reminiscing, however. He reached to the bottom of the box and pulled out a large envelope. It contained Wayne's adoption certificate. It certainly didn't look as though it had been disturbed, but how was he to know?

In any case, Frank knew that there was no address or anything on the adoption certificate. All it showed was how he: Frank James Higginbotham, factory worker of Frederick Street, Barlickwick, West Yorkshire and Doris Edna Higginbotham, housewife, of the same address, had by order of the court adopted the boy Wayne Higginbotham on the 25th October 1963.

Frank stared forlornly at a card showing Wayne's record of injections. He carefully folded the certificate and the injection record and put them back in the envelope.

It certainly didn't look to him, as he sat cross-legged on the floor of his bedroom, as if Wayne had been digging around in the box.

Why would he?

Wayne wasn't the sort of kid who would have gone snooping around anyway. After all, he had no reason. After the debacle of the Higginbotham's first attempted adoption, they had decided that they would never lose Wayne, even if he did have those ears, therefore they had, or Doris had decided anyway, that Wayne would never ever know that he was adopted.

A tear rolled down his cheek. He scratched his head and stood up stiffly. He walked over to the dressing table that stood between the two sash windows that faced out onto Cavendish Street and the gas works beyond. He stared at the face in the huge mirror; the brown eyes, the familiar nose, the hair parted and neatly greased.

Who was that old man staring back at him?

Frank Higginbotham, a man who put thingummys onto widgets and then boxed them.

Frank Higginbotham: a man now in his mid fifties and a long way past his best with his greying hair, expanding waistline and not a single tooth in his mouth that he could call his own.

Frank Higginbotham: a man whose wife seemed almost contemptuous of him and was always nagging at him and comparing him unfavourably with Stanley Houghton-Hughes.

"Stanley has a real job."

"Stanley earns a fortune."

"Stanley has a nice car."

"Stanley wears a suit."

"Stanley doesn't spend every night sat in front of the gogglebox with his mouth open."

Frank Higginbotham: the man who had once dropped a grenade into the open hatch of a German tank, while Stanley Houghton-Hughes had been picking his nose at the back of a classroom at Wormysted's Grammar School.

Frank Higginbotham: the young warrior who had medals in the attic to prove it, while young Doris Wardle had been taking chocolate, gum and Nylons from any American who would provide them.

Frank Higginbotham: from hero to less than zero in thirty years.

He was now a useless old man, powerless to do anything to save the adopted boy that he loved so dearly; powerless to stop him coming to harm. The fact that he hadn't had a son carrying his own genes had never been an issue for Frank. He knew he wasn't bright, or funny, or a great sportsman. What would his biological son have inherited?

Wayne was very bright indeed, sometimes too bright. Frank smiled wryly as he thought of Wayne's continual corrections of Frank's English, or Doris wartime recollections. Wayne had read enough history to do a college degree, Frank was sure of it.

He caught sight of himself in the mirror again and the smile evaporated.

Frank Higginbotham, a sad useless old man with eyes as dead as his soul.

A knock at the front door below snapped him back into the present. His heart leaped so high it almost jumped out of his mouth.

"Wayne?"

He took one last fleeting look at the sad old man in the mirror and then ran down the narrow staircase without seeming to touch a single step.

16

Wayne Higginbotham sat on the bollard watching the gulls dive bomb into the sea in search of breakfast. The wind blew icily cold off the slate grey ocean. A gull swooped, dived, then surfaced and swallowed a fish whole. Wayne decided that he too needed something to eat; in fact, he was absolutely starving. He saw the newsagents shop across the road and decided to buy a bar of chocolate:

"Can I be helping you young fella?"

The man behind the counter asked, as Wayne studied the confectionery display. He chose a Mars bar and passed it over the counter. The newsagent said:

"That'll be 15 pence please."

Wayne took the coins out of his wallet and handed them over. The newsagent looked at him as if he was an idiot.

"Is it taking the mickey you are?" The man asked, seemingly annoyed. Wayne was quite taken aback.

"No" he answered nervously, "I thought you said 15 pence?"

The newsagent frowned at him:

"Well course I said 15 pence you little eejit, 15 pence, fifteen Irish pence. This is English money, it's no good over here. We aren't part of the United Kingdom any more you know."

Wayne's mouth fell open.

"Oh, I'm sorry I didn't realise," he gasped, embarrassed and ashamed by his ignorance.

"No, course you didn't, it's not like people aren't trying that one on me all the time." The newsagent grumbled, furiously.

Wayne quickly placed the Mars bar back on the shelf and sidled out of the shop with a last apology, as the newsagent turned his attention to a man buying a newspaper.

Well, that had blown things. Wayne had just been congratulating himself on his success of getting to Ireland and now he found that he didn't even have a valid penny to his name. He bit his lip, crossed the street and re-claimed his place on the bollard.

For the first time in his young life, Wayne Higginbotham was in a foreign country. The only problem was that he just hadn't realised that Ireland was so foreign that it actually had its own currency. He had previously been to Scotland and they used English money.

Oh well, once again he was going to have to improvise.

Getting to Ireland had been a complete and brilliant success, although when he had got off the train at the Holyhead ferry port, in the middle of the night, he had been convinced that his adventure had come to a sad and premature end. The place was crawling with customs officers and policemen.

The station was very close to the ship, so it was only a short walk for foot passengers before they embarked. Wayne had noticed the policeman standing with the officer collecting tickets, however, and realised that an eleven year old boy trying to get on a ship in the pre dawn darkness, would arouse suspicions that he would not be able to bluff, or explain away.

He had turned away from the embarkation area and had trudged dejectedly along a corridor within the ferry terminal, wondering what he was going to do now. He had been cold, tired, hungry, extremely frightened and very, very homesick.

Wayne Higginbotham, or at least the boy who used to think he was Wayne Higginbotham, had wished that he had never found that stupid immunisation card, with its address and promise of an emotional reunion with his real family. He had wished that he had been safely tucked up in bed with the prospect of another long dreary, boring summer's day, in boring old Shepton, stretching out in front of him.

His eyes had welled up with tears:

"I know," he had thought: "I'll turn myself in to the police. I might get a free ride home in a police car."

He had turned to look back to where his fellow train passengers were lined up to get on the ferry.

The ship looked enormous, like the Titanic, or the Queen Elizabeth 2. Through the glass corridor, he could see lines of cars all queued up outside, waiting to disappear into the bowels of the ship; and not only cars, there were lorries and buses and ....

What Wayne had then noticed had given him a brainwave. He had seen people crossing from the line of cars into the terminal's café. Wayne had turned back down the corridor, in the direction he had been heading, before he had decided to surrender. The corridor led over a footbridge down into the busy main terminal.

Tired, bleary eyed people meandered around the café and the small kiosk area. Wayne had ignored them all and walked straight outside into the vehicle waiting area. Most cars had people sat inside, reading papers, or trying to grab forty winks before their car had to be driven onto the ship. He had walked to the far side of the lines of cars, as far from the terminal as possible, where it was darkest; where the floodlights that turned the pre dawn gloom into amber hued daylight had least effect. This was where the cars towing caravans had been lined up.

It was the caravans that Wayne had spotted from the corridor. He walked as confidently as possible down the line of cars, making it look as if he had a specific aim in mind. No one had seemed to notice him as they checked their tow-bars, or fiddled with the fastenings on their roof-racks.

Wayne had noticed a large brown Rover 3500, with a long white caravan fastened to its tail. The Rover was empty.

Its occupants must have been in the terminal, in the café or buying some rubbishy souvenir. With his heart pounding in his chest and with his tongue sticking to the roof of his mouth, Wayne had brazenly tried to open the caravan door. Naturally, he had expected it to be locked and that someone would notice him trying to get in and they would shout "Thief." Then he would have been arrested and his troubles made even worse, he'd get that free ride home though.

It had come as something as a shock to him, therefore, that when he had twisted the handle of the door, it had swung open easily and with a speed that had taken him totally by surprise. In fact the door had swung open so easily that he had actually fallen into the caravan.

His breath had come in short gasps and he had been convinced that motorists nearby would have been able to hear his heart pounding. He had swiftly closed the caravan door behind him and had then looked around. Amber magnesium light sneaked into the caravan from the gaps in the curtained windows. It was amazingly spacious and Wayne had immediately decided that he needed to find a hiding place, somewhere where he wouldn't be noticed if anyone should chance to enter. He had walked through the dim interior, looking for a suitable space and on his right he had noticed a tall plywood door. Wayne had opened the door as inaudibly as possible; even so, the squeak it had made had forced his heart into his mouth. He had stood rigid, rooted to the spot for what seemed like minutes. When a hundred angry policemen, or even one livid owner had failed to crash in through the outside door, he had continued to open what looked like a huge cupboard. Wayne had noticed that his underarms felt incredibly sweaty.

The cupboard turned out to be a shower and toilet unit, with a little frosted window. It was perfect. Wayne had slid in, closed the door as quietly as possible and had then sat down on the lavatory and closed his eyes.

Now he just had to hope that whoever owned the caravan was not going to need a wee during the next however many hours.

Wayne had been drifting into a very uncomfortable sleep when he had been jolted awake by the sudden sound of the caravan door opening and someone climbing inside. He had heard something being dropped on the table that stood in front of the big window at the front of the caravan and a man's voice grumbling:

"Fancy, leaving the damned door open with all our stuff inside, that woman's an idiot!"

There had been the sound of an irritated "Tut" and then the caravan shook as someone walked towards the toilet.

Wayne's eyes had been as wide as headlamps in his dark little cell:

He had closed his eyes tight when he heard the handle on the toilet door being turned and had cowered on the loo seat, arms covering his head as he prepared to be hauled out by the scruff of the neck.

"No, no, no" He thought to himself in total panic:

"You can't see me, you can't see me."

The door opened, but instead of being yanked out as he had expected, Wayne had heard the sound of an urgent beep on a car horn. There was a hissed curse:

"Damn!"

The toilet door had been slammed shut and the caravan shook again as someone hurried out, banging the caravan door shut as carelessly as he had slammed the toilet door.

"What if he'd been found?" Wayne had thought as he continued to tremble in the darkness.

His thoughts had been redirected, however, by a sudden jolt and the sensation of a slow forward motion. The caravan had begun to move forward; moving towards the mighty ferry that would transport him to Ireland and to his due date with destiny.

161

He had been saved by the simple movement of the line of cars.

Wayne's sigh had been that of a man who, believing himself to be drowning, breaks the surface of the water and realises that he is still very much alive.

Sitting on the bollard in Dun Laoghaire, in the mid morning sunshine, still exhilarated by his success, Wayne found it easy in his mind to dismiss the whole crossing as "a piece of cake."

That would have been to forget what had been the most nerve-wracking six hours of his life. He had tried to guess what was happening from the changing motions of the caravan and the shifting light patterns from the small frosted window. Every bump, shout and clang as the ferry had been boarded caused him momentary panic. Once the sound of people brushing past the caravan had subsided, however, a long silence began. A silence that was broken only by the deep rumbling throb of the ship's engines, somewhere below, and the creaking of the caravan as it shifted in time with the ferry. For Wayne it had seemed like an eternity. An interminable period of constant, sickening, rolling motion, in almost total darkness, as the ferry chugged slowly across the Irish Sea.

Wayne had tried to sleep, but the slumber that he had managed to get had been fitful, filled with dreams of sinking ships and of his being unable to get out of the caravan. He had remembered the movie he had watched with his Dad called "A Night to Remember" starring that Kenneth More. The film had been about the Titanic. The memory of all those people drowning in the ice-cold water had frightened the heck out of him. Wayne had hoped that there were no icebergs in the Irish Sea.

Wayne's Dad liked Kenneth More: he had also played Douglas Bader, the RAF pilot who had lost both of his legs in another film called "Reach for the Sky." Wayne wondered how Mr More had got his legs back to play his part in "A Night to Remember" and how extreme it must have been to have them amputated for the Bader movie anyway. Some actors were really dedicated. "Reach for the Sky" sounded more like a western movie than one about the war. Wayne's Dad liked westerns. He would sit in front of the TV, nodding expectantly as one of heroes: Randolph Scott, Audie Murphy, John Wayne, or somebody, outsmarted the bad guys in the black hats. It was always obvious to Wayne what was going to happen, but his Dad seemed to genuinely enjoy such movies. It fitted really, Wayne loved his Dad, but he had always known that he wasn't very smart, but now it didn't matter because Frank wasn't really Wayne's Dad after all, was he?

And Wayne wasn't really Wayne. So what did any of it matter?

He had then dreamed of being caught by pirate-like crew members and being made to walk the plank by a tall Captain, in a Scarlet hat with long curly, black hair, a thin moustache and a mean looking hook.

A sudden jolt woke him with a start; it must have been a big wave he thought hopefully to himself, when he had remembered where he was. His relief was palpable when he didn't hear thousands of alarms going off and people screaming.

Wayne had soon begun to feel extremely uncomfortable and confined in his hiding place in the small lavatory, so for a while he had sneaked out and curled up on the sofa at the front of the caravan.

The sound of some of the crew shouting nearby, however, had sent him scurrying back into the small claustrophobic WC. The crossing had seemed endless, but the disembarkation had seemed the longest bit of all.

He had suddenly been aware of a lot of banging and metallic clashes, then a sound that reminded him of a huge chain being dragged across metal. All of a sudden what had

163

seemed like hordes of people had begun to brush past the skin of the caravan. Wayne had heard numerous car doors banging and people chatting excitedly:

"We must be there." Wayne had thought, and his heart had begun to pound again.

Soon the caravan lurched forward and after a fair amount of bouncing around; sudden, harsh, daylight streamed in through the frosted glass.

He had heard people talking again after the caravan had travelled no more than what seemed about a few yards. The caravan door had opened and Wayne had heard heavy footfalls in the caravan and the sound of someone's heavy breathing. Wayne had tensed himself, closed his eyes and hoped for the best. Eventually someone with an Irish accent had shouted:

"Yes, it's foine!"

As the heavy footfalls exited the caravan, Wayne realised it must have been a customs check.

"I've made it." Wayne had thought to himself.

"Good job I'm not the IRA. Now all I have to do is get out of this caravan."

His opportunity had come much earlier than he had expected. He felt the caravan come a stop and heard the doors of the Rover slam. After a minute, or so, as no one had entered the caravan; he decided to take a peek.

He snuck over to the front window, pulled the curtain back a touch and peered out.

Wayne Higginbotham's first view of Ireland was of a plain Dun Laoghaire street, with an empty Rover parked just in front of the caravan. The street looked out over an expansive harbour. Wayne had noticed a middle aged couple on the other side of the road looking out over the bay.

"They must be the owners." Wayne had whispered to no one in particular. That had been his big chance, the door was on the left side of the caravan, the opposite side to where the old couple stood; so Wayne had grabbed his duffel bag and had jumped out of the caravan as quietly and quickly as possible. He had closed the caravan door behind him and had sauntered off down the street, like he had lived there all his life.

Now here he sat, on a bollard looking out over Dun Laoghaire harbour; tired, hungry and cold, without a useable penny to his name, but exhilarated.

What an adventure this was turning out to be. He fumbled around in the inside pocket of his jacket and took out the address that Agnes had given him.

Now all he had to do was get to this Oughterard place; but where the hell was that?

And how was he going to get there without any money?

Wayne looked up and took in a huge gulp of fresh sea air.

The answer to his prayers was rumbling slowly up the hill towards him.

17

Father James Malone stood open mouthed in the doorway of the Old Rectory's large drawing room:

"You want me to what?" He demanded incredulously.

"I would like you to hear my confession." Father Dermot Callaghan replied softly.

"It's not too much to be asking now, is it, young fellow?"

Fr Malone blew out a great gasp of air and wiped his brow with the back of his hand:

"No of course not, I mean, well, of course I will, if you really want me to."

"I do, I do!" The older priest responded firmly, before asking:

"Now, before we get down to business. Where's that damned Spaniard today?"

Fr Malone grinned:

"Our esteemed fairy hunter has gone off to the University Library in Galway, for a couple of days, to complete his research. It seems he's had enough of interviewing the "ignorant peasants" in the village, or so he says. He's going to be staying down there tonight, with some contact he has in Galway City. I dropped him off myself in Castlebar this morning, so that he could enjoy the delights of an Irish bus."

Fr Callaghan smiled, seemingly for the first time in days. The atmosphere in the house had not improved, even though some three nights had passed since Fr Callaghan had made his dislike of Fr Pizarro known.

"And good luck to him, may his road be long and rough and may his bus have bad springs. Who's he seen?" He asked, his eyes narrowing.

Fr Malone shrugged:

"We saw old Liam Fogarty and then, after we'd visited Mickey Finn's place we saw old Tom O Donnell and yesterday it was Davy O Driscoll."

Fr Callaghan nodded and bit his lip:

"All the local experts on folklore, eh?"

He shook his head:

"You know, I do admire the man's professionalism. I really thought he would be a lip service merchant; a "say three Hail Marys" sort of fella. I really believed that Mother Church had given up on all this sort of thing these days. I thought they were more concerned with the modern World, with its wayward Priests, like our Friend Fr Burke. By the way, would you be having any idea of the whereabouts of the old shot canon?" He asked, as he walked over to the sideboard and its resident whiskey bottle.

Fr Malone laughed:

"Father Burke is over in Cong visiting a friend. We have the house to ourselves Dermot. Even Mrs. Dolan is not around. I believe she has gone to see her sick mother in Tuam."

Fr Callaghan grimaced and nodded his head as he poured himself a large shot of whiskey.

"Are you telling me that she still has a mother? Jaysus, she must be over a hundred years old herself, so how old is that making her mother?"

He shook his head and the brief glimpse of frivolity quickly evaporated:

"I have a funeral to prepare and a widow to be visiting later this morning." He declared, solemnly staring at the glass of amber liquid in his hand:

"So we better get on with it and get it done and over with."

He drained the glass in one gulp, then turned towards Father Malone, who had sat down on a comfortable couch by the smouldering peat fire.

Father Callaghan took the chair opposite and bowed his head:

"Forgive me Father, for I have sinned."

Fr Callaghan crossed himself and began his confession in the usual manner. Fr Malone felt weird about it, but he was a Priest, so how could he turn down his friend?

"And what do you have to confess my son?" He responded sympathetically. Fr Callaghan slumped back in his favourite armchair and gripped his rosary tightly.

"I would like to confess to hating Father Burke and Father Pizarro and wishing them both ill in all my prayers."

Fr Malone smiled:

"It is only human to have such feelings Father. Say two Hail Mary's for the sin of wishing misfortune on Father Burke and one Hail Mary for hating Father Pizarro, for it is entirely understandable."

"Ach, so it's you who is the three "Hail Marys" man is it, young James?"

Fr Malone laughed, but noticed that Father Callaghan's forehead was covered in beads of perspiration, despite his attempts at light hearted banter.

Father Malone grinned at him:

"Would there be any other misdemeanours for which you'll be requiring absolution Father?"

Fr Callaghan seemed to think for a minute.

He wiped his forehead with the back of his hand and stared at the moisture on his skin as if totally unaware that he had been sweating:

"I would like to confess that I had impure thoughts about young Mrs. Corrigan the other day; but she did look ever so handsome in those tight jeans, wiggling around the village. It wasn't just my head that was turned.

Even so, I wish to confess to being something of a dirty old man."

Fr Malone tried hard to suppress a snigger and only just succeeded. He thought the older Priest was way beyond such thoughts.

"Sure the temptation of the flesh is one of Our Lord's most trying tests Father, especially for those of us who have chosen the path of celibacy. It is no sin to appreciate the wonder and beauty of the female form; it is only the impure thought that follows that needs to be absolved. Two "Hail Marys." Now, would there be anything else at all?"

Fr Malone was puzzled. Why would Father Callaghan ask him to take his confession when he had done nothing more serious than commit the sort of sins that any adolescent schoolboy might be guilty of? It all seemed so unnecessary.

Father Callaghan nodded slowly.

He wiped his forehead with his handkerchief and then blew his nose on it. He stood awkwardly and walked back to the whiskey bottle and poured himself an even larger shot. He took a deep breath, knocked back the whiskey in one and with tears in his eyes and with a voice breaking with emotion, turned to Father Malone and said:

"Yes Father, I would like to confess to the most heinous sin of all. I have to confess to murder."

18

Frank Higginbotham opened the front door of his little, terraced house in the middle of Cavendish Street and failed miserably to hide his immense disappointment:

"Oh, Mrs Ball." He sighed, in a voice laden down with the weight of dashed hopes and broken dreams.

Elizabeth Ball smiled sympathetically:

"I'm sorry to disturb you at a time like this Mr. Higginbotham, but Mr. Braithwaite rang me earlier. He said he'd had the police round and they told him that Wayne had gone missing. I just wondered if there was anything I could do?"

Frank beckoned Elizabeth to enter the house.

"You'd best come in."

Doris was sat on the sofa, with Margaret providing a comforting arm around her shoulder. Doris' eyes were red. She had obviously been weeping for some time:

"Hello Mrs Ball." Margaret said, as pleasantly as possible.

Mrs Ball looked embarrassed:

"I really am sorry to disturb you at a time like this, Mrs. Higginbotham, Mrs Houghton–Hughes, but I wondered if I could help at all; if there was anything I could do?"

Doris shook her head and sniffed:

"Thanks love, but there's nowt anybody can do at the moment."

She took a tissue from a box on the coffee table just in front of her and blew her nose loudly.

Mrs Ball hesitated, but then steeled herself and said:

"Look I know it's none of my business, but is it true that Wayne was adopted?"

Doris scowled at her:

170

"Who told you that?"

Mrs Ball smiled:

"Mr. Braithwaite; you know what he's like."

Doris and Margaret glanced at each other, their expressions speaking volumes of words. Eventually Margaret nodded as Doris heaved a huge sob.

"He was told not to say owt." Doris grumbled, as she rose from the couch:

"I don't want everybody knowing my business. Would you like a cup of tea, Mrs Ball?"

Mrs Ball said that she would, then with a nervous gulp added:

"There's really no shame in his being adopted, you know."

Her voice was soft and reassuring.

"My husband and I have thought about it, you know, if….."

"Aye, if you can't have your own, I know." Doris interrupted as she passed on her way through to the kitchen. She turned and appraised the younger woman:

"You know, the problem is, when you adopt, everybody knows that there's sommat wrong with you, that you're not quite right as a woman, that you've somehow failed. Do you take milk and sugar?"

Mrs Ball asked for just a touch of milk and then sighed and sat down next to Margaret.

Frank had disappeared upstairs.

Margaret shook her head:

"They're convinced he's run away because of that bullying thing, you know, that do Wayne had with Baz Thompson."

Elizabeth Ball nodded her agreement, but then Margaret leaned in towards her:

"I'm not so sure myself." She whispered, conspiratorially.

"Doris has always been too hard on the lad for my liking; far too handy with the back of her hand."

171

She leaned closer and whispered even quieter:

"I've seen her give him some proper good hidings."

She drew back quickly as Doris came back through into the living room carrying three mugs of tea.

"He's seemed alright at school, hasn't he, Mrs Ball?" Doris asked with a sniff, as she handed the mug of tea over to Elizabeth.

"Well, he did seem a bit upset to be leaving all his friends." Elizabeth said with a shrug:

"He's a very quiet boy, very deep; it's difficult to know what he's thinking sometimes. I must admit I knew nothing about this bullying business, until we were told he was in hospital. It came as a complete surprise; everyone in the staff room was in total shock. Wayne Higginbotham was the last boy we ever expected to be involved in a street fight."

"It weren't his fault, it were that Thompson nutcase." Doris blustered defensively.

Elizabeth Ball almost spilt her tea as she vigorously shook her head to alleviate any misunderstanding:

"Oh Mrs Higginbotham, please don't misunderstand me. Everyone knows Wayne hasn't got an aggressive bone in his body and Thompson was always a bad lot even when he was at Gas Street."

She paused for a few moments and sipped her tea before adding:

"It must be very hard for him to be the only one going to Wormysted's, you know. Does he know anyone else there?"

"Our Cedric is there, of course." Margaret interjected; "I'm sure he'll introduce him to a nice crowd of boys."

Doris sat down heavily in an armchair by the window. She took a gulp of tea and Elizabeth noticed that a tear was rolling slowly down her cheek.

The living room was suddenly darkened as a huge lorry pulled up outside the front window.

"I just can't think where he'd go." Doris sighed and then a huge sob racked her chest. She sniffed and in a voice that was cracking with emotion gasped: "I mean it's not like he has anywhere else to go."

The lorry moved away and the slate grey sky and the foundry and gas works opposite came back into view.

There was a long silence then Frank stepped into the living room, scratching his head and clutching a piece of brown card.

"I've just found this." He said, showing the card to all three women in the room.

"I didn't look at it properly when I looked earlier this afternoon. It was in the box where we keep all the papers."

"What is it?" Doris demanded, jumping up and grabbing the card in one swift, surprisingly fluid motion. Frank shrugged:

"It's his immunisation card." He replied flatly. "It's got an address on. I just sort of glanced over it before. I don't know how I missed it."

Doris glared at her husband:

"You don't think...."

Elizabeth hung back behind Margaret who was desperately trying to peer over and see what was on the piece of card that was so important.

Doris shook her head furiously:

"No, he won't have seen this."

She waved the card around dismissively in front of her.

"He can't have seen this. He wouldn't go sneaking through our private papers, not our Wayne. He knows he'd get a damn good hiding if he did owt like that. No, he doesn't know he's adopted."

She thrust the card back at her husband and slumped down in the armchair again:

"None of this has got owt to do with him being adopted. It's that Thompson thing and probably his having to go to that Grammar School."

She looked out of the window, gazing into the yellow hazed space over the foundry, tears rolling down her face.

"I'll kill that Thompson if I ever get my hands on him." She mumbled to herself.

Frank grimaced.

"I suppose I ought to let the police know I've found this. Just in case."

He said quietly to Margaret and Elizabeth, looking hopefully at them both in turn, hoping that his discovery might be of some significance.

"Where did you find it?" Margaret asked, taking hold of the card and glancing at the address on the front:

London County Council
Public Health Department.
Division No......
Immunisation record of Michael Sean O' Brien
Born on 24/3/1963
Address: 24 St. Joseph's Road
Hammersmith

"That wasn't where you got him from was it? That was, now let me see, it was Ladbroke Grove, wasn't it? If I remember right."

Frank nodded:

"Aye, that were t'agency. This must have been his mother's address."

He glanced furtively at Doris, who still sat sobbing and staring into space. He knew that she would have baulked at his use of the word "mother." She was Wayne's mother now and the woman, who had given birth to him, was as she had once told Frank:

"Less than nowt."

Elizabeth couldn't help but glance at the address.

"Look, I know the Shepherd's Bush and Hammersmith areas quite well. My first teaching job was actually in Shepherd's Bush."

Frank and Margaret both turned to her.

Frank's face betrayed a trace of a silent plea, while Margaret looked blank.

Elizabeth knew what she had to do and before she'd even had time to think about it, blurted:

"I'll go down and check it out."

Frank just stood there opening and closing his mouth like an angler's fresh catch, pulled out of its watery habitat to flap uselessly on an alien riverbank. He just didn't know what to do, or say.

He had been stripped of the last remnants of his dignity by this whole affair. The once decisive man of action was now little more than his wife's "batman." He brought in his paltry wages every Thursday night and "tipped them up" to Doris. Every penny earned by his thingummy, widget and boxing was appropriated by his dominant spouse and spent by her on the things that she deemed important. He had got so used to leaving the decision making to Doris, that now he hadn't got a clue what to say. As long as he got to the pub to down his usual two half-pints of Mackeson milk stout at the weekend, he had been reasonably content.

"I'll go down and check it out." Elizabeth offered again:

"If he's been there, to this address, then we know that he did find this card and that he knows he's adopted. You never know, he might even still be there."

Margaret sighed loudly:

"I think we should just tell the police first. They'll check on it."

Frank still stood there dithering, his hand visibly trembling as he held the card and stared at it, as though he could will an answer from it. Had Wayne seen it?

"By the time the police have called their colleagues in London and they've sent some young bobby round, I could be down there." Elizabeth pleaded:

"Anyway, Wayne might be terrified of the police, especially if he thinks he's going to get into trouble for running away."

"Trouble?" Doris' booming voice echoed around the small living room:

"He'll be in trouble alright if he's been sneaking around in that box, in our private stuff, as well as taking that money. He'll not be able to sit down for a fortnight when I get me hands on him. I'll tell you. I'll kill him!"

The outburst was followed by a bout of loud sobbing as she leaned forward and buried her head in her hands:

"Our Trevor wouldn't have done owt like this to us." She wailed.

Frank looked at the card again.

"Just tell the police, Frank." Margaret urged.

Frank looked at Elizabeth Ball; her eyes shining with hope and begging wordlessly for Frank to make her feel useful, in a situation where everyone seemed to be wallowing in a mire of helplessness.

"It's not such a bad journey now, once you've got through Leeds." She said, beseeching Frank to give her his approval.

"It's nearly all motorway and John won't mind taking me down."

She bit her lip. She knew her husband would go mad if he was forced to drive all the way down to London, as soon as he got home from his office, but she also knew that he would do anything for her.

"I think you'll be wasting your time love." Margaret stated tersely.

Elizabeth shrugged and continued to stare at Frank.

"And I think Wayne will trust me much more than any policeman, or woman. He knows me; he knows I won't be angry with him. He knows that I won't punish him."

She shot a glance at Doris, who was still sobbing heavily in the armchair.

Frank suddenly seemed to develop a modicum of resolve.

He grimaced again and then nodded:

"Aye" he muttered: "It'd be very kind of you, if you wouldn't mind."

Margaret raised her eyebrows:

"Well, I think you're being silly, Mrs. Ball. You're wasting your time and your money in petrol. Let the police deal with it."

Elizabeth's face flushed. She had a mission and she was going to fulfil it, whether it was a waste of time and money, or not.

She looked at Margaret:

"Can I take your phone number, Mrs. Houghton-Hughes?" She asked.

"I'll ring you when we get to London, just to make sure that Wayne hasn't come home already, before we go knocking on doors and making fools of ourselves."

Margaret shrugged again and sniffed her disapproval as she srawled her phone number on a piece of card torn from a cigarette packet.

Frank smiled and held out his hand with the brown card:

"You'll need this." He said, his voice grim and determined.

Elizabeth took the immunisation record and shook Frank's hand:

"I better get off, no time to be wasted." She gulped and turned to leave.

She stopped before she got to the front door, however:

"I hope I am wasting my time." She said, mainly in Doris' direction.

"I really hope Wayne comes home long before we've even got to London." She sighed at looked down at her feet.

"But I don't think any one of us can rest until we've explored every single possibility, can we? I'd rather have a wasted journey than do nothing."

Frank nodded and smiled. Margaret sniffed and gave a slight shrug of her shoulders.

Doris stood:

"Are you off then, love?" She asked:

"Thanks for coming round."

It was as if she hadn't heard a word of the conversation going on in front of her after her outburst. Maybe that was a good thing. Elizabeth didn't want to unintentionally raise her hopes, only to see them dashed, by finding when she got to London that the address no longer existed, or that no one there had any knowledge of Wayne.

It was after she had left, after she had hugged Doris and said her goodbyes that she remembered the look of hope and gratitude in Frank's eyes. She felt unbelievably nervous as she climbed into her old Ford Escort.

What if the card was a total red herring?

Why would Wayne have been rifling through his parents private papers?

Why would he have set off, all on his own, to London?

As the car pulled away, Elizabeth Ball, began to think she'd made a total fool of herself. John would be furious with her, and rightly so. He'd often told her not to get too close to her pupils and now she'd gone and got involved in a major missing persons case. She began to prepare her arguments to counter his inevitable:

"You ought to leave this sort of thing to the professionals," argument.

"Oh well Lizzie" she said out loud, as she passed Gas Street School,

"At least when I'm asked what I did during the summer holidays, I'll have something to tell them."

19

"Now what is it that a young fella like yer'self is doing so far away from home, all on yer own at all?"

The burly, bald lorry driver leaned down and peered at the small boy, lifting his spectacles down onto the end of his nose.

The boy raised his hands, his eyebrows, his shoulders and the corner of his mouth in a cheeky shrug:

"I ran away from home and now I'm trying to get back, me mammy'll kill me if I'm not back soon."

Wayne Higginbotham had heard an Irish child outside the newsagents, just behind him, refer to his mother as "Mammy" and thought it sounded more authentic, for a supposedly Irish boy, than his own flat vowelled, Yorkshire word "Mum." Wayne was having to think quickly now, despite his tiredness, hunger and thirst.

Wayne needed to get to Oughterard, in County Galway, to the only possible blood relatives he knew of, if his bravado so far wasn't going to be wasted; and he didn't have a single penny of Irish money on him to help get him there.

The sight of the bright green lorry chugging slowly up the hill away from the ferry port had been like manna from heaven. The lorry bore the legend: "Danny O Doherty Haulage, Galway" on a plaque above its cab and on both of its doors. Wayne had noticed such details at a distance where most people would have been unable to even see the lorry and the writing would certainly have been undecipherable.

Wayne had always had phenomenal eyesight; Doris and Frank had often said that he could see things that even an eagle wouldn't have spotted.

Well now, for once, his more than excellent vision was turning out to be useful.

Wayne had been prepared to try and thumb a lift, but when the lorry had almost reached him, it had indicated that it was pulling over and a man had jumped out and entered the newsagents. Wayne went immediately into deep planning mode and by the time the lorry driver had emerged from the newsagents, clutching a copy of the "Irish Mirror," Wayne felt that he had devised the perfect plan.

It was too late now to worry about Doris' advice to never speak to strangers. Good advice though it might have been. If the man turned out to be a drug crazed, axe-wielding murderer, then so be it, but Wayne Higginbotham had never been so desperate, nor as ingeniously deceptive as he was now.

Wayne had taken a deep breath and put on his best little boy lost look as soon as he had seen the man coming away from the newsagents counter through the shop window.

"Excuse me" he had said, "but you're not, by any chance, going to Galway are you?"

The grumpy looking lorry driver had appeared startled:

"I am that. And why would you be asking, young fella?" He growled suspiciously.

That was when Wayne had explained about needing to get home and not having any money and it was just after that, that the driver had asked him why he was alone and so far from home.

"And it's only a blooming free ride all the way to Galway that you're after is it?"

The lorry driver scratched his head, as he stood back upright.

"P'raps it's a Gard I should be takin' you to. They're the ones who should be dealing with snotty nosed little runaways."

Wayne struggled to understand what the man was saying, his accent was so thick and Wayne had no idea what the reference to the soldiers who marched up and down outside

Buckingham palace, in funny big black hats, was all about. Did they have those in Ireland too?

"Please Mister" Wayne pleaded, his big eyes imploring the man.

"What were you thinking anyway, running away from yer Ma an'Da?"

The man scalded:

"I've a wee one myself and I'd hate it if he was to be taking it upon himself, to go galavanting across the country on his own."

Wayne shrugged and twisted his mouth:

"I was trying to get back to England. We used to live there you see, that's why I've got this accent. We moved back to Galway a few months ago and I'm missing me mates. So I thought I'd go back and see them. When I got here, though, I realised that I'd been stupid and that I couldn't just jump on a ferry. Now I just want to go home. Please mister."

The tear that dribbled down Wayne's cheek was genuine. He did want to go home, it was just that he didn't really know where home was any more.

He stared deep into the man's eyes and concentrated:

"Please. Please, please."

He willed the word into the lorry driver's mind.

The lorry driver screwed up his face and scratched his head.

"I could be getting myself into a whole lot of trouble here, but sure, I know what you're saying. Me Dad moved around a lot when I was a lad, an' I ran away more than once, so I did. What's yer name lad?"

"Michael Sean O' Brien." Wayne replied, without a moment's hesitation. He was getting worryingly good at this lying business, but needs must, as they say.

"Jump up in the cab and don't be touching anything. We'd better be getting you home, before you get yerself into even more trouble."

181

The man grinned and shook his head.

Wayne moved like lightening, clambering up and taking his place proudly on the passenger seat of the lorry's cab.

The driver huffed and puffed as he climbed in on the other side.

"I don't suppose you'll have been having anything to eat either?" The man asked, looking sympathetically at the boy.

Wayne shook his head vigorously:

"Nothing really, since yesterday morning." He stated, truthfully for once.

The lorry driver grunted, turned and pulled a small package from behind his seat, he passed Wayne something, wrapped in a dirty looking piece of greaseproof paper.

Wayne stared at it, horrified at first, as the lorry driver crunched the gears on his truck and the massive vehicle jerked forward and lurched into the line of traffic leaving Dun Laoghaire.

Wayne was so hungry, however, that he decided that whatever was in the package was better than a long slow death through starvation, so he opened it tremulously and found what looked like a stodgy sandwich.

"Thank you" he gushed and then, closing his eyes because the sandwich did not look particularly appetising, even to the chronically starving, he bit into it.

It was probably the nicest sandwich Wayne Higginbotham had ever tasted: fresh Irish Soda bread with lashings of creamy Kerry butter and thick country ham. He devoured it like a wild animal and most embarrassingly let go an enormous belch as soon as the last crumb had tumbled down his throat.

"Pardon me!" He exclaimed, horrified; hoping that his new found saviour would not take enormous offence and abandon him at the roadside before they had travelled much more than a mile. The man laughed:

"It sounds like you were needing that, young fella. Don't be embarrassed, this isn't a national school, or the inside of a church. There's been worse noises than that in this cab, I'll be telling you. My name's Daniel, by the way. You can call me Dan. Everybody else does."

"Daniel O'Doherty?" Wayne asked, remembering the name on the sides of the cab.

"Yes!" Dan replied. "You've sharp eyes."

He glanced at the boy.

"An O'Brien eh? A descendent of the oul'Boru!"

"Pardon?" Wayne asked.

All he had seemed to hear was something that sounded like:

"O'Brien, Eddie sending oldboro'."

Dan shrugged:

"Are they not teaching anything but cheek in the schools today? Old Brian Boru was the first High King of the whole island of Ireland. Yer man who defeated the Vikings at Clontarf, just up the road there. All the O'Briens are kin of his, don't tell me yer Da' never told you that story?" Dan laughed:

"Course there are now more O'Briens than he ever had in his entire army, like all the rest of the great families of Ireland, they're scattered all over the world so they are."

Wayne Higginbotham took a deep breath and every single nerve in his body suddenly seemed to tingle. His stomach did a flip and once again his heart started to pound in his chest, just like it had when he had been hiding in the caravan.

This time though, the cause was not fear, it was pride, a strange sense of belonging. Through a faint buzzing in his ears and the noise of the cumbersome truck, he could hear Dan telling him about his own family, the O'Dohertys. It seemed from the snippets that he took in, that Dan's clan were descended from some guy called Niall of the Nine hostages who had also once been a king and had kidnapped St. Patrick and taken him to Ireland. He also said that they were originally from Donegal, wherever that was. But what Wayne couldn't get his mind around was the fact that he, Michael Sean O'Brien, was descended from a real live King.

As rows and rows of houses, shops and offices passed by and eventually turned into open lush green fields, Wayne dreamed of palaces, castles, knights and serfs.

"Dan." He said eventually, as the lorry driver finally fell silent, having given Wayne almost the entire history of the O'Doherty clan.

"Would you tell me some more about King Brian Boru?"

Dan glanced at him again as he steered the huge wheel guiding the lorry round a corner, in what seemed to Wayne like a long village of brightly painted houses and extravagantly decorated bars strung out along both sides of the road:

"So yer Da' never was telling you the tale? Shame on him." He laughed.

"That's what happens in the diaspora. Folk go away to England, or off to Americay to earn a living and before you know it, they've forgotten the ould country and all the ould tales. 'Tis a roaring shame. Brian Boru was from Limerick, or Clare, or somewhere down in the south west. He wasn't a Kerryman though, no, he was much too clever, so he was. He defeated all the other petty kings, except the O'Neills, so it's said, in a series of awful battles. Then he defeated a mighty Viking army at the battle of Clontarf, near Dublin."

"Wow" Wayne gasped, amazed. "What happened then?"

Dan laughed:

"Not a lot, 'cos ould Brian was dead. Breathed his last in that battle, he did. Shame, if things had been different, we might have invaded England, instead of the other way round. We could have ruled them for seven hundred years and seen how they liked it."

He chuckled at the thought.

Wayne was slightly disappointed to hear of King Brian's demise, but it didn't really make any difference. He was of Royal lineage now, distant royal lineage, ok, but it was something that he had never been as a Higginbotham. They were probably from a long line of grovelling peasants, wallowing in the muck and mire.

As the countryside of Ireland passed by, outside the warm cab of Dan O'Doherty's lorry, the boy who had been Wayne Higginbotham, had one new thought buzzing in his mind:

"I'm coming home. The lost son of the High King, Prince Michael is coming home."

20

Father James Malone could not believe his ears, what he had just heard made no sense to him at all:

"What?" He gasped; his face a mixture of horror and incredulity.

"I would like to confess to murder." Fr Dermot Callaghan repeated, slowly and deliberately, as though explaining something to a small child.

"You know, as in killing somebody, doing somebody in, rubbing them out, eliminating them, not like in war, or any such oul' nonsense, but just, just murdering them."

Fr Malone winced and stared into the older Priest's tired looking eyes.

"Is this some kind of sick joke you're playing on me now, Dermot?"

Fr Callaghan put his whisky glass down and rubbed his eyes.

"By the grace of Our Blessed Lady, I wish it was a joke, I really do."

He sighed heavily.

"Now, are you going to take the rest of my confession, James Malone, or am I going to have to go and find some other eejit in a dog collar, one who might be prepared to go some way towards absolving me of my sins."

Fr Malone stood and leaned on the mantelpiece, staring into the fire.

"OK, Dermot." He whispered:

"Please continue, although if it is murder you have committed, how can I ever even begin to give you absolution?"

He stared at the smouldering peat and watched occasional flickers of flame burst out of the briquette and leap up towards the chimney. It was so natural, so routine, so normal, which made the possibility of Fr Callaghan confessing to a murder seem even more absurd.

Fr Callaghan leaned back in his armchair and closed his eyes:

"For well over twenty years, I suppose, I've been trying to forget every single thing that happened back then, but I can't. There isn't a single night that passes without me seeing it all again, seeing the flames, hearing the screams. My God, those screams."

He paused and swallowed heavily. Fr Malone turned and looked at him, thinking that he might be waiting for a comment from his confessor, but he took a deep breath and continued.

"I have never whispered a word of this to another living soul, James, but now seems to be the right time. If, by my confession, I can help to prevent another such tragedy, then I will. May the Saints preserve me, but I will."

Fr Callaghan bit his lip and then continued:

"I was new to Finaan then; just like you are now, a young Priest, as green as spring grass and just over from a year working as a teacher at a private school over in Yorkshire. I was assigned here to work with a priest who, I was told, had an awful lot of respect locally: Father O'Leary. Yes, your man the Bishop, so he is now.

O'Leary was a strange man, a very intense and driven. He seemed a bit like one of those evangelical types you see on the TV in America; a little bit mad with the fervour and all that stuff. His sermons were always full of Hellfire and brimstone and dire warnings that his congregation would descend screaming into the fiery pits of hell, if they did not lead pure and holy lives.

Anyway, pretty early on in my time working with him, he told me that he had been given a Divine mission, but that it was top-secret stuff. Of course, I took it all with a pinch of salt; we all have divine missions don't we? That's why we have entered the priesthood after all; but he said that his mission was different. I pressed him and pressed him to tell me what the nature of his divine mission was, but he would not tell me, until one night when the bottle opened his mouth for him. Even so, he swore me to secrecy, on the pain of death, he said; and I agreed. Ha! What a fool I was.

He told me that his mission was the elimination of the last of Lucifer's agents on earth. I asked him what he meant and it was a strange tale he told me. I thought the man was a raving eejit at the time; but, as God is my witness, this is what he said."

Fr. Malone sat down slowly in the chair opposite his colleague and friend, hardly daring to breathe. Fr Callaghan's eyes were still closed, as though he was relating his tale in his sleep:

"Bishop O' Leary, or Father O'Leary, as he was then, told me that the "Tuatha de Danaan", the people who came to Ireland after the Fir Bolgs, were not men, as we are men, nor were they what might be called a fairy race, as some believed, but were all demons, in fact, they had once been angels, cast out of heaven. They were the followers of Lucifer, who had once sat on the right hand of God, but who had been expelled for trying to take over the very Kingdom of Heaven. The "Tuatha" had fallen with their master and had crashed ignominiously to earth, here being forced to take a roughly human shape. They were still angelic, even in human form, immortal, beautiful and magical, but fortunately small in number. They could not resist the fast breeding race of men, who were filling every land in the World. Eventually, the last few hundred of the "Tuatha de Danaan" fled to Ireland, from the mainland of Europe, just as the Celts were coming in from the East. It was here, on this very island, that they fought the native Fir Bolgs for supremacy. The "Tuatha" eventually won, but were so reduced in number that they were forced to flee underground when the Celts finally came to Ireland. They then became what we call the fairy folk, the little people."

Fr Callaghan laughed:

"I must admit when O'Leary was telling me this, I couldn't help but smirk. I even said to him: Mother Mary, you'll be telling me next that there is a Santa Claus after all. He wasn't amused. This is no joking matter Father Callaghan, he roared. These creatures are evil servants of Satan who are opposed to every aspect of Our Lord's teaching. Because they were cast out of heaven, they are at war with God's ministry on Earth. He told me that The "Sacred Order of Pope Gregory the Great" had been secretly killing them for centuries even when the Catholic Church in Ireland was itself being savagely oppressed by Cromwell and his successors. Even when the holy mass was having to be taking place in hedgerows, because the churches had been burned down, they were still seeking out the Fairy Folk and killing them at every opportunity."

There was a long silence, as Fr Callaghan seemed to be trying to compose himself. Fr Malone shuffled in his chair but said nothing. After what seemed like ages, Fr Callaghan began to speak again:

"He told me that the only sure method of doing away with the little folk, was to trap or lock them in their barrows, their caves, or cottages, then pour in oil and burn them. It seems burning was the only way to cleanse the Earth of their evil. During the clearances in the last century, the "Order" had been able to cover its activities as being the work of the heinous English landlords. Sometimes the "Order" would hire a band of thugs to do their dirty work, but some members preferred to do it themselves. O'Leary was one of those.

One evening, over dinner, I remember him being in a tremendously good mood. I thought he'd had too much of the wine, but eventually he told me that he had it on the strictest authority that there were now but three of "the Fallen" left in the whole of Ireland and probably, the world.

A male and one female had been found locally; the final victory was at hand. He told me that they were in this very Parish and that he would make sure that they would never be able to raise the "Slanaitheoir mor."

I asked him what that was and he, after much persuasion, explained to me then that the reason the early Church had gone to war with the "Tuatha" so enthusiastically, was because of some very secret old prophecy, supposedly known only in the higher echelons of the "Order."

Essentially, this prophecy stated that, Christ, in his second coming, could only be killed by an immortal, one of the "fallen." Christians would know this immortal as "God's assassin," to the Tuatha de Danaan, he would be known, as the "Slanaitheoir Mor," their "Great Saviour."

The "Sacred Order of Saint Gregory" was founded specifically to ensure that no such immortal would live long enough to be able to take on that "Great Saviour" mantle and assassinate our resurrected Lord.

To prevent the birth of this being, the "Order's" ultimate mission had been to ensure the death of absolutely, every single immortal on this planet. O' Leary really thought that he personally was about to save the Earth. And you can help me, he said."

Fr Callaghan laughed sarcastically at this point:

"Oh and help him I did, James, help him I did. I still don't know why I went along with him that next night. I was not one for believing in such superstitious nonsense, but I went along all the same."

Fr Malone spoke for the first time since Fr Callaghan had begun his main confession:

"Was it not an attempt to prevent O'Leary doing something stupid, perhaps?"

Fr Callaghan opened his eyes and looked at the younger Priest.

"You know James, I would like to think that it was; but I know deep down in my heart, that it was really nothing more than mere morbid curiosity."

"And what happened?" Fr Malone asked, gently.

Fr Callaghan stood sharply, giving the younger Priest a bit of a shock.

He refilled his whiskey tumbler and went and stood by the fire, much like Fr Malone had earlier.

He closed his eyes again and took a deep breath:

"I was awoken in the early morning hours, a couple of nights after O' Leary had told me about the suspected fairy couple, by yer man himself. "Come on, grab some clothes." He told me, so I dressed quickly and we jumped into his old Ford car."

Fr Callaghan turned and meandered over to the window, with its views out over the pleasantly bucolic countryside beyond. He stared out of the window, but saw only the events of over twenty years earlier.

"It didn't take us long to get to the cottage, out in the hills towards Clifden, it was. I asked him who the people were and how he knew that they were the fairy folk. All he would say was that it didn't matter who, what, or why, but that we were doing the Lord's work. He said there was absolutely no doubt that the couple belonged to the sidh.

Maybe I was even beginning to believe him at that point.

We parked away down the lane and walked through the pitch dark as quietly as church mice. O' Leary was carrying a can of some sort, like you'd be using to carry petrol, I suppose.

I don't know what I was expecting to do, but Father O' Leary told me just to stand in the distance and make sure that we weren't seen. He tied something to the front door of the cottage and then he disappeared for a while around the back, I suppose he was closing off the all exits. Then I saw him throwing something over the thatch roof. It was only later that I realised he was throwing petrol.

Once he was satisfied that the thatching was soaked, he set light to a rag and threw it up on to the roof. It went up like you wouldn't believe."

Fr Callaghan's voice began to break.

"I should have done something. I should have stopped him. I should have broken down the door. I should have told the Gardai, but I had sworn to him and he had told me it was the work of the Lord."

He turned towards Fr. Malone, tears coursing down his cheeks:

"Sweet Jaysus, James, I just stood there and watched it, I watched that cottage burn, like a child watching an autumn bonfire. I was transfixed, mesmerised by the flames. I watched the fire consume the thatching on the roof. I stood and watched as burning thatch and timbers fell into the cottage."

Fr Callaghan started to sob as he turned from the window.

He walked slowly towards the younger Priest who was still sat in the armchair. Fr Callaghan fell to his knees before him and clutched his hands as if in prayer:

"I heard the screams, James; I heard them, a male and a female screaming inside that cottage as it collapsed in an inferno around them and I did absolutely nothing. I can still hear them screaming for help. And even worse, I can still see the expression on fat O'Leary's face. He was grinning from ear to ear."

Fr Dermot Callaghan fell forward, his head hit Fr Malone's knee:

"Please give me absolution Father. Please forgive me, for I have truly sinned."

21

The rush hour traffic on 5th Avenue was as crazy as usual, but Terri Thorne was too excited to notice. She sat in the back of the yellow cab and read and re read the telegram from her agent:

"Terri,

> *Meet John Dallas (Director)*
> *Waldorf Astoria, Tues, 10:30 am*
> *Audition for major part in Hollywood feature production.*

Good luck
Tom."

As the cab edged slowly forward, Terri glanced out at the lush summer greenery of Central Park. The cool tranquillity of the woodland stood in such sharp contrast to the heat, hustle, bustle and noise on the street.

A girl could just be seen through the line of trees, strolling along on roller skates, wearing a tee shirt and shorts, as though she was by a Californian beach, not an East Coast city park.

Terri smiled, but for once she was not jealous of people like the carefree roller girl, she was as happy as she possibly could be.

Around her horns blared, cabbies and truckers shouted insults, while a cop whistled and waved traffic on like a man possessed, but Terri could not have felt more serene:

"I mean whadda hell we payin' taxes for?"

The cabby in front of Terri moaned:

"Dis traffic is a joke, where are the cops? Huh? Dose jokers in City Hall doin' nuthin to help us, huh? It was faster to get round Noo Yoik in the days of horses, y'know whaddam sayin?"

Terri murmured an agreement.

"I mean it's like crime, ya can't walk out on da street without bein' mugged, or getting raped, y'know whaddamean. Whadda dey do with all the tax bucks, huh? I tell you what, dey pay off da hoods, da mafia, dats what. Hey, I'm taking a left on East 57th Lady, Ok?

"Yes, sure!" Terri agreed.

The cabby indicated and cut across two lanes of traffic to take a left, answering the honking of horns with horn blowing of his own, accompanied by several rude gestures that Terri had never seen before.

"Da problem wi'dese guys is dey don't have to drive for a livin'. Dey ain't professionals, dey're all schmucks, y'know whaddamean?"

Terri was just beginning to get butterflies by the time the yellow cab swung right onto Park Avenue. She looked at her watch; she knew that at least she would be at the hotel in plenty of time, even in this traffic, for what was going to be the most important audition of her life.

Since Terri's arrival in New York as a naïve eighteen year old, over ten years earlier, she had been to plenty of auditions. Most had led to nothing, but she couldn't really complain. She had rarely been "resting," as actors and actresses tend to call being out of work; and she had been in many lucrative TV commercials and had had many "extra" and bit part roles, both on TV and on the Broadway stage.

This one was different, however, this audition was for a real live Hollywood movie. The famous movie director John Dallas had seen her in a commercial for Chevrolet and had contacted Tom Williams, her agent, saying that she was just what he needed for a mega-budget disaster movie that he was about to start filming in L.A.

Tom had told her all of this a couple of nights earlier, but she had heard it all before. Tom had been saying that she was going to be an enormous star for over five years now and where had it got her?

More young mom and Stepford wife roles in commercials for automobiles, detergents, cheesy snacks and the occasional walk on bit part in cop shows.

Well, this time it seemed that Tom might have actually come up with the goods.

She had received the telegram that morning at 7:00 am in her apartment in the lower Harlem district of New York City and had squealed with delight before rushing off to get ready. She had prevaricated for ages over what to wear, which had almost made her late, but she had been saved when her immaculately dyed strawberry blonde hair had fallen perfectly into place, instead of going all flyaway as usual.

Even so, in her haste, she had still not quite fastened up her blouse when she had hailed the cab outside the front door of her apartment block and had been somewhat embarrassed at the amount of cleavage she was displaying as she leaned down to give her instructions to the goggle eyed cabby.

In what seemed like just a few seconds, the cab rolled to a stop outside the Waldorf Astoria, the prestigious hotel on Park Avenue. She paid the cabby, who glowered at his tip as though it had been paid in used toilet tissue, and danced through the lobby area to the immense reception desk.

"I'm here to see John Dallas." She gushed breathlessly at the gum chewing, disinterested looking African-American girl who approached her as she leaned on the desk.

"Room 234, second floor." The girl replied nonchalantly, already inclining her head as a signal that she was ready for the next customer's request.

Terri almost flew to the lift. Now she definitely had butterflies.

"Keep calm, be cool. Keep calm, be cool"

She repeated the mantra to herself about twenty times in the short lift journey to the second floor.

She exited the lift and turned sharply to the right, following signs for rooms 220 to 240.

Her heart sank as she turned into a new corridor; a line of about thirty girls stood leaning on the wall, or sat on the floor. Just about all of them were chewing gum, chatting, or reading. Some were doing leg stretches. A stunning blonde girl at the end of the line nearest Terri, appraised the newcomer:

"You here to see Mr Dallas too, honey?" She purred, from between shiny scarlet lips.

"Yes!" Terri replied, her heart sinking faster than a stone ship.

"Better join the line then." The girl laughed, "sure looks like he's gonna be a might busy today."

Terri smiled resignedly.

"Oh well, I don't suppose I've anything better to do." She sighed as she sagged against the corridor wall.

"Thanks a million, Tom, so much for today being the first day of the rest of my new, glamorous, ultra successful life." She thought to herself, as she sighed heavily again.

As it happened, Terri Thorne's life was about to change. It was about to change in far more ways than she could ever have imagined, even in her wildest dreams.

Meanwhile, in the eternal City of Rome, a very important Churchman rushed along a marble corridor, his purple robes flying out behind him like wings. His hand was clamped to the top of his head to prevent his skullcap flying off. He skidded to a halt outside a large ornately carved door. He turned the handle; the door creaked open and the man disappeared into the darkness beyond.

A voice somewhere in the darkness growled:

"And......."

The Priest in the purple robes rubbed his hands nervously; he was sweating profusely, more than was natural perhaps even in the heat of the Roman summer. He pushed his spectacles back on to the bridge of his nose:

"Pizarro reports that the last of the demons will be despatched, tomorrow night at the latest, Your Eminence."

"Excellent." The voice rumbled:

"You may leave. Pass my congratulations on to Bishop Donleavy and his team, by the way.

The man with the purple robes bowed:

"Yes, yes, of course, thank you, Your Eminence." He grovelled, as he made his exit backwards.

He closed the heavy door and walked off down the corridor, back towards the sunlight, which gleamed through an open door in the distance. He was breathing a lot easier than he had been and had suddenly stopped sweating quite as much.

Back in the dark room, a figure stood before an ornate tapestry, hanging on a wall, he pulled a golden cord and the tapestry slid smoothly aside, like a curtain. The figure pressed what looked like a dirty mark on the white plaster of the wall. A previously invisible door swung silently open, revealing a hidden dark chamber. The figure stepped in, closing the invisible door behind him. An Alter stood in a small secret chamber, illuminated by candles. The figure knelt on a gilded cushion and bowed his head.

"The very last of your enemies is being dealt with, my Lord. "The demons "Great Saviour" will never be born. It is almost time for you to walk among men once again and for you to rule them. The dominion of glory is almost upon us. The prophecy will never come to pass."

Although the man was alone in the room, another voice rumbled:

"You have done well my faithful servant. When the last of the demonic immortals is consigned back to the realm of

Satan; I shall return in glory and all mankind will tremble and kneel before me. As the prophecy said, only "a child no mortal man shall sire" can harm me.

I shall laugh at their puny bullets and their bombs, their swords and their arrows. They shall all know the true meaning of fear, my servant. Two millennia have I waited for this and my new reign will begin as the third millennium begins. My reign will last forever; and you my son, shall sit at my right hand."

A low laugh began to grow until it filled the chamber.

The man bowed his head to the ground and as the laughter subsided, he closed the curtain and left the chamber. In the darkness, he smiled.

"Pizarro, my faithful sword arm. Tomorrow you will bathe in glory and your name shall live in history as the man who played midwife to the Messiah."

22

"Jesus!" Exclaimed an extremely exasperated John Ball, as he slowed to a stop behind another line of cars, scores of red brake lights glowing in the early evening twilight.

"This is the fourth set of road works we've been stuck in since we got through Leeds."

He looked at his watch and raised his eyebrows:

"You do realise Lizzie that we're not going to get there until midnight at this rate."

Elizabeth Ball fumbled with the map and the A-Z guidebook on her knee:

"It's not that far now darling," she said, reassuringly, "and then all we have to do is get round the North Circular and we're there."

"North Circular, pah!" John moaned.

"One day they will build that blooming London orbital motorway they've been talking about for years and then we really could get there in a reasonable time. Don't suppose it will happen in my lifetime though."

He drummed on the steering wheel for a minute, scratched his head and sighed:

"I really don't know how you managed to persuade me to do this, Lizzie." John said, shaking his head.

"Shhhhh! Elizabeth Ball glared at her husband, nodding her head in the direction of Frank Higginbotham who was sleeping soundly and snoring like a pig to prove it, in the coupe's tight back seat.

Once she had left the Higginbotham house that afternoon, Elizabeth had got straight on the phone to her husbands office.

"Look John," she had said firmly, having told her husband that she was going to London to search for her missing pupil:

"I need your help to do this, but if you won't help, I'll drive down in my own car."

John had held up his free hand and sighed deeply:

"I'll cancel my meetings later this afternoon, don't worry I'll drive you down." He had said, in a voice that reverberated with the echo of frequent surrender.

"Oh, and I'm going to try and get his Dad to come, you know, I think it's wise if one of his parents comes."

"Ok!" John had said, thinking silently, "I don't suppose they'll be helping to pay for the petrol?"

Had Elizabeth said: "I'm going to travel down wearing a gorilla suit with a hole in it where the bottom should be and a banana up my bum."

John would have eventually agreed.

Sometimes it was pointless arguing with Elizabeth Ball and John knew that this was one of those occasions.

John's smart Ford Capri pulled up outside the Higginbotham's house at about five o clock. Lizzie had bounded out and knocked on the door.

Frank opened the door, once again bearing the hangdog expression of a man who has lost a ten pound note and found a two penny coin.

"Frank" Lizzie had exclaimed. "Is Margaret still here?"

"Well, aye." He had replied, looking somewhat nonplussed.

"Could you come with us, just in case?" She had asked eagerly.

"What? All the way to London?"

Frank had looked aghast.

"Yes, of course." Elizabeth had stated.

"What, now?"

"Now would be good!"

Frank looked worried.

200

"But what about…."

"If Margaret will stay with her, until we get back any way, Doris will be fine. It's like I said earlier. Hopefully he'll come back before we even get to London. I mean I do presume he's not back yet?"

The sudden happy thought had hit her that Wayne might have already come home, or had been found and the look on Frank's face was merely coincidental.

"You'd better come in for a minute." Frank said despondently.

"You want him to go to London?" Doris had wailed as soon as Elizabeth had explained that she had thought it best if at least one of Wayne's parents accompanied her.

"What about me? I don't want to be on me own."

"What about Mrs Houghton-Hughes? Could you not stay with Mrs Higginbotham, Mrs Houghton-Hughes?" Elizabeth had asked imploring a positive response from Doris' sister.

"Well, I've got our Stanley and Cedric's tea to do, but I suppose I could come back. Our Stanley could drop me off later."

She looked at her elder sister with a slight amount of distaste.

The prospect of leaving her palatial Ripon Road residence and staying on Cavendish Street, even for a night did not fill her with any great sense of joy. Although, beneath her malaise, she had to admit that it was in a good cause.

Doris looked panicked:

"But what happens if they come and tell me that he's, you know, that he's…"

"They won't, believe me, they won't."

Elizabeth Ball smiled reassuringly and touched Doris' arm.

"Anyway, if we're lucky and I'm right, we'll be back before breakfast time tomorrow, hopefully with a very tired Wayne."

"Oh I do hope so, I do hope so." Doris wailed.

Frank took a deep breath:

"Well I better put a few things in a bag." He said, smiling hopefully at his wife.

"A photo would be useful."

Elizabeth yelled as Frank disappeared upstairs.

So it was that after another couple of traffic jams and a busy trip around the west side of the North Circular, the party of three, in the bright yellow Capri, pulled up outside 24 St. Joseph's Road, Hammersmith. It was twenty past eleven at night and very dark.

"It's a bit late to go knocking on somebody's door isn't it?" John grumbled.

"What do you think Frank?"

Frank rubbed the sleep out of eyes.

"Aye, I suppose so." He stated flatly.

Elizabeth had meanwhile opened the Capri's passenger door and was marching smartly towards the clean, green portal of number 24.

"Oh heck, she's off." John groaned and proceeded to climb stiffly out of the low-slung Capri. He pulled his seat forward, which allowed Frank Higginbotham to also climb out, slowly and painfully.

"Rat a tat tat."

Elizabeth rapped smartly on the door of number 24, then stepped back and looked up at the bedroom windows. Nothing happened. She knocked again and waited.

No lights were switched on, no curtains twitched.

John Ball and Frank were now stood behind her.

"Don't say we've come all this way for nothing." John moaned.

Just then, the door opened slightly,

"Yes, can I help you?" A girl's voice asked, she sounded frightened. Elizabeth suddenly realised that she would too if someone came hammering on her door after eleven o' clock at night.

"I wondered if you could help us?" Elizabeth asked smartly:

"We're looking for a little boy who's run away from home."

The door opened wider, a bit like the two men's eyes, as the young golden haired girl stood framed in the doorway fastening a silk kimono that was only just long enough to be decent.

The girl was completely and utterly stunning:

"A little boy?" She asked, sounding just a little bit sleepy.

"We're looking for a little boy called Wayne Higginbotham and we think he might have been here."

Lizzie continued, apparently unaware that her male companions were both stood behind her, with their mouths hanging wide open in a semi trance like state.

The girl suddenly seemed to snap to attention:

"That's freaky." She exclaimed:

"There was a young boy here, yesterday evening, but he wasn't called Wayne, his name was Michael, I think, yes, Michael, Michael O'Brien. He said he was looking for his mum."

"Frank, have you got that photo?" Elizabeth asked Wayne's spellbound father. Frank reached into the inside pocket of his jacket and handed Elizabeth the black and white photo of Wayne with the monkey in Blackpool.

Elizabeth showed the photo to the girl.

"Oh my God that's him. That's Michael." The girl exclaimed before clapping her hand over her mouth.

Elizabeth looked heavenwards:

"Thank God!" She breathed, while Frank and John looked at one another and broke into grins.

Elizabeth waved the immunisation card at Frank:

"You see, he had seen it. He's even using the name on it." She stated triumphantly before turning back to the girl.

"Oh my God! He had run away, hadn't he?" The girl asked, sounding particularly concerned.

"I knew it, the way he was behaving just before ...oh my God, oh my God and I let him go."

Tears welled up in her eyes.

"Do you know where he went?" Elizabeth asked, the triumph rapidly melting away from her features.

"Look, you'd better come in." The girl said, opening the door wide enough for them to enter:

"I'm Mandy by the way."

Elizabeth held out a hand:

"Hi, I'm Elizabeth Ball, one of Wayne's teachers and this," she indicated one of the ogling men:

"is my husband John and that is Wayne's Father, Mr. Higginbotham."

Both men smiled and mumbled greetings.

Mandy looked confused: "Father?" She asked, screwing up her nose and suddenly looking furious at Frank.

"Are you the one who wouldn't let him see his own Mother?" Mandy demanded angrily.

Poor Frank looked from Mandy to Elizabeth to John with a panic stricken expression on his face.

"Frank is Wayne's adoptive Father!" Elizabeth clarified.

The girl rolled her eyes, clapped her hand to her forehead and blew out a gasp:

"Oh God, now I get it. He was adopted, oh no, how could I have missed that. He was adopted. Michael is Wayne's real name; he was looking for his real mother. Oh no, I was so stupid. I should have realised. Oh my God!"

Elizabeth shook her head as the girl led them upstairs, both men trying desperately not to look up and see anything they shouldn't have.

"Please excuse the mess up here" Mandy chimed:

"I'm afraid I fell asleep watching TV and I haven't even cleared up the dishes from dinner yet. Can I get you anything?"

Lizzie, John and Frank shuffled into the girl's bed-sit flat and stood around looking a bit uncomfortable at the carelessly discarded underwear and wine bottles.

"Ooops." Said Mandy, blushing as she snatched up various items of skimpy clothing off the floor:

"I'd say make yourselves at home, but it's not much of a home I suppose." She laughed nervously. Elizabeth smiled:

"I'm sorry to disturb you Mandy and we don't want to take any of your time, especially at this time of the night, but we are worried about Wayne and really we need you to tell us all you can about what he was doing and where he was going and so on."

Mandy nodded eagerly:

"Yes, of course, I understand, he was such a sweetie with his little pixie ears and his freckles. Can I get anyone tea or coffee?"

"Yes, that's definitely Wayne." Elizabeth laughed:

"No I'm Ok thanks"

The two men also declined the offer of refreshments.

"I feel so bad now." Mandy said sadly as she filled her kettle.

"I was going to take him home. I mean he said he lived nearby and I should have; but he seemed so self-assured, so confident, you know? He said his mum and dad had divorced and that his dad had never let him see his mother. He said he'd found out that his mother had lived at this address at about the time he was born. It just didn't occur to me that he might have been adopted. I suppose I jumped to a few conclusions, you know? I made some stupid assumptions."

She ran her hands despairingly over her face and took a cigarette from a pack on the table. She offered her visitors one and Frank accepted gratefully.

The girl took a long, nervous drag of the cigarette, then sighed and blew out smoke at the same time:

"Oh God, After we'd been to see Agnes, he just went off. I offered to take him but he was like…."

"Agnes?"

Elizabeth interrupted Mandy rather brusquely:

Mandy nodded:

"Oh yes, Agnes next door. I took him there, because I thought she might be able to help. She's lived here since before the war and knows everybody."

Mandy shook her head again:

"I just can't believe I just let him go like that"

"Did Agnes know anything about Wayne's mother?"

Elizabeth prompted Mandy again:

Mandy ran a hand through her long, silky hair and shook her head:

"No, but she did think she knew a woman who might have been her sister, we think anyway. She gave Michael. I mean Wayne, an address."

Frank, John and Elizabeth all jumped in at once:

"Do you have it? Do you know where it was? Do you know where she is?"

Mandy shook her head:

"We could go round and ask Agnes, but I think she'll be in bed by now."

Elizabeth shrugged:

"I'm sorry Mandy, but if we can save Wayne from spending another night on the street, then I think it's got to be worthwhile."

Mandy nodded her agreement:

"OK, I'll just put something on and we'll pop round."

Ten minutes later, Elizabeth, Mandy, Frank and John were all sat in Agnes' front room, just as Wayne had been earlier the day before. Agnes was in something of a state. Not only had she been raised from her bed, in the middle of the night, but she had also found out that the sweet little boy that she had seen the previous day was now missing.

"I can't quite remember where I put that address book," she mumbled as she searched for the book that had Molly O'Malley's address in.

Suddenly with a triumphant:

"Ha!"

The old lady tottered over to the coffee table.

"I must be losing my mind. It happens when you get old you know. I must have left it out here yesterday. Anyway, here it is:

Molly and John O'Malley,

The Old Barn,

Quay Road,

Oughterard,

County Galway.

Republic of Ireland

Mandy looked at the three searchers who had all sunk back into their seats, expressions of shock and disappointment etched on their tired features:

"Surely you don't think he'll have tried to get to Ireland, do you?"

There was a long silence:

"Oh my God!" Mandy gasped again.

23

Wayne Higginbotham fell asleep in the crisp, clean bed almost as soon as his head hit the soft white pillow. He had just enough time to reflect on how nice it was to be amongst his own kind at last and how amazingly lucky he had been in finding such nice, kind people on both sides of the Irish Sea, since his adventure had begun the previous morning, far, far away:

Mandy at the house in Hammersmith, London, who had been as kind as she had been radiantly beautiful.

Agnes, the old Lady, who had given him his Aunt Molly's address, as well as biscuits and orange juice.

Dan O'Doherty, who had driven him all the way to Galway in his lorry and then all the way up to Oughterard, in his own car.

Wayne was even grateful to the tourists who had been kind enough to leave their caravan unlocked, enabling him to sneak undetected over the Irish Sea.

It seemed strange to him that Wayne Higginbotham had never had much luck in his life, but since he had begun to think of himself as Michael Sean O'Brien, his run of good luck had seemed almost endless.

That must have been what people meant when they referred to the luck of the Irish.

As he tumbled down the swirling helter-skelter of slumber, Wayne just didn't have time to wonder whether there was anything behind his good fortune.

He hadn't time to wonder why ticket inspectors and railway staff had let him buy tickets and travel on his own, without too many questions.

Indeed, the strange cause of Baz Thompson's sudden incapacitation, all those weeks earlier, had been pushed right to the back of his mind by his more recent discoveries.

The boy who had been Wayne Higginbotham fell asleep, believing that Michael Sean O'Brien was, purely and simply, just a very lucky kid.

It had been more than two hours since Dan had dropped him off in the centre of Oughterard.

"Good luck lad." he had said:

"I hope you don't take the beating I took, the last time I was for running away."

Wayne had thanked him profusely for his kindness:

"Oh it wasn't anything." Dan had laughed: "I live on the Oughterard road out of Galway anyway, it wasn't so far out of me way. Now are you sure you're not wanting me to be taking you to your door?"

Wayne shook his head:

"No thank you. I'll only get an even bigger telling off for talking to strangers and accepting lifts. They'll have no idea how far I got and I suppose it's best if they never do."

"Sure, well good luck, Michael Sean O'Brien and don't be off running away again. It's a big cruel world out there." Dan said with an admonishing wink. After further wishes of good luck he drove away back down the road towards Galway.

Wayne looked around.

Oughterard was a bigger place than he had imagined it to be. The main street seemed to go on forever, full of shops, pubs, hotels and Irish novelty stores. How was he going to find his Aunt's house and what would happen when he did?

Wayne was alone again and now he was further away from home than he had ever been in his life. That knot began to grow in his stomach again.

"Oh well!" He thought to himself as he aimlessly ambled along the main street.

"Too late to worry now." But worry he did.

209

"What if they don't want anything to do with me?"

"What if I am not Molly's sister's baby?"

"What if this is all some horrible mistake?"

He noticed a middle age man walking along the pavement towards him:

"Excuse me sir." Wayne said in his most polite and posh voice.

"But you couldn't tell me where "The Old Barn on the Quay Road is, could you?"

The man squinted at him:

"I beg your pardon?" he said.

Wayne repeated his question in a voice that betrayed just a hint of nervousness.

The man stood up tall, having leant down to listen to the boy. He turned from left to right looking confused and then scratched his head. Wayne's stomach felt very empty again.

"Well, bless me now, is it the Ould Barn you'll be wanting, down on the ould Quay Road. Now let me think, who is it yer lookin' fer?"

The man's accent was even more indecipherable for Wayne than Dan's had been, but he thought he'd heard:

"Who are you looking for?" So he looked at the piece of paper clutched in his hand and answered:

"Molly and John O'Malley."

A spark of recognition illuminated the man's face and he laughed:

"Oh gracious, why didn't you say so? John O'Malley? Sure he'll be in the big house down the Quay Road there."

He pointed down a nearby street, leading off the main road through Oughterard.

"His is the turd house on the left, when you leave the main built up part of the road. It's about a half a mile down towards the Lough. Ye can't miss it, it's the big, white place wi' the red door."

"Turd house?" Thought Wayne as the man ambled away. He screwed up his nose at the prospect of a house made of some sort of poo, but suddenly realised that turd was merely the Irish way of saying third.

So it was, that less than twenty minutes later, the boy who had been Wayne Higginbotham and was now thinking of himself as Michael Sean O'Brien, stood for the second time in front of a strange door, waiting for an answer to his knock.

Waiting for the second time in two days to meet someone who just might have the same blood running through their veins as he did.

Someone who might even possibly even have the same ears.

The red door belonged to a large detached modern bungalow, with stunningly white walls and a large garden. Over the garden wall, just beyond some trees, Wayne could see an expanse of water in the distance. It looked like an enormous lake, but before he could study the view any further the red door swung open. A small boy of about six peered around it and looked him up and down.

Wayne noticed, with a touch of disappointment that the boy had small ears. The boy screwed up his nose:

"Ma, there's some traveller kid at the door." He bellowed back into the house. He turned back towards Wayne and glowered at him.

A plump, rosy-cheeked woman bustled up behind the boy:

"Hello, can I help you?" She asked, looking more than a little bemused to see such a young boy out knocking on doors at that time of the evening.

Wayne gulped:

"Are you Aunt, I'm sorry, I mean are you Molly O'Malley?" He asked nervously, a lump in his throat choking the words as they came out of his mouth.

"Yes, that's me." She replied, still looking puzzled and now ever so slightly worried.

"I'm er Way, I mean, I'm er, Michael er, Michael Sean O'Brien" Wayne stated, hopefully.

The woman looked even more confused.

"Do I know you? Are you from Patsy's school?" She asked, leaning down peering slightly myopically at the small boy standing on the doorstep in front of her.

"I don't think I've seen you before. I don't think I know you, do I?"

"No, I'm, er, er, no, you don't know me, but I, er, gosh, I think I'm er, I think I'm your sister's son." Wayne whispered timorously.

"My sister's son, but Katie doesn't have….." Molly began, but then she hesitated.

"There's only our Theresa and our Katie and neither of them has children and your not an Aussie, so you're not Siobhan's. Are you sure you've got the right Molly O'Malley, son?

Wayne gulped:

"Erm, did you live in Hammersmith, about eleven years ago?"

Molly scratched her head and nodded:

"Yes, so we did."

Wayne took a deep breath:

"And did your sister come to stay with you?"

Molly frowned:

"Well, now, yes……."

A faint glimmer of recognition slowly began to spread over Molly O'Malley's face like a rapidly spreading red wine stain on a white carpet:

"Theresa came when she was, Oh my goodness! Holy Mary, mother of Jaysus! Our Theresa!" She gasped:

"You're English aren't you? You're not saying you're………., no you can't be."

Wayne gulped:

"I think I might be Theresa's son."

Molly O'Malley gasped then fell flat on her back in a dead faint.

The little boy who had been hiding behind Molly and peeping at Wayne occasionally from behind his mother's skirt, looked at the crumpled figure of his mother, looked up at Wayne, then turned and bellowed back into the house again:

"Da, some English kid just killed Ma."

Wayne didn't know whether to run, try and hide or just stand there. He thought at first that perhaps she'd had a heart attack and that her death would be ascribed to him and that his adventure would come to a sudden and tragic end in an Irish jail. His indecision was fortunate, however, as Molly soon started to come round. Her husband rushed to her side and gently patted her cheeks a few times. John O'Malley was tall and well built with sandy hair. He had come rushing to the door as soon as his son had shouted and had not even really looked at Wayne, concentrating instead on picking up Molly and binging her round.

"I'm ever so sorry," Wayne blurted and tears began to pour down his face.

John now looked at the small boy stood at his front door, as he supported Molly in his arms.

"I didn't mean to upset anybody, I just…."

"Ah she's fine." John said: "Just a faint. I don't know what's gone on, but you'd best come in, young fella."

It took several minutes for Molly to fully recover, long minutes spent in the O'Malley kitchen with the boy Patsy glowering at Wayne, for causing his Ma to faint. John had sat her on a high backed chair and wiped her face with a wet cloth:

"I'm alright, don't be fussing so." She gasped after a few minutes.

"Do you know who this boy says he is, John?" She asked her husband. He shook his head:

"No, no idea." He murmured.

"He thinks he's our Theresa's son: Michael. Jaysus, after all these years."

John's mouth dropped open.

"Michael Jaysus? Theresa's son?" He repeated, looking dumbfounded.

"Not Michael Jaysus, Michael Sean, you eejit" Molly scalded her husband:

"Although Jaysus might have been more appropriate, as our Theresa did claim it was a virgin birth at first."

There was a hint of a sniff in Molly's remark, Wayne noticed, as it sounded like the sort of comment Doris might have made. John ignored it however and perused the boy with his mouth still open.

"Jaysus, Theresa's baby boy, after all these years. How did you find us?"

He asked eventually, drawing out a stool from under the kitchen table and lowering himself slowly on to it. Molly had meanwhile stood and picked up the kettle:

"There'll be time enough for all that later, John, but I don't suppose you'll be having eaten in a while, Michael. Would you be liking something to eat and maybe a cup of tea, or squash?"

"Oh, yes please, anything, but just water to drink, please." Wayne replied as he began to recompose himself. The thought that he might have killed his Aunt from shock had scared him far more than anything on his trip so far.

"And where in the world have you travelled from?" John asked, still shaking his head in bemused wonderment.

"Yorkshire. Yorkshire in England." Wayne replied.

"All that way, on your own?" Molly asked, giving John a shocked glance.

214

Wayne then proceeded to tell them the tale of how he had overheard the Doctors mention that he was adopted and how he had found his real name in his adoptive parent's brass box. He told them about his journey and how he had managed to get all the way from Shepton in Yorkshire, to London and then how an old neighbour of the O'Malleys had given him Molly and John's address.

He told them how he had even managed to get across to Ireland without being stopped and sent home at any point.

"Well, we'd better be phoning your parents, they'll be worried sick." Molly exclaimed as she placed an enormous ham sandwich in front of Wayne.

Wayne looked distraught at such a prospect:

"They don't have a phone." He almost shouted, panicked by the prospect of being packed off back to England, before he could meet his real mother.

Molly looked at John who shrugged:

"Of course, we'll have to let them know that the boy is well." He said, firmly:

"But that can wait 'til first thing tomorrow. He has travelled an almighty long way on his own and it is a bit late for him to be setting off back tonight. Maybe we should let him eat and then rest a while."

Molly nodded and then looked at her watch:

"Talking of resting Patsy, it's time for you to be in bed."

The little boy moaned and was still moaning when his father picked him up to carry him off to a bedroom, after Molly had jerked her head at him in a gesture that meant she needed to talk to their young visitor, alone.

"I suppose it's your Ma that you're after finding?" Molly asked in a matter of fact way, as the squeals of her son subsided down a long corridor.

Wayne nodded eagerly.

"Well, I'll say one thing for you young man, there's no doubt about whose son you are, now that I've seen your eyes

215

and that chin. You look just like your ma. Although I don't know where the ears are coming from. Ah well it's only natural for a child to want his own kin."

Molly glanced nervously at her spouse, then sighed heavily:

"But Michael, I'm afraid I have bad news for you."

Wayne's heart sank.

"I haven't seen your Ma, since, well, not long after you were born."

Molly continued:

"I believe she's in America, but as for where, I've no idea at all."

Wayne's heart hit the pit of his stomach. So it was true what Agnes had said; Wayne's Mum was in America. Now he would never get to meet her. He devoured the sandwich hungrily and tried not to betray his immense disappointment.

At least she was alive.

At least Molly had said that he looked like her. It was the first time anyone had ever said he looked like somebody.

Molly smiled:

"Sure, you must be shattered, travelling all that way. We have a spare bed all set up in our guest room for when anyone comes to stay. You'll be staying here tonight and tomorrow I'll tell you all about your family and I'll take you to meet your Granda' up in Mayo, before you set off home. It'd be a shame for you not to meet any of your family, except me, after such an adventure."

Wayne's face lit up. Well that was better than nothing. Even if he wasn't going to get to meet his mother, then meeting his real Grandfather would be a fantastic bonus. He'd never had a grandparent before. Plus he'd already got to meet a real Aunt and an Uncle. There was definitely no sign of the ears on either of them though.

"Have you had enough to eat?" Molly asked looking concerned, as Wayne dabbed up the last few crumbs from his plate with his fingertips.

"Yes thank you that was marvellous." He gushed.

Molly's face swelled with pride.

"Yes, You certainly have your mother's eyes and her blarney." She said softly, tears welling in her eyes.

"I always wondered what happened to you both." She gave Wayne an almighty hug.

Wayne presumed that she meant his mother and himself, so he gave it no further thought.

Molly went on to tell him about his other Aunts and his four Uncles, who were his mother Theresa's brothers and sisters. She worked out that he had twelve cousins in all, including her own Patsy. Only one of his other Aunts, the youngest, Katie, still lived at home in Ireland. All of his other Aunts and Uncles were in America, Australia, or New Zealand. His Grandma had died only a year earlier and he had a few tears when he thought how close he had been to getting to meet her, but he was delighted to hear that he had such a big family.

Molly's good humour evaporated quickly when he asked the next inevitable question, however:

"Aunt Molly," he started, "Do you know anything about my father?"

Molly's face went white and she turned sharply and stood over the kitchen sink, pretending to look out of the window into the garden beyond.

"No, I don't," she snapped: "Our Theresa never told us who he was, although she did tell someone that he was an American. One minute she was there with us, the next she'd gone. Off to America we believe. One of your Uncles was doing well over there. It was probably your father she went off to find."

She quickly softened again, however, as she related how beautiful his mother had been and how she had been the most

217

sought after, most beautiful girl in all of County Mayo and County Galway for that matter.

So it was that Wayne went off for a bath and to bed, thinking about everyone's kindness and with an air of eager anticipation about the following day.

While Wayne was sleeping soundly, John and Molly discussed what they were going to do. John had to work the next day, but they decided that he would ring the police in Shepton, from his office and see if they could contact his family. Molly meanwhile, would take him up into Mayo to introduce him to other members of his family before he was packed off back to England.

"I'll ring our Katie in a second, she's bound to be at Maire Duke's at this time of night. I'll warn her that Daideo has a surprise arriving in the morning." Molly laughed, moving over to the telephone.

John O'Malley looked intently at his wife:

"What about his Da?" He asked with a grimace.

"I told him what Theresa told our Katie, that he was a Yank." She whispered with a shrug.

"And he probably was. Don't go believing all that fairy folk nonsense that me dad put around. Daideo is just a simple ould man.

"And what about his sister?" John asked, quietly.

"He didn't mention her. Maybe she didn't survive, or they might even have separated them?"

Molly sucked on her teeth:

"Tomorrow, I'll tell him all that tomorrow."

Molly grimaced.

I think tomorrow is going to be a day that will live in a lot of people's memories for an awful long, long time.

24

The old man stood outside the door of his ramshackle cottage and blew a huge plume of smoke into the air. The sky over the Partry Mountains to the east was darkening rapidly. Clouds skittered along from the west as though in flight from something terrible. They disappeared over the mountain range, their tails burning red from the last rays of the setting sun. The Partrys already appeared dark and broody as the darkness climbed towards their flat peaks.

The old man took the pipe from his mouth, drew a deep breath and sniffed the air, filling his lungs with the cool freshness of the breeze that blew in from the wide Atlantic Ocean.

Suddenly his eyes widened, he gasped and he took an involuntary step backwards, clutching at his chest. He dropped the pipe which smashed into several pieces on the stony ground. His breaths came in short sharp bursts, he grabbed the doorframe to steady himself, then he staggered along the wall of his cottage until he could face the mountains that lined the view to the South, away in the distance behind his home. He tried to calm himself and took another deep breath, still clutching at his heart. An ice cold shiver seemed to run down his spine and then all the way back up:

"It can't be true. It can not be true!" He said out loud, although the words he used were certainly not English, nor indeed did they belong to any other recognisable language.

He slowly regained his composure and as soon as he felt able, crept inside, slamming the cottage door behind him.

A couple of minutes later, the old man emerged from his cottage with what looked like an enormous diamond. It twinkled and shone in the evening twilight. All the colours of the rainbow seemed to dart and dance inside it, lines of light bounced off its walls like the reflections within a thousand prisms.

The old man held it up towards the mountains of the South and the colours in the crystal began to converge. Reds ran into yellows, yellows ran into greens, blues coursed into purples and as each colour joined together; a glow of white light began to grow in the centre of the diamond crystal. The light grew in intensity until the crystal shone like a tiny star in the old man's hand. He gasped, dropped to his knees and tears of joy began to flow from his eyes and caress his time worn features. He started to laugh, a soft bubbling chuckle at first, which got louder and louder, until he was roaring like a mad man. Then he jumped up and whooped with joy before doing a merry little jig. He punched the air triumphantly. He kissed the shining crystal and put it back in his pocket. His smile stretched from ear to ear as he re-entered his cottage and closed the door for the night. The gurgling of the babbling brook that passed his back door was drowned out for many hours by the sound of singing; strange, eerie but beautiful singing that lasted almost 'till dawn.

The shadow of the cast iron fire escape staircase and the proximity of the adjoining grey brick building made the small apartment gloomy at the best of times. On this particular evening, however, the apartment was not only gloomy but stifling. The temperature must have been near 95 degrees and lower Harlem was sweltering in the heat.

Terri Thorne was particularly hot. She staggered into the apartment and slammed the bags down on the table. Her apartment had no air conditioning and despite the fact that the window was wide open, it really felt like there was absolutely no oxygen in the room.

Terri had just managed to haul two huge bags of groceries all of four blocks and then up four flights of stairs and she was totally exhausted. She collapsed on her sofa and wiped her forehead on her sleeve.

She had been sat for no more than a minute when the phone rang. Terri ignored it at first but, after four more annoying chirps, she leaned forward with a sigh and picked the receiver off its stand on her coffee table.

"Yeah, Terri here." She stated, sounding tired and more than somewhat annoyed. Her eyes, however, suddenly brightened at whatever the caller had to say:

"What?" She asked, sitting bolt upright. Her mouth stayed open as though her face had been frozen in time. There was another statement from somewhere down the phone line.

"No way! You're kidding me." She gasped as she quickly stood, her free fist clenched and the arm moving up and down. Now she was smiling broadly.

"You mean it, I mean, this is for real?"

She was now pacing backwards and forwards, stretching the cord of the phone.

"Yeah, sure I'll be there. What? Are you kidding? No way, nothing's gonna stop me."

She nodded, listening to whoever and whatever it was; and then, with a grin as wide as the Hudson River said:

"Thanks Tom, I love you, I really do, thank you so much, thank you."

She replaced the receiver with a bang and jumped up and down on the spot and squealed with delight:

"Yes, yes, yes." She cried at the top of her voice.

A voice from outside mocked:

"Enough already, you're making me jealous." But Terri Thorne didn't care. She picked up the phone and dialled a number:

"It's Terri" She yelled excitedly down the line:

"I got it! I got it!" She sobbed with excitement:

"Yeah, I've got to be in L.A. next Saturday and that's it. I'm going to be a movie star."

All of a sudden, the humidity and heat seemed so irrelevant.

Terri Thorne was living the last week of being a "nobody" and it felt better than anything else she had ever felt before.

25

Fr Dermot Callaghan and Fr James Malone sat silently in their drawing room and stared into their respective glasses of whiskey. Fr Callaghan looked flushed, his eyes were red and swollen, his face blotchy and tearstained, while Fr Malone just looked totally traumatised.

James really hadn't been able to believe what he had just heard. That the priest he had respected more than almost anyone else in the World, had taken part in an arson attack. An attack that had resulted in the deaths of two old people: innocent, blameless old folk, who had committed no greater crime than follow the native traditions of their land. Moreover, he was shocked and appalled to hear that such a campaign of assassination and murder had been going on for hundreds of years, all in the name of the Holy Church of Rome. He just couldn't get his head around it.

Where was God in all this?

How could he permit such crimes in his name?

Since Fr Callaghan had finished his confession, the two Priests had sat in silence, one in shame, the other in shock. Eventually, it was Fr Malone who broke the silence:

"So how come the Gardai didn't notice that there'd been foul play?"

Fr Callaghan shrugged. When he spoke his voice was low and cracked:

"There are a number of possibilities. They may have just presumed that it was an accident and not really gone in for the full forensic thing; or maybe they were just paid off. The Church, I mean the "Order" is very rich, you know. They've used bribery many times in the past. Corruption really does make the pen mightier than the sword."

Malone grimaced and sniffed scornfully:

"Bribery and corruption, two of the three traditional curses of the Irish nation, the third, of course, being treachery. I suppose we can find some of that somewhere in the story."

Fr Callaghan looked down at his shoes.

"You have no idea how bad I feel about it, James." He said, resignedly. "But the past is the past and I cannot change those things now. What happened over twenty years ago cannot be undone, it is the now we can manage and the future we have to alter."

Fr Malone stood and glared angrily at his colleague:

"You're right. We have to stop it." Malone stated simply.

"We have to make sure that nothing like that ever happens again and that means stopping Pizarro. We have to bring the "Order's" activities to the notice of the Church and to the appropriate authorities."

Fr Callaghan sneered and laughed sarcastically.

"Oh sure, James, we'll just ring his Holiness, the Pope and everything will be put right. You have simply no idea, no conception at all, of how powerful these people are. Priests, Bishops even, have been conveniently disposed of in the past, if they have tried to be blowing the whistle on them. They are professional assassins, trained killers and worst of all fanatics. Do you know exactly who is in the "Order" and who is not?"

Fr Malone thought back to the office in Dublin where he had first met Fr Pizarro. The opulence had been a testament to the enormous wealth of the organisation and its location a sure sign that they had tremendous influence at the very highest level within the church establishment.

"Then we must tell the Gardai." He spluttered:

"I mean for God's sake, somebody has to know. Somebody has to do something. What about the press?"

Fr Callaghan shook his head:

"Great headline isn't it:

"Catholic Priests burn Fairies, Elves and Pixies. We would be laughed out of house and home. Do you not think people have tried to do something about the Society in the past? Do you not think that the "Order" have prepared for such actions? Do you not think the Gardai have never been told? This is not some fly by night fashionable little clique operating covertly within the church you know. This is not the Opus Dei, or anything like that. This is a fifteen hundred year old secret society that has been working within the heart of the Vatican, almost since the end of the Roman Empire. Think about it lad! Since long before the Crusades, long before the Vikings founded Dublin, long before the English ever came to crush us under the heel of their boots."

Fr Callaghan closed his eyes.

"No, James, I was wrong. I was wrong to believe that by confessing I could help to prevent the same thing happening again. There is nothing, absolutely nothing we can do."

Fr Malone stared, open mouthed at the man he thought he'd known. A man, whose kindness and friendliness was almost legendary in the locality. Everyone knew Father Dermot Callaghan. Even the few Protestants in the area liked the man. Yet here he was, confessing to aiding and abetting murder. Confessing to being complicit in the greatest of all crimes and now pleading impotence in preventing a repetition of such a crime.

Fr Malone drained his glass and put it down on the mantelpiece:

"I thought you said that you would try to prevent anything like this happening ever again? That was the whole reason for your confession, you said."

Fr Callaghan shook his head:

"I know, I know! The more I am thinking of it though, the more I know that it's useless, James. There is absolutely nothing we can do."

He snorted.

"Don't think our Spanish friend is quite as amiable and cuddly as he seems. There is dark power there James, deep dark power, trust me on this. But suppose we did stop him, by whatever means, fair or foul. They'll only be sending another one, probably of even greater power, then another and another. We are just two simple Irish village Priests, one an old fool, the other little more than a lad. What can we do?"

Fr Malone sighed, then turned and walked over to the window.

"I will not allow an innocent old man to be murdered, to be burned alive, by Pizarro or anyone else." He stated flatly.

"The more I see of this, the more I despair of our Holy Mother Church. This is not the work of the God that I worship. This is not the work of a merciful Lord!"

Fr Callaghan stood:

"And how do you think you are going to stop them?"

Fr Malone stared out at the darkening sky.

"I don't know, Dermot, but believe me, I will. I will stop them even if it costs me my Priesthood."

"And what if it costs you your life?" Fr Callaghan asked, his eyebrows raised provocatively.

Fr Malone turned to him, his face a mask of steely determination:

"I will stop this even if it costs me my priesthood, my faith and if it comes to it, my life."

He swept past the older Priest and left the drawing room, banging the door behind him.

Fr Callaghan pursed his lips and poured himself a very large whiskey. He then pulled one of the armchairs around until it faced the fire. He sat down with great care, not wishing to spill the amber liquid. He raised his glass to the flames:

"Good luck to you lad, good luck to you. May the Lord protect you and listen to you more than He ever did to me. May He give you all the help you're going to need. And by God you will need it! Slainte."

He made his toast to the fire.

Fr Malone was sitting at his desk in his room when he heard the car crunch to a stop on the gravel somewhere below his window. His heart missed a beat, was that Pizarro returning? He stood and peered out from under the net curtain. In the ever gloomier twilight he saw the dark shape of a Land Rover, the shadowlike figure of Fr Pizarro seemed to be in earnest conversation with the driver. Despite the darkness, Fr Malone saw Pizarro reach into his robe and pull out a large wad of notes, which he gave to the driver of the Land Rover, before picking up his bag, raising a hand towards the departing vehicle and walking inside.

Fr Malone raised an eyebrow.

"It must have been a Galway Taxi." He thought, "I didn't know any of the Taxi companies down there used Land Rovers though. Looks like he got well ripped off anyway. Serves him right."

He allowed himself a small smile then shrugged and sat back down at his desk and continued to write the sermon he was planning to deliver on the following Sunday. A few minutes later a knock on his door broke his concentration:

"Come in!" He shouted.

Fr Pizarro stuck his head around the edge of Fr Malone's bedroom door.

"My preparations are now complete." He hissed, his black eyes glittering in the light from Fr Malone's desk lamp.

"We shall strike tomorrow night. You will be ready before midnight."

Fr Malone stared into the dark depths of Pizarro's eyes:

It was as though ice began to form around his heart, freezing the very blood it tried vainly to pump around his veins, squeezing its walls like a ship crushed in polar ice. The words of refusal that had been about to emerge from his mouth were choked even before they were uttered. A strange feeling of apocalyptic dread seemed to overtake him and his entire body shivered.

"Yes." He said.

Pizarro's head disappeared and he closed the door gently.

Fr Malone shivered again and looked at the manuscript of his sermon.

He had inadvertently drawn a simple hanged man.

It was just after dawn that the Land Rover bumped and jerked over the mountain road, which led from Tourmakeady to the Westport Road. Its headlights peered through the early morning mist as it crossed the Partry Mountains and headed down into the immense, sparsely populated valley. The driver appeared to be looking for something and it wasn't long before he saw it. A small cottage was almost hidden in a tree-lined hollow, near a small, hump-backed bridge. On the opposite side of the road from the cottage, just by the bridge, stood half a dozen, or so, crazy looking wind chimes and toys, all perched on the dry stone-wall.

The Land Rover driver slowed down as he approached the cottage and poked a large hammer out of the window, which he deliberately smashed into the chimes and toys, while cleverly avoiding the wall. There was an almighty racket as the chimes crashed into the road and an even greater racket as the Land Rover reversed and crushed the flimsy artefacts firmly beneath its wheels.

The old man in the cottage jumped up and ran to his window, but was only just in time to see the tail-lights of the car as it sped off into the distance. He pulled on his coat and walked up his garden path and opened the gate. All of his wind toys were smashed beyond repair.

The old man smiled ruefully:

"So the scouting is over and the war begins now, does it?"

He peered into the darkness and took a deep breath of cold night air.

The Land Rover did not stop for several miles, only eventually pulling over in a lay by on the main Westport road. The driver took a wad of money from his pocket and counted it into his wallet. He smiled, a satisfied wolfish sort of smile and set off again, on towards Westport, where another new day was beginning.

26

Elizabeth Ball was awoken by the sound of her alarm clock, not just ringing, but dancing manically across her bedside table, buzzing and vibrating, like some demonic pneumatic drill biting into solid concrete.

Her arm crept snake like out from under the sheets and her fingers groped blindly in search of the offensive timepiece; eventually she felt cold metal and her hand slammed down violently on to the button on top of the clock, silencing it immediately.

She turned her face into the pillow and groaned, but it was no good, she had to get up, she had something very important to do. First one naked leg, then another emerged from under the blankets, then, an arm, then another, until eventually, the whole of Elizabeth Ball's tired body, had climbed painfully out of bed.

She walked stiffly, scratching and yawning, staggering slowly towards the bathroom, feeling as though she had not slept a wink all night. The look of her eyes in the bathroom mirror tended to reinforce that opinion: bloodshot red orbs, set in deep circles of black.

Elizabeth's husband, John, literally hadn't slept a wink; he had showered as soon as they had got back to Shepton, had some breakfast and gone straight off to his office, muttering darkly about amateur detectives and the comparative professionalism of policemen.

They had arrived home at nearly five in the morning, having driven all night rather than stay in an expensive hotel in London. Elizabeth and John had shared the driving, but had both been so shattered by the time they got back to Yorkshire, that neither had any idea how they had actually done it.

How John Ball was going to cope with a day in the office, Elizabeth had no idea. How she was going to cope travelling all the way to Ireland, she had no idea.

Oh yes, that reminded her, that was what she had to do and why she had to get out of bed.

She had promised Frank Higginbotham that she would go to Ireland in search of Wayne. Her first hunch, that he had gone to London to examine the Hammersmith address, had proven correct. Why would her feeling that he had subsequently set off to find the Oughterard address, that Agnes had given him, prove any less accurate? Just call it women's intuition. John hadn't been so sure. He had felt that having failed to find his mother in Hammersmith, would have meant that Wayne would have become dispirited and would have just given up and become one of the countless homeless, nameless children wandering the streets of London:

"No!" Elizabeth had insisted, as the Capri had negotiated its way back along the North Circular:

"Wayne is too motivated to just give up like that. We know now that he did find his details and that he has set out to discover who he really is. I am one hundred percent certain that he will have set off for this address in Ireland."

John had shaken his head dismissively:

"He would never make it across the Irish sea. With all the security now because of the IRA and the passport checks and so on."

"What do you think Frank?"

Elizabeth had turned to the back seat passenger who had been quiet since they had left Agnes' house. Frank had shaken his head.

"I don't know." He had said, thoughtfully. "I still don't know how he found that card. I don't even know why he would have looked for it."

He had looked away, out of the Capri's small rear window into the darkness.

Elizabeth had suddenly felt incredibly sorry for him.

Even if Wayne was found, and hopefully they now had the leads to say he would be. Even if he did return home safely, the Higginbothams had effectively lost him forever. The very fact that he'd run away to find his real parents meant that he no longer regarded Doris and Frank as his real Mum and Dad.

Elizabeth had bitten her lip and had turned back to look out of the windscreen.

"I tell you, if you go to Ireland, you're wasting your time." John had insisted:

"Just tell the police. They will investigate the London end, the ferry ports and will even contact the Gardai. They have the manpower and the resources, don't they? You are just one person following a series of assumptions. I mean what do you think Frank?"

Frank had frowned, rubbed his chin and had then said:
"Aye"

Elizabeth had sighed and closed her eyes:

"My assumptions have been pretty accurate so far, haven't they?"

Perhaps her husband had been right, perhaps she was going to be wasting her time and money, but she felt strangely connected to the missing youngster; connected in a way that she couldn't explain.

Orange light, orange light, orange light.......The street lamps had passed in quick succession as the Capri sped up the deserted dual carriageway towards the M1 and Elizabeth had begun to dose.

She had felt incredibly weary, and despite the adrenalin burst that their success in tracking Wayne's footsteps to London had generated, she had felt very depressed. Her husband had an annoying habit of being right and he probably was this time too. They should tell the police, it was the only sensible thing they could do.

Suddenly, as if in a dream, she had heard a voice:

"I'm going to go."

She had snapped awake and glanced at her husband at the wheel, eyebrows raised in surprise and looking in his rear view mirror towards Frank.

She had turned in her seat and looked at the grim faced Yorkshire man. His face looked just so miserable, or maybe resolute, she hadn't been able to tell:

"I'm going to go," Frank had repeated:

"I'm going to Ireland, tomorrow, to that address. If it's left to the police and because they're too slow, or sommat and sommat happens to our Wayne, I wouldn't be able to live with meself."

He had glanced at Elizabeth, who had smiled:

"I'll come too." She had said, encouragingly, before turning to her husband, who had been shaking his head and grimacing as he drove.

"I wouldn't be able to live with myself either." She had added.

John Ball sucked on his teeth, but had then patted her knee.

"Ok love, it's up to you." He had said with a resigned sigh.

She smiled as she stared into the bathroom mirror at the memory of that pat and knew that although John disagreed with her course of action, he would support her. Her strength of character and personality were two of the reasons why he had married her, or so he'd said at the time.

She pulled off his Tee shirt which she wore as a nightdress and stepped into the shower. Of course they weren't the only two reasons but on this occasion they were by far the most important.

An hour later, Elizabeth's Ford Escort pulled up outside The Higginbotham's house on Cavendish Street and Frank stepped out of the door:

"Bye Love, I'll be back tomorrow, or the day after at the latest." He shouted as he closed the door behind him.

"Was Doris Ok about you going off to Ireland with a strange woman?" Elizabeth asked with a grin, teasing the older man slightly as he slammed the car door.

Frank swallowed and looked straight ahead:

"She weren't best pleased." He said with a frown: "I didn't dare tell her your husband wasn't coming."

The Escort pulled away from the kerb and rolled along Cavendish Street.

Frank glanced at Elizabeth and asked:

"Was John upset?"

Elizabeth shook her head:

"No, he was just cross with me for going on what he thinks is an expensive wild goose chase." She replied with a rueful grin.

"He still thinks the matter should be left to the police."

"I told Doris to tell them." Frank said, miserably:

"She'll probably go to the station with Margaret later on."

It took over four hours for the Ford Escort and its tired driver and passenger to get to Holyhead, on the island of Anglesey; where they bought tickets for the next ferry crossing of the Irish Sea. During that time Elizabeth Ball and Frank Higginbotham didn't talk much. Frank was worried that if he talked too much, the younger woman would think he was making a play for her, while Elizabeth didn't want to appear flirty. Even so, by the time the car crossed the Menai Straits, Elizabeth and Frank knew that they had done the right thing.

At about the time that Elizabeth and Frank were driving along the North Wales coastline, Doris Higginbotham and Margaret Houghton-Hughes were getting ready to walk to Shepton police station, to inform W.P.C. Harrison that

Wayne had been tracked as far as London and that Frank was following a lead in Ireland.

It was also at about that time that Constable Hartley walked into Shepton Railway Station and asked the booking office clerk if he recognised the boy in the photograph:

"Aye." The clerk replied, looking shocked:

"Do you know? I'm sure as that's him that bought a ticket for London, the day before yesterday. It's a funny thing, though. I wanted to say no, but he gave me some cock and bull story about his mother and I couldn't help but let him have the ticket. It was like he was pleading with me, right in me head, if you get what I mean. He'd only been gone five minutes when I had to see the Station Master to tell him that I weren't feeling right well really."

The clerk looked embarrassed:

"Aye, as soon as he'd gone I got a proper screaming headache. It were so bad that I were off sick all day yesterday."

Constable Hartley took a few notes and returned to the Police Station feeling rather pleased with himself. He put his hat on the desk in the police station back room and screwed up his nose:

"London, he definitely went to London. The booking office clerk down at the station recognised him." He said proudly, as he reclined back on his chair, arms behind his head. The chair rocked back on to two legs.

"What's that? Don't break that chair you big lummox!"

W.P.C. Harrison scalded him as she put a pile of papers and notes into a folder.

PC Hartley stood up indignantly:

"London, that Wayne Higginbotham kid. He definitely went off to London."

"Oh!" WPC Harrison replied nonchalantly:

"Do we know why?"

"The usual reasons, I suppose." PC Hartley pontificated as he poured himself a cup of coffee.

"The streets being paved with gold and all that stuff."

WPC Harrison stared at him, incredulously:

"Do you think that's all it is?"

PC Hartley took a long swig of coffee and shrugged.

"Well, what wi't'Grammar School and the Thompson business, I suppose that'd be enough. But there's sommat else here. I don't rightly know what it is, but I'll tell you sommat, there's sommat very funny about this whole Wayne Higginbotham business. Sommat very funny indeed."

WPC Harrison raised her eyebrows quizzically:

"Like what?"

PC Hartley scowled and paced from one side of the office to the other:

"Well, think about it. That Baz Thompson lad is still totally Gaga, like his mind has gone. Have you seen the size of him? I tell you I'd have to give him the back end of my truncheon a few times to knock him out and I'm reasonably hefty. It's not just that; the booking clerk at the station said he was ill. He had got an headache and all that, straight after this Wayne kid had got his ticket. He said he felt there was something funny about the kid. That he just couldn't say no, when Wayne asked for the ticket, like."

W.P.C. Harrison scowled sceptically at her colleague:

"So one's a nutter, the other has migraines." She shrugged.

"I don't know." P.C. Hartley replied: "But I have a very funny felling about young Wayne Higginbotham. A very funny feeling indeed."

A few hours earlier, a long way away, in a small house in Galway, a lorry driver had jolted awake and sat bolt upright in bed. Daniel O'Doherty's wife stared at her husband as he shook his head and rubbed his forehead.

"Jaysus, I'm feeling terrible." He moaned. "It's like I had a skinful of the porter last night. Yet I wasn't touching a drop."

Dan O'Doherty also had the strangest feeling that he had performed an extraordinary act of kindness, which was odd because he was known by all his family and friends, as an incredibly misanthropic, miserable and grumpy man: a very grumpy man, with a particular dislike of other people's children.

It must have been a dream he decided and put his aching head back down on the pillow, pulled the covers up tight and drifted back off to sleep.

27

Wayne woke up to what sounded like a million birds singing and twittering, right in the middle of his head. It was the loudest dawn chorus he had ever heard in his life. The sound came as such an enormous relief. Wayne had been dreaming that Doris had caught him as he was taking the money from her sideboard. She had grabbed his arm furiously and was about to give him the beating of his life. Her features had been hideously contorted, as people's features tend to be in dreams, so that she looked like some sort of monstrous harridan and her raised hand had been more like a giant claw. But, as so often happens in nightmares, the dream had ended just as it got to the really nasty bit and Wayne had suddenly snapped awake.

Yet, where was he?

The warm comfortable bed was clearly not his own and the birds never sang like that at home. Slowly the events of the two previous days began to trickle back into his mind. He wasn't at home and Doris was not about to beat him senseless for stealing, but he was in trouble, serious, big trouble.

For the first time in the two days, Wayne Higginbotham thought seriously about what he had done. For two days the excitement of his escape from his humdrum existence, the thrill of seeing new places and the prospect of finding out whom he really was, had kept him from worrying about the repercussions of his actions. Yet now, in the confines of a warm comfortable bed, Wayne began to worry. In fact, he began to feel sick with worry.

How would Doris react?

What would Frank do?

Would he ever be allowed home?

Would he be sent to reform school for stealing?

What if, even after everything he had done, he was not accepted by his real mother or father?

His heart thumped in his chest and his stomach felt cold and empty.

Wayne turned on his pillow and clutched it tight, as he struggled to fight back tears. What was he doing to the people who had raised him as part of their family?

Wayne decided that he would ring Auntie Margaret that night and tell her to tell everyone that he was alright; that he would be home soon and that they shouldn't be worried.

His decision made, Wayne began to feel a little bit better. He could feel his heart beginning to slow down as the memory of his horrible dream and his worry began to fade. He took a deep breath and opened his eyes.

The room he had slept in was plainly decorated, with a picture of the Virgin Mary on one wall and a crucifix on another. An old wardrobe, a dressing table and a chest of drawers occupied the walls, while his bed was underneath an open window. The window through which the cacophony of birdsong was assaulting his ears, but another sense now began to attract his attention, the sense of smell: bacon, frying bacon.

Wayne felt his mouth watering as he sat upright, and then kneeled on the bed to peer out of the curtains. The view could not have been more different from his window at home.

Instead of a roofer's stone yard, the auction mart and a behemoth of a mill; rolling green fields, bordered by lines of trees swept down to the banks of the enormous lake he thought he'd seen as he arrived at his Aunt Molly's. The sun was shining, the sky was blue and fluffy white clouds danced overhead, their reflections scooting across the lake. The thought suddenly crossed Wayne's mind that he might have died and this was heaven.

A sudden knock at the bedroom door shattered that illusion:

"Michael, are you awake, son? Will you be wanting breakfast? There's a full Irish waiting for you downstairs."

The voice of his Aunt Molly reminded Wayne Higginbotham of exactly where he was and what his new found relatives had promised for today. It also reminded him of who he really was. No longer was he Wayne Higginbotham, perpetual loser, fuzzy headed, big eared geek; now he was Michael Sean O'Brien. Michael Sean O'Brien, who, somehow, seemed to make things happen on demand.

He was already on his third sausage when his small cousin, Patsy, arrived at the breakfast table.

"Me mam says we're going to Daideo's today."

The small boy announced as soon as he had sat down.

Michael looked up at him, a dribble of egg yolk on the corner of his mouth.

The younger boy stared at Wayne through narrowed eyes.

"Me Mam says you'll probably be given over to the gardai, if Daideo isn't liking yer." He stated as his mother put a plate of egg and bacon in front of him.

"That'll do, Patsy!" Molly said firmly.

"That is not at all what I said and you know it!"

The boy scowled and dug into his egg, raising his eyes just once to glower at his newly discovered cousin.

"That was marvellous. Thank you." Wayne sighed, as soon as he had wiped the last yellow stain from his plate, with his last morsel of fresh, brown soda bread.

"Would you not be liking some more? You look like you need a good feed." His aunt asked, as though he had starved during his long journey from England.

"No, no thank you." He smiled.

"Well, you better get ready then, young man. We've quite a drive this morning." Molly said as she picked up his plate. Wayne couldn't help but notice that she bore a pained expression as she walked over to her kitchen sink.

"You'd better hurry too Patsy."

The weather had changed by the time the two boys clambered into the back of Molly's Austin Maxi. The sky had darkened and spots of rain began to stain the drive outside the house.

"I'm afraid John had to work today." Molly explained as she climbed into the car:

"He's a doctor at the local surgery and time off is a difficult thing to come by. People are just always getting ill."

She started the car and drove out of the short driveway:

"I don't suppose you'll have been to this part of the world before, Michael?"

"Er, no!"

Wayne replied, shaking his head as car pulled out onto the main road through the town, where Dan O'Doherty had dropped him off from his lorry the previous evening.

"Ah well, this is Connemara, or at least it will be soon." Molly smiled.

"We're heading up into the "Joyce Country.""

The Austin bounced along the winding country road and the houses, shops and hotels of Oughterard, soon gave way to open fields. Wayne had dozed for most of his trip with Dan O'Doherty and was now amazed by the sheer, wide, unspoiled expanse of the countryside:

"It's beautiful here." He muttered.

"Just bog!" Patsy scoffed.

"Peat bogs. Da says it's only any good for the cutting of the turf."

Wayne did notice the absence of trees. It was all just so empty and the further they went the emptier it looked.

Soon Wayne noticed mountains looming into view; not fells and hills like in Yorkshire, but real mountains: steep green and grey slopes with rocky pointed peaks. Shafts of sunlight illuminated them like aerial floodlights. Wayne couldn't help but shed a tear:

Where were the satanic mills?

Where were the ranks of grey terraced houses?

Where were the industrial wastelands?

It was like going up into the Dales, but bigger, better and more spectacular.

At a place called Maam Cross, Molly turned right and the car began to climb up a twisty mountain road, bordered by several small lakes. The Austin raced along the road, bouncing this way and that, juddering and jerking at every pot-hole. Molly was a fast driver, unlike Frank, who, when the Higginbothams had hired a car, on the odd occasion that such extravagance had been necessary, seemed to drive as though he was ambling along at the back of a long funeral cortege.

It wasn't long before they were in the middle of the wildest countryside Wayne had ever seen, and it just got progressively wilder and wilder.

Molly passed through the small village of Maam, bearing to the left and eventually took another right turn up a smaller mountain road sign-posted "Tourmakeady."

"Tell me again how many Aunts, Uncles and cousins do I have Aunt Molly?" Wayne asked as the car's tyres screamed for mercy as it rounded a narrow hairpin bend.

Wayne thought he had seen spectacular views in his short life. He'd stood on Ilkley moor and seen the cow and calf rocks. He'd stood on the very top of Shepton moor and seen the entire town with its church, reservoir and castle spread out below him. But Wayne Higginbotham was totally unprepared for the view over Lough Nafooey that his Aunt Molly pointed out as the car came over the brow of a hill and began to hurtle down around several hairpin bends, nor was he prepared for the view of Lough Mask that eventually came into view as they crossed the brow of another hill.

"You've four Uncles and two other Aunts, besides me." Molly stated as she concentrated on getting the Maxi around a bend at what seemed an improbable speed. Wayne went quite white in the back, while Patsy picked his nose, seemingly quite unconcerned at his mother's attempt to become the fastest rally driver in Ireland.

"Well now, let me see: There's Colm, the eldest. He runs a pub in New York City. Him and his wife, Maria have four girls and a baby boy; then there's me and John with Patsy, then there's our Siobhan, who's in Australia. She has four children, two girls and two boys, but she's divorced now. Then there's our Sean, who's also in Australia, he has just the one girl, with his wife Linda.

You've got Dan who's in New Zealand. Then, of course, there's your Ma, Theresa, who's off somewhere in America, then, there's Liam who's just gone off to work for Colm in America and last, but not least, there's Katie who's only seventeen and still at home with your Grandda. Do you know Michael, you'll be the eldest grandson? Colm's eldest girl has only just turned ten."

Patsy pointed towards a small white house coming in to view just over the brow of a hill.

"That's where your Daideo and me Auntie Katie live."

Molly stopped to open a gate in the road.

The house looked small, but it stood next to various farm buildings and sheds and it was difficult to tell it was so high up. A rough track wound its way up to another gate where two sheepdogs barked and circled excitedly. The Austin bounced up the track like a rally car, coming to a screaming stop by the gate. An old looking man came out of the cottage and walked towards the car, calling off the dogs as he pulled the gate open, Molly immediately sped through and stopped by the house. Wayne's heart was beating so hard he was sure that Patsy would be able to hear it.

Molly turned to the white faced boy sitting next to her son on the back seat and gave him a reassuring smile:

"Well, Michael, are you ready to meet your Daideo, your maternal Grandfather?"

A little further back down the lane, where clouds of dust thrown up by the Austin Maxi now settled, an old bicycle stood propped up against a wall. There was no sign of the rider. A black and white border collie cocked its leg against a fence post, sniffed the air and then sat down patiently by the bike.

The two sheepdogs that belonged to Daideo, glanced down towards the collie and barked once each, before retreating back towards a shed whimpering softly with their tails between their legs.

Daideo, or Tom Mick a John O'Brien, to give him his full name would have noticed the dog's strange behaviour, had he not been in an extremely deep state of shock.

Molly had climbed out of the car, walked over to her father, given him a hug and then stated simply, as though commenting on the weather:

"Da, I've a bit of a surprise for you. There's someone in the car you have to meet."

The old man looked bemused:

"And who would that be now?" He demanded sternly: "None of ye're posh friends I'm hoping."

Molly opened the rear door on the Maxi.

"Do you remember when our Theresa disappeared Da, all those years ago?"

The old man's face darkened at the mention of the name.

"Humph, she's no daughter of mine that one! I haven't been setting my eyes on her for eleven years."

Wayne's heart was pounding again. The old man did not seem well disposed towards being friendly.

"Well," Molly announced:

"This young fellow is one of the reasons she disappeared. This is your long lost grandson, Michael Sean. One of the babies our Theresa ran away to London to have. The poor child was given up for adoption and now he's gone and run away from his own home to come and find us."

Wayne clambered, somewhat reluctantly, out of the Maxi, still pale and looking terrified.

The old man staggered to the car and leaned on the roof for support as his mouth opened and closed soundlessly, like a landed fish gasping for air on a river bank.

Tears began to roll down his cheeks as he stared at Wayne and he shook his head. Wayne stood by the car door, looking uncomfortable, shifting from one leg to the other and glancing at Molly for support.

Finally the old man recovered his composure:

"I knew about ye, ye know? I always knew about ye. I knew she was in trouble when she was for running away like that. What she did to ye was wrong. I am so, so sorry."

The old man began to sob. He looked haunted, guilty even; as though Wayne was the ghost of Christmas past rattling his chains threateningly.

"It was all so wrong."

The old man sobbed again as he staggered forward and hugged Wayne, so tightly that the boy found it difficult to breathe.

"Jaysus, thank Jaysus, ye've come home now. Ye're home at last. Come on in son, come on in."

The old man burbled as he put his arm firmly around the boy's shoulders and gently guided him towards the cottage. His grip was strong for a man who looked so old. A lifetime of labour had given him a strength that belied his small stature and advancing years.

A pretty, young girl had appeared at the front door, holding a tea towel. Patsy ran up to her:

"Auntie Katie, Auntie Katie...this is me lost cousin, Michael Sean. Look! He's got ears like a leprechaun."

The girl smiled.

"I know, Patsy." She said. "Your Ma rang me in the pub last night."

She looked knowingly at her elder sister and winked.

Once inside the old man bent down and grabbed Wayne by the shoulders, staring straight into his eyes.

"Ah you're our Theresa's alright." He muttered, squeezing Wayne's shoulders until it almost hurt.

"You have her eyes. She was the most beautiful of all me daughters, still is, I suppose."

Molly and Katie both erupted into laughter:

"Thanks Da!" They both chimed in chorus.

Back down the lane, the black and white dog poked its nose through the five-barred gate and sniffed, then it sat back and cocked its head, its ears pricked up vertically. It whined and shifted from paw to paw. It had watched the small party of humans disappear into the small white house. When they had all gone, it had led down behind the gate and let go a soft whimper.

The two farm dogs watched the Border collie from a safe distance. Both were shivering.

28

Fr James Malone knelt before the Alter, his hands clasped together in prayer, his head bowed. The Church was empty and his mumbled prayer echoed eerily off the bare white walls and in the wooden rafters:

"In the name of the Father, the Son and the Holy Ghost, I beseech you, Holiest of Holies, to grant me strength. Grant me the strength of Samson and the courage of your servant David. Grant me the wisdom of Solomon and the faith of Abraham, but most of all, my Lord, grant me the sort of miracle that thou granted Moses, to get him and the Israelites out of Egypt, for I will sorely need such a thing. Amen"

The young Priest looked up at the stained glass window behind the Alter. The image of Christ, hands spread in supplication, stared down at him sympathetically.

James Malone sighed deeply:

"Ah well, thanks for listening anyway." He said as he scrambled to his feet:

"Pity I haven't got the time to chat a bit longer, but you know how it is. Mrs. Doyle's husband died yesterday and I've got to visit her and then I have to go to the abbey up at Kylemore."

He shook his head:

"Now look at me talking to myself. Come on James, pull yourself together."

Another voice echoed in the empty church.

"That would be a good idea, I think."

Fr Malone's breath caught in his mouth in shock.

Fr Burke emerged slowly from the shadows behind one of the columns.

"You seem edgy, Father. Talking to yourself is never a good sign."

He said in his clipped, almost English, accent.

Fr Malone blew out a large gasp of air.

"Yes, a good friend of mine told me it's the first sign of madness. Thank God, it's only you Father. You gave me quite a turn."

Fr Burke responded with a cold smile.

"I thought I'd pop in and speak to you in private, James." Burke stated as he walked down the small church's short aisle, his fingers caressing the wood of each rank of pews as he moved slowly towards Fr Malone.

"That's nice of you." Malone smiled, without a single hint of sarcasm.

Burke' mouth twisted upwards again in what cold have been mistaken for a grimace, or a faint smile:

"Mmm. I wanted to discuss tonight's events."

"Tonight?" Fr Malone managed to sound genuinely surprised.

"Yes, tonight." Burke replied curtly.

Fr Malone turned his back on his colleague and aimlessly moved a small silver cup on the Alter.

"What about tonight, William? Am I forgetting something?"

Do not play games with me boy!" The older priest snapped.

"Do you think I am ignorant about Francisco's mission? It was I who initially notified Bishop O'Leary about our friend Finn, many, many years ago. Oh yes, we have known about him for a long time, Dermot and I, but as you know Dermot lost his courage long ago. Finn knew I was watching him, though. He is far too old and wily to make the usual sort of mistakes that these demons make. Isn't it simply delightful that it was trust in you that finally caused his undoing?"

Fr Malone turned back to face Fr Burke, a look of horror on his face.

"Yes, my young friend. These demons usually get drunk and are caught in the act of carelessly shape-shifting and some other drunkard confesses in horror to what he saw whilst intoxicated. Either that, or they brag about their supernatural abilities to those with shallow pockets and big mouths. Ha, Finn always thought he was too clever, but then he went and gabbled to you."

Burke laughed; a malicious, mocking sound that echoed through the empty church.

"The old fool trusted a Priest of all people. Ha ha. I suppose he got over confident because he thought that you were so innocent and naive. Ha ha ha."

Realisation spread across Malone's face and he closed his eyes in shame.

"Oh yes, it was you who signed his death warrant, James. But don't feel too bad, you merely, deliciously and unwittingly, confirmed long held suspicions, my young friend. Oh yes, it was you who brought my old friend Francisco here. Did you know that Francisco and I dealt with four of the last six demons exorcised here in Connaught? Your friend Dermot and the Bishop himself, dealt with the last couple. Do you also realise that we believe Finn to be the last of his species on God's good earth?

Thanks to you, my young friend, you could serve the shortest apprenticeship in the history of the Order and taste the sweetness of the final victory, after what will be your very first battle."

"I want no part in this, I………." Malone stammered.

"It is too late for that my young friend!" Burke interrupted sharply:

"To put it bluntly, even crudely, James, you know too much about the "Order" not to be part of it. You are one of us now, whether you like it, or not."

The last two words were delivered in a low threatening voice.

Fr Malone stepped down from the Alter and faced the older Priest.

"You don't scare me William." He whispered through gritted teeth.

"Don't I?" Fr. Burke responded with raised eyebrows.

"Oh dear, the old magic must be fading. That drunken, old fool Dermot seems to have been scared of me for twenty years or so.

In fact, he still seemed somewhat terrified of me this morning when I left him, hanging around in a squalid little church on the very edge of civilisation; such a waste of an experienced Priest's training and abilities."

Fr Burke shrugged at Fr Malone's enquiring scowl and turned to walk back down the aisle. He took two steps and then turned back to the younger Priest.

"You might not find me scary, James, but were I you, I would give Francisco Pizarro the respect he deserves. He is far more than he seems. The Holy Ghost truly walks by his side."

Fr Burke smiled his twisted little smile and walked to the end of the aisle. Fr James Malone did not move an inch.

Burke turned again.

"You will be ready in the Rectory hall by midnight. You will wear black, no collar. You will bring a torch."

His footsteps echoed off the cold stone as he marched out of the church door.

Malone was suddenly aware that he had not breathed since he had walked down the alter steps to face his old colleague. He took a long, deep gulp of air into his lungs. His mouth felt as dry as the Kalahari in a sandstorm and his heart was pounding.

He had no choice; he had to get Dermot to join him. Together, with God's help, they could defeat Pizarro and Burke.

He took off his surplice and ran into the little chamber that served as his office, cloakroom and storage area and put on his jacket, before picking up his keys and walking quickly out of the church.

It wasn't far from the Finaan church to the old rectory, but he ran almost the entire distance. He was quite exhausted when he burst into the house:

"Goodness, Father Malone, ye'll be giving me a heart attack, so ye will." Mrs Dolan exclaimed as he stormed into the hall almost knocking the tray of dirty tea cups out of her hands.

"Have you seen Father Callaghan?" Fr Malone demanded through gasped breaths, as he grabbed Mrs Dolan by the shoulder, his eyes wide and wild.

"Not since breakfast, Father Malone, sir."

The woman responded looking a little bit terrified:

"Has something happened, at all?"

Fr Malone didn't wait to answer. He charged up the stairs to Fr Callaghan's room and banged on the door:

"Dermot, Dermot, are you there?"

There was no answer so Fr Malone tried the door. It was locked.

"Dermot, are you in there?" He shouted again.

Mrs Dolan her breath short from running up the stairs as fast as she could after the young Priest, having safely put the tray down on a table in the hall, gasped:

"He went out Father, phew, he went out this morning, straight after breakfast. Oh dear me, I'm too old to be running around like a wisp of a girl. He said he was going to the old church at Finool."

"Did he take the car?" Fr Malone demanded, grabbing the old lady's shoulders this time.

"Well yes, I think so, he was with Fr Burke. I must say he …………oh"

Fr Malone had already let go of Mrs. Dolan's shoulders and had leapt down the stairs taking four at a time.

"Well I never!"

The old Lady opined, her fists planted indignantly on her hips.

The bicycle that Fr. Malone found in the shed by the house was not exactly the height of fashionable transport, but it was serviceable and although every turn of its wheels forced the emission of a horrendous squeak, it could move quite quickly when ridden hard. Unfortunately, riding the bike hard also produced a deafening clunk as one pedal bent inwards and caught on the frame. The rapid squeak, squeak clunk, squeak, squeak, clunk stopped passers by in their tracks, as Fr Malone hurtled through the village, like a mechanical bat out of hell. The noise soon slowed down to a painful squeeeeeeeek, squeeeeeeeek, clunk, as the Priest began the long ascent to Finool.

About half way up the first hill out of Finaan, Fr Malone became aware of the sound of a siren from somewhere behind and he slowed almost to a stop, as the tinny neeh naah, neeh, naah, got closer. Soon a Gardai mini van pulled up alongside the panting, exhausted Priest.

"Ah come on now, Tom, I wasn't speeding surely." Malone protested with a grin as the Gard wound down his passenger window alongside him.

Tom Lydon, the local police officer, half smiled:

"You better get in, Father. Leave the bike there, it'll be alright."

Fr Malone frowned, leaned the bike against the wall and climbed into the Gard Lydon's van:

"What's going on, Tom?" He asked: "Sure, I was only joking about the speeding thing."

Tom grimaced:

"I've just had a phone call, looks like there's been an incident in Finool. I'll have to check it out before I'm telling you, Father. But it sounds like a bad business. I'm glad I bumped into you. I think your services might be needed."

Tom Lydon shook his head as he pushed the screaming mini as hard as he could along the narrow country road, eventually getting stuck behind a caravan bearing German number plates:

"Bloody tourists!" He snapped, looking in his mirror and moving out to overtake:

"Neeh naah, neeh, naah, neeh naah"

Fr Malone wondered whether he should tell Tom about the whole "Order" thing and about Burke and Pizarro. Dermot's words stuck in his mind however:

"Do you not think the Gardai have never been told?"

Could Tom be a member of the order?

Or might his silence have been bought at some point?

Burke did say he'd dealt with a number of such "incidents".

Tom might have been involved in the investigations and wasn't it more than a little strange that no one had ever discovered anything suspicious in all the deaths that had occurred?

Fr Malone pursed his lips and decided that he would be wise to keep his own counsel for the moment. The mini pulled into the small village of Finool, siren still blazing:

"Neeh naah, neeh, naah, neeh naah"

A tractor pulled half out of a side street and Tom swerved around it.

"Jaysus Christ, sorry Father, but you'd think they'd hear the hooter wouldn't you?"

The car pulled up outside the village church and Lydon jumped out and put his Garda peaked hat on his head, pulling the brim down as far as he could, in an attempt to cement his look of authority.

Fr Malone also climbed out of the mini, his back and the backs of his legs aching after his exertions on the bike, but the pain would have to wait. An old woman with a grey shawl wrapped around her shoulders was gesticulating, weeping and gabbling at the guard, all at the same time:

"I'd just gone in to offer a prayer and that's how I found him. Jaysus, it's such a shame. He was a lovely man."

"What time was that?" Tom Lydon asked the woman, pen poised above his notebook.

Fr Malone walked past him and opened the church door.

"Hey wait a minute, Father! You can't go in there, that's a crime scene!" Tom Lydon bellowed from somewhere behind.

Fr Malone hardly heard him; he merely stood rooted to the spot, his mouth open in horror.

Hanging from the raftered ceiling of the tiny church of the picturesque village of Finool, his feet dangling about a foot above the stone paved aisle, was the body of Father Dermot Callaghan

29

Elizabeth Ball had decided that Frank Higginbotham was not the World's greatest conversationalist long before they had even got as far as the Welsh border, a mere two hours into their journey from Shepton.

Now that they were more than half way across Ireland, she had totally given up trying to engage the man.

Her questions about his work had been met with little more than monosyllabic responses.

Her questions about Wayne had been met with uninformative replies and Frank had seemed to show little interest in her commentaries on the passing landmarks and changes in scenery.

It came as something of a shock to her, therefore, when, after nearly half an hour of total silence, (the radio in the Escort, having died some weeks earlier,) Frank spoke:

"Wayne's a good lad, you know."

Elizabeth glanced at the Yorkshire man, with his almost totally grey hair, which was greased and combed back in the fashionable manner of the late forties and his large, sad, brown, puppy dog eyes.

"I know." She said.

"I mean he wouldn't do owt to hurt anybody."

Frank added, ringing his hands as he stared out of the windscreen at the seemingly eternal rolling green landscape.

Elizabeth simply nodded.

There was another long silence and then Frank continued:

"I think our Doris is a bit hard on him sometimes."

Elizabeth glanced at him again:

"What do you mean Frank?" She asked.

Frank frowned and looked down into his lap:

"Well, you know, she gives him good hidings and what have you."

Elizabeth flinched:

"Why?" She asked, a little too sharply for her own liking, but Frank responded.

"She wants him brought up right, you know, to turn out a good 'un, I suppose."

"She seems to be succeeding admirably so far." Elizabeth stated flashing a smile at Frank:

"You both do, he's a credit to you both."

Frank looked embarrassed:

"It's shame you see." He said, looking out of his side window at a passing farm.

Elizabeth turned but saw only the back of his head. A signpost showed Galway to be only sixty miles away.

"Shame?" Elizabeth prompted.

"Because she couldn't have one of her own."

Frank's voice was almost a whisper.

Elizabeth glanced at him again. He was still looking away from her.

"She always wanted a baby. Especially when Margaret got pregnant; they were always jealous of one another them two. She'd had a few miscarriages and the Doctors said it were unlikely that she'd ever carry one to term. So when Margaret said she were in the family way, like, Doris decided she'd have to adopt."

Elizabeth nodded and smiled:

"It must be an awful predicament, finding out that although you want a family, you can't have a baby, yourself. Is that when you set out to adopt Wayne?"

Frank grimaced as though he had a serious pain in his stomach:

"No." He said quietly. Elizabeth came to a stop by a zebra crossing in a small Irish town.

A small group of children crossed the road in front of them, one small boy stuck his tongue out at Elizabeth who laughed and stuck hers out in return.

"That's when we went through all the checks and stuff and got John." Elizabeth who was looking for signs indicating the route the Galway, absent mindedly said:

"John?"

Frank gulped, his mouth seemed to dry up:

"Aye, he was the one we adopted before Wayne. John, he was called. We were going to change his name to Trevor. That's what Doris still calls him, although we never got the chance to change his name, properly."

His eyes misted over.

"Ha!" Elizabeth suddenly exclaimed and turned into down a street that had appeared little more than a side road.

"The road signs here are appalling." She moaned.

It was only after another few moments of silence that Frank's statement registered in her mind:

"Oh" She gasped, "So Wayne wasn't your first attempt to adopt?"

Frank shook his head.

"No, that were John." He sighed, oblivious to Elizabeth's stare.

The car suddenly made a lurch to the right as Elizabeth realised that she was driving towards a ditch.

"Aye, John was a beautiful baby, perfect. It broke Doris' heart when his mother took him back. She changed her mind at the last minute you see. We were offered Michael, or Wayne as we called him, as a replacement."

Elizabeth was now driving with her mouth hanging open in shock. Frank continued:

"Our Doris were a bit disappointed with Wayne when we picked him up, John having been so perfect like. It were the ears more than owt else. Doris hated his ears. She cried for days. She weren't keen on the fact that his mother had been

Irish either. She's not over fond of the Irish, our Doris. She always used to say you can't trust 'em. Like the French, you know. It was even worse when we were told his father had supposedly been a Yank. Doris really hated Yanks."

Elizabeth frowned uncomprehendingly:

"She hates Americans, why?"

Frank shrugged:

"She thinks they're all big heads. It's all to do with the war, I suppose. Them being over here, being flash and all that. I was once told sommat happened between Doris and a Yank who was billeted in Carelton for a week, or so before D Day. I was away, so I don't know if owt happened, but I do know she's never told me."

Elizabeth shook her head:

"Let me assure you Frank, I've taught a lot of children and not come across many who are as polite, courteous, honest and as bright as Wayne."

Frank nodded and smiled, weakly:

"I know; he's a grand lad. I just wish our Doris had taken to him a bit more. You know, treated him a bit more like one of her own."

He paused and then coughed to clear his throat:

"It was only a few weeks ago that Doris threatened to send him to a children's home, if he didn't do as he was told."

A tear rolled down his cheek.

"I wonder if he knew then that he'd been adopted, like; and all this is because of that, him beating her to it, as it were."

Elizabeth blinked to clear the tears from her eyes.

At least she felt she knew now why Wayne, solid, dependable Wayne Higginbotham, had done something so extreme. Why he had gone and done something so out of character.

Thinking about Doris Higginbotham and her:

"He'll not be able to sit down for a fortnight, I'll tell you. I'll kill him" remark, Elizabeth couldn't exactly blame him.

258

Wherever thirteen-year old John Albert Watson was in the world, his ears must have been burning. Not only had he been discussed in a Ford Escort speeding along the country roads of Ireland, but he was also the subject of a melancholic reminiscence in Shepton, Yorkshire:

"Our Trevor would never have done owt like this to us." Doris wailed as her sister Margaret nodded her head sympathetically.

"That's what we were going to call him, you know." Doris blubbed.

"His proper name was John, the name his mother gave him, but we were always going to call him Trevor. He was such a lovely little baby, always smiling, not like the other ugly little beggar. I cried all the way home with him. Do you remember Margaret?"

Margaret made a hushing sound as Doris continued.

"I knew he'd be trouble as soon as they said his mother had been Irish. The Irish have always been trouble, coming over here taking our jobs. Getting drunk and fighting. I mean look at 'em now, trying to blow us all up."

Margaret grimaced as she squeezed her sister's shoulder:

"Sssshh, you're just upset, love. Wayne's a good lad."

Doris loudly blew her nose into a tissue:

"They said his father was American, no wonder he's too big for his boots, bloody Yanks. Over sexed, over paid and over here, that's all they were."

"Mrs. Higginbotham."

WPC Harrison's soft voice interrupted Doris' tirade.

The sisters were sat in the reception area of Shepton Police station, where Doris had reported the previous evening's discoveries and told PC Hartley about Frank rushing off to follow the lead to Ireland.

259

"PC Hartley has contacted the Gardai in Galway and told them to look out for Wayne. Are you sure you can't remember the address that your husband has gone to?"

Doris wiped her eye and shook her head:

"It were Ocht, Oct something."

She shook her head sadly.

"I should have written it down, but we never thought. Frank just wanted to get off there and then and find him."

WPC Harrison smiled:

"Why don't you go home and have a nice cup of tea. Mrs Higginbotham. He'll turn up don't you worry. At least we know he's alive and well, even if he is leading us a merry dance."

The young policewoman ushered the sisters out of the station and watched them walk away, arm in arm back towards the High Street.

She turned and went back into the office where PC Hartley was studying the Daily Mirror's racing page:

"Well did you ring'em?" She demanded.

PC Hartley looked up, his expression one of contemptuous disbelief:

"Oh aye, course I did." He replied sarcastically.

"Hello Mick, it's PC Hartley in Shepton, England. There's an eleven year old runaway boy heading your way. He's going to a village called Oct sommat. Keep your eye out. Do you think I'm daft? If I ring 'em wi'that they certainly will. I can see 'em now, rolling around saying: "Hey Mick have you heard this one...and they call the Irish thick." No you listen to me and mark my words well. There is no way that kid would have gotten all the way to Ireland. He didn't have enough money, he didn't have a passport and as for the way security is now. No, no way. I tell you I'll eat my hat if that's where he's found."

He rocked back on his chair with his arms behind his head:

"I bet you a pound to a penny that"….CRASH…the chair leg snapped depositing the rotund constable in an undignified heap on the floor.

"Blast!" He shouted as other officers passing the office back room laughed.

WPC Harrison couldn't help giggling.

"That never happens in the Sweeny!" She laughed.

PC Hartley stood up dusted himself off and grunted.

"Humph! Anyway as I was saying…"

He picked up the broken chair and examined the leg as he spoke, shaking his head at the unfairness of it all and wondering why such things only ever happened to him.

WPC Harrison sat down on the remaining good chair: "Well?"

PC Hartley threw the remnants of the chair into a corner:

"Bloody rubbish." He muttered.

"You were saying, about Wayne Higginbotham?" WPC Harrison prompted with more than a hint of exasperation.

"Oh, aye….well I bet you a tenner, he's still in London. I did ring the Met earlier on and gave them a description."

WPC Harrison shook her head and then picked up a pencil. She put it to her mouth, thought for a minute and then waved it at her colleague.

"Something worries me, you know?" She said, her forehead ridged in a frown.

"What?"

PC Hartley plonked himself on the corner of the table that they used as a desk.

"Don't break the table now!" WPC Harrison laughed. Hartley jumped back and glowered at the policewoman.

"I'm not that heavy you know. It's just that that chair was bust already."

He blustered as his cheeks reddened.

WPC Harrison snorted:

"Anyway, doesn't it worry you that the Father has suddenly run off to the Republic of Ireland?"

PC Hartley looked blank:

"No, why?"

WPC Harrison leaned forward and stubbed the end of the pencil on the table:

"What if this Ireland lead is a red herring? What if he's done the kid in?

What's the current extradition status with the Republic?"

PC Hartley's mouth dropped open:

"You don't think……..""

WPC Harrison put the blunt end of the pencil back to her lips and nodded knowingly :

"Aye…I'm beginning to think, only a hint mind, but we just might just have a murder case on our hands. Anyway, I need some lunch."

It was another two and a half hours before Elizabeth's Ford finally entered the small town of Oughterard:

"We'd better find somewhere to stay." Elizabeth remarked; her voice almost a drawl as tiredness overcame her. The sun was already lying low in the western sky, despite the long summer evening.

"We'll try that Guest house over there. They may be able to tell us where this "Old Barn" is."

Frank agreed.

"Let's just hope he managed to get here, one way, or another."

The first Guest house Frank and Elizabeth tried: "The Corrib View," was full. Oughterard being a very popular tourist haunt, particularly for fishermen, who find Lough Corrib to be one of the finest fishing grounds in Ireland. The woman on the reception desk directed Frank and Elizabeth to a small "bed and breakfast," which only had one room available, but they decided to take it anyway. They put their bags in the Spartan room while the owner of the house took a phone call

"I'll sleep on the chair." Frank declared, looking at the small bed with more than an amount of trepidation.

Elizabeth laughed:

"Oh, what a disappointment!"

Then seeing the embarrassment etched all over Frank's face, she gently squeezed his hand:

"I'm only kidding. You're a proper gentleman, Mr Higginbotham."

The owner reappeared as the couple emerged from the room:

"Would the room be alright for the two of you?" She asked, a suspicious gleam in her eye as she saw the awkwardness in the way the couple were behaving. She already suspected that Elizabeth and Frank were a runaway couple, having an illicit affair and hiding from their respective spouses. Well, that's how things were now in England what with all the divorce and the contraception and the free love and so on. Why, she'd even heard about wife swapping parties in some posh parts, where husbands put their car keys into a dish and the women took pot-luck as to who took them home. Shameful!

"That's what you get in heathen, Protestant countries." She had thought to herself, thanking goodness that she lived in God fearing Ireland."

She sniffed, somewhat contemptuously.

"Fine, fine." Elizabeth smiled:

"You couldn't do me a favour could you?"

Mrs Hanlon, for that was the owner's name, nearly had a heart attack. What were these immoral scoundrels going to ask of her? Whatever it was, she would have no part in their sinful perversions:

"Could you tell me where I might find the "Old Barn?" I'm looking for a Mr and Mrs. O'Malley." Elizabeth asked sweetly.

Mrs Hanlon crossed herself and heaved a huge sigh of relief:

"Oh Jaysus, thank goodness, yes, of course," She laughed.

Elizabeth wondered what she had said that had caused the woman to be so relieved, but quickly forgot about such concerns when the woman told her than John and Molly O'Malley lived no more than two hundred yards away. Elizabeth and Frank looked at one another and nodded a silent agreement:

"We may be a little late." Elizabeth gasped as she and Frank bundled towards the door.

All feelings of fatigue were forgotten as a flood of adrenalin burst into their systems.

Mrs Hanlon looked surprised:

"What? You're going out now? But you've not even had a cup of tea yet and nothing to eat at all. And it's nearly nine o'clock. The key's under the mat by the way, just in case you are late."

Frank shouted a quick "Ok" as the pair swiftly disappeared along the street.

"Strange folk, the English."

Mrs Hanlon muttered as she ambled back into her kitchen.

"Very strange folk."

30

The sound of the phone ringing was absolutely the last thing that Terri Thorne wanted to hear. She tried to ignore it at first, but it wouldn't go away. She put her throbbing head under the pillow, which seemed to deaden the sound at first but then the incessant ringing pierced the foam and struck right to the core of her brain.

"Arrrgh" She screamed as she threw the pillow onto the floor, tossed back her sheet and climbed out of bed.

Terri had spent the previous evening and the early hours of the current morning, celebrating her success in the audition; success that would see her going off to start a new life in Hollywood.

"Urrgh," she grunted as the foul taste in her mouth registered on her taste buds:

"Never again!"

She moaned as she found a silk kimono, that was untidily curled up on the floor and she pulled it on.

The phone continued to ring.

"Alright already." She bellowed:

"I'm coming, dammit! Jaysus, Son of Mary, don't these people know when a phone just ain't gonna be answered?"

She padded across her bedroom, avoiding the detritus of the previous evening, her clothes, commencing with the last things she took off, her underwear, leading to her T shirt, which was rolled up, on the couch, by the phone.

She glanced blearily at the clock on the wall.

"9:30...who rings at goddam 9:30 in the morning." She groaned.

She picked up the phone.

"Oh Katie...hi." She croaked, trying to overcome the sudden feeling of nausea and sound enthusiastic about hearing from her youngest sister, back home.

"How are ya? ...God, news travels fast. Did Colm tell you?"

The voice on the other end of the phone sounded taken aback.

Terri snorted:

"About the audition you eejit....I got the part. I'm going to L.A. next week.

Yeah, L.A."

She flopped onto the couch and propped the phone between her shoulder and her chin, while she lit a cigarette.

"Yes, The L.A. as in Los Angeles, California, you know, like California, USA...you know, Hollywood, fame, fortune... stardom! God don't you know anything in that backwater."

She shook her head disappointedly at her youngest sibling's apparent lack of amazement and her voice betrayed her impatience and indignation at what she perceived as a lack of interest.

"Yes kiddo, you're going to have a movie star as a big sister. I thought Colm must have rung and told you, last night. I told him straight away, mind you, I'm going to have to get a loan off him for the flight though. I'm stony broke."

Colm O'Brien was the girls' big brother, who had lived in New York for a number of years and who ran a bar in Manhattan. He had provided Terri's funds and her first job when she had arrived penniless in America, eleven years earlier.

"Anyway if you're not ringing to congratulate your beautiful and soon to be extremely rich and famous big sister, then why the hell are you ringing at this ungodly hour?"

There was something about Katie's voice that had worried Terri, even through the fog of her hangover.

Katie had always been her favourite but she had only been six when Terri had urgently left Ireland for London. She was certainly the only one of her siblings that she kept in regular touch with now, except for Colm, of course, and her younger brother Liam who had only recently arrived in the United States.

"It's not Daideo is it? Is he Ok?"

Terri's head was clearing rapidly, something was obviously wrong back home, but Katie was having difficulty articulating exactly what it was:

"So our Molly arrived, yes, this morning, OK, and there was an English kid with her, yes and ……..."

Terri Thorne who had been very white from the effects of her hangover, suddenly went what Procul Harum in the Sixties, would have described as "A whiter shade of pale."

Her mouth dropped open and she dropped the cigarette on the couch. She then dropped the phone as she moved rapidly to stop the couch catching fire. She stubbed the cigarette out in an ashtray on a table positioned by the couch and put the phone back to her ear.

"Tell me this isn't some kind of sick joke, Katie?" Terri whispered, softly and a touch threateningly.

"He's really there, really, really there?"

She started to sob.

Theresa O'Brien, who had been calling herself Terri Thorne since she had arrived in New York all those years earlier, was, for once, lost for words. She had always called herself Terri; the Thorne was an abbreviation of her mother's maiden name: "Thornton." She had felt that Terri Thorne would be a better stage name than Theresa O'Brien.

She put the phone down, after telling Katie had said that she would ring her back later, when she had recovered her composure. She cried for an hour and then she was violently sick.

Some two hours after Katie had phoned; Terri picked up the receiver again and dialled a number:

"Colm? No, I want to speak to Colm O'Brien please. Yes, it's Terri, his sister. Oh, Hi Liam, look get Colm would you? It's urgent, very urgent." Terri cradled the phone for a moment while she nervously lit another cigarette:

"Oh hi Colm, look, it's Terri…. oh yeah, very sober now… …I know you're going to be pissed, but I need to borrow the money for another flight….no Colm listen, please, this is real important. I've got to get home……to Ireland you eejit."

Terri held the phone away from her ear as a torrent of expletives exploded down the line:

"I know, I know Colm but…..no Colm listen……..Colm listen to me."

Terri was now shouting:

"Colm, ye're not going to believe this, but your nephew is at Pop's right now……No, not one of Siobhan's sons, you eejit….mine…… Yes, my son……..yes, exactly……I'll see you in less than an hour Ok?

Terri replaced the receiver and sighed heavily.

She walked back into her bedroom and pulled an old holdall out of the wardrobe.

"Great timing kid!" She muttered under her breath.

"Great timing!"

31

Katie O'Brien poured tea from a large brown teapot into three mugs:

Are you sure you're OK with tea, Michael?" She asked the curly haired youngster sitting at the kitchen table.

"Yes, thank you." Wayne replied, a little shyly.

Katie was quite pretty and at 17, only six years older than him. She smiled brightly:

"You'll be having none of this though!"

She poured a small amount of whiskey into one of the mugs, which she then pushed along the table, to where Tom Mick a John O'Brien was sitting, staring intently at the boy.

Molly picked up the other mug:

"Katie, would you be taking Patsy for a walk, for a while?"

Molly asked her younger sibling.

"Sure!" Katie responded with a grin:

"We'll leave you with the prodigal for a while. Be nice to him Daideo."

Wayne felt somewhat uneasy at the way the old man, his real, actual, live grandfather was looking at him. He wanted to stare back at him. He wanted to see if his Granddad's eyes were the same as his, if he smiled in the same way, if he had the same hair and the same mouth and chin.

Wayne wanted to see if he could see anything of himself in the old man, but he was just too shy. He had, however, already carefully examined his Grandfather's ears. They were rather large and they did stick out somewhat perpendicularly from his head, so that was encouraging. However, Wayne was slightly disappointed to see that neither of Daideo's ears was, in the slightest bit, pointed.

When the old man finally spoke again, Wayne couldn't understand a single word he said. It sounded like he was speaking in a foreign language. Then, suddenly Wayne realised that it was a foreign language: Gaelic.

Molly answered her Father in the same tongue, looked a touch embarrassed and shook her head.

Wayne noticed that a word that sounded like "the fire" had been repeated a number of times. He looked at the huge hearth where a peat fire glowed brightly. Perhaps they thought he wasn't warm enough. It was the way that Molly sat down and looked at him pityingly that told him he was going to be told something really serious. The fact that she reached across the table and gently took his hand confirmed it. The only time Doris did anything like this was when a relative, or a favourite pet had died. Wayne steeled himself for bad news. He noticed his grandfather had stopped looking at him and was now staring intently into his mug of whiskey-laced tea.

"Oh no" he thought, silently: "She's going to tell me my mother's dead and that she just hasn't been able to bring herself to do it yet."

"Michael." Molly whispered, looking into his eyes: "There's something I haven't told you, that you should know. I could be being wrong and be making a bit of a "tater" of meself, but I don't think you do know, so if you do know don't be cross with me. "

Wayne felt his skin tingle as he braced himself for the inevitable bad news. He heard Daideo say something very sharp to Molly and then the old man glanced at him from the corner of his eye.

"Yes" He gulped.

Molly hesitated momentarily:

"Well, do you know? Did you know? You er, have….you have a twin."

Wayne stared blankly at her.

"A twin?" He repeated vacantly.

"Yes," Molly nodded. "A sister. It seems she was adopted too, but by a different family."

Wayne stared at her open-mouthed:

"The lady in London didn't say that. No-one, no-one mentioned a sister." He stammered in disbelief.

"The old lady only mentioned that my Mum had been pregnant when she came to stay with you."

His voice was choked with emotion.

"Agnes wouldn't have known that she was carrying twins." Molly whispered as she glanced back at her father.

"I have a twin." He muttered, looking towards the window.

"Your Mother was desperate to have you both adopted together, but for some reason it just didn't happen. " Molly sighed, glancing at her father again, who was nodding approvingly.

"We heard that Theresa was furious when she found out that the adoption agency had separated you both and had you farmed out to different families. She was convinced that if you ever did find her you would hate her and treat her as a total pariah."

"A what?" Wayne asked uncomprehendingly.

"It just means a bad person." Molly smiled reassuringly:

"And your Mum is anything but a bad person."

"She was being foolish to be sure, but not bad." Tom O'Brien agreed, in an accent so thick that Wayne though his English almost as incomprehensible as his Gaelic.

"Have you told the boy about the rest of the family?" Tom asked Molly. Molly nodded.

"Do you have any idea where she is?" Wayne asked.

"Who? Your Mother or your sister?"

Molly raised her eyebrows.

"My, my sister." Wayne grimaced as he said the unfamiliar alien words.

Molly shook her head:

"No, like you, they didn't tell us where they were taking her. Theresa heard some six months after you'd both gone your separate ways, that you were both fine and doing well with your respective new families. That was the last she ever heard about either of you. That was the way of it in those days. It was just after that, that Theresa, your mother, went off to America."

"Was she looking for my Dad?" Wayne asked his Aunt.

Tom O'Brien coughed and took a long draft of tea. Molly glowered at her father:

"Maybe." She whispered. "Maybe!"

The front door of the cottage burst open and Patsy charged in.

"Can I have a drink Ma?" He gasped, panting from some huge childish exertion.

Katie stood at the door, obviously curious about the events taking place inside.

"Of course you can my fine young warrior!" Molly laughed, grabbing her son playfully by the arm. She looked at the shocked youngster sat at the table:

"Katie, why don't you show Michael around the place a little?" Molly asked her sister:

"I'm sure the boy needs a walk, after all that time in the car and it will be nice for him to see where his mother grew up."

"Sure." Katie replied.

Wayne stood, smiled weakly at his Aunt and Grandfather, turned and walked slowly out of the cottage. It seemed as though a great burden had been placed on his shoulders.

"What do you think of our bit of old Ireland then, Michael?" Katie asked; a hint of mischief in her voice.

"Have you ever been over here before?"

A few paces took them to the edge of a small rise, from where Wayne was sure he could see at least a hundred miles into the distance. A rolling patchwork of fields fell away from the hill upon which his grandfather's farm was built and tumbled down to an immense, shimmering silver lake, dotted with innumerable tree bearing islands. The sun poked through from behind a cloud, and the lake turned from shimmering silver, to a vivid Caribbean blue. Swallows and swifts darted around the sky and a black and white martin chirped noisily as it emerged from a gap in an old outbuildings roof:

"No, never. I've never been out of England before." Wayne replied.

"Cept Scotland, I went there once. What's that huge Lake called, Katie?" Wayne asked his young Aunt.

"That's Lough Mask." Katie responded and then pointed to the huge mountains that were all around them, except for the distant far side of the Lough.

"And these are the Partry Mountains. They're some of the finest mountains in Ireland. They're not the biggest, but they are impressive aren't they?"

A buzzing noise grew quickly behind Katie and Wayne as Patsy emerged and ran past them, arms outstretched, as he pretended to be a jet fighter.

"Daggadaggadaggadagga" He shouted as he ran over the brow of the hill and disappeared as quickly as he had just materialised.

"Yes," Wayne smiled: "It's so beautiful here, so much nicer than where I live."

The mountains reminded him of a picture of the sea. They were like great rolling waves of rock caught in a single instant of time. Rising in great green mounds and breaking at the top in bare rock and tumbling shale.

Clouds, like an ocean's white foam stuck to the flat peaks.

He could not only see the nearest range, from his high vantage point, but also, behind them, the dark outlines of a larger range and through gaps, great hills beyond.

Wayne imagined that the land might actually be rolling and churning like a storm tossed ocean, but it was too slow to be detected in the short insignificant life of man.

Maybe, Wayne thought, microscopic bacteria on the surface of the sea thought that the waves were hills and mountains, because their lives were so short and the speed of their momentary existence so exaggerated, that the sea actually seemed to be solid and stationary to them. He stared at the wall-like mountain on the other side of the valley.

Is the life of man similarly exaggerated?

The sound of Katie's voice echoed in his head.

"I'm sorry?" He responded, noticing a slight exasperation in her tone.

"I said, where's that?" Katie asked.

"Where's what? Wayne answered looking confused.

"Katie laughed and shook her head:

"You really did phase out on me there didn't you? You said it was nicer than where you live and I asked where that was. I mean I know it's in England but where? Near London?"

"Oh No!" Wayne shook his head and took a deep breath of air.

The day was turning out quite warm and the suns fleeting appearances from behind swift moving, fluffy, white clouds, were getting longer and longer.

"I live in a town called Shepton, that's in Yorkshire. It's a long way from London. It's a long way from anywhere, as a matter of fact. The countryside around Shepton is beautiful, so they say, we get lots of tourists coming to the Dales, they come from as far away as Leeds and Bradford, but it's not as beautiful as this."

"If you're wanting far away from anywhere, then that's here." Katie replied: "Anywhere in England would be better than here. There's no jobs; so everyone has to leave to make a living. Daideo says the view is a very fine thing, but you can't eat it. There's nothing to do, except go to the pub. England sounds so exciting. Having said that, America sounds even better."

Wayne smiled sadly.

"Yeah. I wonder where my real Mum is. I wonder what she's doing, what she's like."

Katie smiled knowingly:

"Oh, don't worry about her. I'm sure she'll be having a whale of a time."

Katie knew exactly what Theresa O'Brien was doing, but this wasn't the right time for her to tell her new found nephew.

The couple walked over the brow of the hill and sat down in a buttercup and daisy strewn field. Sheep nibbled the lush, green grass nearby and looked dumbly up at the humans, preparing to flee if they came any closer.

"Did you know her?" Wayne asked.

"I mean you're a lot younger than she is, aren't you?"

Katie frowned and shaded her eyes from the sun:

"Yes, of course I did, I mean, of course I do, know her. She's not dead you know."

Katie cast him a furtive glance:

"But I was only about six when she left here."

She cleared her throat and decided to change the subject.

"How long have you known?"

She asked, as she mindlessly picked a daisy and threw it down the hill.

"Known what?" Wayne replied, squinting as the sun reappeared.

"That you were adopted."

Katie whispered, her eyebrows raised inquisitively.

Wayne stared at the ever-changing view of the shimmering lake. He shrugged and copied his Aunt by tearing up a buttercup. He contemplated it for a moment as though the answer to his questions might be found there. Then he tossed it down the hill.

"A few weeks." He muttered.

"A few weeks. Is that all?" Katie squealed.

"You mean you weren't even knowing that the people who you thought were yer Ma and Da, weren't?"

"No!" Wayne shrugged again, throwing another wildflower down the hill.

"Jaysus, so how did you find out? How did you find us?"

Katie asked incredulously. So Wayne once again related the story that he had already told his grandfather upon arrival, while Katie had been busy elsewhere: The tale of the careless whispers in the hospital, the immunisation card in the brass box, then the journey to London, meeting Mandy and Agnes, the trip to Ireland, the caravan and Dan O'Doherty.

"Jaysus." Katie repeated, her mouth hanging open:

"It's been a hooley of a time you've been having, that's for sure. What an adventure."

She gasped as she fell back onto the grass.

The two led in silence in the sunshine for a while, then, eventually, Katie stood up:

"Patsy!" She shouted. The boy was right down by the gated entrance to Daideo's farm, at the bottom of the track.

"I better go and get him." She grumbled.

"Come on, I'll show you a secret mountain Lough, it's up the path behind Daideo's."

She set off to run down the hill.

Wayne couldn't help but feel a little disappointed.

Somehow, despite the fact that he was looking out over the landscape that his mother had known and as impressive as it was, it didn't seem to bring her any closer to him.

Yes, he had met two of her sisters; that had been nice.

Yes, meeting Daideo had been great.

Wayne had never had a grandfather before, so meeting Tom Mick a John O'Brien, had been fantastic.

So why did he still feel so empty?

Why at this moment, looking out on the most beautiful vista he had ever seen, did he feel crushingly disappointed?

He threw another daisy down the bank then stood and followed his young Aunt.

In the distance Katie was laughing and talking to Patsy.

As he watched his Aunt and his cousin walk hand in hand in the sunshine, Wayne realised why he felt so empty inside.

He had not set out to find a nice view, nor had he intended to see the world. He had not set out to be a tourist and if he was really honest he had not imagined at any point that he might find Aunts, or Uncles, or cousins, or even Grandparents. He had risked everything to find one or two people: his real mother, or his father and he had failed to find either.

Not only that, but now he had discovered that he also had a twin sister and he had absolutely no chance of ever finding her at all.

The sun disappeared behind a single dirty black cloud and the shimmering lake below turned a dull grey colour.

In the cottage Tom O'Brien wiped his mouth on his sleeve.

"'Tis a shame, the boy's come all this way looking for his Ma and Da and we can't be helping him meet either of them, at all."

Molly walked over to the window and smiled.

"He's found two Aunts, his Grandfather and he's seen where his Ma was raised." She sighed.

"It could've been an awful lot less."

The old man nodded:

"What are you going to do with him now? His people will be worried."

Molly turned away from the window.

"John was going to ring the police in this Shepton place, you know, to see if he's been reported missing and so on. When

I get home we'll see how things are and how we're going to get him back home to England."

Tom Mick a John O'Brien nodded sagely:

"He's knowing where we are now. If his parents will allow it, he could come back and see us, maybe even stay once in a while."

Molly cut a loaf of bread into slices and began to lather them with soft, creamy white butter.

"I would doubt they'll be doing that. People that adopt children don't usually like contact with the real family. Just in case they might be for taking 'em back. It's understandable really; they want the child to look at them as the real Ma and Da. It would be a nice thought though."

Lunch was a quiet affair: Piles of sandwiches, with thick slices of ham and cheese and even thicker brown tea. The conversation was light and concerned the wider family and their doings.

Once everyone had finished, Molly and Katie cleared the table, while Tom O'Brien regaled his grandsons with tales of high adventure and legends of local characters:

"Now Granuaille, she was a mighty pirate Queen, a fierce woman who even faced up to Queen Elizabeth of England in her own capital, London, itself."

The cottage kitchen had been a recent addition to the house. It contained a sink unit, a Calor-gas oven and a cupboard. A curtain separated it from the main room, which Katie drew as soon as all the dishes had been carried through. Katie elected to wash the dishes while Molly picked up a tea towel.

"You decided not to tell Daideo last night then?" Molly asked her youngest sister, barely getting above a whisper so that her father and the boys couldn't hear.

"No." Katie hissed in response: "He was asleep by the time I got back from the pub."

Molly nodded:

"I'd just hoped to be making it less of a shock for him, he's getting on you know."

"I know." Katie grimaced. She took a deep breath and turned to her sister:

"I suppose you saying that makes me think there's something I ought to be telling you."

Molly scowled:

"What?" She whispered impatiently.

Katie shifted uneasily and avoided her sister's inquisitive glare.

"Maybe Michael isn't the only surprise Daideo's going to be having this week."

"What do you mean?" Molly looked aghast.

"Jaysus, Katie you're not, are you?"

Molly glanced down at Katie's belly.

"Jaysus, no!" Katie whispered indignantly.

She looked her older sister right in the eye.

"I know you haven't been speaking to our Theresa for many years, Molly, but I have. When you rang last night, well, I just had to ring and tell her."

Molly blanched:

"Theresa knows? She knows about Michael? Is she coming home?"

Katie shrugged:

"I've no idea. She just burst into tears and said she'd ring me back. She never did, of course."

Molly O'Malley shook her head:

"She's no heart, that one. I for one would be betting she doesn't come home."

Katie shrugged:

"Well, she knows now. It's up to her I suppose."

Molly grabbed her sister by the shoulders:

"Whatever you do don't mention it to the boy, or Daideo. I wouldn't want to be breaking either of their hearts."

All too soon, Molly approached Wayne as he sat alone on the cottage's small garden wall.

"Admiring the view again are you?" She asked jovially.

"I'm afraid it's time to go home, Michael."

"Back to Oughterard?" Wayne sighed.

Molly nodded and put her arm around his shoulder:

"And then back to England, young man. We really must get you sorted out!" She said with a pained expression.

"It's not right that your people will be worrying themselves to death over there. I'm sure there will be other times when you can come to your Daideo's."

Wayne smiled sadly:

"Yes, Aunt Molly. It's been fantastic to meet him and Aunty Katie. It's been even more fantastic to see all this."

He waved his hand at the panorama spread out before them.

"And thanks for showing me the secret lake Katie. It was a bit spooky though."

Katie laughed:

"Ah sure, that's only a mist that gets stuck under the caldera. It's always like that, even on a sunny day."

Wayne hadn't a clue what she was talking about but he nodded knowledgably all the same.

Tom Mick a John O'Brien gave Patsy a big hug before standing back and smiling sadly at Wayne:

"It's been good to be seeing you, Michael." He stated gruffly:

"I hope you'll be coming back soon."

Wayne smiled and nodded:

"I hope so too, thanks for everything."

Tom Mick a John O'Brien hugged his long lost grandson and wiped away a tear.

"Be taking care of yourself Lad." He said:

"I can go to me grave a little happier knowing you've turned out a fine boy. May the road rise with you!"

"Bye Daideo" Patsy shrilled from the open back window of the Austin as Molly turned to leave.

Katie waved furiously from the door of the cottage as the car rolled slowly down the track towards the gate.

It was about a mile further down the lane that Molly had to slow down behind a man walking slowly, seemingly totally unconcerned, right in the middle of the road.

"Now who would be walking right in the middle of the road like that, like a total eejit." She grumbled.

The man turned and smiled at the car. He was quite a thick set man, wearing an old tweed sports jacket and a farmer's tweed flat cap:

"Hello there, would that be Molly O'Brien?" He bellowed.

Molly wound down her window:

"Dan Joyce, you're a long way from home are you not? How are you?"

The car rumbled alongside the man who had to break into a half trot to keep up.

"I am well and I am a long way from home, you're right about that. My old bike had a puncture." The man laughed:

"I was hoping ye'd be giving me a lift in that fine posh shiny motor car of yours. Just as far as the crossroads in the village would be a great kindness."

Molly laughed and stopped the car.

"Sure Dan, as ye're related. Climb in."

Dan Joyce ran around the back of the car and climbed in through the front passenger door.

"Dan is a third cousin of me mother's. Her mother was a Joyce. That would mean he's related to you, Michael" Molly explained:

"He lives up in the hills over towards Westport."

Dan thanked Molly as he settled into the passenger seat and then turned towards the boys on the back seat:

"Hello Patsy," he said with a grin and then he turned to Wayne:

"And who would this fine young fellow be? I don't think we've met."

Molly laughed:

"He's a bit of a surprise, this young man is our Theresa's long lost son, all the way from England."

Dan nodded knowingly.

"Theresa's boy is it? And how old would you be, young fella?"

"Eleven." Wayne whispered shyly.

"Ah, yes, I thought you would be, so I did."

The first things that Wayne had noticed about Dan Joyce were his piercing green eyes. They had seemed to look straight into Wayne's head, almost as if he could see what he was thinking. They were warm eyes, kind eyes, surrounded by laughter lines and they seemed to emanate a nice warm, cosy feeling. Wayne had then noticed Dan's ruddy, cheerful, if unshaven face, he also noticed the curly wiry grey hair sticking out from under Dan's cap.

What had taken the breath right out of his Wayne's lungs, however, were Dan Joyce's ears.

Like Wayne's Grandfather's, they were large and stuck out from the side of his head, almost at right angles, but unlike Daideo's or anyone else he had ever met, Dan Joyce's ears were distinctly pointed.

Pointed, like Mr. Spock's,

Pointed, like an elf's,

Pointed, just like his own.

32

The afternoon and evening of Thursday the 14th of August was the most miserable period of time Father James Malone had ever experienced in his life.

He had been forced to stay in Finool, while the Gardai took Fr Callaghan's body down from the ceiling and he had been questioned at length by the officer on duty, about the dead priest.

Naturally, Fr Malone made no reference to the "Sacred Order of St Gregory," Fr Pizarro, or Fr Burke. He did inform the officer that Fr Callaghan had been depressed and in his opinion, had been drinking far too much.

The officer seemed to think that might have been a reasonable cause of suicide. The corpse did reek of drink. But wasn't it an unusual thing for a Catholic Priest to be going and committing suicide?

Tom Lydon drove Fr Malone back to Finaan and regaled him with a multitude of anecdotes about good old Father Dermot.

Once back in the village, Fr Malone climbed out of the car, thanked the gard and then stood transfixed outside the old Rectory. Eventually, he took a deep breath and walked in.

Mrs Dolan was just crossing the hall towards the kitchen:

"Hello Father, I wasn't expecting you back so soon." She twittered.

"Would you be liking a nice cup of tea? I was just going to make one."

Fr Malone shook his head:

"Er no, no thanks Mrs Dolan. Look, I have some bad news, I'm afraid."

Mrs Dolan stopped dead in her tracks and looked at him expectantly.

Fr Malone gulped:

"You'd better come into the drawing room and sit down."

The woman did as she was told. The couple entered the drawing room and Mrs. Dolan sat down, while Fr Malone helped himself to a large glass of Fr Callaghan's best whiskey. Mrs Dolan raised her eyebrows in surprise and even more so when Fr Malone knocked the entire tumbler of whiskey back in one quick gulp and then poured himself another.

"I don't like to be interfering Father, but isn't that Father Callaghan's whiskey?" She asked nervously.

Fr Malone nodded affirmatively.

"Is Father Burke here? Or that Spaniard?" James asked brusquely, his lip twisting as he almost spat the word: "Spaniard."

Mrs Dolan shook her head:

"No Father, they're both out about their business and Father Callaghan is in Finool, I think." She added helpfully.

Fr James Malone wiped his forehead and then rubbed his eyes:

"That's just it Mrs Dolan. I'm afraid he isn't. He isn't anywhere, anymore. Father Callaghan is no longer with us."

Mrs Dolan stared uncomprehendingly at the young Priest:

"But I saw him myself this morning, so I did. He was on top of the world. Sure, as I served him his breakfast he said to me that he felt great. He said he was going to do something that he should have done a long time ago. I asked him what he meant, but he said I'd know soon enough."

She paused and thought for a minute, while Fr Malone took another large swig of the dead man's whiskey.

"What do you mean he's no longer with us? Has there been some kind of accident?"

Father Malone nodded gravely.

"Father Callaghan has been found dead in the church at Finool." He said slowly and deliberately.

Mrs Dolan went white and her mouth dropped open.

"Dead?" She gasped:

"How, Father?"

Father Malone bit his lip:

"It seems he was depressed, very depressed. It seems he took his own life."

Mrs Dolan crossed herself:

"Holy Mother!" She exclaimed:

"I would never have thought it. He seemed like a man with a mission this morning. I would never have guessed in a million years that it would be to go and be doing himself in. Well I never!" She crossed herself again for good luck:

"I'll be making that tea now Father. You'll be wanting a nice cup of tea, would be my guess."

She bustled out of the room.

Father James Malone slumped into the cosy armchair that Fr Dermot Callaghan had usually occupied. He took a sip of whiskey, put the glass on a coffee table and then closed his eyes. Thoughts tumbled in his mind like washing in a spin dryer.

What had she meant "a man with a mission?"

How had he decided to make right his mistake of long ago?

Had he decided to "blow the whistle" on the "Order?"

Had he decided to take matters into his own hands?

If so, had it cost him his life?

Or, was it the case that old Father Callaghan could not cope with the truth any longer, now that he had confessed his sins?

How had it all come to this?

"Jaysus, I know nobody said it was going to be easy, but how hard does it have to be?"

Fr Malone had rocked forward and was holding his head in his hands when his last question, spoken out-loud, was answered.

"As easy as Our Lord Jesus Christ chooses to make it, James. Still talking to yourself, I see."

Father Burke's pompous tones broke the young Priest's meditation. He opened his eyes, Father Burke stood before him, a sad look on his long face:

"I have just heard the sad and terrible news. I will inform his next of kin and the Bishop, of course. Such a terrible business. Such a shock."

Fr Malone glowered at him:

"What?" He gasped.

Fr Burke's eyes did not flicker, nor did his expression betray any sign of the incongruity of his behaviour.

"Father Callaghan's untimely death is a great shock to all of us. Such a tragic waste. It is vital that we pull together now, in the light of this, unfortunate tragedy. I know you were close to him, James. You have my deepest sympathies."

Fr Malone gaped at the figure before him.

"I...I..." he began to speak, but Fr Burke held up his hand:

"No, I understand James. All of this must be very traumatic for you. If you need to talk to me, please feel free, any time."

He turned and walked towards the drawing room door.

"By the way James, do go easy on Father Callaghan's whiskey. We wouldn't want you to start on the same downhill path, now would we?"

For just an instant there was the intimation of a threat in Burke's syrupy voice and the faintest hint of evil in his eyes. He smiled:

"It is at such times of sadness James that the words of our Lord truly manifest themselves as being true pearls of wisdom:

"He who is not with me, is against me and he who does not gather with me, scatters."

Do not forget my son that Christ himself spent much time casting out demons, remember the parable of the "legion and the swine."

Fr Burke turned and walked out.

Late that evening as Father Malone sat at his desk in his room; he heard a soft tap on his door:

"Come in!" He muttered, almost inaudibly. Fr Pizarro entered slowly, his dark eyes down cast:

"I am sorry about Father Callaghan. May Our Lord grant him the peace in death that he craved in life."

He muttered and then crossed himself:

"It is sad whenever a man of God dies, Father. I did not agree with Father Callaghan about many things, but he was a good man at heart."

He turned to leave Malone's room:

"Even in such unfortunate circumstances, the Lord's work must continue. I am sure the late Father would have understood. Tonight at midnight my work will be begin in earnest. Tomorrow, once our work is done, I shall return to Rome and I do hope I will be able to convey to the highest authorities of the "Order" the magnitude of your service."

He bowed his head:

"Until later, Father."

He left the room and closed the door behind him.

Father Malone bit his lip.

"Well, Jimmy boy. It looks like the moment of truth is drawing near."

He whispered quietly, to no one in particular.

33

The ringing of the phone in the police station, echoed loudly throughout the reception area. An extra bell was situated on a wall behind the reception desk, although it was extremely annoying, it did make sure that no call could be missed, no matter how noisy the station was.

WPC Harrison was just emerging from the back office as the phone rang. The desk sergeant came out behind her, carrying a steaming mug of tea.

"I'll get it!" She said chirpily and picked up the receiver:

"Hello Shepton Police Station, WPC Harrison speaking. How can I help you?

Yes, why yes, we have..........

Yes that's right.....

Monday morning it seems........

Yes..........Wayne Higginbotham............

Yes, adopted in London, it seems.........

Yes, brown curly hair, freckles and er, biggish, pointed ears.....

Yes, that's him alright and where did you say you were Mr. O'Malley?

Octerhard? Could you spell that for me please......

Thanks Mr. O'Malley. We'll be in touch with his mother right away, you've made a lot of people heave a big sigh of relief, I can tell you. I believe his father is on is way to you, right now though......

Yes, set off this morning, with one of Wayne's teachers.....

Yes, someone in London gave them your address, which is how Wayne found you........yes that's right

Tonight I would think....

Yes………..

Thanks Mr O'Malley. Goodbye.

WPC Harrison swaggered into the back office:

"Constable Hartley. I've just had a major lead in The Wayne Higginbotham case." She stated, hardly able to contain her glee.

PC Hartley who was in the middle of his lunch, spluttered half a mouthful of sandwich all over his desk:

"A body? Have they found a body?"

WPC Harrison looked grave:

"Yes, sort of." She sighed, as she slumped onto a chair

"What do you mean, sort of?"

PC Hartley spat out more Ham sandwich.

"Well they have a found a body, but it's not that as concerns me." She said, unable to prevent a small grin cracking at the side of her mouth.

"Whaddya mean?" Hartley asked, horrified, his mouth agape and his eyes almost popping out of his skull.

"Well….." WPC Harrison drew out the word:

"I was wrong about him being murdered. The boy is fine. Very much alive, in fact, but what concerns me, is which hat are you going to eat first, the flat cap, or the helmet. I mean that helmet would take some chewing. The boy is in Ireland. The far west of Ireland!"

It was dark by the time Elizabeth Ball and Frank Higginbotham knocked on the front door of The Old Barn, in Oughterard.

"Nice house." Elizabeth commented as they waited for an answer.

"Aye." Frank agreed

Someone inside came bounding up to the door, it swung open and an anxious looking man gasped:

"Mr Higginbotham?"

Frank stepped back and nodded:

"Aye!" He said, totally taken aback: "But how............"

"Come in, come in."

The man beckoned the couple inside and closed the door.

"Come through" he said, taking them through into the kitchen.

"I'm Johnny O'Malley and you must be Michael, I'm sorry, Wayne's teacher?"

He held out his hand towards Elizabeth, who accepted it with an expression of utter bewilderment.

"Welcome to Oughterard." John intoned, removed his hand and repeated the gesture to Frank.

"And you must be Mr Higginbotham, Wayne's father?"

"How on earth do you know who we are?" Elizabeth asked.

John had turned to switch on the electric kettle.

"Ah there's no mystery in it." He said, turning back towards her.

"Young Michael, or Wayne as I believe you know him, arrived late last night and I phoned the police in Shepton this morning. Wayne told us where he was from. They said you were on your way."

Frank still appearing bewildered, looked around the kitchen:

"Is Wayne here?" He asked.

John shook his head and suddenly looked very worried.

"I'm afraid he's not. Look, we didn't mean any offence, but my wife thought he should meet his grandda, after coming all this way. You know, he came to find his Ma and stuff and she's not here. Molly thought meeting his grandda would make up for it a bit. She took him up to Mayo this morning."

Frank looked at Elizabeth, who was visibly tiring in front of his eyes.

"When were you expecting them back?" Frank asked.

John squirmed.

"Now that's just the thing. I was expecting them back hours ago."

Elizabeth slumped on to a chair and put her head in her hands. The two men turned to her.

"It's Ok, it's Ok." She said with a note of embarrassment, looking up at the two gaping men.

"It's just been the most incredible 24 hours. I've never driven so far in my life and after going to London and back last night, I just can't even start to think straight."

Frank put his hand reassuringly on her shoulder.

"Can you not ring the Grandad?" Elizabeth asked, as the kettle switched itself off and John turned to make tea.

"He hasn't got a phone up at the house, but I rang my sister in law, who has a part time job at a pub near Tom's house and she said they'd set off hours ago."

He passed mugs of hot steaming beverage to Frank and Elizabeth:

"Milk and sugar are on the table if you'd like to be helping yourselves. I must say I've been itching to set off up the road, but I knew you were coming, so I felt I ought to wait."

"What about the police?" Elizabeth asked, the tone of her voice betraying her acute disappointment. She couldn't help it. They had come so far with little expectation, but John's greeting at the door had convinced both her and Frank that they had found Wayne, that he was going to be sat inside waiting for them. Now, her high hopes had been dashed again.

John sighed.

"If there's been an accident they'll be in touch, but Molly is a good driver and she knows the road to Tom's, Michael's grand da, like the back of her hand."

He glanced at Frank:

"I'm sorry, Wayne's grand da." He corrected himself with a shake of the head.

"Himself turning up like that out of the blue, it was quite a shock I can tell you."

291

Elizabeth looked at Frank and grimaced:

"I'm sorry Frank, I'm going to have to go and lie down. I don't think I can go on tonight. I'm dead on my feet."

Frank squeezed her shoulder.

"I know. Thanks for getting me here." He smiled:

"We'll find him, don't you worry. We're very warm now. Very warm."

"Would you like to be ringing home the pair of ye? To let your people know you're here safe and sound as it were." John suggested helpfully.

Both eagerly agreed. Elizabeth went first and while she was on the phone, John asked Frank if he was prepared to drive up to Mayo with him.

Frank agreed, despite being shattered himself.

"If we're so close, it'd be daft to wait until morning to find out if owt's happened to him." He stated bleakly.

His own phone call home, to Stanley Houghton-Hughes, was extremely brief. Margaret was staying at Doris' house during Frank's absence. Stanley agreed to pop around with the news that they were very close to finding Wayne, there and then, despite the lateness of the hour.

As he put the phone down, Elizabeth stood:

"John tells me that you're going up to Mayo to try and find out what's happened?" She asked. Frank nodded:

"Aye."

"Please forgive me Frank, but I couldn't get back into a car tonight. I know it sounds stupid to give up now after coming so far but I just couldn't."

She began to sob.

Frank put his arm around her, obviously embarrassed.

"It's possible that they've stopped off on the way back and Molly has lost track of the time." John chipped in, doing his best to sound optimistic.

"You get yourself off to bed." Frank whispered to Elizabeth.

"Wayne will be here to see you in the morning."

He looked at John hopefully.

John smiled back, but his eyes betrayed the fact that he was very, very worried indeed.

34

"Tis a great, great kindness that you're doing me, Molly O'Brien. You're a queen amongst women. So you are."

Dan Joyce's chitchat was infectiously cheerful.

"It's Molly O'Malley, now Dan, you know. I got married." Molly chided her passenger with a grin and feigned annoyance.

"Now less of your blarney, or I'll be dropping you off right here, instead of taking you all the way home."

"Are you sure that it's no trouble at all?" Dan asked.

Molly shook her head.

"No, of course not. I can take the Westport road back down home, once I've dropped you off."

She couldn't help feeling, deep down inside, however, that it was a lot of trouble. The drive from Tourmakeady up over the mountains, past the remote farm where Dan lived, was probably adding at least fifty miles or so to their journey and Patsy had started to whine about being hungry. Even so, she just didn't feel that she could say no to the jocular individual, who she had known since childhood.

It was strange though. Even though she had known Dan since she was about six, he never seemed to get any older. It was also weird that the family link had never been mentioned by anyone but Dan.

Daideo had once warned her that Dan Joyce was "away with the fairies." But he was jovial company and it just seemed right that she should take him all the way home.

Wayne sat silently in the back of the car, wondering what it was about this strange Irishman that worried him, or made him feel strange, he wasn't quite sure how he felt about him.

The passing scenery was stupendous, especially once the Maxi began to struggle up the mountain road above Lough Mask and the splendour of the colossal lake began to emerge back down below them.

Wayne, however, just couldn't stop staring at Dan's ears. Eventually Dan turned in his seat:

"Would you be looking at that" He stated breathlessly as the view of the lake filled the entire back window of the car.

"Tis a fine, fine sight."

He looked away from the view and turned his bright green eyes on Wayne:

"And where would ye be living now young Michael?" He asked.

"In England." Wayne replied, feeling a little bit uncomfortable as Dan's eyes probed him.

"Ah, across the wide water." Dan nodded:

"And how is that beautiful mother of yours, herself?"

Wayne couldn't help but stare into Dan's eyes, which was unusual because he didn't usually make eye contact with strangers.

"I'm sorry?" He asked, his initial thought being how Dan would know Doris and wondering how on earth he could think of her as beautiful.

"Your Ma?" Dan laughed: "Have ye forgotten all about her already?"

The realisation that he meant Theresa made Wayne squirm uncomfortably in his seat.

"I, I don't know." He stammered.

Molly sighed:

"Theresa gave him up, Dan. She had him adopted almost as soon as he was born. Michael hasn't seen his Ma since he was a tiny baby."

For the first time since he had climbed into Molly's car Dan Joyce's face lost its jolly demeanour. His mouth dropped open in shock and he took a deep breath. He turned back towards Wayne:

"I'm sorry about that, lad." He whispered.

Wayne was staring at his lap, but couldn't help but draw his eyes up to meets Dan's.

As clear as if he had been wearing Frank's stereo headphones at home in Cavendish Street, Wayne heard a voice, smack bang in the middle of his head. It was so clear and sonorous, yet so unexpected:

"She should not have done that, but the ways of women are like the ways of the sea and the sky, unpredictable. Welcome home, my son." The voice said.

Wayne let out an audible gasp.

Are you alright there Michael?" Molly asked, turning and glancing at the boy who had gone quite, quite white.

"These roads are very twisty." She said:

"Do you want me to stop?"

"I think he's going to puke, Ma." Patsy chipped in enthusiastically.

Wayne shook his head feverishly:

"No, no, I'm fine really. I think I must have been daydreaming."

He looked at Dan who had raised his eyebrows and was smiling knowingly.

"Ah, 'tis the view, it takes the very breath away. Isn't that so Michael?"

He winked and turned away.

Wayne felt a shiver run up and down his spine. His entire body seemed to be tingling, yet he felt strangely relaxed. It was almost as though the tension that had been occupying his mind since the moment he had closed the front door of Cavendish Street behind him, on Tuesday morning, had evaporated. Maybe this was it. Maybe he was losing it. After all it had been a traumatic few weeks. At least he would have a good explanation for his actions for Doris when the time came for him to face the music.

"Sorry Mum, but I'm a lunatic. Burble, burble, burble."

Dan glanced back at him.

"Are you alright, son?"

The voice in his head asked.

Dan had not moved his lips and he was not throwing his voice like that Ray Allen bloke, the ventriloquist on the telly did.

The voice didn't even sound like Dan's. The accent was different for a start, in fact the voice had no accent and it was definitely much deeper than Dan's. Yet there was a look in his eyes that suggested that he knew what was being said.

Wayne decided to try and answer in the same way. He concentrated on Dan's eyes and said the word ***"Yes"*** as clearly as he could. The Irishman, nodded, almost imperceptibly, smiled and turned away.

"I'm hungry!" Patsy moaned.

The car had crossed the apex of the pass through the mountains by the Lough and was now winding down a mountain road into an immense, bleak valley:

"Will ye be popping in for a bite to eat?" Dan asked cordially.

Molly glanced into her mirror at the boys in the back.

"I think we better had Dan, or it'll be moaning from our Patsy all the way to Oughterard. Do you have any crisps? Tayto's? Or anything that would be keeping these boys going until we get back home?" Molly asked.

"I might, I just might at that!" Dan grinned.

By the time the car pulled up, a quarter of an hour later, in a gateway near to a small white-washed cottage, which was almost hidden in a dip by the side of the road, Wayne was convinced that he had imagined the voice.

He was certain that the pressures of the last three days had sent him totally insane. He'd just better not mention it to anyone. He'd heard about people who heard voices. They usually turned out to be a few sandwiches short of a picnic, at best; or sometimes they turned out to be mass murderers.

"Here we are at last!" Molly assured the boys:

"We'll just get a little something to eat and then we'll be on our way home as quickly as possible. We can't be staying long, Dan. John'll be worried."

"Sure, sure." Dan huffed as he clambered out of the car.

"I hope he's got Tayto's" Patsy whined. "Cheese and Onion Taytos!"

"Come on, come on."

Dan called as he walked across the road to a small gate in the wall.

Molly, Patsy and Wayne, followed the farmer through the unkempt garden and into the ramshackle little cottage.

Wayne noticed a pile of broken wind chimes by the garden wall.

The cottage was dark and full of shadows.

Dan seemed to only have a small table lamp for illumination.

"I'll bank up the fire first." He called out cheerfully:

"There's quite a nip in the air for the time of year. Make yourselves at home."

The interior of the cottage was, to say the least, somewhat Spartan.

Old newspapers and magazines were scattered haphazardly around the bare stone floor, while the only furniture seemed to be an old worn armchair, a table upon which stood an ancient T.V. and a dresser leaning against a wall. A hearth, complete with antique range, filled an entire end of the room.

Dan put a couple of turf briquettes onto the fire and poked it, so that tongues of flame soon began to lick hungrily around the fuel.

Molly sat in the old armchair and Patsy climbed on to her knee. Wayne sat on a stool near the TV.

Dan stood back and admired the now roaring fire, which sent flickering shadows dancing around the bare whitewashed stone walls.

"There!" He declared:

"Now Molly, you look awfully tired. A little nap would be doing you the power of good."

He stared at the woman who was gazing into the fire:

"I do feel incredibly sleepy all of a sudden." She yawned and shook her head:

"But we should be getting down the road, I awwwww"

She yawned again. This time Patsy joined her:

"Ah go on!" Dan laughed:

"A quick forty winks won't be hurting you at all."

He smiled at Molly who smiled back.

"You could charm the hind legs off a donkey, Dan Joyce." Molly drawled drowsily and then closed her eyes and immediately began to gently snore. Patsy snuggled down on her lap with his head on her chest and also closed his eyes.

"Tayto's" He moaned and then he too seemed to drift off into a sudden deep sleep.

Dan grinned:

"They must have been worn out, poor devils. And so now we can talk freely, young Michael O'Brien."

What Wayne found peculiar was that Dan was now talking in the same accent and tone as the voice that he had heard in his head.

Wayne scowled. His madness was obviously accelerating.

Dan turned to Wayne and laughed:

"I'll bet a pound to a penny that you weren't quite expecting to find anything like this in old Erin's Isle?"

Wayne shook his head. He had to admit that he felt a little concerned for his safety now that Molly was asleep, but he was very concerned indeed about his sanity.

Dan glanced at the sleeping mother and child as though he'd read Wayne's mind.

"Oh, they're alright." He said reassuringly:

"It's a useful little trick I learned long ago. It has granted me much needed peace and quiet, many times."

He winked at Wayne and then left the room, only to re-emerge seconds later pulling a rickety old chair. He turned the chair back towards Wayne and then straddled it, sat down and leaned on the back, like a TV cop about to begin questioning a suspect.

"So, have you worked out who I am yet?" He asked, his mouth twisted in a lop sided grin.

Wayne swallowed and frowned:

"I don't know, I really don't." He declared, hesitantly.

Wayne couldn't help staring at Dan's ears and a strange possibility began to slowly creep into his mind.

"Are we, are we related?" Wayne asked with a gulp:

"Molly said you were like part of the family."

"Ah, now, you could say that." Dan laughed:

"Go on, search your heart, my boy. Think! Look at me."

Wayne screwed up his face:

"I don't think I look like you, your eyes are green while mine are not quite green, but not blue either. You don't have any freckles, and........."

Dan nodded eagerly:

"Yes, go on, go on."

Wayne grimaced:

"I suppose, you do have the same sort of ears as me."

"And very fine ears they are too, my son. Have you ever seen anybody else with such fine looking ears perched proudly on the sides of their head?"

Wayne shook his head:

"No, I suppose not, no, no I haven't." He mumbled:

"Not in real life anyway."

"So, go on. Have another guess as to who I might be." Dan cajoled the boy.

Wayne took a deep breath:

"Are you, are you? No that would be mad, totally mad."

"What would be mad?" Dan asked; sounding to Wayne, somewhat annoyingly amused.

"You're not, you're not, by any chance, my father, are you?" Wayne suggested nervously.

Dan nodded and smiled:

"Yes, my son, I am indeed your father."

Wayne's mouth dropped open and Dan smiled sympathetically:

"Sorry, I know that wasn't the best way of introducing myself, but I couldn't think of a better way to do it. I just knew I had to see you, to talk to you, alone, as soon as I knew you were somewhere nearby."

"How did you know I was here?" Wayne asked, shaking his head in disbelief:

"No one knew I was coming. I didn't even know I was coming here myself."

His voiced was raised, almost in panic.

Wayne didn't want to admit it, but the thought of his father being a smelly, old farmer, in the filthiest, tiniest cottage he'd ever seen, did disappoint him a little.

Dan stood up, strolled over to the small, dirty, cottage window and sighed: "We have so much to talk about, you and I. I have so many questions for you and oh, so much to tell you. So much to explain, so very much! There would not be enough time for me to tell you everything, even if you stayed here all summer long, or even for several summers."

He turned to the boy and raised an amused, knowing eyebrow:

"Ah, Michael, please don't be disappointed in your ould Da."

Wayne blushed:

"I'm not, I'm not. I'm just a bit shocked, I suppose."

Dan held out his hand and raised the boy's chin so he could look into his eyes.

"I know many things, my son and I know disappointment when I see it. You have travelled far, to find out whom you really are and this is not what you had looked for and hoped for."

Wayne looked aghast:

"No, it's just that..........."

Dan held up his hand and smiled sympathetically.

"Peace, my son, be not embarrassed by the truth. Your line is not so depleted that it has yet come to this."

He walked back to the window and wiped a finger along the window ledge:

"All of this is necessary, this hovel, this decrepitude. Even so, perhaps I should dust more often, especially when I've got visitors coming."

He cast a mischievous grin in Wayne's direction.

Wayne smiled.

"There's no need, Father." He said, throwing out the last word as quickly as he could say it.

What felt really weird was that he'd hoped to find his real Mum, maybe to punish Doris, somehow; but he loved Frank, the man he'd always assumed to be his Dad and now that he'd met his real father, that fact seemed to have emerged at the front of his mind.

Wayne Higginbotham was confused.

Dan sighed:

"I can see bewilderment in your eyes, my son. I shall cut to the chase quickly, as they say. I must show you myself, as I really am, Michael. Please do not be alarmed."

Dan turned towards the boy and removed his jacket.

There was no flash of light, nor pall of smoke, yet suddenly Dan had changed.

Instead of a ruddy faced, jolly Irish farmer standing by the chair, there was now a taller man with long straight, dark hair and an ageless unlined face. The kindly emerald green eyes had not changed, nor had the pointed ears, nor even the friendly expression. Yet, the man standing in front of Wayne could not have looked any less like Dan Joyce.

He now appeared clean shaven, strong featured, handsome even, and his clothes were not now the scruffy corduroy trousers and holed woollen sweater that Dan had sported, but looked more like the sort of things that Wayne had seen in history books, the clothes someone might have worn long, long ago: A long green tunic, brown belt, loose green trousers and high boots that looked almost like brown, suede riding boots. The man's long shiny hair was held in place by a gold circlet, which he wore around his forehead.

"This is really it!" Thought Wayne:

"I'm either dreaming this and I'm going to wake up in a minute, or I'm as nutty as a bloody fruit cake."

The man who seconds earlier had been Dan Joyce, laughed:

"Don't worry, young man, I'm not a hippy. I'm not even in one of those new heavy rock groups and I can assure you that you are not losing your mind, nor, is any of this part of an idle dream."

He ruffled the boy's hair.

"The raiment I wear is seldom seen in this day and age, but it is my true apparel, for I am Aillen the last of the sons of King Fionnbharr, himself."

He took on a more solemn air and sadness crept into his eyes.

"I am the last Prince of the immortals. I am the last of the ancient, Royal line of the once mighty, Tuatha De Danaan."

He looked back at Wayne and his green eyes twinkled again.

He bowed low and courteously, like Wayne had seen people do in movies about the middle-ages, when gallant, chivalrous knights would bow in such a manner to beautiful maidens, or to Kings and Queens.

"But now that you have returned home, my son. That honour belongs to you, my young Prince."

Wayne's eyes grew large and round, like shining blue-green saucers. His mouth dropped open:

"What? You mean I'm a, a Prince?"

The man, who had been Dan, gave an affirmative shrug.

"The last Prince of a Royal Line going back many thousands of years."

Wayne Higginbotham closed his eyes and rubbed his forehead.

"I'm going to wake up any second, come on alarm clock, go now. Doris is going to wake me up. Doris is going to wake me up."

He pinched himself, hard.

"Ouch" He gasped.

Wayne Higginbotham opened his eyes.

He was still in the Spartan cottage, with its flickering, black shadows dancing on the orange, flame illuminated, walls. His Aunt Molly and Patsy snored peacefully in the old armchair and the tall medieval looking man with the long hair was still stood there, smiling down at him

"Bloody Hell!" Wayne exclaimed.

"I'm not dreaming!"

35

Doris Higginbotham was not best pleased. In fact, she was cross, very cross, well no, actually she was almost apoplectic with rage. Her face was set in a mask of fury as her sister Margaret passed her a cup of tea.

"He'll not be able to sit down for a week, I'll tell yer! I'll bloomin' well kill 'im when I get me hands on 'im. Running off to Ireland like that, the light fingered little beggar! I'll chop his fingers off, I will!"

An hour earlier Stanley Houghton –Hughes had delivered the news that Frank and Elizabeth had traced Wayne to some remote part of Ireland and that they were confident that Wayne would be accompanying them back to Yorkshire, some time the following day.

Doris had been so relieved that she had hugged her rotund, bald, brother-in-law. Stanley had been so surprised that his round spectacles had popped down to the end of his nose and his red face had puffed up to a deep embarrassed purple:

"Now, now Doris, decorum, love, decorum. I did tell you they'd find him, alive and well, didn't I? I said alive and well!" He spluttered, easing her arms from around his waist.

"Thanks for letting us know, Stanley." Doris gushed.

"Eeeh I don't know what I'd have done if owt had happened to him."

"Aye, well" Stanley had blustered:

"It's late and I've a very busy day tomorrow. Can't have the wheels of commerce grinding to a halt now, can we? Harumph! Always delighted to be the bearer of good news, I am. Aye, it's sommat that's in short supply these days and I'll tell you this for nowt, it'll be even shorter if that bloomin' idiot Wilson gets his way, now that he's back in. There'll be more three day weeks, you mark my words."

"Stanley, that's enough of your politics. Let Doris be happy!" Margaret scalded her husband, who gave a loud "harrumph" and bade the ladies goodnight.

The intervening hour, however, had seen Doris' relief and delight turn to annoyance and then to outright anger:

"I mean what the heck was he doing looking in that box anyway, Mags?"

Margaret shrugged:

"I don't know, I 'm sure love. You see that's the thing when they're not your own, I suppose. You don't know what goes on inside their heads."

Doris had glowered at Margaret. She always felt that her sister looked down on her for having been unable to conceive her own child and used it to belittle her.

"You don't allus know with your own." She had snapped, but she knew that Margaret had a point. She didn't really understand her adopted son.

Wayne had strange opinions about an awful lot of things that she found irritating and annoying. He would correct her when she related various anecdotes because she had got dates wrong, or people mixed up.

He would laugh at things that she didn't find at all funny and he read stuff that she regarded as being a total waste of time.

The most irritating thing of all was that he was useless at doing practical things, like woodwork and the sorts of things that other boys were good at, like Meccano and Lego.

All of Doris' male family line had been immensely practical men. Builders, joiners and plumbers all ran in the family.

"I just don't know how he's going to make a living." She had remarked to Frank one evening just before Wayne had disappeared.

"He might be good at art and history and all that stuff, but you can't make a living painting pretty pictures and reading books, can you?"

Frank had sighed:

"He might turn out to be a teacher, or sommat."

"Pah!" Doris had spat:

"He needs a proper job. The likes of us don't make teachers. Trevor would have got a good job. He'd have made sommat of himself."

The thing that had most annoyed Doris as she reflected on the reasons for Wayne's flight to Ireland was the supposition that he had gone in search of his real family:

"I mean are we not good enough for him?" She had moaned to Margaret. "We've done everything we can for that boy and this is how he rewards us; by throwing it right back in our faces the first chance he gets."

Margaret heaved a frustrated sigh:

"He's probably just curious, Doris. It must have been a shock for him finding out that he's adopted. How he found out is another matter altogether."

Margaret's soft words only fuelled Doris' anger:

"Shock, I'll give him shock, sneaky little beggar, rummaging around in our private papers. Shock made him steal that money did it?"

Margaret bowed her head, it was obvious to her that anything she said would be twisted by her sister and would only deepen her resentment and annoyance. It was like trying to put out a fire with paraffin.

"There's never been any thieves in my family, or in Frank's." Doris moaned.

"I can't abide them as are light fingered. I mean what was he expecting to go and find? If his mother had been heartless enough to give him up as a baby, then she certainly won't want a big, ugly, hungry eleven year old turning up on her doorstep, I can tell you that much for nowt."

In her heart, however, Doris was terrified that Wayne's real mother just possibly might welcome him with open arms. What would be even worse was the possibility that she might be younger, prettier and richer than Doris Higginbotham.

Margaret gave her older sister a long hug as she dissolved into tears:

"He's just not like us Mags." She wailed:

"He's nowt like us at all."

36

"Hail Mary mother of grace.............

Hail Mary mother of grace............

Hail Mary mother of grace............"

Father James Malone sat at his desk, in his room, his head in his hands, repeating the prayer over and over again.

It was difficult for him to believe that out there, out of the window in front of his desk, birds were singing in the evening twilight. Lush, thick green leaves were rustling in the breeze that caressed the branches of the trees in the garden.

Out there, beyond the tall, stone garden wall, people were exercising their dogs, lovers were out walking hand in hand, people were filling Finaan's pubs, swilling porter and whiskey, laughing, joking, chatting, gossiping and arguing.

Cars and Lorries were passing through the village and the drivers and passengers were totally unaware of what was happening in the unremarkable house, behind the wall, behind the screen of stunted apple trees.

Even further away; his family and friends in Dublin would be doing the things they always did on average Thursday nights: watching TV, going out, eating, sleeping, just going through the mundane routine of another ordinary weekday night.

The Earth was still turning and it was still travelling through space, just as it would tomorrow and the day after and the day after that.

Somewhere out there, God was watching all of that stuff.

Was he watching Father James Malone?

Would he help Father James Malone?

"Hail Mary mother of grace............

Hail Mary mother of grace............

Hail Mary mother of grace............"

From somewhere in the distance James heard a shout. He took a deep breath, wiped his eyes, stood and walked over to his dressing table. He ran his hand through his hair and studied the reflection in the mirror. A faint trace of a smile curled the corner of his mouth:

"Do you expect me to help you kill an innocent man?"

He heard a voice inside his head, it sounded strangely like Sean Connery's.

"No Father Malone, I expect you to die." Came a voice that sounded equally strangely like Father Pizarro's.

He remembered the first time he had met the Bishop's henchman Pizarro in the Bishop's palatial office. He remembered how he had compared the Bishop to the megalomaniac bad guy in the Bond movies, with the obligatory, white cat on his knee. James Malone's left eyebrow lifted as he turned from the mirror and the voice of Sean Connery voice filled his head again.

"Sorry Mr Pizarro and Bishop Blofeld? Your little plan to take over the world is going to have to be put on hold for a while. Who am I? The name's Malone, James Malone."

As he slammed his door behind him, however, Fr Malone's bravado seemed to evaporate all too quickly.

"Hail Mary mother of grace............." He whispered.

Father William Burke replaced the receiver of the hall telephone on its cradle and looked at his watch.

"The hospital will carry out a post mortem on poor, dear Father Dermot tomorrow. It is likely, barring complications, that the body will be released to us here on Saturday, so that he may lie in state here at home for the wake."

Mrs Dolan dabbed her eyes with her handkerchief.

"Poor dear man." She sobbed:

"I'll be going home now, Fathers. It has been a terrible, terrible day. God bless you all."

She crossed herself, blew her nose loudly and left the house.

Father Burke sighed:

"I was beginning to think that snivelling woman would never leave." He declared with a sneer. Father Pizarro almost smiled. He looked at his watch:

"I think it is time to call our reluctant apprentice, Father William." He said as he strolled towards the drawing room door.

Fr Burke nodded and shouted up the staircase:

"Father Malone. It is time!"

Burke turned to the Spanish Priest:

"Are you sure he should be involved. He is a risk, a risk that we can ill afford." He hissed.

Pizarro smiled his thin humourless smile:

"He has his purpose in the eyes of our Lord. Even if he knows not what it is."

Burke shrugged:

"I hope you know what you are doing, Father." He whispered.

The sound of a door being slammed carried down the draughty staircase. Father Malone appeared and trudged disconsolately down the stairs wearing black trousers and a navy blue, roll neck jumper.

"Good." Pizarro sniffed, while Burke eyed the young Priest suspiciously:

"You are fully prepared, Father Malone?" Burke asked.

Fr Malone lifted his eyes from the carpet just long enough to cast a withering glance in Burke's direction.

"Oh yeah, I'm ready. Well and truly ready." He almost spat out the words.

Burke glowered at him, his eyes blazing.

Pizarro held up a hand to silence the other Priests:

"My brothers, tonight we stand on the brink of a historic victory. The "Order" is convinced that this "Mickey Finn" creature is the very last of the cursed demonic horde that we have been fighting for well over a thousand years. Our triumph, the triumph of good over evil is at hand. You must listen carefully and carry out my orders to the letter, if we are to succeed and if Glory is to be ours, by the grace of Our Lord. These demons derive much power from an energy source, a stone, sacred to their kind. It is their most precious item and they always hide it in a place they believe to be safe. The demons call this thing their crock of gold, for they confuse its power with wealth."

Pizarro paused and appraised his colleagues, anticipating their surprise and delight at what he was about to say:

"I know where this monster keeps his stone and without it, his powers will be reduced to almost naught."

Pizarro's dark eyes moved from Malone to Burke and back again.

"But how? How do you know where it is?" Burke asked, looking puzzled. Pizarro glared at him impatiently:

"Fr Malone and I searched the creature's hovel while it was out. They usually hide such items near their bed, or near the hearth, the centres of spiritual strength within the home. Finn was no different. Now, if I may continue. You two will provide a distraction, while I take the stone from its hiding place. We will crash your car into a wall half a mile or so from the fiend's house. You, Father Burke will go and ask for Finn's help. Father Malone, you will feign injury. I will go over the fields and remove the stone from his hearth; while Finn is helping you both with the car. You must detain him there for as long as possible. I will then place four blessed devices, of my own, around the cottage."

He reached into a black leather bag and pulled out a crucifix: A fabulously ornate golden crucifix, the base of which had been sharpened, like a stake. The top of the crucifix appeared to be surmounted by an enormous, glittering diamond.

"There are four of these stones," Pizarro stated, as he caressed the crystal with the tips of his fingers.

"They create a Holy sanctuary, where demonic powers can not be used. The beast will not be able to shape shift, play mind games or summon any other forces of darkness. Tonight, my friends, we shall complete the work of our Lord. We shall rid Ireland of demons just as the Blessed Saint Patrick expunged it of serpents. Our names shall be blessed and venerated on high."

Pizarro turned his black eyes on to Malone and he started to laugh:

"Even those of us drawn to the Lord's work with the reluctance of the weak of mind, will be venerated."

Fr Burke joined in the laughter and slapped Fr. Malone on the back:

"Come Malone." He bellowed: "Time to be a hero."

Fr Malone stared at the black garbed Priests as they put their cloaks over their shoulders and stepped out of the house into the darkness.

Father Burke opened the passenger door of the car, bowed sycophantically and Pizarro stepped in. James climbed into the back.

Whatever else happened, Fr Malone knew that his sole mission on earth was to stop the madness that was manifest in Father Francisco Pizarro and his greasy acolyte. It was all so easy for James Bond to be a hero in the movies, the director could just yell "cut" if things went awry, but James Malone was going to have to give it a go in real life. He would stop the bad guys, even if it was to be at the cost of his own life.

37

The silver Volvo estate looked like it was in the hands of a suicidal madman as it hurtled along the dark, narrow country roads of County Galway and then into Mayo.

"I'm sorry I'm driving like a total eejit!" John O'Malley explained to his terrified looking passenger:

"But I've got to admit that I was expecting to be seeing the Maxi at some point up this road. I just don't know what Molly is doing, staying out this late."

Frank Higginbotham desperately clutched on to his seat and gasped an acknowledgement. He was used to driving on country roads; in his younger days, before Wayne had come along, he had possessed an old Ford Anglia and had toured the narrow Dales roads extensively, but he had always been a sedate driver. At points the Volvo had approached ninety miles an hour as it sped along the unlit road:

"I would only drive like this at night." John shouted by way of explanation:

"At least you can see the other fellers coming in the dark. It's the lights."

The Volvo skewed round a tight corner, tyres squealing.

Frank wondered if he was going to live long enough to ever see Wayne again. He looked at his watch, five minutes to midnight.

John knocked the stalk by his steering wheel and the Volvo turned off the main road to the loud tick-tock sound of the indicators and a noisy scrunch of gravel.

The road was bleak and dark, the Volvo's headlights struggled to illuminate much of what lay ahead and John was forced to adopt a slower pace.

There was no moon and the stars cast very little light, but Frank could make out huge looming dark shadows, outlined in what little light there was.

"Are we in a mountainous area now?" He asked.

The car was climbing steeply.

"Yes. We are in County Mayo, in the Maumturk and Partry mountains. It's where your boy's birth mother is from."

John explained as he guided the Volvo around another tight bend, tyres squealing all the more and spitting gravel in protest.

Frank, although desperately tired, found that he couldn't sleep, he was being bounced around too much for slumber to overtake him.

"What's she like?" He asked eventually.

John O'Malley glanced at the obscure figure sat next to him.

"Who?" He asked as he yanked the steering wheel and the Volvo spun like a rally car around a double hairpin bend.

"Wayne's mother?" Frank continued, eyes wide with fear, as the headlights showed another bend before what looked like a long straight downhill road.

The car successfully negotiated the bend, its tyres protesting noisily and Frank let out a long relieved sigh, as an unperturbed John scratched his head nonchalantly.

"You better not be letting Molly hear me saying this, but she was by far the catch of all the O'Brien girls, all four of them, though young Katie is going to be quite a looker, so she is."

The Volvo picked up speed along the straight and Frank was soon grabbing the base of his seat again as the road ahead disappeared into another tight bend.

"It was a strange business when she turned up at our flat in London all those years ago, you know, in the family way as she was. She was only a kid herself, sixteen at the time. Molly asked her who's it was, the baby that is. She swore it was some

American fella's. She said his name was Finn, or something, but refused to tell us his full details. All she would say was that she'd met him back in the village, that he was a young buck who'd left Ireland as a baby and was back visiting his folks in the old country, while he was based in England in the air force. Anyway, she said he'd already gone back to England, that she didn't have his address and that he knew nothing about the baby at all. So that was why she'd run away from Daideo and from Mayo and had turned up on our doorstep. It turned out the baby she was expecting was, in fact, a pair of twins and that was a surprise in itself, and then she was up and............."

"Twins?" Frank gasped incredulously as he grabbed the dashboard. The Volvo careered around a bend and seemed to defy all the known laws of physics, simply by staying on the road.

"Did they not tell you when you adopted Michael that he was one of twins?" John seemed momentarily surprised:

"But, of course, they were split up by the adoption agency."

He shook his head:

"It would have been easier for them to place one, than find a family prepared to take two, I suppose."

Frank swallowed hard.

So Wayne had a sibling that he didn't even know about, poor little devil. The Volvo started to climb a steep mountain road, still travelling at breakneck speed:

"It won't be long now." John shouted, above the noise of the screaming engine:

"We'll be finding 'em, don't you worry."

At that particular moment, it wasn't the prospect of finding Wayne that was causing Frank any worry at all.

Tom Mick a John O'Brien looked at his watch. It was after half past twelve. He rubbed his eyes and drained his whiskey glass:

"Be getting me another small one, would ye, Katie?" He asked.

Katie O'Brien acquiesced without a sound. She had been home from the pub for half an hour and had raised her father from his bed as soon as she had got in. Katie had told him how Molly, Patsy and Michael had failed to get home and that John was on his way to look for them. Katie had already telephoned the Gardai, in Westport, from the pub, Maire Duke's, to see if there had been any accidents locally. They hadn't known of anything untoward happening in the area. Somehow that hadn't been too reassuring. Mayo covered a big area.

The strangest thing that had happened had been one of the pub regulars who had driven up from Tourmakeady had reported that he had seen a red Austin Maxi driving up the mountain road to Westport, earlier on.

"I was as certain as the day is long that it was your sister Molly who was doing the driving." The man had said:

"I've been knowing her long enough and I know that she lives now in some grand place in Oughterard, so I did wonder why she was away driving in the wrong direction. There was a feller in the car with her who had the look of old Dan Joyce from up o'er the hills, but I couldn't be too sure."

Tom Mick a John O'Brien stroked his chin thoughtfully.

"So old Martin said Dan Joyce was in the car with Molly? You're sure o'that now?"

"Yes Dad!" Katie replied with more than a touch of exasperation, as she plonked the whiskey glass down on the table in front of her father.

In the distance the sound of an rapidly approaching car, crunching noisily up the rough track to the house, could be heard.

Tom Mick a John O'Brien stroked his chin some more and suddenly something clicked in his brain.

He jumped up with a shout.

"Jaysus, I've got it. I've got it, I tell ya"

Katie had opened the front door of the cottage and the headlights of the Volvo shone into the room as the car swung around in front of the house.

John O'Malley and a shaken looking Frank Higginbotham clambered stiffly out of the Volvo, Frank bent over, put his hands on his calves and gratefully sucked in several huge gulps of air.

"This is your wee man's Grandda." John explained to Frank, as a figure stormed out of the cottage pushing past the young girl who was framed in the light of the doorway:

"Come on Katie and be shutting that door behind you." The old man shouted, as he rushed over, yanked open the rear door of the Volvo and ushered her urgently into the back of the car.

John and Frank looked at one another in bewilderment:

"Tom?" John asked in bewilderment:

"Get in and drive will you, you eejit." Tom O'Brien bellowed:

"We'll do the introductions and all that malarkey later. I'll explain it on the way, but I think I'm knowing where your wife and child are. I'm sure of it, or my name isn't Tom Mick a John O'Brien."

38

"And that is the tale of the children of Lyr." Aillen, Son of Fionnbharr declared with a wave of his hand and a melancholic smile:

"But it's so sad. Why does it have such a sad ending?"
Wayne shook his head and frowned:

"Are all the stories of old Ireland as sad as that?"
Aillen laughed:

"Most of them, I'm afraid. Ireland is a very wet land; a land of bogs and puddles, pools and lakes. Some say it is because of the rain, but we who have been here long enough know that it is because of all the tears that have been cried over the years."

There was twinkle in his eye as he lifted a foot on to the chair next to him.

"Remind me to tell you about Dagda's bottomless cauldron and Lugh's mighty spear one day, oh yes and about Nuada's magnificent sword, now there was a mighty weapon that made your Excalibur look like a boy scout's little penknife."

He looked at the cottage windows:

"Ah but look, it's getting dark. I'd better be waking these good people before the search parties are sent out for them."

"No, please…Dad?"

Wayne still felt strange using that word and Aillen looked more than a little embarrassed.

"I mean, please tell me more. Not the myths and legends. Tell me what really happened back then. How old are you? Where are you really from? How do you do all this magic and stuff?"

Aillen laughed again and held up his hands.

"Well, well! I suppose you've told me about your life, where you live and the people who have cared for you. It would only be right for me to tell you something about your past, your heritage. I will tell you about the blood that rushes through your veins, young Michael, or Wayne, or whatever it is you wish to be called young Mac Aillen. I will tell you the truth of it, for there are many lies and falsehoods that have been spread maliciously about my people, about your people."

He puckered his forehead in concentration and sat down.

Wayne sat bolt upright in his chair, eagerly awaiting the story of how he came to be.

"The Tuatha de Danaan, the tribe of Dana, came to this island long before the Celts. I was very young then, a child with a keen desire to be a warrior; although my people had long since stopped their warlike ways and adopted more peaceful means of resolving their petty disputes."

"Where were you before you came here?" Wayne interrupted him.

Aillen nodded patiently:

"The world then was not as it is now. Some say we came from the place now called Denmark. Some say that is how we got our name, but it is not true. Dana was the water Goddess, The Goddess of the sea; and because we seemed to come from the sea, the Fir Bolg, the people who lived here, gave us the name: Tuatha de Danaan: The people of the sea Goddess."

He laughed again:

"We liked to call ourselves: "The chosen ones," but then doesn't every bunch of people who ever set foot out upon the road, claim to be the "chosen people."

Aillen closed his eyes and continued to speak:

"All I remember of our arrival on this shore is the smoke of our burning ship. It is said we set our ships on fire as soon as we had landed; it may have been that we crashed our ships. I know not whether we came from the water, or indeed from the sky and those who did know ne'er said. Possibly we came from amongst the stars. I was so young then and am as subject to the course of the facts that make up history being exaggerated into legend and then fading into myth and eventually obscurity, as anyone else. I never knew our four fair cities: Finias, Gorias, Falias and Morias. They were destroyed long before I was born.

There was a very fine English Lady, a very fine Lady indeed, who compiled the tales of the Tuatha de Danaan during the latter years of the Nineteenth Century. She was called Lady Gregory and her work was considered to be the most accurate history of our race. Yet it was the Irish that gave her the tales she took to be gospel. It was the Celts and the descendents of the Norman invaders who told her their versions of our legends, who we were and the tales of our heroes."

Aillen shook his head:

"At least she saw us as more than being simple little fellas, wearing little, green top hats with brass buckles, sitting on our pots of gold waiting to trick innocent mortals. Can you believe there is an entire industry made up now selling Hong Kong made plastic leprechauns and such junk to American tourists? Pah!

What is true is that we were always different. So different that we were chased and harassed by the other peoples, because we did not die of disease and old age like they did. Naturally they were jealous, they did not trust us.

Our immortality has been both our greatest gift and, believe it or not, our greatest curse. If you do not die, then you do not feel the need to multiply in the way that mortal men do, so our numbers were always small. Thus it was that, although we were much smarter than mortal men and could often control them and use our powers against them......"

Aillen sighed as his voice cracked with emotion. He turned and wandered over to the dirty, window. His voice took on a mournful tone.

"We lost out in the end, due to sheer weight of numbers, as they say now. We were always retreating before the horde of mortal man, which is how we ended up hiding in the holes, the barrows and the caves, another species ready to join the dodo in the extinct file."

"Dan O Doherty says that you smashed the Fir Bolgs." Wayne added excitedly.

Aillen turned to him and smiled:

"Oh, we had a few scuffles in our time, but we tried to avoid trouble as much as possible. Yes, we had a few skirmishes with the hairy Fir Bolg and the Formorian tribes, who were here before us, but it was the Milesians, and the Celts who came looking for the fight. By then we were almost spent, exhausted, our numbers too few for great pitched battles. We could hardly raise a decent shield wall."

"So did not all of that fighting stuff take place?" Wayne asked; a hint of disappointment in his voice.

Aillen frowned but his eyes betrayed his humour:

"Ah you're a bloodthirsty little man. Yes, we fought for our lives. I was a pretty hot swordsman and archer in my day, but there came a time when fighting could no longer save our race. The day finally came when we had to resort to magic to survive. To stay alive we had to shift our form."

He clicked his fingers and all of a sudden it was Dan Joyce who was stood in front of Wayne:

"I think we've met." Dan declared before he clicked his fingers in turn and became a little old man with wiry white hair and green clothing that reminded Wayne of a picture book leprechaun:

"BeJaysus, Mickey Finn, at your service."

The old man declared with a bow.

"This is how I'm seen most o' the time in these parts altho' "my nephew" Dan does have his uses."

The little old man did a little jig and started to sing: "Patrick McGinty" in his musical broad Connemara accent:

At the line "bought himself a goat," Mickey morphed into a goat and bit a lump out of the side of the armchair in which Molly and Patsy were sleeping soundly.

Wayne was laughing so much, he thought he'd fall off the chair, especially when the goat turned into a sheepdog, which ran up to him and started to nip at his ankles.

Just as quickly as he had morphed into Dan Joyce, Aillen reappeared:

"It's just a little trick I learned in the forces." He laughed.

Wayne pondered what he had heard for a minute and then asked:

"Why do they call you the little people?"

Aillen laughed and immediately shrunk before Wayne's eyes until he stood no more than a foot tall.

"It's easier to hide when you're only this big." He squeaked before re-assuming his normal stature before the astonished and delighted boy who clapped his hands and laughed gleefully.

"Then we could do this, if things got really tough." With a wave of his hand Aillen simply disappeared. His disembodied voice was as clear and loud as it had been when he had stood right in front of Wayne.

"Mind you, life in the forces was a bit different in the days before the Romans."

Suddenly he reappeared, right in front of the astonished boy.

"Wow! How do you do that?" Wayne asked in amazement.

Aillen shrugged:

"Magic, my dear boy, magic."

Wayne scratched his head:

"They didn't come here though, did they?" Wayne asked.

"Who?" Aillen looked confused.

"The Romans!" Wayne screeched with all the exasperation that an eleven year old can muster.

Aillen shook his head:

"Ah no, only to trade, but the impact they had was unbelievable. I suppose it was the Romans that finally brought the disease that finished us."

Aillen grimaced as though a sudden cramp had gripped his belly. He slumped onto his chair.

"They were the ones who first brought the word of the Christian God to Britain and it was through them that the first Christians came to this island. Even when they'd been kicked out of Britain, they lingered here. Intolerent, humourless zealots, the lot of 'em. God this, God that. Jesus loves and forgives all...then they maim, burn and kill if you have the audacity to disagree. Jesus loves you, oh yes, unless you don't happen to follow exactly their way of worshipping him."

Aillen stood up again and marched around the cottage, gesticulating wildly.

"I have met "gods," conversed with them, drunk with them, fought with them,"

He paused and winked at Wayne,

"And on one occasion, with a particularly gorgeous goddess, made love with them. Not one of these "Christians" has ever even seen this God that they claim to worship."

Wayne's mouth was hanging open again:

"You've met gods?" He gasped incredulously.

"Of course I have!" Aillen declared, the twinkle eclipsing the anger in his shining emerald green eyes.

"Loads of them."

He walked away from his window towards his hearth, casting a cheeky glance back at the boy who sat totally awestruck:

"They were only other immortals who men used to get down and grovel too. They weren't grumpy old men, with long white beards, sitting up in the clouds, you know."

"So the Tuatha weren't the only immortals?" Wayne asked.

"Oh no, there were others, once."

Aillen looked wistful again.

"All long gone now, I'm afraid. Immortality only means that you don't die naturally, as they would say now. An arrow in the heart, or a knife in the back, will kill an immortal just as well as any mortal man; as will the loss of your head or being burned to death. The "Sacred Order of Saint Gregory" has spent the last fifteen hundred years hunting down anyone that may, or may not be immortal, just because of some old prophecy they happen to hold dear."

"The Sacred Order of what?" Wayne asked with a confused grimace.

Aillen laughed:

"Sacred Order of Saint Gregory." They are like a Christian gestapo. Their speciality is hunting down magical beings because of some ancient prophecy related to the Second Coming, or something."

Wayne's mouth hung open in amazement.

"You're a magical being, so are you a leprechaun?" Wayne asked with a frown, struggling to sort out his categories of magical beings.

Aillen laughed and slapped his leg.

"Sort of!" he said scratching his head:

"The Irish, as I shall now describe the mix of peoples who live on this island have always called us the Sidh or the fairy folk. Leprechaun is just an Irish term for any old magical being. Some call us the "the little people" as you said. It's a bit insulting, I mean I was nearly six feet seven inches tall in my prime."

He noticed Wayne's sceptical frown:

"Well they do say you shrink as you get older......... and I am over three thousand years old, you know."

He ruffled Wayne's hair:

"Look maybe the best thing is if I show you what happened. Would you like to be seeing how we ended up where we are now?"

"Sure." Wayne replied, jumping up, excitedly.

"Let me just get me crock of gold." Aillen laughed.

He walked over to the hearth and pushed a loose brick, which swung open. He pulled out an old and quite small, ornately carved wooden box. He lifted the lid and took out a piece of grey stone. He handed it to Wayne.

"It's a piece of granite." Wayne snorted.

Aillen just stared at him expectantly.

Wayne screwed up his face:

"What does..............whoa."

The shard of grey stone had miraculously turned into a crystal, as clear as any diamond. Light and colour danced within, trapped within its glasslike walls. It seemed to glow brighter and brighter, until it was like he was holding a miniature star in the palm of his hand. Then the light seemed to burst out of the crystal.

Wayne felt as though his skin had just burst into flames and someone had hit him on the back of his head with a cricket bat.

Every nerve end on his body tingled, while his heart seemed to accelerate. The hearth, the cottage and Aillen, all disappeared in a whirl of colour and light that engulfed the boy and then just as suddenly, disappeared.

Wayne found himself standing in a small clearing in a forest as thick and dark as he had ever seen.

The bemused boy looked around, wondering what had happened to Aillen's cottage. Was he in the small copse outside Aillen's house?

Wayne looked up. Through the dark green canopy of leaves and branches he could see that the light was fading. The harsh calls of hundreds of black crows echoed through the treetops like so much mocking laughter.

"Aillen?" Wayne shouted: "Father, where are you?"

"Don't worry, I'm right here." His father's voice answered, as he suddenly materialised right next to his son.

"Aillen, what is going on? Where are we?"

Wayne Higginbotham was terrified, why had he ever left his cosy, little house, in Shepton?

Was he really experiencing this?

Or was it all part of some weird dream?

Was he awake?

Was he hallucinating?

Had the man claiming to be his father given him some of them drugs that his mum, Doris, had warned him about?

The bird song ceased abruptly as the sound of something large could be heard crashing through the dark undergrowth nearby.

"Aillen?" Wayne wailed.

"Stay calm, son." Aillen urged, quietly as he reached out and took Wayne's hand. The something became many things, as twigs snapped and the sound of crashing branches echoed all around the clearing.

Suddenly, Wayne imagined that he could see several dark shapes moving through the bushes and branches. Lots of shapes that slowly gathered substance and form as they began to crash out of the bushes into the clearing, right in front of Wayne and his father.

Wayne bit his lip, closed his eyes and waited to meet his end.

39

Constable Hartley eased himself into his armchair and picked up his steaming mug of hot cocoa. He pressed a button on his remote control and the channel on the TV in front of him changed:

"I was watching that!" Mrs Hartley moaned as she stood up.

"I might as well go to bed."

"There's a good film on here."

The off duty policeman declared, before taking a loud slurp of cocoa.

"Oh aye, What's it called?" His wife asked, turning back towards the screen.

"Village of the Damned." PC Hartley stated with relish.

"It's one of them sci-fry films isn't it? Load of rubbish." Mrs Hartley sniffed and promptly marched out of the living room.

An hour and a half had passed before Constable Hartley wearily climbed up the stairs and fell into bed.

"Well? Was it any good?" Mrs Hartley asked, somewhat huffily from her refuge underneath the blankets.

"It was alright, I suppose." PC Hartley replied as he pulled the sheets up to his chest:

"But it's made me think."

"Oh aye."

His wife's sceptical tone passed straight over his head:

"That'd be a first."

PC Hartley stared at the bedroom wall.

"Are you ever going to turn out the light?" Mrs Hartley demanded.

"I think there's an alien from outer space living down on Cavendish Street."

The rotund policeman whispered.

His wife turned and looked at him. He was still staring at the wall:

"Have you gone totally daft?" She barked.

Constable Hartley shook his head:

"No, love, but I'll tell you sommat for nowt. If that Wayne Higginbotham turns up back in Shepton. I'm going to be keeping a very close eye on him. A very close eye, I tell you. I'll not be having the invasion of Earth by mind controlling aliens starting off in Shepton. Not on my beat."

Mrs Hartley stared disbelievingly at her husband and then shook her head in disgust and settled down to sleep:

"I don't think you should watch any more late night movies." She said as she began to drift off to sleep:

"They're giving you nightmares."

Constable Hartley shivered and then switched off the light and settled down into bed:

"Yorkshiremen don't have nightmares!" He declared pompously, seconds before noisily breaking wind and then almost immediately letting out an enormous snore.

There was a muffled whisper in the darkness:

"No, that's true, they *are* the flipping nightmares."

Far away, high above the dark, stormy Atlantic Ocean, a Jumbo jet lumbered through the inky black night sky.

A stewardess bit her fingernails as she peeped around the galley curtain at the haunted looking woman sat by the window:

"Whaddya think is the matter with the blonde in 17A?" She drawled at a colleague, who stopped what she was doing and took her turn in peering at the forlorn looking passenger:

"Jesus, the Lady looks like she's going to her own funeral." She whispered.

"Go and have a word with her. We don't want her going nutso when we hit Shannon."

"No way." The first stewardess replied:

"She might be going to a funeral. A lot of New Yorkers have family in Ireland. Maybe her Mom's just died, or something."

"Or maybe she's just pissed at having to go to Ireland to see the folks when it's over 100 degrees in the city and Ireland still seems to be in the grip of winter." A camp steward chipped in as he tossed a tray of empty glasses on to the work surface.

"You girls are just so nosey. Why don't you get on with the clearing up and mind your own business." He hissed, as he pushed through the curtains and marched off down the aisle.

The first stewardess bit her nail again:

"I'm going to check on her." She stated, with steely determination and with that she pushed through the curtain and walked up to row 17.

Most passengers were asleep.

The cabin was full of snoring, coughing and wheezing forms, haphazardly positioned in their seating areas; some covered in grey blankets, others not. The stewardess leaned across the sleeping figure of a man who's head had fallen right back onto his shoulders so that his face, with its wide open mouth, faced the aircraft ceiling. He emitted a loud snore, just as the stewardess leaned over him.

She glanced at him with more than a little distaste, before reaching out across the empty middle seat and touching the blonde woman's shoulder.

The woman jumped and gasped with shock. Her pallid face took on an even whiter hue, as she looked at the stewardess:

"Ma'am would you mind closing the shutter on that window? People are trying to sleep."

The stewardess whispered.

The woman glanced at the slumped figure in the aisle seat, who emitted another loud snore, shrugged and slammed down the shutter and closed her eyes.

"Are you OK Ma'am?"

The stewardess' nasal tones did convey an amount of concern.

The woman opened her eyes and looked up at her inquisitor.

The stewardess smiled as sympathetically as she could manage:

"You look like you've seen a ghost." She whispered, as the occupant of the aisle seat shuffled and moaned in his sleep.

The blonde woman nodded slowly:

"I haven't seen one, yet." She said slowly and deliberately:

"But I guess I am on way to meet one. In fact I'm on my way to see a lot of ghosts. It's just that one of them has been haunting me for an awful lot of years."

The stewardess squeezed her shoulder gently:

"Hey, it won't be as bad as you think. It never is!"

She smiled reassuringly.

The woman responded with a half smile and a single tear ran down one cheek.

"I hope not." She sighed.

The stewardess stood away from the snoring male and waved her hand over her mouth:

"Eugh!" She moaned and grimaced: "Garlic overkill! Can I get you something to help, a brandy maybe?"

She raised an inquisitive pencilled eyebrow.

The woman nodded eagerly.

The stewardess turned and walked away. Back behind the curtain, as she was pouring the brandy into a plastic glass, her colleague tapped her arm:

"Well?" She asked impatiently.

"Man trouble!" The stewardess replied:

"I'd know that look anywhere, believe me honey. Man trouble. She's going to see an old boyfriend!"

The blonde woman lifted the shutter a couple of inches and stared out into the darkness again.

Somewhere down there, down in the nothingness way below, she had a son and a daughter: Two children that she had carried, given birth to and loved with all her heart, in the all too brief time that she had been allowed to spend with them, but now she didn't know either of them. They could have walked right by her in the street and she would never have known.

Yet now, after years of guilt and ceaseless anguish, she could maybe, just maybe begin to start putting things right. The timing was appalling. This jaunt could totally mess up her career just as it was about to take off, yet this had to be the priority. She would never be able to mend her broken heart, nobody could, but maybe this trip would be the first stitch in repairing the wound. Terri Thorne, actress, model and budding superstar would have to wait. Theresa O'Brien still had some unfinished business to attend to, somewhere way down there.

40

Wayne Higginbotham stood totally transfixed and more than a little terrified, as whatever the beasts were that had trampled noisily through the undergrowth emerged into the twilight of the clearing in the dark, thickly wooded forest. He looked up at his father nervously. Aillen smiled at him encouragingly, squeezed his hand and put a finger to his lips to maintain the silence of the moment.

Wayne turned back and watched a small, bedraggled band of long haired, bearded warriors stagger wearily into the clearing. Bloodied and exhausted they spoke not a word. Some slumped to the mossy ground, curled up and went to sleep immediately, despite the arrival of a cloying drizzle that seemed little more than a swirl of mist at first but soon soaked everything. Others moaned softly and tended their wounds, or sat in morose, silent contemplation. One particularly savage looking individual took a whetstone out of a bag and started to slowly and carefully sharpen his sword. Another grunted as he pulled several arrows from his leather-covered shield. All bore the haunted look of the recently vanquished. One wept quietly, taking care not to let others see.

Wayne quickly realised that both he and his father were invisible. Not one of the warriors had noticed them, although they were stood quite clearly in view despite the failing light.

Thick, grey clouds rolled over the forest, as the twilight shadows grew and the light faded even more.

A solitary bat swooped over Wayne's head making him duck.

A huge bear of a man, bearing a torc of solid gold around his neck and a circlet of silver on his brow, strolled into the clearing and glanced at the physical debris and ruin sprawled out before him.

"Is this how thou greets thy king?" He bellowed angrily.

Some of the men, those least wounded, or weary, scrambled to their feet and bowed or nodded respectfully, others just looked at the new arrival with blank, crushed expressions, some slept on, oblivious.

Unknown to Wayne, more than one had already passed on to the next world in their sleep.

Fionnbharr, High King of the Tuatha de Danaan shook his head sadly.

"So this is what it comes to?" He moaned to another new arrival just behind him.

"Demoralised, dejected and defeated. So ends the last of the great immortal races. Men will now hold sway upon the face of the earth, until time itself suffers a long, slow lingering death. So it was prophesied, so shall it be."

The warrior behind the King nodded sagely.

"There are no more than a score of warriors here my Lord Fionnbharr. I believe thy son has a band of at least two score with him. He is making his way back to the mountains."

Wayne glanced up at Aillen as he recognised the name Fionnbharr. Aillen nodded and mouthed the words:

"My father."

Fionnbharr sighed heavily and stroked his bushy red beard thoughtfully as he leaned back, exhausted, against the trunk of an ancient oak tree

"I saw Lugh taking a small band to the South west, but again they were no more than a score strong. We will number no more than five score, even if we pull together every last warrior in the entirety of Erin's isle."

He coughed, a harsh racking cough and quickly and covertly examined his hand for any specks of blood.

At that moment a small wiry, warrior seemed to appear from right out of the thin air before the king.

Wayne flinched and glanced back at his father who just shook his head and pointed back towards the King.

"Did I not warn thee that we needed to use the magic, my Lord?"

The skinny warrior gasped urgently, as he panted like a man who had just run half way up a mountain.

"If we continue to fight like mortal men, so we shall be doomed to die like mortal men."

"Achill" The King's voice sounded strained, he had been shouting commands on the battlefield all day.

"Achill, my old and wise friend. Thou hast reason, but we have been sworn since the time of Great Nuada, to fight them on their own terms. It has been our code of honour since before the fall of our fair cities."

The King looked and sounded as though all his energy had been drained from his scarred and bleeding body.

Achill shook his bald-head violently, his pointed ears, the most noticeable feature of his race, almost waved, his movement was so sharp:

"With the greatest of respect, my Lord, as honourable as it might have been deemed in the elder days, if we continue to fight without using our magic, it will be our death sentence. Thou hast been a great and wise King, O mighty Fionnbharr, but thou wilt soon see us all in Tir Na Nog, unless we resort to the magical gifts that the Gods gave us. Mortal men are numbered as the ants that march to spilled honey and they breed like the flies on the corpses of the dead. Honour is a mighty gift, my King, but when all of the great and mighty are dead and there are no bards left to sing of legendary deeds, then what of honour?"

The King sighed and rolled his eyes.

Achill continued:

"And begging thy pardon, my Lord, fighting men on their own terms has already resulted in the destruction of thy Kingdom. We cannot flee to the West this time, as we have done so oft before. Ever since the demon and his legions of the damned, cast us from our fair cities. There is nothing further West, My Lord, only the great wide grey ocean. We were doomed to make our last stand on this island and that stand we have already made. The Tuatha de Danaan are all but spent and at length when the last of us passes, so passes the prophecy of the "Slanaitheoir mor," the great saviour."

King Fionnbharr frowned and sighed heavily again.

"Alas, that I should have been cursed to be the King that should see the utter desolation of my people."

Achill grimaced:

"The only hope we have, my Lord, is to convene a last Council. The Council must be convinced that if we are to survive then we must make full use of our magical gifts. We must go and dwell in the underground places. We must inhabit holes in the earth, caves and the ancient barrows, the dark places that mortal men dread and fear. Men already call us the sidh, the fairy folk; because we have the gifts of immortality and magic, well, let us fulfil their superstitions and their many legends about us. We have a host of other gifts that "honour" has forbidden us from using thus far. If the prophecy about the saviour of the world is to come to pass, then thy line must survive, or the souls of every living thing in the whole world shall be doomed, even those of the heinous scourge that is mortal man."

Achill stared defiantly at Fionnbharr. The small, wiry warrior had taken at least fifty heads before Fionnbharr had seen him vanish from the battlefield. Had he not used his magic, as the Tuatha de Danaan had long been forbidden to do, then he would have been one of the twenty score Tuatha dead now lying dead on the battlefield. The once mighty warriors, that now provided food for the crows and the vermin of the fields, along with the hundred score of their enemy.

Fionnbharr cursed under his breath. Achill was right about the prophecy. The witch Fenalla of Gorias had sworn that one day, a child born of mortal womb, but sired by the line of King Nuada, would save the world from eternal darkness, in an age that was yet to come to pass. If the Tuatha de Danaan were totally wiped out, then no such child would ever come to exist.

Fionnbharr gestured for the warrior by his side to help him stand.

The warrior and Achill both gasped with dismay when they saw the arrow shaft sticking out of Fionnbharr's side.

The King laughed:

"I for one will not need to hide like a rat in a hole, but thy counsel is just and wise, Achill, as usual. The witch's prophecy must be fulfilled. Even if it means we lose our honour and become as cowards. Let us make haste to the last long house by the round lake in the belly of the mountain. There we shall summon the last Council of the Wise."

Wayne watched, entranced, as the great King, supported by the much smaller but evidently strong warrior was escorted out of the clearing, followed by several of the warriors.

Wayne looked back up at his Father:

"Come now, we shall go now to a place you will recognise." Aillen whispered.

Wayne closed his eyes and without feeling any sensation of movement or motion, opened them in an entirely different location. It was the little round Lough high in the semi-circular caldera of the mighty mountain, Buckaun, near his grandfather Daideo's house. The secret "Lough" that Katie had shown him that very morning. Just like then, it was shrouded in a low grey mist that seemed stuck under the walls of the valley.

As he grimaced in the harsh light, Wayne noticed that the sun was now quite high in the sky. He had passed from near darkness to what looked like late morning in the blink of an eye. He shook his head in wonder.

Aillen let go of Wayne's hand and folded his arms. He nodded in the direction of a long wooden building with a golden thatched roof:

"That's the last long house of the Tuatha de Daanan. Once there were hundreds of them. Two days have now passed since you saw my father, King Fionnbharr, in the clearing in the wood. The survivors of the last great battle fought by the once mighty Tuatha de Danaan are now gathered in that hidden hall The women folk, the wives of the living and the more numerous widows of the lost, are gathered in a cave on the other side of the mountain, waiting for the Council's decision: Honour, or survival."

Far below, Wayne could see Lough Mask, the huge lake, dotted by small islands that stretched almost as far as the eye could see. It looked exactly the same as it did in Wayne's own time, but he did not have time to think any more about it before Aillen touched his shoulder and in the blink of an eye they were standing at the back of the horribly smoky, stinky, dark hall

Wayne recognised the form of King Fionnbharr, although he was slumped on his plain wooden throne. It seemed that he was now almost too weak to speak. Wayne noticed the familiar shape of Aillen Mac Fionnbharr, Fionnbharr's eldest son, stepping forward to represent his father, the High King. Wayne gasped and turned to look at his father who was still stood behind him:

"But how can you be in two places at once?" He whispered.

Aillen grinned.

"Tuatha magic, think of it like watching a telly." He whispered back, then he touched his lips again as Achill, the steward of the King, banged the reed-strewn floor with the shaft of his spear to silence the gathering.

The other Aillen stood and walked forward into a shaft of light shining through a crude hole in the thatched roof, that permeated the smoky hall like a spotlight.

"Great Lords and noble warriors of our people. We gather here this day to decide the course of our future. Almost since the day we of the Tuatha de Danaan came through the mists of the air and the high air to this Earth, cast out of our great cities: Fair Finias, Mighty Morias, Glorious Gorias and Fine Falias, by the demon and his horde, we have been harried and chased by those who are jealous of our bounty, even unto our doom. The mortal scourge, to whom we once taught the fine arts of civilisation, have finally condemned us to the nether world of Tir Na Nog: The land of the dead. The defeat that even the demon Lucifer, cursed be his name, could not inflict on us."

A sad consensual murmur arose around the hall.

Aillen nodded, his clean-shaven face grim, as he perused the last few surviving warriors of his race. Tall and serious, his large pointed ears stuck out through his long black straight hair.

Wayne looked back at his new-found father, both Aillens wore a simple circlet of gold around his forehead and both the same long black robe, edged in gold.

Wayne shook his head. This was all getting just too weird for words.

The Aillen of the hall's time glanced back towards his father, the King, slumped on his throne and it was obvious that his heart ached. He turned back towards his meagre audience:

"My people, for I speak to thee as my father's son and as a Prince of my people. There is but a slender hope for us, but it is a hope. We of the Tuatha de Danaan are children of the age of magic. Our great cities may have long since crumbled to dust, yet our hope rests in the arts learned there and in the craft of our ancestors. We shall vote on a course of action in a few moments, but we now need to gather the treasures of our race. Who now wields the sword of Gorias, that the great Nuada wielded even before he became the silver handed?"

A young warrior near the front shouted "Aye," stepped forward and handed over a beautiful sword with a blade of burnished steel, a golden guard and pommel and a hilt wrapped in soft brown leather.

Aillen took it and thanked the young warrior who bowed and returned to his place.

The Prince placed it by the throne of the King.

"Who now bears the Spear of Finias, that Lugh threw in his righteous anger at the battle of Magh Nia?"

The wiry warrior Wayne recognised as Achill shouted "Aye!" stepped forward and handed an enormous, silver-tipped spear to Aillen, who again placed it by the throne of Fionnbharr.

Aillen stepped back into the beam of light:

"Who now holds the bounteous Cauldron of Murias? Once the pride of King Dagda."

Queen Oonagh, consort of Fionnbharr and Aillen's mother stepped from the shadows behind the throne. It looked like she was the only female in the hall:

"The gift of rich Murias rests o'er there." She whispered demurely and pointed to a brass cauldron resting on the floor near the huge table in the middle of the hall.

Aillen gestured to two warriors who picked the heavy vessel up and carried it to the throne, placing it by Fionnbharr's feet.

Aillen nodded his gratitude and once again retook his place in the light.

"The King himself has the greatest of all the gifts of our heritage: The great stone of destiny, the treasure of the once great city of Falias and creation of the wise wizard Morias. Now behold his judgment."

Fionnbharr stood up painfully, Achill holding one arm and Oonagh the other. From a pocket inside his robe, the King pulled out a large stone ball, which he held aloft gritting his teeth.

"I call upon my esteemed ancestors and the counsels of the wise long passed, to help us in this the hour of our need." He bellowed as best he could.

A green mist seemed to swirl up from the reed floor and soon enveloped the central part of the hall. The gathering gasped in surprise and bewilderment. Not since the ancient days had the portal of Tir na Nog been opened.

Wayne's mouth fell open in disbelief.

Four figures slowly emerged from the mist, a tall stern looking warrior wearing what looked like a knight's gauntlet, or a prosthetic silver hand. His hair and beard were as black as a raven's feathers.

Then came a giant of a man with a shaggy red mane and beard, followed by a portly, bald headed man who looked more like a merchant than a warrior. Lastly a small, wizened figure with a long white beard, a shock of white hair and a long wooden staff ambled out of the mist.

Wayne's eyes were so wide he wondered if he'd ever be able to close them again.

The gathered warriors were also amazed as one they all respectfully knelt on the reed strewn floor.

King Fionnbharr put the stone down, carefully, on the seat of his throne then crouched slowly and picked up the sword. He handed it to the silver handed warrior:

"Great and mighty King Nuada, who first led us to this island long ago and smote the Fir Bolg. I return to thee this mighty sword so that the enemy may not make use of it."

Fionnbharr tried to shout so that all could hear, but his voice was husky and the shout came out as little more than a loud croak.

The ghostly figure of the once mighty King Nuada accepted the gift of the sword, bowed graciously and stepped back.

The giant red bearded warrior now stepped forward expectantly.

Fionnbharr bent to try and pick up the spear, but grimaced, gritted his teeth in agony and pulled back. Achill quickly grabbed the spear and passed it to the King.

"Mighty Lugh, I return to thee the spear that once thrown in anger never missed its target."

The King gasped through clenched teeth.

Lugh nodded curtly, took the spear and stepped back behind King Nuada.

King Fionnbharr gestured the bald man forward.

"Wise Senias, who made sure that the blight of hunger never affronted his kin, or indeed any in his City. I return to you the Cauldron of Plenty."

Senias shook his head:

"While there is still one of my people who breathes the air of life, then the cauldron will stay in this world. I bequeath the cauldron to Prince Aillen, so that hunger will not mark him, or any of his kin. In years to come, the mortals of this island will suffer great hunger and will die like fish in a poisoned pool. Such will not be your fate, Aillen Mac Fionnbharr."

Aillen bowed low and thanked the rotund apparition who grinned, then turned and took his place behind King Nuada and the warrior Lugh.

Wayne quickly turned back to his father:

"He's talking about the great potato famines isn't he?"

The modern day Aillen smiled and nodded, impressed at his son's knowledge, but he put his finger to his lips again and whispered:

"Watch!"

Finally Queen Oonagh lifted the stone of destiny off the throne and passed it to King Fionnbharr.

The white bearded wizard Morias stepped forward.

Fionnbharr swallowed, his mouth was getting drier and drier:

"Oh wisest of the wise and greatest sage of my people, Morias, I return to thee the Lia Fail, the Stone of Destiny, the last great treasure of the City of Falias."

The wizened old man stepped forward and took the stone, then to the amazement of all, he hurled it to the ground where it shattered into many pieces. Every mouth in the hall fell open as a horrified Fionnbharr collapsed back on to his throne in a palpable state of shock.

Morias held up his hand to quell the murmuring:

"The Lia Fail is yet the mightiest of our treasures. From it, we derive much of our strength and much of the magic that you will need to survive."

He bellowed in a deep powerful baritone that belied his ancient wizened appearance. He peered myopically at his small audience:

"The fate of the Tuatha de Danaan is not to end here, nor shall the Stone of Destiny. There are some amongst you here, who will live to endure the long passage of many, many Centuries. Some here will live long enough to see mortal men sailing the seas in great ships wrought of iron. There will be some who will live to see mortal men ride in machines made of iron, that fly and spit fire and death from their wings, even as did the dragons of old. Aye, and there are a few of you will see other machines that roll along the ground, greater even than the huge, tusked, iron-flanked beasts of the hot lands of the South. You will see all the nations of mortal men engaged in wars where the count of the dead shall number greater than the grains of sand on the shores of this island."

Wayne nodded knowingly, as he folded his arms and turned to his father.

"Planes, tanks, battleships. World War One and Two." He whispered, before turning back to hear the old man continue.

The murmuring in the audience grew as Morias held up his wizened claw like hand again.

"The shards of the Stone of Falias shall be held by the last of the line of our Kings and by his trusted servants. The shards shall be kept apart until such a time that destiny decrees that the pieces shall be brought together once again. That is the time when the witch's prophecy shall truly be tested. Only then will the stone reform. That day will come, either at the end of all things, or at the very beginning of a new age of light. Even I cannot see what capricious fate has in store for this world at that point, so far distant. Like my learned and wise friend Senias did with the Cauldron of Murias, I would ask that King Nuada and mighty Lugh make the Sword of Gorias and the Spear of Finias available for the use of the Slanetheoir Mor. The future champion who shall attempt to fulfil the witch's prophecy."

The old silver handed King and the giant beside him nodded their assent.

Morias grinned and picked up a small piece of the stone. He took a ring off his little finger and placed the piece of stone on the golden circle that decorated the ring. He waved his hand over it, breathed on it and whispered a short incantation. The wizard Morias then passed the ring to King Fionnbharr who placed it on the little finger of his right hand.

"So passes out of this age of the world the Stone of Destiny. I swear to all of thee that it will return. I call upon all gathered here to use every magical trick thou possesses to endure, to ensure that the prophesied champion will be born and that he might have all that he shall need to overcome the great darkness that shall then threaten the world. I wish thee well."

With that the wizard turned swiftly and disappeared into the mist, followed by the bald, rotund Senias.

The giant warrior Lugh walked forward and swung his spear over his head:

"Only the one who is blessed with all the magic of the Tuatha de Danaan shall be able to find this Spear. This I swear!"

Nuada held the Sword of Gorias aloft:

"And this I shall hide where one day it may be found only by the one whose destiny it is to wield it in anger."

Then both turned and disappeared into the mist, which evaporated into the smoky air of the hall as swiftly as it had arrived.

The hall was almost in uproar as Aillen Mac Fionnbharr stepped back into the beam of light:

"The great treasures of the Tuatha de Danaan are now safe. I will pass shards of the stone to the members of the Council of the Wise. I now ask the surviving members of that Council to step forward.

Wayne counted eight warriors as they stepped forward.

Aillen sighed as he glanced at the few surviving members of the once great council.

He took a deep breath:

"Do we now deem it worthy to go underground, to use magic as we may and to endure?

Do we choose to live, that the witch's prophecy might one day be fulfilled and the world saved even for mortal man?

Or do we fulfil the long held vow to fight with honour and join our ancestors in Tir na Nog?"

The eight venerable warriors, the last survivors of the Council of the Wise, bellowed to a man:

"Life!"

Aillen looked at his father who nodded and then at Achill who clenched his fist and punched the air triumphantly, his grin as wide as his face.

Aillen grinned too. There was still hope:

"The Council of the Wise and the High King are in agreement. Then it is decided. We shall now scatter like rabbits before the fox. We shall become the spirits of the bog, the rivers, the woods and the mountains. Mortal men shall use our names to scare their children in their beds."

In the far distance the sound of the barking of huge Celtic hunting dogs could be heard.

Aillen grinned:

"So the hunters are already searching for their prey. Leave now my brothers. Use any means thou canst to survive and even try to multiply. The world has yet to see the final passing of the mighty Tuatha de Danaan."

Aillen handed out the shards of the stone to the Council members and to several other warriors, including Achill.

As the hall emptied, King Fionnbharr beckoned his son to him.

"I now pass into Tir Na Nog." Fionnbharr gasped.

"I am sorry you shall never be truly the King of thy people, my son. Look after my lovely Oonagh, thine own wife, sweet Celebdhann and my grandchildren."

Aillen smiled sadly:

"I am sure capricious fate, as Morias described her, has a plan for me, My Lord."

Fionnbharr nodded:

"Achill will help you with the Cauldron, my son. I........."

There was a slight gurgle in the King's throat, as his head fell forward and his eyes closed.

Ooonagh closed her eyes and bit her lip. She deemed it unbecoming for a King's consort to weep.

So passed Fionnbharr, last true King of the Tuatha de Danaan.

Wayne glanced up at his father and saw tears in his eyes even after all the centuries that had passed.

The modern day Aillen took Wayne's hand and suddenly they were once again standing outside the hall.

Aillen explained that he, along with Achill and Oonagh had moved the cauldron into a small cave by the little hidden Lough and they were now setting the hall alight.

Wayne watched sadly as his ancestors hugged, bade their farewells and parted.

Aillen gazed at his old self and his mother as they kissed for the last time.

"Oonagh declared that she would go south and live in the warmer fields and watch the sea until the World ended, or death found her." Aillen explained sadly, as he watched her walk slowly off across the grass alone.

"Could you not have persuaded her stay?" Wayne asked, his voice choking with emotion.

"Her will would not be bent." Aillen whispered sadly.

Achill had wished Aillen luck and set off in his turn to lose himself in the wild mountains of Donegal.

Aillen and Wayne stood and watched the old version of Aillen Mac Fionnbharr as he stood and gazed at the last long hall burning for a while. Then as he heard the mortals approaching, attracted by the smoke, he slipped off down a narrow pass through the rocks back to his own hiding place. The modern Aillen shrugged and smiled a melancholic smile.

"He is going to where his beautiful wife, Celebdhann, daughter of Dagda and their five almost fully grown children are waiting. I am so tempted to follow him, so that I might once again set my eyes upon my greatest love and upon my fine sons and daughters, but I fear my heart would break and this time there would be no mending it."

He heaved the heaviest sigh Wayne had ever heard:

So there you have it, Michaeleen, last of my boys. That is how the survivors of the once mighty and immortal race of the Tuatha de Danaan were scattered, like a few pitiful leaves in the wind. They spread throughout the entire island of Ireland, the reign of men had begun and in turn, so had the legends of the sidh, the fairy folk, the little people."

He took Wayne's hand again:

"And now we must return at last to the time that Morias spoke of: The time of the fulfilment of the witch's prophecy. For I am the last of the pure blooded Tuatha de Danaan and for you my son, it is possibly your destiny to become the "Slanaitheoir mor." Come; let's go home."

40

The green Morris Minor chugged slowly along the dark country road, between tall, looming black hedges.

Fr. Pizzaro looked at his watch:

"Hurry, William. Can this car not go any faster?" He asked, impatiently.

In the back of the car Fr Malone was formulating his plan to thwart any action that Pizarro and Burke might have in mind.

He had hidden a kitchen knife in the lining of his cloak and hoped and prayed that he would not be forced to use it. Fr Malone abhorred violence in any shape or form and the prospect of using a weapon filled him with dread, but he still couldn't think of any other way of preventing Pizzaro and Burke from carrying out their diabolical scheme.

Pizzaro looked round at him:

"You are sweating Father Malone."

The Spaniard gloated over James' nervousness. Even in the darkness of the Morris interior the sheen of perspiration could be seen on James' face:

"Do not worry, your part in the plan is to play nothing, but an innocent bystander, there will be no blood on your hands, my young friend."

He smirked knowingly.

James caught Fr Burke glancing at him maliciously in the rear view mirror.

"There will be blood on my hands if I do not prevent this madness."

James thought to himself as he clutched and rolled the beads of his rosary in his fist.

Fr Burke coughed nervously:

"You're absolutely sure that this Mickey Finn and Dan Joyce are one and the same person?"

Pizarro nodded:

"I think this is the tenth time that I have told you, William. Finn is a shape shifter. The only things it cannot change are its ears."

He blew out a long sigh.

"Is there anything else that troubles you? Either of you?" He asked; his voice laced with sarcasm.

The car struggled up over the mountain pass and began to slowly descend into the valley where Mickey Finn's cottage was located.

Even in the light of the old car's weak headlights, the road ahead could be seen to disappear into a series of tight perilous hairpin bends. There was no fence or wall by the roadside to prevent cars from crashing off the edge and tumbling helplessly down into the black void below.

"If I just lean over, grab the wheel and steer the car over the edge, then I will have done my duty." Fr Malone thought, biting his lip.

Yet, for all his determination to stop what he knew was going to be an act of terrible wickedness, he just couldn't force himself to take decisive action. He thought of what Father Callaghan had said to him:

"I should have done something. I should have stopped him" and "I was transfixed...and I did nothing."

Father James Malone's heart was pounding against his ribcage.

He had to do something.

He had to do anything, but what?

What was the point of his killing himself as well as Burke and Pizarro?

How would he prevent the "Order" from simply sending out replacements?

He tried to swallow but his mouth was as dry as crisp sandpaper.

There was something else that he couldn't quite shake out of his mind either, although he hated the thought of it.

Just what if they were right?

What if the old prophecy was true?

What if Mickey Finn was somehow related to this: "Slanaitheoir mor"? What if Mickey Finn was "God's Assassin" as James had heard Pizarro refer to him?

What if Christ in his second coming was assassinated, by this "Slanaitheoir mor" and all because Fr James Malone had sabotaged the "Order's" mission?

No, that was all rubbish, The "Order" were just zealots. A bunch of fundamentalist fanatics who believed in fairy tales about vampires, werewolves and the like.

Father James Malone had always been a good Catholic boy.

He had grown up loving the Church and had dedicated his life to it.

How could the Church, even if it was only a few covert fanatics within the main body of Catholicism, have got it so wrong?

A bead of sweat dripped off Father Malone's nose. He put his head in his hands and prayed as hard as he had ever prayed, for some degree of guidance.

Fr Pizarro turned to him again:

"Feeling sick, Father?" He asked somewhat sarcastically.

James looked up at his dark features, every angle and wrinkle was outlined in the faint light of the glowing dashboard. It made Pizarro look even more malevolent than usual. His black eyes glittered in the darkness:

"A bit." James retorted defiantly.

Pizarro's lip curled in a pale imitation of a smile.

"Do not worry, my son. It will soon be all over."

Fr Malone frowned and put his head back in his hands.

The old car finally pulled round the last bend and turned on to a long straight piece of road. The beams of its lights peered like children's torches into the blackness. The night was heavily clouded and not even a single star could cast its light on the gloomy valley that stretched out before them.

Fr Burke frowned as he peered at the road ahead:

"How far now?" He barked, his voice betraying tension and nervousness.

Fr Pizarro looked calmly across at him:

"About half a mile, William. Only half a mile now."

James sighed quietly. He had missed his chance to take action on the pass road. Just like Fr Callaghan, so many years before, cowardice had got the better of him. He had preferred to save his own skin than that of a potentially innocent old man.

Malone squeezed his rosary tighter and tighter until it was hurting his own hands. Like St. Peter, he had lost his courage at the moment of truth. A strange, uncharacteristic rage began to boil up inside him, as he thought of the years of suffering that Fr Callaghan had endured: the agony of knowing what he had done, the years of guilt; the endless nightmares; the waking in the middle of the night, hearing screaming voices: The years of knowing that he had helped to kill innocent people in cold blood.

Fr Malone thought of Dermot's last confession and his apparent suicide. Had he killed himself?

Or, had Fr Burke murdered him, before he could rectify his mistake?

Before he did something to stop what he, Father James Malone, was about to let them get away with?

He glared at the back of Fr. Burke's head and the significance of Burke's words echoed in Fr Malone's brain:

"He still seemed somewhat terrified of me this morning when I left him........Hanging around in a squalid little church."

Fr Malone's mouth opened, but no sound came out. He swallowed, cleared his throat and tried again:

"I will not allow this sacrilege."

The words came out as little more than a whisper:

He saw Burke glance in his mirror and Pizarro turn slowly in his seat.

"I will not allow this..."

Fr Malone shouted, jumped up from the back seat and dived between Pizarro and Burke, grabbing the Morris' steering wheel and yanking it hard to the left. The car veered into a low stone wall and smashed into it with an almighty bang and crash. The Morris came to a sudden halt and Father Malone was thrown into the front over the other priest's shoulders, smashing his head on the large central speedometer. There was an explosion of light in his head as he fell backwards.

Fr Malone groaned and moved to touch his head to see if it was bleeding but instead felt his hair being grabbed. His head was pulled back sharply and was then slammed forward into something unyielding and hard. Then it all went dark.

Father Pizarro opened the door and stepped out of the car. There was a squelching noise as his feet landed in the soft, wet boggy ground at the side of the road. He groaned in distaste and disgust:

"I hate this miserable, wet, cold, heathen country." He spat, as he leaned back against the car door. Then he began to laugh. Father Burke dabbed the side of his head with a blood stained handkerchief as he scrambled out of the wrecked car:

"I smashed my head on the window." He moaned: "That was not part of the plan."

He walked round the back of the car to join the Spaniard. Father Pizarro laughed even harder:

"It was even better than we planned, William, my friend. We were only a few yards from where we planned to fake the accident. I was going to use this on our impetuous young friend to make it look realistic."

353

He took a small cosh from his pocket:

"Yet the fool went and did it for real. He has played his part far better than we could ever have imagined."

He laughed even harder and crossed himself:

"Thank you, Lord!"

Fr Burke looked worried:

"Is he dead?"

Pizarro opened the door and leaned into the car. He pulled Malone's prone body on to the passenger seat. Malone's face was covered in blood. Pizarro felt his pulse.

"No, there is life there; but I do not think he will interfere with our plans again this night."

Burke looked around nervously.

"But if we can't get the car going again, how do we get away, you know, once we have set the cottage on fire?"

Burke's voice was edged with panic.

Pizarro took a deep breath.

"Have faith, my friend, the car will start. It will get us away from here." Pizarro stated as he pulled the damaged wheel arch off the front nearside tyre:

"Although it seems we shall have to travel with only one headlamp. It is not of concern on this side of the mountain, of course; for the night sky will soon be lit by burning thatch."

He walked around to the car boot and took out a petrol can and a black leather briefcase, while Fr Burke mournfully dabbed away at his wound. Pizarro glowered at him:

"Come William, you know what to do. The cottage is only a few hundred yards, or so, from here. Let us get on and carry out our duty."

The two Priests walked off into the darkness, their silhouettes outlined in the forlorn single beam of the one remaining headlight of the car.

In the battered Morris, Fr James Malone, groaned and shifted slightly, then fell silent.

41

Wayne opened his eyes. He was standing in the rustic cottage, exactly where he had been stood, seemingly hours earlier. Yet Molly and Patsy seemed not to have moved at all. He glanced at his Timex watch. Only five minutes had passed.

His father put the piece of stone to one side and shrugged:

"So now you've seen how we became what the Irish call the little people."

Wayne nodded but so much still confused him.

"What was the prophecy that the wizard talked about? You said we'd come to it now: the time of prophecy."

Aillen scratched his head:

"I don't really know it myself." He blustered, somewhat evasively:

"The prophecy was supposedly made by some old witch in one of the ancient cities of the Tuatha de Danaan. She prophesied that a great Tuatha champion, would be born of a mortal womb and would save the world. He would be a descendent of Nuada, our greatest King and he would be of the direct line of a great King of the mortals. She said he would face three great tasks before overcoming the king of all demons. He would be known as the "Slanaitheoir mor," the Great Saviour."

Aillen coughed:

"The "Sacred Order of St. Gregory" was founded to fulfil a Christian prophecy, I believe. A prophecy that stated it would be the person we call the "Slanaitheoir mor," that would murder the Christian Messiah in his second incarnation. They call the last of our line: "God's Asssassin." They intend to make sure that our prophecy never comes true, our purpose is to ensure it does and to ensure theirs doesn't."

Wayne frowned.

"So you said we've come to the time of prophecy now. Have we?"

Aillen coughed again:

"The thing is, I'm not really sure. We could have, but then again, we might not have. It's all a bit perplexing."

"Mmm" Wayne murmured as the next question came into his mind.

"So what happens when the Tuatha de Danaan do die. I mean you told me they can be killed, but they're meant to be immortal, so how does that work?" Wayne asked plaintively.

Aillen rubbed his chin:

"It is a good question, my son. The Tuatha were immortal in that they did not suffer from the ravages of time, or from disease. However, like all living things, the Tuatha de Dannan are not indestructible. Indestructibility and immortality are two very different things."

Wayne nodded:

"So you're not like Captain Scarlet?"

Aillen frowned:

"Who?"

Wayne shrugged:

"It doesn't matter. He's just a puppet bloke on the telly."

Aillen smiled kindly:

"Once killed on this plain, our spirits live on, in another place: Tir Na Nog. It is a place that lies between the realm of mortal man and the great beyond. It is not life as you know it, but then it is not what you would call death either."

Wayne shook his head, bewildered:

There was along silence, while Wayne considered everything he had seen and heard. Then he took a deep breath and decided to ask the question that he'd wanted to ask ever since he had entered the cottage:

"All this magic and the story of Tuatha de Danaan and all that stuff, well it's great, but what I really wanted to know is, well, it's sort of difficult."

Aillen smiled sympathetically:

"Go on, my son, ask whatever it is you wish to know."

Wayne looked straight into his father's eyes:

"Why did I have to be adopted? Why didn't you marry my Mother?"

Aillen opened his mouth, then thought better about what he had been about to say and closed it again. He raised his eyebrows, stroked his chin and sighed:

"Ahhh, Your mother!"

Aillen Mac Fionnbharr repeated, suddenly looked terribly guilty.

He looked away from Wayne and frowned, then walked slowly over to the window and stared wistfully out into the blackness:

"Ah, yes, your mother; young Theresa O'Brien. I first saw her in the fields, high above the great Lough. She would have been about fifteen summers old, I suppose. I was cycling down the road, in the guise of Dan Joyce and there she was, running through a meadow of wildflowers, her long red-gold hair, shining like the very sun. Ha! It sounds like a stupid woman's tale, doesn't it?"

He turned towards Michael and screwed up his face, mocking himself, but Wayne noticed that his bright green eyes were swimming with tears.

He turned back to the window.

"She reminded me of somebody. Somebody I fell in love with a long, long time ago. She was also beautiful beyond words."

"Celebrian?" Wayne asked, his voice soft and sympathetic.

Aillen turned to him again and smiled:

"Celebdhann." He gently corrected his son.

"Long before the Christians came to Erin's isle, I met a young Tuatha maiden, a princess, although I did not know it then. Her name was Celebdhann, and she was the daughter of Dagda and his Queen Boann, a client king of my Father. She was as fair as a summer morn, just like your mother." He added quickly.

"We were wed on a Midsummer's Eve, my Celebdhann and I and the hooley that followed lasted until the leaves began to fall."

He laughed a sad wistful laugh and then knelt down before Wayne.

"We had two sons and three daughters, all of them fine children like you. All of them grew tall and fair, just like you will; and life was good. So very sweet."

He stood and anger clouded his eyes:

"Then the invaders came, in their turns, the mortals who hunted us like vermin. We were forced underground, as you have seen and after the Celts, came the Northmen, then the Normans and then the cursed English. Despite our powers, despite our magic, over the centuries all of our children perished before the mortal axe, the arrow, the sword, or the flame. It was all too much for Celebdhann, she wanted to go away, to leave these shores. She wanted to start again, I suppose; while I just sat brooding in a cave in the mountains and seethed in anger, misery and resentment."

Aillen was silent for a moment. The only sounds came from the hiss of burning turf on the fire and somewhere in the distance the hooting of an owl.

Aillen scowled and pressed his nose to the window, peering out into the darkness. After a couple of moments, he shrugged, stepped back and started to speak again:

"Nearly four hundred years ago, during the time that the first Elizabeth ruled in England and while Granuaille O'Malley ruled the waves off Connaught; a great Spanish ship was wrecked off Clew bay. All of the crew who made it ashore were massacred by the O'Flahertys, as was their wont, save one who they kept for ransom. He was a nobleman, the captain of the ship, Felipe Dom Albaya de Greco."

A wry smile creased Aillen's lips.

"He managed to escape from the O'Flahertys, our friend Albaya de Greco. He ran into the mountains and hid. He was cold, wet, starving and scared out of his wits, when we found him. The fools that we were, we took pity on him and took him in. We saved his skin and our reward was his treachery. Oh yes, our Spaniard was a handsome devil. His skin was dark, his eyes, his hair and beard were as black as the sky beyond the stars and his tongue was as smooth as a snake's belly, with his poetry and ballads and his tales of the Americas."

Aillen shrugged and let out a short ironic laugh:

"I suppose also, that some wives might get a bit bored after two thousand years of marriage to the same man. She'd heard all my poems and songs and ballads a thousand times over. Anyway, my Celebdhann ran away with that wily Spaniard, first to Galway City and then across the sea to Spain."

Aillen snorted:

"I never saw sight, nor sound of her again."

Wayne sighed:

"Will she still be alive? I mean, if she's immortal like you, she was, is, isn't she?"

Aillen shrugged:

"I doubt it. Even for an immortal, life is full of unexpected hazards. I thought she had returned when I first saw your mother. I was certain that my Celebdhann had come back to me, but no."

He smiled sadly.

"So although she wasn't Celebdhann, she was a fine and beautiful maid. I knew that Dan Joyce would not turn your mother's eye and Mickey Finn certainly wouldn't, so I wooed her in this guise:"

Aillen turned towards the window, then spun back, looking incredibly like Elvis Presley in tight blue jeans, white T shirt and black leather jacket:

"I pretended my name was Danny Finn, Mickey's grandson, all the way from Tupelo, Mississippi."

Aillen drawled in a fair imitation of a deep Southern accent. He pulled a pair of black sunglasses from his inside pocket and put them on.

"Now do I look cool or what, boy?" He demanded, striking an Elvis like pose, arm in the air, knee pushed forward and his hips swaying to imaginary music.

"No!" Wayne laughed.

"You look like a Nineteen Fifties teddy boy."

Aillen turned back to his natural appearance:

"Cheeky devil!" he laughed:

"It worked for your mother anyway. We dated for six months, until her sixteenth birthday and then, well......"

"What happened?" Wayne asked. "Why did she run away?"

Aillen knelt again and took the boys hands in his own.

"I, I fell in love with her, just as I had with my own sweet Celebdhann. I think she was in love with me, or rather the handsome, cool American that she thought I was. One night after we had...well, I felt it was time to tell her the truth. At first, she didn't believe me and then, when I showed her my true self, she just went mad. She accused me of cheating her, lying to her and so on and she ran away. I tried to follow her, but by the time I got to her house, she had already left. I heard she had gone to England."

Wayne frowned thoughtfully.

Aillen shrugged and continued; a mischievous glint in his eye:

"Ah well, I suppose it was the age difference that proved a bit much for her, you know. They did warn me that my being a few millennia older would be a bit too much of a gap."

Wayne didn't laugh, instead he began to look hurt and upset.

"Why didn't you go after her?" He asked; his voice breaking:

"Did she not mean that much to you?"

Aillen looked pained.

"I have not left this island in well over two thousand years. I suppose I was afraid."

He stood and went back to the window.

"I knew that she carried my child." He whispered.

"I just knew. I also knew that one day you would come looking for me. I knew you would find me."

Wayne looked down at his feet:

"Children." He muttered.

Aillen looked confused.

Wayne looked earnestly up at him:

"Children, not child! She was carrying two babies. It seems I'm a twin. I have a twin sister, although I've never met her."

Aillen opened his mouth, as if to speak but before any word was uttered, his expression changed, he suddenly turned towards the window, his eyes wide and alert. There was the sound of footsteps outside and then a harsh and heavy banging on the door.

"Just a minute. Oi'll be there in a minute."

Aillen Mac Fionnbharr had disappeared.

Dan Joyce picked the dull looking stone up off the table and handed it to Wayne.

"Be looking after that for me would ya?" He winked at Wayne.

42

The two priests marched briskly along the dark road, until the light from the Morris had faded. Fr Pizarro reached into his bag and took out a small torch. He seemed to be looking for something in the road side. Eventually a white stone could be seen in the torchlight just by the wall.

"The cottage is just around the next corner. I will hide here, behind this wall, until you have passed with the demon. Make sure you get him to help you carry Malone back to his cottage and do not be too quick. Now go!"

Pizarro leapt stealthily over the wall, while Fr Burke scurried along the road.

In the distance, the stream that passed by Mickey Finn's little house could be heard, trickling over rocks and pouring into pools under small waterfalls, as it flowed down the valley.

Fr Pizarro crouched in the darkness and clutched his rosary with its enormous golden crucifix:

"In Nomine Patris, Filiis et Spiritus Sancti…" He began, his eyes closed and his face raised towards heaven.

An owl hooted. Pizarro pricked up his ears; a hoot was the signal that Burke and he had agreed to, if there was a problem.

He waited for a moment, the same hoot echoed over the boggy fields. He cursed and leapt over the wall, then moved quickly down the road, running with his back bent in the shadow of the wall, like a soldier using it for cover. He bumped into Burke just around the corner, knocking him over in a heap:

"What is it?" He hissed angrily.

Fr Burke picked himself up and brushed down his cassock:

"We have to abort!" He whispered as loudly as he dared: "Look."

He pointed into the darkness. Pizarro pointed his torch in the direction Burke was pointing and the red glint of an Austin Maxi's tail lights glimmered in the gloom.

"He has visitors. We have to abandon this." Burke demanded.

Pizarro shook his head:

"Continue! We can not give up now. It is probably just another peasant, or even better, maybe there is another demon, despite what we have been told."

He grinned and his white teeth gleamed in the darkness:

"We will improvise if there is a bigger problem, my friend. Have courage!"

He turned and scurried back towards his hiding place, while the wild eyed Fr Burke took a deep breath and made his way back towards the cottage, trembling like a leaf.

He walked through the small gateway, down the short path, then banged wildly on the door and waited:

"Just a minute. Oi'll be there in a minute." He heard someone's muffled shout from inside. He banged again, more urgently this time.

"Help! There's been an accident!" Burke shouted, sounding every bit as nervous as he felt.

The door swung open and the figure of Dan Joyce stood framed in the light:

"Oh, Father. What is it?" Joyce asked, pulling his tweed jacket on.

Fr Burke began to gabble:

"There's been a terrible accident up the road, there's a young Priest badly hurt in the car. He needs help. I found your cottage and saw the light. Please help us."

He began to run back up the path beckoning Dan to follow:

"Come quickly. He's bleeding badly. Please hurry."

Burke passed through the gate, quickly followed by Dan. The two men soon passed by where Fr Pizarro was hiding. As soon as the sound of their footsteps disappeared around the corner, the Spanish Priest leapt over the wall and ran towards the cottage, as quietly as possible.

"Look he's in a bad way; do you know first aid at all?" Fr Burke cried while Dan Joyce examined the shape of Fr Malone:

"It's a terrible blow to the head he's had." Dan stated, wiping blood from his fingers on to his trousers:

"It must have been a nasty smash you were having."

He scratched his head.

"We'd better get him back to the cottage. It's a lucky thing; I've got someone there that can go and get help."

Father Burke and Dan Joyce carefully pulled Malone out of the car and began to carry him, as gently as possible, down the road; Dan holding him under the armpits, while Fr Burke gripped him by the ankles. Fr Malone moaned and stirred, but soon fell back into deep unconsciousness.

Fr Pizarro meanwhile, had placed his four crucifixes in the ground around the cottage, in a pre arranged ritual order. Each time he stuck one in the ground he crossed himself, kissed his rosary and muttered some incantation. Then he walked boldly up to the front door and knocked gently, before twisting the doorknob and letting himself in:

"Is anyone here?" He called, quietly.

He noticed a woman and child fast asleep in the armchair. He tip toed quietly into the room and sighed deeply.

"Forgive me Lord for I know what I am about to do." He whispered.

Then he quickly and quietly crept to the fireplace and prodded the brick, behind which Aillen kept the stone. He cursed under his breath when he realised that the cavity behind the brick was empty. He glowered around the room and saw the carved box that had carried the stone on the old dresser. He tip toed over to it, constantly glancing towards the sleeping woman and child and wrenched it open.

It was empty.

"Damn!" He mouthed silently before sidling back to the front door where he had left his black bag. He picked out the can that he had brought from the old Morris and began to quietly and carefully splash the contents around the room.

He stopped when the woman turned and snored loudly.

When she didn't wake, he continued. Then, satisfied that he had spread the liquid evenly around the room, he went outside and began throwing the stuff up onto the thatched roof.

Eventually Pizarro hastily re entered the living room and went over to the armchair. He lifted the rosary with its large crucifix from his belt, held it over the woman and child and crossed himself then he motioned the stations of the cross over the sleeping couple; that done, he positioned himself carefully behind the front door.

The Priest took something black out of his pocket, crouched down and waited. All the time, watching the sleeping woman and child, just in case either stirred, neither did, not even when the front door clattered open and Fr Burke and Dan Joyce entered carrying Fr Malone:

"We'll take him through to the….." Dan called, but his instruction was cut short by a savage blow to the head from behind. He dropped to his knees, his face blank. He then released the supine figure of Fr Malone and fell forward, right over the unconscious Priest.

Fr Pizarro stood behind him, a black cosh in his hand and an expression of smug satisfaction on his face. He glanced over at the sleeping woman and child then jerked his head at Fr Burke, indicating that he should get out.

Burke's mouth fell open when he saw the figures in the armchair and he looked at Pizarro, his face horrified. He shook his head:

"It's a woman and child for goodness sake." He whispered angrily.

"What crime have they committed?"

Pizarro shook his head:

"I have blessed them." He stated calmly. "They will enter paradise. It is an unfortunate consequence I am afraid. All wars have their innocent casualties."

The beatific look on his face disappeared:

"Now get out, before I decide that you should join them."

Burke looked back towards the armchair and crossed himself:

"And what about Malone?" he asked, although he had already anticipated Pizarro's response.

Pizzaro grinned, his teeth gleaming white in the shadowed cottage.

"Like I said: innocent casualties."

Burke glanced at Joyce and Malone as they led in a heap on the floor, then he whimpered and fled.

Pizarro spat on the motionless Dan Joyce and then glanced for the last time at the woman and child with a look that was almost remorseful. He then turned and followed Burke out of the door, closing it behind him.

Something heavy scraped along the ground outside and was moved in front of the cottage's front door.

Wayne Higginbotham materialised from out of the thin air, just by the old dresser. He knelt down and cradled Dan's head in his arm and slapped his cheek with his free arm:

"Aillen, Aillen, wake up…come on, you've got to wake up. Dad, please wake up."

Dan Joyce remained motionless. Wayne bit his lip, then shouted:

"Aillen Mac Fionnbharr: Wake up for God's sake!"

He grabbed the stone in his pocket and concentrated for all he was worth.

There was a sudden thud on the roof, as though something had been thrown up onto the thatch.

Wayne looked up and heard the unmistakeable sound of crackling flames, as thick black smoke and the pungent aroma of something burning began to filter down into Mickey Finn's cottage.

43

"Now when are you going to be telling me, Tom, why in the name of Mary, Mother of Jaysus, we are driving through the middle of nowhere, in the early hours of the morning?" John O'Malley exclaimed impatiently, as he steered the silver Volvo through the lakeside village of Tourmakeady.

"I mean what makes you think they're up this way?"

"It's the ears." Tom Mick a John O'Brien explained:

"I recognised the boy's ears."

"What do you mean?" John asked incredulously.

Tom O'Brien clutched the corners of the two front seats as the car hurtled towards the mountain pass road.

"The boy's ears are the ears of a *sidh*."

"A what?" Frank asked, screwing up his face, totally mystified.

He could hardly tell what the old man was saying anyway, but now he really was talking a different language.

Tom patted Frank's shoulder. Introductions had already been carried out on the road from Tom's farm to the lakeside village of Tourmakeady:

"Don't you be worrying about it, Frank. It's an Irish thing. The sidh are the little people, fairies, or whatever you want to call them. The word comes from barrow, because they say they all used to live underground in barrows. It's a load of ould twaddle."

"Are you saying my son's a fairy, or sommat?" Frank asked in disbelief.

"Not in that way, Frank." John laughed:

"He means like a leprechaun."

"That is not what I mean!" Tom shouted angrily: "I mean he is of the "Tuatha de Danaan.""

He turned towards Frank:

"You should be knowing this John O'Malley. The "Tuatha de Danaan" lived in Ireland before the Celts; it was they who killed off the Fir Bolg, of Dun Aengus. When the Celts came, they went off and hid underground."

Wayne's grandfather turned to face Frank:

"So they've been living in caves for hundreds of years, generation after generation and your adopted boy is the son of one of them."

Frank frowned:

"Folks living in caves and such? There's been nowt on the news about it."

"It's an old wives tale." John interjected with a sceptical shake of his head.

Tom patted Frank's shoulder:

"Like I say Frank, it's an Irish thing. John, do you remember old Mickey Finn?"

John nodded.

"And do you remember his nephew, Dan Joyce?"

John nodded again. He had visited the area many times when he had been courting Molly and had met both characters on many separate occasions in Maire Duke's pub.

"Do you remember anything strange about them?" Tom asked insistently:

John shrugged:

"Not really. Two farmers is all I remember."

"Think man!"

Tom bellowed.

John shook his head:

"No!" He sighed.

The Volvo sped around a corner, tyres squealing in protest and began the ascent of the mountain pass road.

Tom let out an exasperated sigh and continued:

"There's many a man in the village who is convinced that Mickey Finn and his nephew are one and the same person.

They've never been seen together though Uncle and nephew they are supposed to be. The "Tuatha" are well known as shape shifters."

John shook his head and laughed:

"Those are just old wives tales, Tom, rural superstitions." He said, looking at Frank and raising a very sceptical eyebrow."

Frank just looked very tired and very, very confused.

Tom Mick a John O'Brien sucked his teeth indignantly:

"Ah, there's more to the world than you young folks know. I think you were away in London too long, John. You think like an Englishman. Anyway, before our Theresa was for disappearing off to London, or wherever it was she went, she was supposedly seen around a lot with Mickey Finn's American grandson."

John nodded:

"She did swear on the grave of her mother that the father of the twins was an American."

He glanced at Frank, whose forehead was creased in concentration as he tried to interpret everything that was being said.

"That's the whole point." Tom shouted triumphantly.

"Everyone who claims to know Mickey Finn knew he never had children, let alone grandchildren in America."

John shook his head and shrugged:

"Tom, that doesn't prove anything."

He threw his hands up in despair, the car swerved and everyone grabbed whatever was close at hand as John struggled to regain control:

"Jaysus, John are you for killing us all?" Katie shouted from the back seat.

"No and I'm not in for a leprechaun wild goose chase, either." John moaned, his cheeks reddening with embarrassment.

Tom Mick a John O'Brien sat back in the rear seat disconsolately.

"Don't be for believing me then. But I'll tell you this, I noticed the boy Michael's ears this morning and the only ears I've ever seen like them are the cab doors on the sides of Mickey Finn's head and Dan Joyce's.

It's just a bit more than a coincidence that our Theresa was courting a relative of theirs, just before she runs away and gives birth to a pair of babies, one of them at least bearing big pointy ears."

Katie and John both rolled their eyes, while Frank closed his tight. It wasn't just fatigue, it was also fear. The Volvo had almost reached the summit of the pass and was taking hairpin bends like a competitor in the Monte Carlo rally.

He opened them again when he heard a huge intake of breath and felt both Tom and Katie move to stare through the gap between the front seats. The car had finally got to the top of the pass and had it been daylight they would have had a clear view right over the valley. As it was the only illumination was a furiously blazing building way down in the distant valley bottom.

"Jaysus Christ!" Tom gasped: "That's Finn's place!"

44

"Wake up father!" Wayne heard himself shouting, although since he had clutched the stone he seemed to have somehow moved away from Aillen. Wayne almost felt like he was watching the events before him unfold on a TV screen. He was there, but somehow, he wasn't. Nothing seemed real any more. It was like when he had heard someone knocking on the cottage door, for reasons he had not understood, he had suddenly felt afraid. He had clutched the stone and wished for invisibility. Suddenly it was as though he had been floating, weightlessly, peering out at the room through a thick green mist. He had watched the weird looking, long haired Priest come into the cottage and had seen him searching fruitlessly for Aillen's stone. When he had failed to find it, he had poured some liquid all over the place. His face had been twisted in a manic grin as he had glanced furtively around the room, ensuring that the liquid was evenly spread.

The Priest obviously hadn't seen Wayne, even though the boy had been watching every move that he had made. It had come as quite a shock to Wayne to realise that he really was invisible. He had wished for it and it had happened. Before he had the time to fully appreciate his new magical power, however, Wayne's attention had flicked back to the black-eyed priest.

It worried Wayne that the mad looking clergyman was making some strange gesture over Molly and Patsy. It was what he'd seen Priests do over dead people on the TV. They weren't dead were they?

Wayne had then heard voices outside. The mad Priest had looked around urgently and had then rushed over to the front door and hidden himself just behind where it opened.

There had been a clamour as the door of the cottage suddenly burst open and a second Priest had barged in with Dan Joyce. They were struggling to carry an injured younger Priest.

Wayne had been glad that he had seemed invisible, when he saw the black haired Priest club Dan unconscious. What the heck was going on?

The mad looking priest and the one who had just burst into the cottage had fled out through the door as quickly as their legs would carry them, leaving Dan and the younger Priest in a heap by the door. Wayne had heard something heavy being pulled across the door outside and with a sinking feeling in his gut, he had finally begun to understand exactly what was going on.

Now he was clutching the stone tightly in his fist again, willing Ailleen to wake with all his might. He was aware of the strange fog billowing around him, but this time shadowy figures began to emerge and surround him. The bearded red haired King Fionnbharr and several others, younger looking men and women. Could they be Aillen's late sons and daughters? Wayne wondered.

Was he in Tir na Nog already?

Was he dead?

Wayne was so amazed that he almost forgot the urgency of the situation. Then he heard Fionnbharr shout at Aillen in a language Wayne didn't understand. The others joined in, although he didn't understand the words, Wayne could understand that they were shouting encouragement and warnings.

Aillen's eyes flickered open and he groaned as he pushed himself up on one elbow and put his hand behind his head where the priest had clubbed him:

"Ohhh, my head." He moaned.

Wayne quickly put the stone back in his pocket; the fog and the shades of Wayne's ancestors and kin quickly vanished, revealing a room filling rapidly with thick, choking black smoke.

"Father, you've got to wake Molly and Patsy. They've set the roof on fire and one of them poured some stuff all over this room."

Wayne desperately informed his father, trying his best not to sound as though he was panicking.

Aillen blinked and put his hand to the back of his head again:

"Oh my head, my head is bursting. Help me up son." He said weakly. Wayne did his best and Aillen, still in the shape of Dan Joyce clambered to his feet, painfully.

"The demon yellow spleen." He gasped:

"It's what they've always used to burn us out of our houses and homes, or to burn us in them."

He reached down and touched Fr James Malone's forehead:

"This one must be on our side if they intended to burn him with us. I've met him before. I felt he was a good man even then. Wake Christian, wake quickly!"

Aillen commanded, softly, as he shook the young Priests shoulder.

Fr Malone, blinked, grimaced and then groaned and twisted his body. His eyes flickered open like Aillen's had moments earlier and he began, slowly and painfully, to rise:

"Where am I?" He gasped, before coughing as smoke billowed down into his mouth.

Wayne helped him to get upright while Dan rushed over and woke Molly and Patsy. Smoke was now billowing down into the living room in great clouds and burning stalks of thatch were beginning to float down into the room.

"I'm afraid you've woken up in a house on fire." Wayne informed the groggy, young Priest:

"That's a nasty cut on your forehead."

Fr Malone shook his head vigorously:

"Oh my Lord!" He gasped again, as he realised where he was and saw the smoke filling the room. Molly and Patsy were both coughing violently as Dan helped them to the door.

Dan tried to open the door, but it was jammed shut. Somehow the Priests had wedged something against it from the outside.

Dan covered his mouth with a filthy old handkerchief:

"The back way, come on!" He commanded.

There was a sudden rush of heat as the liquid that the priest had poured, ignited at the far end of the living room. Rivers of flame danced quickly around the Spartan furniture.

A groggy looking Fr Malone, Molly, Patsy and Wayne all followed Dan into his bedroom, all were now coughing and flames were beginning to lick through the bedroom ceiling as he slammed the bedroom door shut. It would only be seconds before clumps of burning thatch fell through onto the fuel that Pizarro had sprinkled around the bedroom and that went too. The whole house was going up in flames like a tinderbox.

"There's no door in here." Fr Malone coughed desperately.

Dan picked up a table allowing a jug and bowl to fall onto the floor and smash. He hurled the table against the window, which smashed, allowing smoke to billow out. Then he pushed with all his might against the wall underneath the window.

"Help me!" He barked at Malone who put his shoulder to the wall and began to push too. Both men were struggling to breathe let alone push. Molly and Patsy's faces were now black and tear streaked and their terrified eyes betrayed just how desperate they had become.

The wall gave way surprisingly easily. Flames licked through the bedroom door as the interior of the cottage quickly turned into an inferno and the smoke was now so thick that none of them could see more than an inch in front of their noses. Dan pushed the coughing Molly, Patsy and Wayne unceremoniously out through the hole in the wall, they obeyed quickly and without question, then Fr Malone squeezed through, followed by Dan. A wall of flame exploded behind him, igniting his tweed jacket as he emerged into the night. Dan threw himself forward and rolled on the ground as the others collapsed where they stood, coughing and gasping for breath, their faces blackened and their clothes and hair scorched.

Behind them the sound of timbers cracking and crashing into the cottage living room reverberated throughout the wooded copse. Flames danced high above the cottage into the inky black sky.

All five figures led on the grass coughing and moaning for what seemed like several minutes, but was probably only seconds before Dan stood:

"That was too damn close. Molly, take Patsy and Michael through those trees and run over that field to the road. Get to your car, get in it and stay there." Dan shouted between coughing fits. Despite the serious predicament they had just escaped and the gravity of their situation, Wayne couldn't help but smirk as he noticed that his father's face was comically blackened with soot, like one of the black and white minstrels off the telly. Dan's eyes shone in the dark, like the headlamps of a distant car:

"What's going on?" Molly demanded, totally confused:

"What time is it? Why did you let me fall asleep?" She coughed violently again.

Dan glowered at her blackened face:

"Do as I say woman and do it quickly! You and the boys are in great danger. All will be explained later."

There was something about Dan's voice now that was much nearer to Aillen's. It certainly didn't invite dissent. Molly put her arm around her coughing son:

"Come on Patsy and you Michael." She shouted.

Dan looked at Wayne.

"Go, boy!" He shouted.

Wayne's teeth showed up white from his sooty face as he grinned back at his father:

"What? And miss all the fun? You take Patsy, Aunty Molly, I'll be along shortly."

Molly glanced at Dan who glared at Wayne momentarily then he turned to Wayne's Aunt and nodded. She ran off into the trees, dragging a still coughing Patsy behind her.

Fr Malone had crawled off across the rough back garden and was lying coughing and spluttering in the darkness near the trees. Dan marched around the edge of his garden towards the front of the humungous bonfire that had been his home:

"How did you break the wall so easily?" Wayne asked, trotting beside him. Aillen, still in the shape of Dan, looked down at his son and grinned.

"When is a door, not a door?"

"When it's ajar?" Wayne suggested, familiar with the old riddle but somehow convinced that that wasn't the right answer in this case.

"Correct." Aillen agreed:

"But also when it's a simple pile of loose bricks, cunningly disguised as a wall. You remember to always have an escape route planned, my son, when you've been persecuted for as long as we have."

He looked up as they edged around the walled garden to the front of the burning house. Wayne noticed that Aillen was now glaring at two black robed figures standing motionless in the road, their faces illuminated red in the light of the cottage inferno.

"It's not the first time I've had my house set alight and burned down around me." Aillen spat, staring straight ahead, his eyes betraying his naked fury.

Aillen Mac Fionnbharr dispensed with the Dan Joyce disguise and morphed into his natural shape. It was no longer a rotund, middle aged Irish farmer that stood by Wayne's side, but a tall, regal warrior of the "Tuatha de Danaan."

"This time you will do my bidding my son. Hide under those trees and stay there. This could get nasty." Aillen warned Wayne, as he walked crazily close to the flaming ruin, so that his silhouette stood out clearly in front of the conflagration.

Even from where he stood Wayne could feel the heat burning his skin. This time, sensing his father's mood, he did as he was told and retreated into the shadows under the trees.

Aillen seemed impervious to the heat as he walked across the front of what had once been his home.

Fr Burke was the first to notice the tall imposing figure of the medieval looking warrior, striding purposefully across the front of the burning cottage. He began to tremble and point:

"The, the, the…"

Pizarro, who had been smiling smugly, indulging his body in the warm heat of the fire, his eyes closed in anticipation of his "Order's" final victory; glowered at his colleague:

"What?" He hissed.

Before Burke could answer, however, he followed the Irish Priest's terrified gaze and saw the lone figure seemingly emerging, phoenix like, from the flames.

Pizarro's black eyes glittered in the flickering orange light and his lip curled contemptuously:

"Demon!" He bellowed charging forward through the cottage's gateway into the blistering heat of the front garden.

It was all too much for Fr Burke.

He screamed like a terrified little girl and ran. He ran for all he was worth back up the road, in the direction of the battered Morris.

Aillen and Fr Pizarro stood before one another, like gunfighters in a western movie, on either side of the small garden:

"Why do you persecute me?" Aillen asked; his forehead creased in a puzzled frown:

"Why has the Church that you represent murdered my people? Why does your God fear us so?"

Pizarro's face contorted with fury:

"How dare you ape the words of our Lord." He spat:

"We do not fear you. My God fears no one. We hate you because you are the unnatural servants of Satan. You are the "fallen," the would-be killers of Our Lord, Jesus Christ. We will not endure the prophecy. The Lord, our God, does not condone immortality, only God the Father, the Son and the Holy Ghost, can be truly immortal and he will return and reign for a thousand years."

Above the crackle of the flames and the crashing of beams and timbers, Aillen had to shout to make himself heard:

"We have never harmed your God, your Church, or you. We have no intention of ever harming your God. Your God is supposed to represent love. What love is it that would murder women and children as they sleep?" He held out his hands, as though mimicking the crucifixion.

Pizarro moved towards Aillen, his face purple with rage, his eyes reflecting the fire before them, his hands punching the air, emphasising every word as he spoke:

"You do not fool me, demon. We know you are the last of your kind, the supposed "Slanaitheoir mor.""

Aillen flinched as though he had been struck. Pizarro laughed:

"Oh yes, I know all about such things. I am as cursed as you are, demon. My mother was as you. An Irish witch who charmed my Father with her evil incantations and spells. My cursed mother was a "Tuatha" sorceress, who told me such tales as that of this so called "Slanaitheoir mor," before I was wise enough to stop listening to her. She bewitched my father into falling in love with her when he had been cast helpless upon the shores of this miserable rock. She didn't even have the good grace to grow old as he did. Everyone could see that she was an enchantress. Everyone could see it, except for my poor fool of a father who refused to denounce her, even unto his death. Both of them were burned by the blessed inquisition when I was but a boy of twelve years.

My father had made sure that I was a good Catholic, despite his devotion to the witch. Even so, I was only saved from being cast onto the flames with them both, by a Bishop from within the "Sacred Order of St. Gregory." A Bishop who was wise enough to realise that the best way to fight demons, was to use one of their own against them.

When my inheritance was taken from me, my title, even my name, the "Sacred Order of St. Gregory" was good enough to spare my life and raise me. I am the sword arm of Our Lord. I have repaid them a thousand-fold, by taking your kind, her kind, to the very brink of extinction."

He brushed his long black hair behind his large and now obviously pointed ears and held up his hand, palm forward.

"It ends here, demon." He screamed.

There was a flash like lightening and Aillen was blasted off his feet, landing heavily on his back, almost by the wall of the burning cottage.

It seemed like all the air had been blasted out of his lungs and he struggled to raise himself up on one elbow, coughing and wheezing in the intense heat.

Pizarro walked across the grass, his face set in an arrogant sneer, the flaming building reflected in his cold black eyes.

Aillen climbed onto one knee:

"It is your own kind you are murdering, you fool. What was your father's name?" Aillen spluttered, as the last of the cottages roof joists crashed into the room below, just behind him.

"What is my name to you, fiend?" Pizarro shouted.

"It is important that I know the name of the one who wishes to kill me, especially as he is one of us." Aillen answered.

Pizarro smiled his thin smile and raised his right hand.

Aillen was lifted from the ground and dragged like a limp rag doll towards the black eyed Priest.

"You shall die, cursing in ignorance." The Priest grinned:

"I have placed four pieces of the stone of Falias around the cottage, pieces emplaced in crucifixes. Pieces that respond to me and now work in the name of the Lord of Hosts. They are the remnants of my own mother's stone. I found the hiding place of your stone when we first searched your hovel, demon. It was my intent to remove it, so that you would be weakened beyond measure, but fortune is with you tonight. It is unfortunate that you can still call upon the power of the stone, but shape shifting and invisibility tricks will not save you now. Prepare to feel the bitter sting of mortality."

He raised his hand again.

Aillen raised his right hand in defence, as if to fend off a punch.

There was an intense flash of light as Aillen's palm seemed to absorb the magical energy that Pizarro had hurled.

Pizarro staggered backwards, looking confused.

Aillen jumped up and put his hands confidently on his hips:

"Ah, my friend, it is not I who am the fool. I lured you here. I knew my careless words to a young Priest would eventually worm their way to the Roman snake pit that you slither around in. I knew you would come. I needed to find out if my suspicions were correct and that our main tormentor over the last four hundred years was indeed, one of our own."

Pizarro thrust his palm forward. There was another flash of light. This time Aillen staggered and coughed as the energy bolt hit him squarely in the chest, but he continued to stand:

"I hid the stone this night, because I knew who you were when you came here and violated my home. I can more than match your power, traitor, stone, or no. Yet know this now, that I am not the "Slanaitheoir mor." Even if you succeed in killing me, you have failed. The prophecy refers to one who is of both Tuatha and mortal Royal blood. I can only claim the former."

Pizzaro cursed and raised his palm again.

A ball of light flew from his outstretched hand. Aillen caught it in his own hand, like a child catching a ball.

"Your entire life has been a failure for the "Slanaitheoir mor" is not what you think. He is a power for good, not evil."

"Liar!" Pizarro cried as he fired another bolt.

The "Slanaitheoir mor" is God's assassin.

Aillen brushed the bolt aside.

"Do you see how the shards of your stone have no dominion over me? That can only mean, as I suspected, that your stone was once part of mine. It was given freely, as a token of love and it still bends its power towards me." Aillen shouted, raising both hands.

Two bolts of white light hurtled towards the Priest, who was knocked flat onto his back.

Pizarro turned over and crawled up onto his knees. He used the gate to clamber upright, looking shaken, the arrogance drained from his face.

Aillen walked slowly towards him, contemptuously glancing aside another weak energy bolt that the Priest fired at him.

"And now I finally know who you are, no matter what name you hide behind: Senor Albaya de Greco."

"How do you know that?" Pizarro snarled; agony etched all over his face:

"How do you know that? That name has been banned from utterance since the year of our Lord Sixteen Hundred and Three. How did you know?"

He now seemed genuinely worried.

Now it Aillen's turn to snarl as he lurched forward and grabbed Pizarro by the scruff of his neck:

"Because your wretch of a Father stole the only woman that I had ever loved, the woman I worshipped for nearly two thousand of your years. I saved his miserable skin and that is how he repaid me. He stole my wife, the mother of my children and the light of my life. I am only glad that, in the end, he loved her enough to die for her. You are the half brother of my own long dead children. You probably even killed some of them."

His voice choked and he pushed Pizarro away.

From the shadow of the trees Wayne had watched as the two immortals had engaged in magical combat with his heart in his throat. He had been transfixed, totally incredulous as he had watched the warrior and the Priest hurling balls of energy from the palms of their hands.

Then he thought back to his confrontation with Baz Thompson. How he had held his hand up, palm outwards and Baz had flown through the air as though he had been punched by Mohammed Ali.

It was all beginning to become clear to the eleven-year old boy, that things were never going to be same again.

Another flash snapped him out of his reverie.

Wayne had only just found his Father; he was desperately worried that he might lose him before he had really got to know him. Yet he knew that there was nothing he could do to help. He felt an arm creep around his shoulder. Fr James Malone stood by him, his sooty, blood streaked face looking haggard in the firelight:

"Are you OK?" Fr Malone gasped. Wayne nodded:

"Yeah, are you?" he whispered.

The priest nodded back:

"What were you doing here?" Malone asked.

Wayne hardly dared turn away from the combatants, but he glanced quickly at Malone.

"I'm sorry, I suppose I was responsible for bringing the others along." Malone whispered regretfully:

"Pizarro lied to me. I knew from the first time I saw him that there was something evil, something otherworldly about him. He told me some cock and bull tale about losing a sister and; fool that I am, I believed him."

Malone's face had coloured in anger even in the darkness and his voice had got slightly louder as he spoke.

"Because of him a good Priest died today. I wonder how many more he has killed over the years. Well, there will be no more. It ends here!"

He let go of Wayne's shoulder, picked up a large broken branch from the ground and began to stagger forward out of the shadows.

Wayne looked on totally petrified, rooted to the spot.

"You are the evil one, Pizarro." Fr Malone bellowed:

"Not him, leave him alone."

Aillen turned his head towards the advancing young Priest.

The next few seconds seemed to Wayne to happen in slow motion.

As Aillen turned to see Malone charging furiously out of the shadows, his concentration was momentarily distracted; Pizarro swiftly unclipped the golden crucifix from his rosary chain and pulled it apart. The silver blue glint of a cold steel blade shone brightly in the firelight. Wayne, horrified, saw that the crucifix contained a knife:

"Noooo!" He shouted, rushing forward, but it was too late.

Pizarro leapt forward and plunged the knife deep into Aillen's chest, once, then twice.

Aillen turned back to face Pizarro, a look of total surprise on his blackened face then he fell to his knees, his hands clutched to his chest.

45

The silver Volvo raced down the twisting pass road, as though hordes of demons were hanging on its tail-lights. At every hairpin bend its rear end swung around almost as if it wasn't connected to the rest of the car, tyres screaming and smoking in protest.

John O'Malley was driving as fast as he had ever driven in his life and he had spent years rallying in his younger days.

A white-faced Frank Higginbotham clutched the door handle, hanging on for all he was worth, while in the back, Tom O'Brien and Katie held on to whatever they could.

No one had spoken since they had first seen the burning cottage from the top of the pass. Everyone in the car had their own thoughts and fears. Not the least of which was whether they would actually reach the cottage alive. As the car spun around the last tight bend on the hill, John noticed a single headlight bumping up and down in the road coming in their direction. The powerful halogen headlights of the Volvo soon picked up a strange sight, an ancient smashed up Morris Minor, with a front wing missing, only one headlight and a very flat tyre was skidding along the road towards them. Sparks were flying up from the bare wheel rim and the driver was obviously drunk, or mad, because the car was veering from left to right all over the road and the driver was obviously struggling to control it. At the speed John was travelling he knew he could not stop in time and all four in the Volvo watched horrified, as the Morris and the Volvo careered straight towards one another.

Then at the last moment the Morris veered straight off the road right in front of them. The solitary headlight flicked up into the air like a small searchlight and then disappeared, before shining up again as the Morris tumbled and rolled down a steep bank.

"Jaysus." John gasped:

"We'd better stop!"

Tom O'Brien grasped his shoulder:

"We've Molly, Patsy and Michael to be finding first. We'll come back and see what happened here, once we've made sure they are not in that fire. The man must have been out of his mind to be trying to drive that wreck anyway."

Frank, shaken as he was, was relieved to hear Tom's decisiveness. He had travelled too far to find that his son had been reduced to charcoal.

John nodded, took a deep breath and stamped on the accelerator and the Volvo surged powerfully forward again, hurtling down the road towards the flames.

46

Fr Pizarro turned towards Fr James Malone as he staggered across the cottage's garden.

"You?" He hissed and held up his hand, palm towards the young Priest.

"Your part in this is over, you fool!"

Malone was thrown up into the air like a loose leaf being tossed in the wind. He landed with a thud dangerously close to the burning cottage.

The young priest cried out in pain, his arm still clutching the branch, was bent at an acute angle underneath him. He struggled to get up, but howled again when he put weight on his obviously broken limb.

Pizarro smiled and turned his attention back to the kneeling figure of Aillen in front of him.

"So demon, it was the power of steel, not the stone that finally killed you."

He began to cackle.

"And trust me, if you are not the last of the "Tuatha de Danaan," then I shall find them and kill them. I will kill them all. There will be no "Slanaitheoir mor". Whatever it takes, God's assassin will never be born."

Wayne looked on horrified. Pizarro did not seem to have heard his cry, nor had he noticed the boy's approach, he must have presumed that the voice shouting "No" had been the young Priest and he was too busy gloating over the fallen Aillen.

Wayne was shaking all over, just like he had been when Baz Thompson had been mocking him, just like he had been when Baz had been ready to finish him off. It was strange, it seemed like all of that had taken place a million years ago, so much had happened in the few short weeks, since Baz had cornered him on the corner of Cavendish Street.

Wayne could see Pizarro laughing in the light of the flames.

He was laughing at Wayne's father, just like Baz Thompson had laughed at him.

Wayne felt the hairs on the back of his neck start to rise as he walked forward. A strange buzzing sound began to sound in his ears.

Wayne Higginbotham could fire energy bolts too. He had done it before.

"Oi, freako!" He shouted: "Leave my Father alone."

This time Pizarro did notice him.

The Priest's black eyes flicked up as he saw the small boy walking towards him.

Aillen sank onto his haunches. He turned too:

"No, run boy, run." He gasped, weakly.

A wicked leer creased Pizarro lips:

"What is this? A child?"

Aillen grimaced and coughed:

"Run boy!"

Pizarro edged forward:

"Yours? He is yours, is he not? Yesss, I can see the ears even in this light. Oh sweet winged victory. You have a son, so you are truly not the last. It is this one who is the "Slanaitheoir mor" isn't it?"

He grabbed Aillen by the hair and pulled his head back.

"Deny that this is the one, if you dare."

He began to laugh out loud.

Aillen's face creased in agony and his mouth moved, but Pizarro couldn't hear him.

"Ha, You have lived long enough to see your last hope die." The Spaniard snarled as he threw the limp Aillen down to the ground, twisting his body round so that he was facing Wayne and would be able to witness his son's demise.

Wayne just kept marching forward.

All he could see was the Priest in the black cassock, with a bloody knife in his hand.

All he could hear was the Priest laughing dementedly.

Wayne walked determinedly across the grass; the heat from the fire seemed to grow suddenly cold. He got closer and closer to the Priest, with the black hair, who suddenly stopped laughing.

The Priest held up his hand, just as he had against the younger churchman.

Wayne felt as though he had been hit by a blast of hot air, but he kept on walking.

Baz Thompson, black-haired, evil Priest, what was the difference?

They both wanted to hurt him, both wanted him dead and that made Wayne Higginbotham cross. The fact that this one had hurt Wayne's true father made him very cross indeed.

Wayne lifted his right hand, his palm facing outwards. He felt energy surge through him, just like it had back on Cavendish Street.

Father Francisco Pizarro scowled. His blasts had not harmed the boy.

Doubt crept into his eyes for the first time.

Wayne's first blast hit the "Order's" prime assassin squarely in the middle of his chest.

The black haired Priest flew up into the air and fell backwards, his arms flailing like windmills, just like Baz Thompson had done.

For the first time since that fight, Wayne knew that he had power. Little Wayne Higginbotham had power beyond imagination and he now knew how to use it.

He also realised that Aillen's stone somehow amplified his powers.

Wayne Higginbotham realised that he could do the sort of things that Superman did and he didn't even have to wear his underpants outside his tights.

He was even more powerful than Mr. Spock

He continued to walk forward.

The Priest scrambled up on to his feet.

Wayne noticed that the black robed figure certainly wasn't laughing now. His black eyes showed something else now, something more than the reflection of flames. The Priest's eyes showed fear.

Wayne gripped the stone in his pocket and the green fog began to envelop him.

The Priest grimaced, baring his shining white teeth, then he screamed with rage and held up his hand to deliver his most powerful blow.

Wayne was suddenly aware of a crowd walking with him. There, right next to him, marched mighty Fionnbharr, High King of the "Tuatha de Danaan," next to him his consort Oonagh and behind them Aillen's other sons. My half brothers, Wayne thought with pride. On his other side marched other figures: including a tall mean looking warrior figure wearing a gold circlet around his brow and bearing an enormous club

"You must be Dagda." Wayne thought, remembering the tales of Dan O'Doherty and what Aillen had told him. The warrior turned and nodded gravely. Next to him stood a younger figure, but who looked strangely similar:

"Angus Og? Son of Dagda?" Wayne wondered.

The second warrior smiled.

Before he could identify any of the others another hot blast hit Wayne and he noticed the Tuatha warrior's hair blowing back as though they were standing in a very strong wind.

Wayne turned his attention back to the mad priest who was standing with a look of total amazement all over his face. He had concentrated all his venom and spite into one huge expulsion of power that he had fully expected to incinerate the audacious brat of a child who had dared to challenge him.

The boy hadn't even flinched.

Pizarro's mouth fell open.

Wayne continued to walk towards the confused Francisco Pizarro:

"Vicars are supposed to be nice. You're not a very nice Vicar are you? You just stabbed my father. I don't think God will be very happy with you."

Wayne felt anger surging through his body, he saw the red mist fall over his eyes, just like it had in Shepton, he bared his teeth aggressively and lifted his hand.

Wayne felt a great surge of power rush down his arm and a sensation like an electric shock as a bolt of energy left his outstretched hand.

The Priest was lifted off his feet and flew straight back into the garden wall. The impact of his body on the stone making a satisfying, bone crunching thud.

The Tuatha surrounding Wayne nodded approvingly:

Fionnbharr grinned and motioned a finger across his throat.

Wayne turned back to the Priest who was crouching and cowering by the wall, his breath knocked out of him:

"Don't hurt me." The crestfallen Spanish assassin wheezed pathetically:

"They made me do it. I am like you. Look, I have the same ears."

He scraped his hair back behind his ears again:

"I could help you. I could protect you. I know the lore of our people. I know who you are....."

He started to breathe violently:

"It is you, isn't it? You are the one, aren't you?" He cried:

"It was never him, was it?"

He pointed at the figure of Aillen, who had struggled back on to his knees:

"It was never him at all. They were wrong. It's you. You are the "Slanaitheoir mor." You are God's assassin. It is you who is the subject of the prophecy."

Father Francisco Pizarro crossed himself and started to mutter some prayer while fiddling with his rosary beads, his eyes wide and panicked, reflecting the reds and oranges of the furious conflagration that was consuming Aillen's home.

Pizarro's words seemed to freeze Wayne.

Although Aillen had told him about the prophecies of the "Tuatha de Danaan" and "The Sacred Order of St.Gregory," the apparent confirmation that he did have a key role to play in the climax of some ancient apocalyptic power play, suddenly seemed to overwhelm him.

How could he, little Wayne Higginbotham from Gas Street Primary School in Shepton suddenly have become so important?

Fr Pizarro took full advantage of Wayne's fleeting lapse in concentration and seemed to suddenly leap up and rush forward, all in one rapid, fluid motion. The rosary was cast aside and the knife that had been hidden in the crucifix was held high above his head. His black eyes were ablaze as he rushed towards the boy. Madness had seized Pizarro and momentarily Wayne didn't have a clue what to do.

"Oh bum!" was the only thought that passed through his mind.

Even before Wayne had a chance to raise his hand to defend himself, however, a large dark shadow flew swiftly straight over the garden wall.

Wayne had no idea where it had come from, nor had Pizarro.

The shadow landed on two very firm feet right in front of the insane Priest and before he could do anything about it, the shadow swung a mighty right hook, which caught Pizarro squarely on the chin. Pizarro's head flew back forcing him to let go of the knife, which dropped to the ground. The shadowy figure crouched slightly, instinctively, like a boxer, and threw a second punch, a haymaker this time, which sent the mad Priest stumbling helplessly back down the garden path towards the burning cottage.

Pizarro tripped and fell onto his bottom, his face dazed and his facial expression even more confused. His eyes still burned with the same malevolence, however, and years of combat experience had taught him never to allow his opponent an advantage. He shook his head quickly and recovered enough to jump upright in two rapid movements that would have shamed an Olympic gymnast.

Pizarro's mouth, despite the fact that blood was pouring down his chin, began to twist in an arrogant sneer, as he faced the shadow that had come between him and his prey. What he had failed to notice was that the figure had stooped every bit as quickly as Pizarro had risen and had picked up the blade. Wayne watched, transfixed as Pizarro's own knife, the knife he had used on Aillen, arced gracefully through the air, its aim straight and true. It hit its owner right in the middle of his chest.

Pizarro looked down in disbelief at the sight of his own weapon sticking out of his body, his eyes now wide with shock. He frowned, completely unable to comprehend what had happened. He looked up at the shadowy figure, mouthed something unintelligible and shook his head in disbelief.

Pizarro gritted his teeth, grabbed the hilt of the knife and pulled it out of his chest. He lifted his face once more to face whatever it was that had become his new nemesis.

Wayne thrust the palm of his hand out towards the evil Priest once more.

He felt the power surging up through him again, a warmth that seemed to course through his veins. He could feel something inexplicable leaving the palm of his hand, as though a thunderbolt of pure rage was blasting out of his body.

Pizarro was lifted into the air and flew swiftly through what had been the door of the cottage, disappearing into the flames with a searing scream of anguish and pain. No more than a millisecond later, the final remnants of the roof and the entire front wall of what had been Mickey Finn and Dan Joyce's cottage collapsed into what had now become a funeral Pyre.

47

It was John O'Malley who had first noticed the Austin Maxi parked in the gateway in the side of the road, near the burning cottage:

"Jaysus, that's Molly's car, there." He had gasped, as the Volvo's headlights picked out the tail-lights and Galway number plate.

"Holy Mother of God, don't let them be in that cottage." John had cried as he slammed his foot on the brake pedal

"There's someone getting out." Frank had commented as the Volvo screeched to a halt. Molly had emerged from the Maxi and had run towards the Volvo as all four doors had been thrown wide open and John, Frank, Tom and Katie had jumped out simultaneously.

"John, thank God. Thank God it's you. They tried to set us on fire." Molly had wailed as she fell into John's arms:

"Who? Who tried to set you on fire?" John had demanded as he had wiped his hand over her soot blackened face.

"I don't know; they looked like, like Priests."

Molly had shaken her head uncomprehendingly.

"Is Patsy OK?" John had shouted. Molly had nodded:

"Patsy's in the car asleep, he's fine, but Michael's still over there."

She had turned and pointed towards the burning cottage.

Frank Higginbotham hadn't needed to hear any more. He had already been running down the road towards the burning building, long before Molly had finished her sentence. Despite spending almost forty-eight hours constantly travelling, sitting immobile in cars, or on ship. Frank had known somehow that he now needed to move faster than he had ever moved before. As he had closed on the cottage, his heart pumping, he had begun to discern dark shapes silhouetted by flames in front of the burning building. One figure had been crawling away from the building, another was kneeling on the garden path, his head bowed, but most crucially one was rushing towards a much smaller figure, with what looked like a knife raised above his head.

Almost thirty years of forced inaction, suddenly evaporated from Frank Higginbotham's life.

Over Twenty odd years of screwing thingummys onto widgets and then packing them into boxes was forgotten within the blink of an eye.

Twenty odd years of suppressed rage suddenly exploded into action.

Private Frank Higginbotham, once a desert rat of Monty's Eighth Army was back at war.

He had approached the wall at speed and at an angle, like an athlete approaching the high jump and with just a single hand briefly touching the top of the wall; he had vaulted over it, in one clear bound, landing on his feet right in front of the surprised knife wielding assailant. Just like all those years earlier, Frank hadn't wasted time thinking about tactics or plans, he had simply acted with instinctive perfect timing, his well aimed blow striking home with devastating force, right on the knifeman's chin. The follow up punch had caught his cheekbone and forced him to stumble back towards the cottage.

It had all seemed so strangely familiar to Frank, burning ruins, the wounded and the dying lying around nearby. He hadn't even had to think when the knife landed blade down in the grass at his feet. He had just snatched it up, taken aim and hurled it with all his might. Just like his Sergeant-Major had taught him, so long ago.

It really was as though he was still fighting the Nazis, just that now the uniforms were different and this time he wasn't throwing a grenade, he was throwing a knife.

It was only when the enemy had fallen back into the house and it had collapsed around him that Frank had taken time to think. Time to breathe again; he certainly wasn't as fit as he had been, all those years earlier:

"Dad?" He heard a familiar voice coming from somewhere behind him. He bent double, rested his hands on his knees and took in several great gulps of air before turning and receiving a flying Wayne into his arms.

"That was brilliant Dad. Just totally, bloody brilliant."

Wayne was crying his eyes out, as he hugged his Dad.

"Language! Wayne, please." Frank whispered as relief and joy flooded his mind.

"You saved me." Wayne's eyes shone with pride as he pushed back and stared incredulously at the face of his adoptive father.

Frank couldn't help but cry too.

There had been times over the past few days, when he had imagined that he might never see his son again. Wayne and Frank held each other tight; then suddenly Wayne pushed back again.

"Just a minute Dad. There's something I've got to do."

He rushed over to the kneeling figure on the path.

The figure struggled to raise its head.

Wayne knelt down and the figure collapsed into the boy's arms.

"Don't die father, please don't die, Aillen." Wayne sobbed. Aillen Mac Fionnbharr coughed and then grinned painfully.

"He was right my son. The Spaniard was right. You are the "Slanaitheoir mor." Your power already surpasses mine. It is as was foretold."

"How can I be something I can't even say?" Wayne sobbed and laughed at the same time.

"You are a descendent of a High King of the "Tuatha de Danaan" and now I have realised you must also be a direct descendent of the mortal High King: Brian Boru: The last

High King of Ireland. Your mother is an O'Brien. It has truly come to pass: the Union of the High Kings of the "Tuatha" and of mortal man. There is no doubt now, my son. You are the "Slanaitheoir mor."

"But what does the Slanathy moor thingy do?" Wayne asked plaintively.

Aillen smiled:

"You will know that when the time comes. Look after that stone, my son, and gather the four that our friend planted around the cottage. They will give you more strength than any immortal has had for many hundreds of years."

He coughed, more violently this time.

"I will always be there with you, with my father and his kin. We will watch over you, my son. You must find your sister, we will watch over her too."

He coughed again and his entire body seemed to convulse.

Wayne was aware of a hand on his shoulder and looked round to see Frank staring down at the being who was Wayne's real father.

Aillen looked up at him and held out a hand. Frank gripped it:

"You are the boy's only father now. Look after him well, for he is a Prince of two great races and there will always be those who will wish to do him harm. His destiny is one of greatness."

Aillen coughed, this time blood splattered the path in front of him. He gritted his teeth and continued:

"You are a true warrior, rarely have I seen a mortal show such bravery and skill."

Aillen coughed again and closed his eyes.

"I will guard him with my life for as long as I live." Frank whispered, with tears now coursing from his own eyes, as he realised that the dying man was his adopted son's real father.

"Then you shall be truly honoured amongst the "Tuatha" and shall drink with us in the last long hall at the final reckoning."

He beckoned Frank to lean closer and his voice became little more than a croak:

"Dig below the little hut behind the cottage. There is great wealth there. Wealth fitting for a Prince of the "Tuatha de Danaan.""

With that Aillen Mac Fionnbharr gasped, shuddered and with a last faint smile, a squeeze of Wayne's hand and a barely noticeable wink, died.

48

All of those who saw Aillen Mac Fionnbharr die, never forgot what happened next.

And of those who watched the passing of the last of the true, pure blooded "Tuatha de Danaan," few of them would ever know that they had witnessed an event of such significance.

Father James Malone watched.

He had finally managed to get up and had struggled over to where the weeping boy knelt, by his immortal father. Fr Malone was about to offer Aillen the last rites, but he was too late.

Tom Mick a John O'Brien watched.

He had hugged Molly and then he had jogged as quickly as he manage down the road to find out what had happened to his newly discovered grandson Michael. He had just reached the wall and had watched in silence as Aillen had passed away.

John and Molly O'Brien watched.

They had followed Tom down the road once John had checked on Patsy. They had arrived at the very moment of Aillen's dramatic passing.

And, of course, Frank Higginbotham and his adopted son Wayne watched.

For Wayne, the passing of Aillen Mac Fionnbharr, was the saddest moment of his young life and it would be many years before his heart was to be broken in such a way again.

The one thing that everyone there agreed upon, was that as he had died, Aillen's body had suddenly been surrounded by a sort of glowing, swirling green mist that had risen from the ground like smoke. Everyone there swore that they had seen the shapes of people moving within the mist and that they had seen the shapes pick up Aillen's body, which had seemed to miraculously recover, dust itself down and then wave at the boy and the man standing nearby, before disappearing into the vapour. When the mist had blown away, as though dispersed by a sudden warm summer breeze, Aillen's body had miraculously disappeared.

"He's gone to Tir Na Nog." Wayne whispered sadly.

Fr Francisco Pizarro's remains were also never found, even though the local fire brigade and the Gardai spent many hours sifting through the remains of Mickey Finn's cottage over the following days.

As the sun rose over Lough Mask, the small party was still to be found watching the smouldering ruins of Mickey Finn's cottage.

Frank had agreed with Wayne that they would dig up whatever was hidden under the small hut at the back of the cottage at first light.

John and Tom agreed to help. A shovel was found in the hut and after moving the tiny hut to one side, a large iron cauldron was found about three feet underground. Inside the cauldron they found an ancient bronze spear-head, a golden torc, along with several emerald brooches of varying sizes and designs. There was also a perfectly preserved sword, wrapped in oiled cloth and a large horde of gold coins.

"I suppose this will help pay Mum back." Wayne sighed sadly. Frank ruffled his hair.

"Aye, I suppose so." He said.

John stroked his chin:

"It should all be going to the museum in Dublin." He proposed thoughtfully. Wayne nodded:

"I'm just taking a little bit of the gold to repay Mum and a few brooches. The other stuff can go to the museum. Do you think I might need that sword to defend myself from mad vicars someday."

Fr Malone laughed:

"No, I don't think so. Let it go to the museum. I think you've seen the last of mad vicars for a while and from what I saw, you don't need swords or any other weapon for that matter."

John patted Frank on the back and put his arm around Wayne:

"Well, let's be going. There's nothing more we can do here."

Wayne nodded:

"Oh just a minute" he said as he raced off and collected the four small crucifixes that Pizarro had placed just around the garden wall. He pulled the stone off each crucifix and put them in his pocket before throwing the crosses into the cauldron, which his Dad and John struggled to lift into the Volvo.

The Volvo and the Austin Maxi set off back towards the mountain pass.

Wayne turned once and looked at the pall of smoke rising from the valley floor; he couldn't help but shed more tears.

"Why Dad? Why did my other Father have to die, as soon as I'd found him?" Wayne pleaded plaintively.

Frank shrugged:

"I don't know lad. I really don't. Life can be a bit like that."

The only stop the two cars made on the way back to the pass was to look over the brow of the hill where they had seen the Morris Minor crash off the road during the night. Tom and John walked down the steep hill and came back up a few minutes later, shaking their heads sadly.

"There's another Priest in the car I'm afraid. He's dead, quite dead." John stated with a shrug. Fr. Malone nodded:

"Sure, Finaan will be in mourning today. To lose one priest is sad, to be losing two is careless, to lose two and a half is downright stupid."

He raised his broken arm as far as he could without wincing.

"We better be telling the Gardai." He added after a moments thought.

"I think it's better if the details of last nights events weren't made public knowledge, I'll just say that Father Burke and I crashed as we were on our way to Westport. We had started to rush when we saw the burning cottage, you know, to see if there was anything we could do, but old Father Burke lost control on that corner and I fell out of the car as it rolled. You good people found me this morning."

Everyone agreed that that was the best version of events and that the real story was best kept secret.

"Who'd believe us anyway?" John smiled.

The party stopped in the village of Tourmakeady, where Fr Malone was going to report the tragic accident and the death of Fr Burke to the local Garda Siochana.

He gave Wayne a huge smile.

"Good luck young man." He grinned:

"Stay away from all evil looking Priests and God speed back to Yorkshire. And if I were you, I'd avoid Ireland for a while. The "Order" is damaged; but they are very, very powerful and will always be looking for anyone with power like yours."

Wayne nodded and Frank shook Malone's hand:

"If you're ever in Shepton.........., well, you know."

Malone smiled:

"I'll look you up, I promise."

The young Priest watched grimly as the cars disappeared into the distance, he then took off his white collar and threw it into a nearby stream. If he did go to the Gardai there would be too many questions and exactly who could he now trust? No, James Malone had a better plan, one which might give him a few more years of life. He had seen things that had shaken his faith too much for him to continue his life as a Priest. Fr James Malone knew exactly what he was going to do.

Meanwhile, John, Frank, Wayne and Katie carried on back to Tom's house in the Volvo, followed by Molly and Patsy in the Austin.

After a restorative cup of tea, John set off back down to Oughterard with Patsy. Frank asked him if he would pop across to the "bed and breakfast" and let Elizabeth know that Wayne was OK, and that they'd be following on later, with Molly.

Wayne asked if he could spend a few minutes alone, watching the lake and the mountains before he began the long journey back to Shepton. He wanted to remember the things his mother had grown up seeing every day. Frank agreed, with a heavy sigh. He was already wondering how he would explain Wayne's reunion with his natural family to Doris.

"Do you think the boys alright?" Molly asked him when Wayne had wandered off up the hill by his Grandfathers house.

Frank blew another sigh and ran his hand through his hair:

"Aye, I'll give him a few minutes. He's found something here that he never knew he had. I can't say I understand what he's going through, because I don't, but if it was worth him running away for, then it must mean a lot to him. Sadly, he's already lost a big part of what he found, before he ever even really got to know it."

He grimaced and stared through the window at his adopted boy, who was disappearing over the brow of the hill, where he had sat with Katie, only the day before.

Once over the hill, Wayne ran down to the gate and then as fast as he could up to the hidden Lough in the belly of the mountain where his father had shown him the last long hall of the "Tuatha de Danaan."

Wayne had the time to now stand and admire the view. The Lough stood dark and motionless, not a ripple moved on its surface, no fish, no insects, no birds disturbed its rest. To the boy the Lough's depth was unimaginable; maybe it was as deep as Lough Mask, way, way down below. The water, like a mirror, perfectly reflected the semi circular like cliff of rock that surrounded it on three sides. Katie had described it as a caldera, whatever that was. To Wayne it looked like he was stood in a Volcanic crater and only the bit behind him had collapsed down into the valley and the lake way behind and below him. The lip of the crater jutted out, trapping the cloud inside, giving the Lough a climate all of its own. When Katie had shown him the lake he had been amazed by how quiet it was. Not a bird had sung, no insects had buzzed and even the wind had seemed strangely silent.

Now, as Wayne stood, taking in the almost other worldly atmosphere, he started to imagine that he could hear music. He glanced around, half expecting to see a car bouncing up the track with its windows down and its radio blaring out, rudely disturbing the precious tranquillity.

There was nothing.

The more Wayne listened, the more he recognised singing. An angelic choir chanting a haunting sad song, their voices in perfect harmony, soaring and stretching up the sides of the mountain, echoing melancholically over the Lough. It was such a haunting melody, so sad that it made Wayne want to burst into tears.

He shook his head; maybe he really was going mad this time.

Wayne tightly clasped the stone in his pocket, the green mist immediately ascended around him and the music suddenly grew much louder, almost deafening.

Aillen appeared before him, a smile creasing his lips.

"For God's sake, cheer up, lad." The phantom laughed:

"You look like someone's died!"

Wayne twisted his face:

"Ha ha, very funny. Someone has died actually. You!"

Aillen adopted a mock serious demeanour:

"No way. You mean I'm dead?" He gulped, then leaned towards Wayne with a twinkle in his eye:

"So who is it exactly that you are talking to, then?"

Wayne sighed and then smirked:

"OK. I suppose this is a bit different."

Aillen laughed:

"You wouldn't have liked Dan and Mickey anyway. They were very smelly you know."

Wayne couldn't help but laugh:

"Yeah, that cottage was a bit whiffy. What's that beautiful music?" He asked, his face a mask of wonderment.

Aillen smiled sadly:

"That is my people's lament for me, my son. They mourn my final passage into Tir Na Nog. Indeed, they mourn all of our passages into the nether world. I was the last of the true Tuatha de Danaan to exist on this earth. They sing of the loss of our four fair cities, our travails and finally of our love for the Isle of Erin and the sanctuary it provided."

His eyes misted over as he stared out over the little Lough.

Wayne nodded:

"Oh" He breathed as his lip began to tremble:

"It's just so beautiful."

Aillen clasped his son's shoulder:

"The last lament of the Leprechauns."

He grinned and then began to laugh.

"Don't tell the Bord na Failte. The tourists will stop coming."

Wayne smirked and sobbed at the same.

Aillen crouched and looked into his son's eyes:

"Don't be sad, my little warrior. It was all pre-ordained. I was only prepared to pass out from your world when I knew that my son, my heir was safe, secure and fully aware of his heritage."

"Oh sure. So you knew you were going to die?" Wayne demanded incredulously and with more than a little venom.

Aillen shrugged:

"Die, pass away, pass over. Such terms are immaterial to an immortal. You don't need the stone to see me young Mac Aillen. At least for a while you only need to think of me. You have the power. I felt it many weeks ago, when you used it in anger for the first time. Even though you were so far away. I suspected even then that you were the "Slanaitheoir mor." In all my years, I have never known such power. You proved that last night. Pizarro had killed many much older, wiser and supposedly more powerful immortals than you my son. Admittedly, your Northman father helped, but you were good.

I knew it would not be long before you found me, as soon as I sensed you using your magic. I knew my time had come. That's why I set up the young Priest. Besides I was getting bloody lonely being alone all those years."

Wayne sobbed:

"You needn't have been lonely. You had me. We've only just met. Anyway, how did you know I'd come to Ireland at the same time as that Spanish nutter?"

Aillen shrugged:

"Well I will admit that I didn't know for sure, it was all a bit quicker than I'd expected, but sometimes, things just have a way of happening."

Aillen laughed:

"The Northman warrior who is raising you, he is a good man?"

Wayne nodded:

"Aye, I suppose so."

"Good! He is a mighty warrior. Learn from him, my son. His wife, the woman who has nursed you and raised you, she is good?"

Wayne nodded and shrugged:

"Suppose!"

Aillen looked stern:

"You know who you are now Mac Aillen. Dry your tears, you are a mighty warrior of the "Tuatha de Dannan" now, you have the last blood of our kind. The "Order" like to see themselves as a thin red line in the fight against what they purport to be evil. They will try again. They will send others to try and finish the job that Pizarro failed to complete, so that they can fulfil their prophecy. You were prophesied to face three great tests before you can truly take the title: "Slanaitheoir mor." You have passed the first test, my son, but I am sure the "Order" will make the next two more difficult. You are going to have to be very, very strong."

Wayne nodded again and sobbed.

Aillen bit his lip:

"Be not sad son. Our time together was always destined to be short. I will be able to come to you for a few years yet. The portals of Tir Na nog are many and will open when you need me and will me to be there. One day, however, the portals will fade. Then there will be only one way to speak to me. The last portal is up there."

Aillen pointed up the mountain-side, to a distant cairn high above Tom O'Brien's cottage.

"You will always be able to find me there. Until the very end of the world."

He stood upright again and smiled down at his son. His eyes shone with pride.

Suddenly his head snapped up and he sniffed the air, his forehead creasing into a concerned frown.

Then Aillen Mac Fionnbharr gasped in anguish and tears filled his eyes as he stared down the track that led to the main road by Lough Mask. He gritted his teeth as he turned back to Wayne.

"Go now, my son and quickly. This journey's final fruit is at hand. Your bravery is about to gain its just reward."

He smiled sadly:

"I must go now. We will meet again, Micheal Sean O'Brien. We shall meet again, my son. Now go boy, do not tarry, run down that hill, someone comes. Someone of such importance, someone......"

His words trailed off as he gazed longingly down the track, his eyes misted over again, then he quickly turned and disappeared into thin air. The green mist that surrounded him evaporated almost as quickly as it had arrived and the beautiful sound of singing faded until it seemed little more than a breeze-like whisper whistling over the Lough.

Wayne stared at the small mountain Lough for just a few more seconds. The clouds still hung around it, spookily, just as they had the day the long hall was burned down before the advancing Celts, all those centuries ago.

Just for a second Wayne thought he could see the Last Long Hall floating in the air above the Lough, intact again, its golden thatch shining in the sun. Wayne shook his head and rubbed his eyes. The Hall disappeared, just like his father had. So the boy started to walk back down the track, his hands stuffed in his pockets, his shoulders drooping disconsolately. Now he was going to have to face the wrath of Doris. That was even worse than mad old Pizarro. At best he could look forward to a continuation of life doing shopping errands in Shepton, at worst she would have him sent him to the children's home for stealing from her, which she had threatened to do when he had committed other minor misdemeanours. Bet she wouldn't have threatened Trevor with the Children's Home. Perfect bloody Trevor.

Wayne had just crossed a small hump of a hill on the way down from the hidden Lough when he noticed a white Ford Cortina bouncing up the track towards Daideo's house. That must have been what Aillen had been referring too when he had said: "someone comes."

Wayne's heart started to pound for no apparent reason and he had suddenly started to run. The hairs on the back of his neck were rising and he could feel his skin tingling.

The Ford stopped at Daideo's gate and stood, motor running for a few minutes. A girl got out, her long blonde hair blowing free in the soft summer breeze. A man took a holdall out of the boot of the car and dumped it on the track by the girl, before jumping back into the driver's seat, swiftly backing up, turning around and driving away.

Wayne could just make out the taxi licence plate on the car's rear end.

The girl began to laboriously push open the large, green, five barred, steel gate; but then noticed the boy running down the track towards her.

She peered at him curiously, brushing her hair out of her large blue-green eyes, then something seemed to click and she dropped the holdall and began to run towards him up the unmetalled track, with its centre and verges of grass and wild flowers. The sun broke from behind a cloud and the girl's hair shone like flaming, red gold. Even from a distance Wayne could see that this girl was even more stunning than the incredibly, beautiful Mandy had been, back in London.

Wayne stopped and stood motionless as she reached him, his mouth agape, tears began to pour down his face in anticipation of what he already knew:

"Michael?" She suggested timorously;

"Are you Michael, by any chance?"

Wayne didn't know how he'd known, but now he really knew for certain.

"Mum?" He cried and ran straight into her open arms.

49

Elizabeth Ball was beginning to panic. Elizabeth Ball was definitely panicking and it was pathetic. That's what she kept telling herself.

"Panicking is pathetic and pointless." She muttered as she prowled around Mrs Hanlon's guest living room.

"Would you be liking more tea, Mrs.....?" Mrs Hanlon asked as she collected a row of dirty mugs. Elizabeth jumped. She hadn't heard the owner of the "Bed and Breakfast" enter the room.

"Oh, er, no thank you Mrs Hanlon. I think I'll turn brown if I drink any more." She laughed, embarrassed that the Irish lady might have heard her talking to herself.

"No sign of them, yet?"

Mrs Hanlon looked at the English woman with genuine concern.

"I'm sure they'll have just stopped off and stayed the night somewhere. It's quite a drive up into Mayo, you know."

Mrs Hanlon carried the mugs off into the kitchen, shaking her head and muttering to herself about strange folk and weird goings on. Elizabeth bit a fingernail and strolled over to the room's big bay window:

"Do I go over again? The neighbours are going to think I'm insane. What on earth could have happened to them?"

Elizabeth had walked over to the "Old Barn" four times already that morning and it was still only ten o'clock. She pulled back the net curtain. The main street was already busy and the road down to the Lough had seen quite a number of cars passing down, fishermen mostly, enjoying their Saturday off.

She was just dropping the curtain when she saw a glint of silver in the corner of her eye. She snatched the curtain up again just in time to see a silver Volvo turn into the Quay Road.

Elizabeth did not hesitate for a moment. She pulled on her jacket and ran out of the B&B's front door. John O'Malley and Patsy were only just climbing out of the car, when she arrived at their front gate, panting and quite out of breath.

"Where are they? What's happened? Are they alright?" She wheezed, as John picked up his son and smiled at her:

"Calm down, calm down, Mrs." He laughed, reassuringly.

Molly will be bringing Frank and Michael, sorry, Wayne, down just a little bit later. He's OK. The boy's had quite an adventure."

Elizabeth burst into tears:

"Oh thank God, thank God." She sobbed.

John grinned:

"It was quite a night I can tell you and if I was telling you a less than a half of what had happened, you wouldn't be believing less than a half of what I said and probably no more than a quarter of that."

Elizabeth laughed and cried at the same time.

"As long as he is safe and well." She said between sobs.

John opened his front door with some difficulty with his son half over his shoulder:

"You'd better come in for some tea." He said.

Elizabeth heaved a sigh and wiped her eyes with a handkerchief:

"Just what I need." She lied.

"Our Michael's a leprechaun." Patsy informed her from over his Father's shoulder as they walked through the hall.

Some hours later, Elizabeth looked at her watch and smiled meaningfully at the shattered looking figure of Frank

Higginbotham. They were sat in Molly's kitchen, all having eaten a huge Irish stew:

"I'm sorry to be a party pooper." She sighed, "and I'm sure the last thing you need right now Frank, is to be getting back into a car, but we are going to have to catch that ferry and it's a long haul over to Dun Laoghaire."

Molly was clearing away the dishes:

"How are you ever going to separate them?"

She inclined her head towards the drawing room where Wayne could just be seen through the interconnecting door, sitting with his head on the blonde woman's shoulder.

"How do you take a boy from the mother he's only been knowing, for a few hours?"

Elizabeth noticed Frank wince and look down at his lap, his forehead puckered with lines.

"It'll be OK, Frank." She whispered.

He looked up at her, nodded and produced a brave smile.

"Aye, I know." He said.

Surprisingly, after a last long hug, Wayne seemed relatively relaxed about leaving Theresa O'Brien's arms. They gazed into each other's eyes and then she laughed and ruffled his hair:

"Thousands of miles and hundreds of bucks, all for half a day with this young ruffian."

Wayne laughed too. She knelt down and held his hands and stared into his eyes again:

"It would have been more than worth it even for just a single second." She whispered.

"I will never lose touch with you again, my son. I will write every week, I promise. Your Dad has given me your teacher, Elizabeth's address and I will send my letters there so your … your Mum doesn't get upset."

She had struggled to say "Mum," yet it seemed right. "Mum" was an alien word to her. She looked up at Elizabeth, who nodded encouragingly:

"Mrs Ball will make sure you get every letter."

She smiled and kissed Wayne's forehead.

"I love you, Mum." Wayne whispered.

The image of Doris, arms folded under her bosom, her face set in indignant fury; flashed into his mind.

"There's something I want you to have." He muttered, as he groped in his pockets for something he had found in Aillen's cauldron. He looked concerned for a second but then relieved as he pulled an emerald brooch out his jeans:

"He would have wanted you to have this." He whispered:

"And I do too."

He handed the brooch to Theresa who looked totally shocked.

"Who would have wanted me to have it?" She asked, but the question went unanswered as her breath was taken away by her first glance at the jewel.

The brooch was the largest emerald any of them had even seen, surrounded by a gold design, topped by a crown:

"It once belonged to a Queen." Wayne whispered as he looked up at his natural mother, who burst into tears and hugged and kissed him one more time.

"But where did you find it?" She asked.

Wayne smiled enigmatically:

"It was a gift someone gave me, with you in mind."

Theresa frowned in wonderment as John touched her shoulder lightly:

"They'd better go Theresa." He whispered gently.

Theresa released her son and gulped back a sob.

Wayne turned sadly and picked up his bag, as Theresa hugged her sister, Molly and Frank:

"Thank you for looking after my baby." She wept. "I will stay in touch, I promise. Maybe, if your wife would ever agree to it, he could visit me in L.A. or...."

Terri Thorne, known in these parts as Theresa O'Brien, dissolved into floods of tears.

Molly kissed Wayne:

"We know where you are and we'll get to see you." She smiled kindly:

"You might have lost one member of your new family, but you've gained dozens, most of whom you'd probably be better off not meeting, but I am so glad you have got to be meeting the one you really came to find."

Wayne turned and put her arms around Theresa once more as all the other goodbyes were said and more hugs were hugged and kisses were kissed.

All too soon Elizabeth's Ford Escort was pulling away on to the main street and on to the road back down to Galway.

Wayne turned and looked out of the back window of the car at the huddled group stood on the Old Barn's drive in the warm summer breeze, all waving, some weeping. A golden wave of soft blonde hair blew in the breeze as a tiny figure disappeared:

"Bye Mom." Wayne whispered, having found the name that he knew would separate her from Doris, but would give her the title she deserved. Somewhere in his head he heard Aillen's voice:

"You can see now why she stole my heart, my son."

50

The last couple of weeks and long days of the long summer holiday seemed to drag on forever for Wayne Higginbotham. As the memory of his adventures in London and Ireland slowly began to fade and get mixed up with the dreams and wild imagination of a child, it began to seem unlikely to Wayne that any of it had really happened at all. Yet he did have some proof. He had hidden the five stones in the safest place he knew: the top drawer of the chest of drawers in his bedroom and although he had tried to summon Aillen several times, nothing had happened, since he had heard that disembodied voice as he was leaving Oughterard.

In fact, apart from a quick visit to the police station on the day after he got back home to Shepton, nothing at all had happened to remind him of his adventure.

Doris had been so relieved that he had returned home safe and well, that she hadn't even chastised him for stealing the money from the sideboard, let alone causing her so much worry.

Guided by Frank, Margaret and Mrs Ball, Doris had been persuaded to avoid asking Wayne what had happened to him in London and Ireland. They had told her that some painful things had happened to him and it would be for the best that he be allowed to forget some of what he had experienced.

"What happened over there was extremely traumatic for him." Elizabeth Ball had assured her.

"Nothing physical happened to him, but he did see and experience some things that boys of eleven shouldn't have to see."

Even though Doris' curiosity was almost insatiable, she controlled herself and life in the Higginbotham household soon returned to normal.

Doris' resolve remarkably lasted over two whole weeks. Then, one morning, Wayne had cheekily answered her back, when she had asked him to do something:

"You've got too big for your boots since you passed for that Grammar School." Doris had bellowed and had then begun to look all hurt:

"I suppose you met her didn't you?" She had whimpered.

"What?" Wayne had asked, dumbfounded.

He had been quietly ignoring her while he read the back of the packet of Cornflakes.

"I suppose I'm not good enough for you, now you've met her." She had sniffed.

"Who?" Wayne had asked, turning in his chair, looking totally bemused.

"Your real mother." Doris had almost spat the words.

"What?" Wayne had screwed up his face.

"I know you met your mother in Ireland. That's why you went isn't it? We're not good enough for you now, are we? Had to find something better didn't you?"

"But I..." Wayne had started to protest.

"Oh aye. I know you've always wanted more than we've got. That's why you went fishing in them papers isn't it? Hoping you'd find out you weren't ours, so that you could get away, go back to where you came from. Our Trevor wouldn't have done owt like this to us."

She was getting angrier with every word.

"Well, my lad, she didn't want you then and she won't want you now. I'll tell you that for nowt."

She had burst into floods of tears:

"If we're not good enough for you. You can beggar off wherever you like, whenever you like."

Wayne had stood and had reached out to hug her:

417

"But Mum, I am happy." He had whispered as she backed away from him.

"Then why?" Doris had barked. "Why? Why? Why?"

The pain and agony etched into her features had made Wayne feel guiltier than he had ever felt in his life.

For the first time, he had actually felt sorry for his Mum.

"It was while I was in hospital." Wayne had admitted after a long tense silence as Doris had continued to sob heavily:

"I was half asleep and I heard a doctor say that I'd been adopted. I didn't believe it, but I had to know. That's why I searched the brass box. I didn't know what I'd find, but what I did find told me the truth. I was adopted."

Doris let him put his arms around her:

"Did you meet her?" She had asked plaintively, gripping his arms and glaring into his eyes.

Wayne had nodded:

"But it doesn't matter."

He had closed his eyes and concentrated. He had then opened his eyes again and had looked straight into Doris' eyes with one word on his mind: "Forget!"

"Well, that's alright then." Doris had sniffed.

"We'd better get your uniform sorted out. You start your new School the day after tomorrow."

Wayne had heaved a huge sigh of relief.

"I've only got one "Mum", you know." He had said quietly.

Doris had looked at him as though he had just spoken Japanese.

"Well how many do you expect?" She had snorted, looking quietly pleased with herself, before she had turned and bustled off.

Wayne had sighed again, his relief almost palpable:

"And only one real Mother, one Mom."

He had whispered as he turned to walk up the narrow staircase to his bedroom:

"And there couldn't be two more different people."

As for Frank, he had returned to the task of screwing thingummys onto widgets and then putting them into boxes. Five days a week, eight hours a day. What was different was that Wayne now respected and loved him more than he ever had. Wayne knew that his Dad was a hero, even if other people didn't think much of him. Their conversations initially grew longer and Wayne tried to involve his adoptive father in much more of his life.

Frank, however, although he was desperately pleased to have a better relationship with his son, was a simple man at heart and Wayne's interests and passions just weren't the same as his. By the dog days of Wayne's summer holidays they had resumed the old routines, Frank nodding away at predictable western movies and Wayne rudely correcting his grammar and pronunciations at every available opportunity.

Elizabeth Ball had gone off with her husband John for a couple of weeks in the sun when she had finally got back to Shepton. John had had a lot of humble pie to eat, having been convinced that his wife had engaged in a wild goose chase.

"Leave it to the professionals eh?" She had mocked him.

The version of the tale that she related to John and to her friends and colleagues, had been expunged of the magical elements, and was pretty much what she had been told in the car and on the ferry by Frank and Wayne.

As a thank-you for all she had done, Wayne had given Elizabeth a ruby and emerald green brooch from Aillen's horde, which later turned out to be worth well over a million pounds. Not that she ever knew, nor did she ever sell it.

Constable Hartley had behaved quite strangely when Doris had marched Wayne to the Police Station to make his apologies for wasting all that Police time. WPC Harrison had been very nice and said that it was great to have him home, safe and sound. Constable Hartley, however, had taken him to one side on the pretext of giving him a little lecture:

"Now then, young Higginbotham." He had said, leaning down so that his face was on a level with Wayne's:

"You gave us all quite the run around didn't you?" He sniffed:

"Now I have me suspicions about you young man. Serious suspicions!"

He looked around cagily and then prodded Wayne's chest and began to whisper:

"It wouldn't surprise me to find out that you were one of them there aliens from outer space, or sommat like that, young man. I know you brainwashed that booking office bloke. You can bloody well forget about trying any of that nonsense on me."

He had straightened his back and his expression had become one of extreme satisfaction, as though he had just apprehended a villain who thought that he'd got away with it. He had prodded Wayne's chest again:

"Oh yes, I know your type. You remind me of that Dr. Spock fellow from the telly. I bet you can do that Vulcan death grip, can't you?"

Wayne had just screwed up his nose indignantly.

The rotund policeman had smirked arrogantly:

"Well I'll tell you sommat for nowt, you'll not be doing your death grip in Shepton. I'll be keeping my eye on you, young man. Mark my words; I'll not have this town turning out like the Village of the Damned."

He had straightened his jacket pompously, before glowering at Wayne one last time, he had then sniffed contemptuously, turned and walked away. Wayne concentrated on the policeman's legs as he walked off and it might have been a coincidence, but PC Hartley tripped over his own feet and fell flat on his face. He jumped up quickly, turned and glared towards where Wayne had last been stood, but the boy was no longer there. As Doris escorted him out of the police station she had to ask him why he had a self-satisfied grin all over his face.

On the very last day of the summer holidays, the day after Doris' outburst, Frank surreptitiously passed Wayne a blue envelope with "Air Mail" stamped on the front and stamps from America. Wayne rushed to his room and ripped it open:

"My Dear Son," It had begun:

"It was so lovely to meet you at last, up on the hill where I spent so many happy days in my childhood. I knew it was you as soon as I saw you. The ears were the dead giveaway I suppose. I cannot believe you've grown up so fast and so handsome. Not a day has gone by when I haven't thought about you and your sister. One day let's hope we might find her too and then we can all be together.
I didn't tell you why I ran away and had you both adopted did I?

I guess the truth is: I was frightened. It wasn't because I didn't love you both, because I did. I loved you so much. You were both such gorgeous babies, but I was so frightened. I was frightened of being poor and struggling to bring up two babies alone and with no money.

I was frightened of the stigma of being an unmarried mother.

But most of all, I was frightened because I thought that I'd gone mad.

They told me that I'd had a breakdown and that unless I surrendered you, your lives would be ruined too. Even the Priest told me that because I had had a breakdown, the best thing to do was to have you adopted.

The mother superior said that you should be adopted separately, that two children were harder to place than single babies. She said someone had already asked for a little girl like your sister. A rich family and that she would have servants and all that stuff. They said you'd get the same. How could I have refused?

I really had loved Danny, had he asked me, I'd have married him like a shot. I must have freaked when I found out I was pregnant. I guess that was why I had the breakdown. For a while I actually believed that Danny had told me that he was one of the fairy- folk.

It must have been a dream, or a wild fantasy or something.

Hah! Now that you know I'm mad, you'll probably run for the hills like he did. By the time I'd sorted myself out, Danny had high tailed it back to America. I never saw or heard from him again.

Well I've got to go now. I'm on set in a moment. Maybe you'll see me on TV in England, if they ever show this movie over there.

Take care my beautiful son.
Your Mom, Terri."

PS Write back soon and tell me all about that posh new school"

Wayne read it twenty times at least; then settled back on his pillow and kissed the envelope. He smiled happily.

He was suddenly aware of a green mist seeping up from the floor and surrounding him.

"Looks like I should stayed on as Danny."

Aillen laughed, appearing in his Danny Finn disguise and speaking in his mock Southern drawl.

"Hey, this is private." Wayne had grinned as he turned the letter over and hid it behind his back.

"Anyway, where've you been?" Wayne asked, laughing with pleasure at the sight of his spectral ancestor.

"Where you need me to be. Right in the centre of your heart."

Aillen replied, as he turned back into himself.

"And that's not just a load of old blarney. I will only appear like this when you need me, or when I need to help you." Aillen remarked, looking all serious all of a sudden.

"If you want to talk to me at any time though, just talk. I will hear you as long as you call my name. Anyway, it looks like things are going to be a bit quiet for a while."

He stroked his chin and then added:

"Anyway what are you waiting for?"

"What?" Wayne asked.

"What are you waiting for?" Aillen demanded more insistently

"What do you mean?" Wayne sounded puzzled.

"Write back to her." Aillen shouted and then began to laugh:

"Don't go losing her, like I did, you eejit."

Aillen's voice faded, as did his image, as did the mist.

There was a knock on Wayne's bedroom door.

He quickly hid Theresa's letter under his pillow. The door opened a touch:

"Were you talking to somebody?" Doris asked.

"No" Wayne smiled "Just myself!"

"They'll think you're away with the fairies if you go talking to yourself." Doris laughed, closing the door.

"And maybe I am." Wayne Higginbotham whispered, smiling.

"Maybe I am."

51

"This was all that was found, Your Eminence."

Bishop Donleavy croaked as he placed the blackened gold crucifix blade, that had belonged to Fr Francisco Pizarro on the desk.

"Bishop O'Leary has had the area very well searched. There is no sign of the demon. We believe that he perished in the conflagration with Pizarro. There is blood on the blade."

The blade was examined and then tossed contemptuously back onto the desk:

"And you are convinced that Pizarro perished too?"

"Yes, yes."

Donleavy nodded as vigorously as his old neck would allow.

"A pity. He was our best operative."

Donleavy crossed himself:

"He was not the only casualty, your Eminence."

"Yes, I saw the media reports. We get them even here in Rome."

A copy of the "Irish Independent" was thrown across the desk, with a small front page article about a small village in Ireland losing two priests and the disappearance of a visiting cleric all within the space of 24 hours. The article was circled in thick black felt pen.

"And what of the other? The young one who reported this creature's bravado."

"Ah yes, Father Malone. It was he who reported the death of the creature, Your Eminence."

"Good, bring him to me. I would very much like to speak with him."

Donleavy looked even more embarrassed:

"I am afraid that will not be possible, Your Eminence."

There was no reaction from the other side of the desk. Donleavy swallowed nervously:

"I am afraid he has disappeared, Your Eminence. I believe he has ….."

He hesitated:

"He has totally disappeared. The Gardai are looking for him now. They think he has either committed suicide, or was murdered by some visiting Spanish Priest, who was reportedly seen with him in the area."

"Oh dear. Three deaths and a disappearance. We are beginning to operate like the CIA aren't we? May I remind you Bishop, that we are the "Sacred Order of St. Gregory" and that we have not witnessed such a debacle in well over a thousand years?"

The voice from the other side of the desk was now raised in anger.

"If this Malone has disappeared, how do you know that he saw the creature die?"

"Bishop O'Leary talked to him on the telephone, Your Eminence, on the morning after the mission. O'Leary said that Malone was quite unhinged and that he had shouted that three Priests had died in vain, one good, one bad and one downright evil; but that the worse thing was that an innocent man had died too. He said that the "Order" was a sham and that it had committed genocide because of a stupid prophecy. He hoped that His Grace was happy. He has not been seen, nor heard of since."

There was a long silence. Donleavy took a deep breath.

"Father Malone's collar and rosary were found on a riverbank in a village called Tourmakeady, Your Eminence. They think his body might have been washed into a nearby lake, Lough Mask."

Donleavy had gone quite white and his hands were visibly shaking.

"And the stones have not been found?"

"No, Your Eminence."

"Nor the creature's treasure?

"No, Your Eminence."

"I would not be inclined to believe that this Malone is dead until his body is found. And if he is alive you will find him, Bishop Donleavy. You will use whatever means are necessary but you will find him. Do I make myself clear?"

"Yes, Your Eminence. Very clear."

"And when you have found him, should he still be alive, you will bring him here. It is absolutely vital that we are one hundred per-cent certain that the last of the immortals has perished."

"Yes, Your Eminence."

"You know the prophecy, Bishop Donleavy."

The old Priest nodded, and in his best croak repeated the lines:

> *"A child no mortal man shall sire*
> *By mother's blood Royal line acquire,*
> *Shall suckle he no milk white breast,*
> *Shall rise in exile, unwelcome guest,*
> *Shall learn to change his form at will*
> *His shape, his face, his ways to kill*
> *Unseen, unheard, his telling blow,*
> *His doom to lay The Messiah low."*

Cardinal D'Abruzzo, the supreme head of the ancient "Sacred Order of Saint Gregory" nodded his approval.

"Good, I think that is all, Bishop Donleavy. You may return to Dublin. Oh yes, you can tell your Bishop O'Leary to pack his things. I have a nice little job for him in equatorial Africa. Where it is somewhat more difficult to fail quite so spectacularly."

"Yes, Your Eminence."

"Good day, Bishop Donleavy. Let us hope that our mission has finally been accomplished and that we have indeed seen the last of those who threaten Our Lord's return."

A blast of hot air flew into the room as the door was opened and the heat of the Roman summer penetrated the marble halls of the Vatican.

Some moments later in a darkened room nearby, a figure stood before an ornate tapestry, hanging on a wall, he pulled a golden cord and the tapestry slid smoothly aside, like a curtain. The figure pressed the dirty mark on the white plaster of the wall, opening the previously invisible door into the hidden dark chamber. The figure stepped in, closing the invisible door behind him.

The figure bowed before the small Alter, which he illuminated by lighting two candles. He knelt on a gilded cushion and bowed his head again.

"So you have succeeded?" A low voice rumbled, seemingly from the Alter itself.

"I am told that they have finally killed the creature. There are no more, as far as we know."

The bowed figure gulped.

The voice chuckled:

"Then the fulfilment of the cursed prophecy is now impossible. Excellent! You will complete the arrangements for my return to earthly form immediately. Now that all the immortals are gone and there is none left who can harm me, I can begin my return to Earth."

"Yes, my Lord. Would it not be wise to wait until…..?"

The bowed figure, his voice betraying his nervousness began to make a suggestion but was unceremoniously interrupted by the disembodied voice:

"No! You will carry out my orders without delay. I have waited in the darkness long enough. Ten long years ago you told me that you thought the last of those foul creatures had been dealt with, but that you needed to make sure. Ten long years I have waited. Is your "Order" so incompetent that it has taken all of ten years to find just one immortal and has left others yet unfound?"

"No, My Lord."

The bowed figure whispered.

"Cardinal, if your "Order" has failed me, I will hold you personally responsible. Do you understand?"

The voice rumbled menacingly.

The bowed figure gulped:

"Yes my Lord. Everything has been prepared, just as you commanded."

The figure crossed himself.

"You may leave, now." The voice rumbled.

"Soon you will meet me, in the flesh, as it were."

The disembodied voice chuckled again.

The bowed figure whispered:

"I cannot wait, my Lord."

Then he then scuttled off back through the invisible door.

"And so shall begin a new age for mortal man. All shall fear me. All shall despair. The strong shall bow down and worship me, the weak shall grovel on their bellies in the dust. And it shall avail them not!"

The disembodied voice hissed and then once again began to chuckle menacingly.

In the city of San Francisco, California, a young Irishman jumped off a street car. His thick, dark, long hair tumbled over his collar in a mass of curls. His sideburns were long and trendily styled in the manner of a Victorian patriarch, his eyes a deep, rich brown.

He looked more Mediterranean than Irish, but Irish he was and a Pop star he intended to be. With his duffle-bag strung over one shoulder and a guitar case in his hand, Jimmy

Malone was starting a new life. The wind from the bay caught his hair and he laughed as he dodged the traffic.

"It's great to be back in the Twentieth Century." He shouted, his arms aloft.

"God bless America."

Some passers by looked at him disdainfully, most ignored him.

There were plenty of lunatics in San Francisco. What was one more?

Epilogue

Wayne Higginbotham almost skipped over the swing bridge that crossed the Leeds-Liverpool Canal as he made his way home from Wormysted's Grammar School.

His first day had been a resounding success, although he had found his first French lesson somewhat difficult and the prospect of having to do homework for the very first time in his life had taken a slight edge off the day. Even so, the curly haired boy wearing his brand new navy blue blazer, with its smart badge, his blue and yellow schoolboy's cap, his matching blue and yellow striped tie and his finely pressed, grey flannel trousers, could not have been much happier.

He had already made several friends, Paul Harland, a teacher's son from a village up the Dales somewhere, had been really nice, as had Martin Taggart and Liam Riley, a boy from Ireland. Wayne had even discovered another boy, who liked "Star Trek," although he had been a bit on the large side, wore thick glasses and smelled a bit.

The only scary thing about the School had been Dai Davies, the Deputy Headmaster. He was a large bald Welshman and Cedric Houghton-Hughes, Wayne's cousin who was now in the Second form had told Wayne all about him. Even the Upper Sixth were supposedly scared of Dai Davies and they looked like proper men, as opposed to schoolboys.

Dai had spoken in the first Assembly that morning and had warned the entire School population that the impeccable standards of Wormysted's Grammar School would be maintained. No transgression would be allowed. Any rule breakers would have Dai Davies to contend with. Over five hundred boys had gulped in unison.

Wayne broke into a run as he crossed the Barlickwick Road by the huge cotton mill.

He just couldn't help smiling. The next day, Wayne's timetable had promised his first Latin lesson. How cool was that? Wayne Higginbotham was going to learn the language of the Caesars.

Wayne shook his head in wonderment and in feverish anticipation of the days to come.

"Oi Lugsy, you little Grammar School poof!"

The harsh voice snapped Wayne out of his reverie as soon as he had turned onto Cavendish Street.

"Don't he look sweet in his lickle cap n'tie?" The voice continued to mock.

Andrew Cooper, one of Baz Thompson's closest friends was standing by the wall of the mill's canteen building; which occupied the first twenty yards of Cavendish Street, along with two other Baz acolytes from St. Swithin's Secondary Modern School.

Wayne didn't know the other two, but he knew Andrew Cooper. He had been at Gas Street Primary and had been a bully even at the age of ten.

"He's the one who done Baz, inni?" One of the other thugs suggested as he peered at Wayne suspiciously.

"Yeah he's the one: it's Doctor Spot." Andrew Cooper laughed derisively:

"And look at him, all done up like a proper lickle Wormystedder."

Wayne smiled:

"The name of the character, as I told Baz, is Mister Spock."

The three thugs laughed again:

"Hey Andy, you got it wrong, you moron. The lickle poofter just told ya."

The thug who hadn't spoken yet, mocked the new leader of Baz Thompson's gang, who glowered at him threateningly, wiping the smile off the boy's face immediately.

Andrew Cooper was now a fifth form pupil at St Swithins, a fifteen-year-old skinhead with an obsessive hatred of Wormysted's Grammar School and every single boy who had ever attended the place. He glared at Wayne and his mouth twisted in a gloating grin.

The fact that the boy standing before him was four years younger than him, outnumbered three to one and skinny looking even for his age, just made the prospect of the anticipated sport, all the more pleasurable.

"We're gonna get our revenge for Baz, Doctor Spot. We're gonna do you good and proper, just for him."

Cooper snarled.

"Yeah, there'll be no lucky punches this time." One of the others grinned maliciously.

Wayne Higginbotham smiled as the three thugs approached him, their fists clenched, their obligatory eighteen-hole, tan, Dr Marten boots shining in the September sunlight.

"How is Baz, by the way?" He asked, raising an eyebrow provocatively.

The three thugs started to run towards him.

"Never mind, I suppose you can ask him yourselves."

Wayne grinned, as he raised his right hand, palm outwards.